PRAISE FOR
PREJUDICIAL ERROR

"A fast-paced tale of the L.A. crime scene."
—Scott Turow

"The courtroom procedures have a nice, nasty snap to them . . . a treat."
—*New York Times Book Review*

"A well-constructed thriller . . . carries the ring of authenticity."
—*Publishers Weekly*

"Impressive behind-the-scenes courtroom drama."
—*San Francisco Daily Journal*

"A winner."
—*Seattle Times*

"Moves with swift confidence . . . memorable."
—*ABA Journal*

"Entertaining courtroom suspense drama."
—*Library Journal*

THE FACE OF
JUSTICE

BILL BLUM

AN ONYX BOOK

ONYX
Published by the Penguin Group
Penguin Putnam Inc., 375 Hudson Street,
New York, New York 10014, U.S.A.
Penguin Books Ltd, 27 Wrights Lane,
London W8 5TZ, England
Penguin Books Australia Ltd, Ringwood,
Victoria, Australia
Penguin Books Canada Ltd, 10 Alcorn Avenue,
Toronto, Ontario, Canada M4V 3B2
Penguin Books (N.Z.) Ltd, 182–190 Wairau Road,
Auckland 10, New Zealand

Penguin Books Ltd, Registered Offices:
Harmondsworth, Middlesex, England

First published by Onyx, an imprint of Dutton NAL,
a member of Penguin Putnam Inc.

First Printing, July, 1998
10 9 8 7 6 5 4 3 2

REGISTERED TRADEMARK—MARCA REGISTRADA

Printed in Canada

PUBLISHER'S NOTE
This is a work of fiction. Names, characters, places, and incidents either are
the product of the author's imagination or are used fictitiously, and any resemblance to actual persons, living or dead, events, or locales is entirely
coincidental.

For Max and Sam

ACKNOWLEDGMENTS

Thanks once again to my wife and chief collaborator, Gina Lobaco; my editors, Ed Stackler and Todd Keithley; my agent, Mike Hamilburg, and his associate Joanie Socola; and to readers Verna Wefald, Carol Richter, and Eric Blum.

Chapter One

Tami Darling stared into the camera, the wireless remote microphone gripped loosely in her manicured but child-size right hand. An easy smile creased her preternaturally youthful face. Motioning the studio audience with her free hand to hush, she listened to the director's final countdown to air time, unable to stop her thoughts from drifting to the sharp upward spiral her career path had taken.

It felt good, almost too good for words, to know that she was the center of attention, the idol of thousands, if not millions, of devoted fans. The story in last week's *Variety* had dubbed her "the next Oprah, the heir apparent to the queen of talk shows, only younger, more provocative, and light-years more sexy." From her neatly layered shoulder-length blond bob to her striking blue eyes, deep Malibu tan and well-cut Donna Karan suit, Tami was the picture of poise and confidence, a role model for aspiring women everywhere. And now, after three respectable seasons, her show was taking off like a Patriot missile. Her Nielsens had increased every week for the last three months. She was a woman fulfilled, what the TV syndicators called a "headliner," and her every move and gesture communicated that she was at one with her success.

Finally, the countdown was over, and with a flicker of adrenaline Tami returned her attention to the present. "What would you do if you fell in love with a man who had been convicted of armed robbery, rape, kidnapping, or murder?" she asked forthrightly as she stepped gingerly from the stage and began to stroll up the studio's center aisle, receiving admiring glances from the members of her mostly female audience. "Think it couldn't happen? You'll meet three women this evening who will convince you otherwise. You'll also meet a psychologist who will tell you they're not all that different from you or me. So stay tuned for 'Prison Groupies—Women Who Fall for Men Behind Bars.' That's the topic of the day on tonight's *O Darling!*"

On cue, the studio audience broke into loud applause. Tami flashed another irresistible smile, and the applause grew louder still as she exchanged a spontaneous high-five with a sixty-year-old woman whose hard face melted into a crimson blush as her hand made contact with Tami's.

Back on stage after the first commercial break, it was time for the opening, semi-serious segment of the program. Tami slipped into a plushly upholstered easy chair behind an expensive high-gloss wooden coffee table. On the table, perched upright in a plastic display stand, was a hardback book with a black-and-white cover photo of a physically well-endowed woman in a short skirt and spiked heels entering the gates of a penitentiary. To Tami's right, on the other side of the table, a thin, intense-looking woman in her late forties fidgeted in a matching easy chair, waiting to be introduced. Outfitted in a no-frills dark blue blazer and matching skirt, her hair tied back in a schoolmarm's bun, Tami's guest had the subdued demeanor of a professional, the perfect foil to Tami's boundless energy.

"It gives me great pleasure," Tami began, her gaze shifting from the woman to the audience, "to introduce tonight's first guest, Dr. Nancy Pollard. Dr. Pollard is a board-certified clinical psychologist practicing out of Beverly Hills, and a former consultant to the California Department of Corrections. She is also the author of the recently published book, *Looking for Mr. Wrong: The Groupie Phenomenon in America's Prisons*."

Tami lifted Pollard's book from its display stand and cradled it in her hands for a TV close-up. Then, as the camera pulled away, she added with a palm outstretched in Pollard's direction, "Welcome!"

Tami and the doctor exchanged greetings as the studio audience stirred restlessly, anticipating the raunchy tales of jailhouse sexcapades that would soon be coming their way. Tami knew that her fans would tolerate only so much academic banter before the groupies were brought on stage and the real fun began. Still, she believed that what Pollard had to say was important and would lend a certain integrity to her show, distinguishing it from its trashier competitors without any slippage in her ratings.

Tami's goal would be to elicit a general sociological overview of the groupie phenomenon from Pollard so that the viewers could better appreciate the personal stories they would hear directly from the groupies. This was the same format she had followed to great advantage in her programs on child abuse, teen pregnancy, infidelity, the sex lives of female bodybuilders, and innumerable other topics. To succeed with the approach meant that Tami had to be an all-purpose performer, informative as well as entertaining. As she had proven day in and day out, there wasn't a talk-show hostess in the nation more equal to the challenge.

Donning what she referred to as her "journalist's hat," Tami turned to Pollard and asked, "How did a straitlaced psychologist like yourself become interested in a subject like prison groupies?"

Prompted by the subtle motions of Tami's left hand, Pollard shifted in her seat and angled her face toward the camera. "In my work as a consultant to the state prison system, I directed a major research project on the conjugal visiting program that allows prisoners with good behavior credits to have sleep-over visits with their wives."

"Now, wait a minute," Tami interrupted as a rumble of disapproval rippled through the audience. "You and I may know that prisoners can receive these visits, but most people might be surprised, even shocked, to learn that their hard-earned tax money is used to finance a roll in the hay for men convicted of serious felonies."

"Well, the intent behind conjugal visits is really quite sound. The visits are designed to serve as a reward for good behavior and as a tool to keep families intact while the husband is incarcerated. The problem is that"—Pollard arched her eyebrows and adopted a more folksy tone—"the privilege can be abused, and it's not the only way that enterprising prisoners can spend time with willing female partners."

"And when did you become aware of this groupie phenomenon?"

"I was at Folsom Prison interviewing a prisoner convicted of ADW—assault with a deadly weapon—about his conjugal visits with his wife when the inmate suddenly received another female visitor."

"And the new visitor wasn't of the married variety?"

"Not only was she unmarried, she was one of about six other women this particular prisoner was receiving regular visits from."

"And then what happened in terms of your research?"

"Well, the inmate at Folsom—let's call him Bobby Joe, for short—told me that a lot of the inmates develop these friendships with women through responses to classified ads or by word of mouth from other prisoners, or even by contacting dating services. He gave me some names. I made a few inquiries and went to the library to review existing literature on the subject. Before long I had enough material for over twenty case profiles and a book."

"And one of the research materials you discovered, if I can toot my own horn for a moment, was a three-part series I wrote on the topic back when I was a reporter with the *Los Angeles Times*." Tami mugged lightheartedly for a close-up, drawing a round of cheers from the audience.

"Your articles were an invaluable source of information," Pollard acknowledged, looking slightly chagrined at Tami's chutzpah in plugging her own very modest contribution to the body of work on the subject.

"But what kind of women would fall for a complete stranger convicted of committing a violent crime?" The incredulity and indignation in Tami's voice, though entirely contrived, sounded genuine.

"Apart from their taste in men, the women I've talked to aren't all that unusual. If you saw them shopping at the mall or driving down the freeway, you'd hardly notice them. Most are employed and live fairly ordinary lives. The majority, I've found, come from modest working-class backgrounds, but I've interviewed several professional women, one of them a psychologist like myself, who developed love interests with men who had been sent to prison."

Pollard tittered softly to herself at her reference to the psychologist groupie. "It's only when they visit their friends in prison that they begin to act—and sometimes look—like the stereotypes we might hold of them."

"And what do these convicts have that guys out on the street don't? Is it just about sex?"

"Now, that's the sixty-four-thousand-dollar question." Pollard arched her eyebrows again. "Sex is usually the driving motivation for the prisoners, but the women are more complicated."

"Isn't that the truth," Tami remarked with a shake of her blond hair.

"In my book I've divided the prison groupies into four overlapping categories. First, and in my view most significantly, you have women with rescue fantasies. These are women who see their mission in life, whether consciously or unconsciously, as redeeming, taming, or improving wayward men."

"Well, I guess that's something we all can relate to, isn't it, ladies?" Tami asked, turning her palms upward and raising them to the ceiling cheerleader-style to arouse a response from the audience. "There are a lot of guys out there who need to clean up their acts." Several members of the audience reacted immediately with laughter and knowing nods. An attractive twenty-something woman was caught on camera giving her smirking male companion a playful swat across the top of the head.

"The role of the rescuer-redeemer is really quite a traditional position for women," Pollard added agreeably, "and if you're looking for a pool of readily available men in need of redemption, prisons are probably the ideal place to find them."

"And in addition to the redeemers?"

"You have women who are looking for the excitement and controlled danger of befriending a man convicted of a serious crime, and women who want to rebel in some way against mainstream social values or make a political statement of some kind. You also have women who may initially fall into another category but who eventually fall in love with a man they meet behind bars. Some of them even wind up marrying the inmate."

"I understand that prison marriages are becoming increasingly common."

Pollard nodded in agreement. "On both death row and in the general prison population."

"And lastly"—Pollard hurried to complete her inventory on the groupies—"you have women, who like the male inmates, are just looking for undisguised sexual titillation."

Pollard's comment drew a round of hoots and hollers from the audience, forcing Tami to wait for the commotion to subside before continuing. "Just one last question before we take our next commercial break and come back to meet our next round of guests," she said, pausing to take a deep breath as if contemplating how to phrase the inquiry. "Other than through conjugal visits, which are supposed to be reserved for married prisoners, how is it possible for an inmate to have sex with a female visitor?"

"Well, I wasn't exactly around shooting film for the eleven o'clock news," Pollard quipped, warming to her role as the purveyor of amusing anecdotes. "But as long as there are benches, chairs, and dark corners where busy hands can reach, and rest rooms in the vicinity . . ."

From the fifth row a half-dozen unruly young women wearing nose and eyebrow rings launched a chorus of catcalls, exhorting Tami to bring on the groupies. The tail end of Pollard's answer was drowned out in the process.

"Let's just say," Pollard said good-naturedly, recovering from the interruption, "where there's a will, there often is a way."

"Thank you, Doctor," Tami broke in, "I couldn't have said it better myself. You've been most enlightening, and good luck with your fascinating book." Tami smiled for the camera as the audience cheered in approval at the impending commercial break. "We'll return in a moment with round two of 'Prison Groupies.' Stay with us."

The muscular man in the white nurse's uniform diverted his eyes from the TV and turned his head toward the long blue couch along the far wall of the second-story living room. "I hate commercials as much as the next guy, Larry, but you're going to miss the entire show."

There was a touch of irritation and disappointment in the man's tone. "Ol' Randy works hard all day," he said, referring to himself. "The least you could do is show some appreciation."

Randy removed the plastic name tag from his uniform and dropped it on the end table next to the easy chair where he sat. The tag came to rest facedown alongside a large hypodermic needle. Randy stared for a moment at the needle and took another quick glance in the direction of the blue sofa. He shook his head in disgust, waiting for some kind of acknowledgment from Larry.

Larry, for his part, could manage only a weak and unresponsive moan. He was stretched out on the sofa in a clean white hospital gown, with an IV drip inserted in his right forearm and his right hand heavily bandaged. His puffy pink face bore the vacant expression of a man unable to comprehend his surroundings. Opening his eyes haltingly and with great effort, the only emotion he seemed to register was fear.

Frustrated by what he took as Larry's disinterest, Randy hit the mute button on the TV's remote control. Then he walked across the room and, after a second of indecision, unlocked the sliding glass doors that opened onto the bi-level cabin's redwood deck. He stepped outside.

It was a warm night, even for mid-July, and the sun setting behind the tree-lined ridges of the San Jacinto Mountains was turning the lush green colors of early summer to successively darker shades of brown, gray, and black. The mountain air was still and clean. Randy inhaled deeply and lifted his eyes to the sky, taking in its vast expanse, pausing to study the faint glimmer of the first stars of evening and the moon rising full and luminous. This was how he liked it. Only the sounds of the bluejays, crows, and sparrows that made their homes in the forests south of Riverside broke the tranquillity of the setting. The nearest neighboring cabin was more than a hundred yards away, and with the Independence Day holiday come and gone, its owners were not due to return for several weeks.

Such quiet evenings always brought out the philosopher in Randy. "It's funny when you think about it," he said in a voice resonating with thoughtful reflection. "Technology has completely changed the way we experience the night."

Even if Larry had been listening, he was long past comprehension. Still, Randy was determined to share his insights aloud. "Our ancestors would retreat to their caves, mud huts and tepees to recite magical chants to make sure the sun would come up in the morning. And they'd build fires—great death fires that danced at night." Randy paused to consider the solemnity of the ancient imagery he had conjured, then shook his head, as if jolting himself back to the present. "Nowadays, you have to come to a place like this to get back in touch with the rhythms of nature.

"But even here," he continued, stepping back inside, "the experience is adulterated by the roof over your head, air conditioning, and color TV. Still, I can't complain, all things considered."

His soliloquy completed, Randy resumed his seat in front of the tube and clicked off the mute button, bringing the sound of the *O Darling!* hour streaming back into the cabin.

Back on stage, Tami was well into the heart of her program, interviewing her three groupie guests. Each guest, Tami explained, had been asked to appear in the kind of clothes she normally wore on dates, and each had been asked to share something of her most outrageous visiting-room experiences.

Brenda, an overweight black woman in her early thirties, came dressed in a black leather mini-skirt that would have been a size too small for a woman twenty pounds lighter. Claudia, a busty twenty-eight-year-old Latina, arrived outfitted in shorts and a halter top that exposed a heart-shaped tattoo on her abdomen. Although each held down responsible full-time jobs, Brenda as a cashier and Claudia as a word processor, they warmed to the task of allowing the audience to glimpse their seamy sides. Using contrived "gangsta-bitch" slang and exaggerated head movements to spice up their stories, they eagerly related their sessions giving under-the-table hand jobs and oral cop to inmates they had met on recommendations from other women. Only the "bleeps" from the show's censors and occasional catcalls from the audience interrupted their presentations.

The clear audience favorite, however, was Jessica, a matronly white woman with a degree in accounting, whose expensive maroon business suit might otherwise have led viewers to mistake her for one of the show's executive producers.

"Jessica met her 'friend' at Folsom Prison after answering a classified ad she saw in a local throwaway paper," Tami said, reading from the prepared script on the TelePrompTer.

"That would be the *South Coast Inquirer,* a weekly published every Monday in Los Angeles and distributed throughout Southern California," Jessica interjected.

"And is this your normal visiting room attire?" Tami asked incredulously.

"William, who is now my fiancée," Jessica answered with a straight face, "made it clear from the beginning that he didn't want me looking like a streetwalker. I let him know that I was an accountant. It was his preference that I always wear a business suit."

"And your most outrageous visiting room experience?"

Jessica paused to think, her lips curling into a playful smile. "I suppose that would have to be sex in a rest room. We managed to slip away when the guards weren't looking."

The audience roared with laughter, drowning out Jessica's attempt to provide more lurid details.

"No, we've checked with the authorities," Tami shouted, quieting down the audience with a downward motion of her hands, "so we know you don't have a criminal record. Didn't you realize that what you and William were doing was against the law?"

"I suppose, but at the time I didn't think about it, and I just didn't care." Jessica shrugged her shoulders as the audience hooted again.

"Who would have thought that life behind bars could be so exciting?" Tami shouted once more above the din. "But say no more. We've got to leave something to the imagination."

"She doesn't know squat about life behind bars," Randy grumbled, his face bathed in the reflected blue light of the TV. "She's nothing but a crass, self-promoting cunt. You know that, Larry?"

Larry moaned another feeble reply, which Randy took as an expression of agreement. Shifting restlessly in his easy chair, Randy rolled up his left pant leg. Then he lifted the hypodermic needle from the end table and inserted it deep into his thigh, releasing the needle's contents into a large vein. "Maybe I should lighten up on your Demerol, Larry," he said. "I'm getting tired of talking to myself."

Back on TV, Brenda was receiving a surprise visit from her boyfriend, a studly white guy who had just been paroled after an armed-robbery stint. Crying tears of joy, Brenda collapsed into her boyfriend's arms as Tami proposed to open up the show to questions from the studio audience.

"Fucking cunt," Randy grumbled again. "But I have to admit I like her show. How about you, Larry?"

Larry's silence prompted further annoyance. "Don't die on me, Larry," Randy commanded. "Not yet anyway." He walked slowly to the sofa and stared at the pathetic figure below him. "That's not how the game is supposed to go."

Chapter Two

"Number fifteen, *Evans* versus *Eckhart et. al.* Counsel may approach." The harried-looking clerk hardly looked up from her desk as she called out the next case on Judge Brian Hanson's busy Wednesday morning law-and-motion calendar.

Judge Hanson, the grand vizier of Department 305 of the Los Angeles County Superior Court, pulled another large manila legal file from the stack of two dozen others resting on his bench. Peering through a set of thick black horn-rimmed glasses, he began to leaf through the file, refreshing his memory of the medical malpractice trial that recently had concluded in his courtroom. "Has counsel reviewed my tentative ruling?" he asked, staring impatiently at Attorney David Nova.

Standing at the lectern in his best pinstripe three-piece, David Nova knew that he had little chance of prevailing on the motion he had filed for a new trial. Worse still, he knew that Judge Hanson would spare him a scant five minutes before giving him the bum's rush and moving on to the next loser on his morning calendar.

"If it pleases the court," Nova began politely enough, "I've raised a number of points in my papers.

And while Your Honor has addressed all of them in your tentative ruling, I'd like briefly to discuss our jury-instruction issue."

"And if it doesn't please the court?" Judge Hanson asked testily. "Would that change anything in the greater scheme of civil justice? There are nine other matters I have to wade through before noon, Mr. Nova."

"I'm aware of the court's time pressures," Nova said, trying to contain his anger at His Honor's imperious manner. As cynical as he had become about the lawsuit lottery, he believed he had deserved to win the trial and that only Judge Hanson's judicial miscues had prevented him from walking away with a seven-figure verdict.

"Then get on with it."

Nova gritted his teeth and glanced at his counterpart, attorney Molly Carpenter, seated in the defense counsel's chair to his left. "As the court knows, my client's husband entrusted himself to the care of Dr. Eckhart and Saint Thomas Hospital for a routine coronary-bypass operation. He was told that he would be in the hospital for no more than a week postoperative and that within a matter of months he would be able to resume a full range of normal activities. Instead, he contracted a drug-resistant staph infection after the operation and died two weeks later."

Judge Hanson frowned and glanced at his watch. "And the jury, after due consideration of the expert testimony proffered by both sides, determined that neither the doctor nor the nursing staff committed malpractice. This sort of thing happens all the time. In medical malpractice trials, like other trials, one side wins and the other loses. I fail to see the point of your motion."

"The point I'd like to make, Your Honor, is that

you refused to instruct the jury on the p.
res ipsa loquitur." Nova always loved it when ₁.
drop a Latin phrase in court, and he warmed t₁
opportunity to use one now.

"Literally translated as 'the thing speaks for itself,' "
he added condescendingly, as though addressing a
first-year law student, "that's the doctrine which holds
that when the patient sustains an injury that does not
ordinarily occur in the absence of negligence, it will
be presumed that negligence, or malpractice in this
context, caused the injury. Twenty or thirty years ago,
bypass surgery was a risky procedure. Today it's routine. Otherwise healthy people don't contract lethal
infections from a bypass unless there was negligence.
Had Your Honor given our requested instruction, as
we were so entitled under the law, the jury would
have found for the plaintiff. I'd be here today defending against opposing counsel's motion for a new
trial rather than making one myself."

Nova's voice grew louder and perceptibly less defer-
ential as he spoke. His face hardened, and his dark
eyes narrowed into accusatory slits. A faint rumble of
excited conversation rose among the lawyers seated in
the gallery, who were waiting to argue their own cases.
It wasn't every day that an attorney had the balls, or
poor judgment, to stand up in court and deliver a
personal dressing-down to a judge. Yet that was exactly what Nova was doing. Since he had no prayer
of convincing Judge Hanson that he had fumbled the
jury instructions, Nova hoped that his remarks might
prompt the judge into saying something equally intem-
perate or ill considered that he could exploit in a possible appeal.

As a strategy, Nova's approach was the stuff of desperation. It was also a professionally risky one with a
judge like Hanson, who had a reputation for re-

warding smart-ass attorneys with stiff monetary sanctions and referrals to the state bar. Nova, however, had long since lost his reverence for the staid traditions of the courtroom. He might have lost the trial, and this morning's motion, but he was not about to genuflect or grovel in front of Hanson or any other inferior intellect in a black robe. He had kissed ass and played the game for too many years, he reminded himself, as he waited for Hanson's response.

"The trial your clients received in this court was fair and impartial," Judge Hanson replied icily but refusing to take Nova's bait. "Ms. Carpenter?" he asked, turning away from Nova. "Is there anything you'd care to add on behalf of the defendants?"

"Just briefly, Your Honor." Molly walked to the lectern and directed a sympathetic glance at Nova, who remained standing at the counsel table. Dressed in a tasteful gray suit, she was a tall, slender woman— at five ten just two inches shorter than Nova—with straight brown hair cropped just below her chin in an economical pageboy. From her plain gold hoop earrings to the single strand of white pearls around her neck and the sensible black low-heeled pumps on her feet, she was the image of the no-nonsense female lawyer. Rock solid, reliable, and incisive.

"No one ever wants to see a patient die, least of all a physician with as long a history of first-rate medical service as Dr. John Eckhart. But contrary to counsel's contention, every surgical procedure has risks. Sometimes even the best surgery and the best postoperative care cannot prevent infection. Evidence that a bad result is rare does not, by itself, warrant a presumption of negligence. The law on this point is quite clear. On the facts of this case, Your Honor correctly instructed the jury that the plaintiff bore the burden of proving Dr. Eckhart's negligence without the aid of any presumption. The plaintiff simply failed to meet that burden." Molly turned toward Nova and gave him a consoling half smile, as if to say that there would be other cases and other trials, that she, too, knew how it felt to lose a close one.

Judge Hanson reached for the next file on his list even before Molly had completed her statement. Almost as an afterthought, he intoned, "The motion for new trial is denied." To his clerk he added, "Call the next case."

Nova pushed his way through the crowded corridor outside of Hanson's courtroom and managed to catch up with Molly just before she boarded the elevator. "Can we talk?" he asked. He brushed a few wayward strands of black hair from his forehead and gave her one of his charming smiles, the kind he liked to think his lady friends found so disarming.

"If it's about the trial, maybe some other time. I've got to get back to the office." With her briefcase tightly gripped in one hand and her car keys already pulled out of her jacket pocket and gripped in the other, she looked in a hurry. It was the way she let her eyes linger on Nova's smile, however, that made her protest sound less than fully convincing.

"It's not about the trial," Nova assured her. He glanced at his watch, determined to change her mind. "Come on, it's nearly eleven forty-five. Even a hard-driven type A like you has to eat lunch. After kicking my tail all over court, it's the least you can do." Slowly, the smile gave way to the kind of earnest expression Molly knew she had to take seriously.

"We can go to Swanson's," he continued. "I'll buy."

Located a block from the downtown civil court-house, Swanson's Bar & Grille was a Los Angeles institution and a favorite hangout for refugees from the legal system and reporters from the nearby *L.A. Times.* Founded in the late fifties by two transplanted New Yorkers who brought the oak-and-leather motif of the Big Apple's watering holes with them, Swanson's boasted the strongest mixed drinks and the best cheeseburgers in the downtown area. It was also a place where people could talk—about sports, earthquakes, the weather, politics, the latest fashions, and above all, the law.

Arriving ahead of the main lunch crowd, Nova and Molly found a quiet booth in the back. Nova ordered a single-malt Scotch rocks and a London burger for himself, a glass of chardonnay and a Caesar salad for Molly. His eyes trailed after their waitress, a leggy blonde with a tight rump and a low-cut black nylon top.

"Still thinking with your pecker, I see," Molly observed, noticing Nova's momentary distraction.

"No harm in looking."

She frowned in disapproval.

"Can you tell me honestly that she doesn't enjoy being looked at?"

"Maybe we should ask her. She'll probably tell you that you're ten years too old for her, or that she only goes for guys with nose rings, or that she finds *me* more attractive." Molly smiled and shook her head, as though reproaching an incorrigible schoolboy. "Now, I'm sure you didn't insist on lunch just to let me see you ogle the hired help. What gives?"

Despite Nova's earlier urgency, he was unwilling to open their conversation with anything but small talk. "So how long has it been since we came here together?" he asked, gazing idly at a row of 1920s-era black-and-white wall photographs depicting a very different-looking downtown Los Angeles. "Four, five years?"

"About that."

"I nearly lost my breakfast when I learned that Dr. Eckhart's insurance carrier referred the case to you."

" 'Med mal' has become something of a specialty for me. The docs, the hospitals, and the carriers seem to like what they're getting, so the referrals just keep on coming. I've even had to turn down some cases."

"You've become one hell of a trial lawyer."

"Well, I had a pretty good teacher."

Nova smiled at the compliment, revealing a set of dimples in his cheeks that gave him a boyish appearance despite the five o'clock shadow already forming on his face. It had been twelve years since Molly had resigned her associate's position in the small law firm Nova had headed at the time. Although she said she just wanted to start her own practice, Nova always thought that Molly had somehow sensed that Nova's firm had no future. Not long after her departure, the firm fell apart under the weight of insufficient revenues and personality conflicts between Nova and his two partners.

The waitress returned with their drinks. This time Nova kept his eyes, if not his mind, entirely on Molly. "And how's your social life been? I think I heard awhile back you were getting serious with some guy, a fellow member of the bar, if I have my facts right."

"It wasn't anything serious, just the same old, same old," she sighed. "You know, girl lawyer meets boy lawyer. They exchange phone numbers and e-mail addresses, see a few movies, hop in the sack, and move on to the next retainer. Actually, I met him on the firing range of my gun club. We did some camping together, and he liked the way I handled a thirty-eight."

"Maybe that's what scared him off. It's not every day you meet a woman who can write a supreme court brief in the morning and plug a hole through a beer can at thirty paces in the afternoon."

"Hey, a girl's got to protect herself. Learning how to shoot was one thing my daddy taught me."

"Good old Colonel Carpenter," Nova said, recalling that Molly had spent much of her youth shuttling back and forth between various military bases until her father, a career officer, finally retired to Southern California. "How is he?"

"Passed away three years ago."

"I'm sorry." Nova sounded like he meant it.

"Thanks." She sipped her wine. "He left me some property and his old dog, who went to fido heaven last spring."

Molly's story was interrupted by the arrival of their food. Famished from her morning in court, she began to dig into her salad but not without noticing the enormity of Nova's London burger and the mound of calorific steak fries that came with it. "Heart attack on a plate," she observed wryly. "You never did take particularly good care of yourself."

"What do you mean?" Nova objected, tapping his stomach lightly with the fingers of his right hand. "I've got the abs of a seventeen-year-old." Even if he was pushing forty-five and on the down side of hunkdom, Nova was still a more than presentable specimen, with a healthy olive-toned complexion, a strong masculine jaw, and a full head of straight black hair that had only begun to show the first traces of distinguished salt and pepper above the ears.

"You've also got the eating habits of a seventeen-year-old," Molly replied. She took another sip of wine, then added, "So how's *your* personal life?"

"That's what I wanted to talk to you about." Nova

reached into his briefcase and pulled out a thick legal file. His demeanor suddenly became serious.

Molly's eyes widened, as if she knew just what was coming. "It's about you and Tami, isn't it? I've heard about the divorce, but that was quite some time ago. Has something else happened?"

"The divorce was a piece of cake. We had no problem with the division of property. I kept the house in Topanga. She kept her place in Malibu, and we agreed to waive any claims on each other's earnings. It's Jamie that's the problem. Tami's TV show is relocating to New York in the fall, and she wants to take Jamie with her. She's filed an order to show cause, asking the court to modify our joint-custody arrangement. I'm afraid things have gotten pretty ugly."

Nova removed a thick, single-spaced document from the file and handed it to Molly. "It's the original and supplemental report and recommendation of the psychologist who prepared our family evaluation for the court," he said sarcastically. "I had high hopes, but she's siding with Tami."

Molly gave the report a quick perusal. The evaluator, a local clinical psychologist with a specialty in family counseling, had conducted in-depth interviews with the parents—Tami Dawson, aka Tami Darling, and David Nova, as well as their ten-year-old daughter, Jamie. The interviews were summarized at some length, and were followed by a series of findings and conclusions, all couched in the vernacular of contemporary therapeutics. The bottom line was the shrink's recommendation that primary physical custody be awarded to the mother and that Jamie be permitted to move with her mom to New York. The report also indicated that a copy had been served on both parents and on Tami's counsel, Thomas Brockman.

"Thomas Brockman," Molly said, sounding impressed.

"Tami's retained one of the nastiest pit bulls in the biz. Who's representing you?"

"I *was* being represented by Bud Baker," Nova said, emphasizing the past tense of the relationship. "He handled the initial separation and dissolution."

"But?"

"He wanted me to approve the move to New York and settle for liberal visitation. I fired him."

"So now you're unrepresented. Am I right?"

Nova nodded sheepishly. "Bud's a compromiser, not a fighter. He's just not right for this kind of case."

"Where is Jamie now?" Molly asked, growing more exasperated.

"That's where things also get complicated."

"You mean that's where you screwed up." She waited for an explanation.

Nova swallowed the last of his Scotch. "Long before I learned about Tami's transfer to New York, I agreed to let Jamie go to summer camp in the Catskills. Tami's sister Barbara has an apartment in Manhattan, and Jamie begged me to keep my promise. Tami agreed to pay for the camp and to bring Jamie back for the custody hearing if we need her. So I figured, 'Where's the harm'?"

"I'll tell you where the harm is," Molly lectured. "Tom Brockman's going to eat you for dinner. He'll point out that Jamie loves camp and has shown she is already well on her way toward making a smooth transition to life in New York."

She put down her fork, intent on making her point. "The judge is going to take a long, hard look at you and Tami, and ask himself who is better equipped to raise a teenage girl. On the one hand, he'll see a middle-aged man who thinks that every woman on the planet craves him like no-calorie chocolate. On the other, he'll see a self-made professional woman who seems like she just stepped out of the pages of *Working Mothers* magazine. Even with a good lawyer, you'd be lucky to come away with some kind of joint custody. But you're not even represented. Jesus, David, get real."

Nova gazed at Molly expectantly.

"So that's what this is all about," she said, putting two and two together. "You want me to take your case."

"You handled my first divorce," Nova said contritely. "You're the best."

"That was ages ago, right before I left your office, and it was uncontested. As your employee I was in no position to say no. Things are different now. A custody hearing takes a lot of work. With my current caseload, it's just not in the cards."

"I'm prepared to pay top dollar, and I've already done most of the legwork," Nova countered. "I've found some disgruntled former employees from Tami's show who will swear up and down that the only difference between the real Tami Darling and a snake in the grass is that the snake has a heart and a soul. So most of the grunt work's already done. All you have to do is step in for the hearing. *Badda bing, badda bang,* as they used to say back in Newark." The Italian section of Newark, New Jersey, was where Nova was born and where he was raised until high school, when his father, a machinist, got a job with Douglas Aircraft that enabled the old man to move the family to Long Beach, California.

"If I were you, I'd forget about the cute expressions you picked up from the old neighborhood," Molly said, suppressing the urge to laugh at Nova's comical attempt to imitate an East Coast "made guy." "The last thing you want is for the court to think you're some kind of transplanted sleazy dago with custom-made leisure suits and boyhood friends named Jimmy the Weasel. After nearly thirty years out here, you ought to know better.''

"Hey, my grandmother used the same expression," Nova said in mock protest.

"Oh, right," Molly said, recalling, as best she could, the bits and pieces she had learned of Nova's family history while she was an associate in his office. "She was the one who really raised you and your sister, and who was always imparting little pearls of wisdom about the good life."

"We used to call them 'lessons in life.' *Fear God, and always wash behind your ears* was her favorite," Nova remarked, hoping to coax another chuckle out of Molly.

Sensing that she was unmoved, he decided to plead. "Look, I know that I'm a skirt chaser, but Jamie never sees any of that. I'm a good father, and Jamie is all I have. If Tami takes her to live in New York, I'll lose her, no matter what kind of joint-custody order the court issues."

"But Tami has just as much to lose if Jamie stays with you, doesn't she?"

"All that Tami cares about is her career. Her idea of spending quality time with the kid is a phone call from the studio while someone from the makeup department works on her hair and another retouches her nails. Christ, she wasn't even home when I picked Jamie up to drive her to the airport. The only person to say good-bye was Tami's Central American housekeeper. I don't want my daughter raised by a retinue of servants."

Molly appeared to mull the matter over. "So you want me to make America's talk-show sweetheart look like the reincarnation of *Mommy Dearest*. That's what you're saying."

"You'd only be bringing out the truth." Nova slid the rest of the file across the table to Molly. "There's a settlement conference tomorrow before Judge Fowler."

"Tomorrow?" Molly asked, nearly choking on her wine at Nova's nerve.

"It will only take an hour or two," Nova said apologetically, "and I've already submitted our brief for the conference. All you have to do is read through the file, show up, and make a few brilliant remarks on my behalf."

"That and rearrange my morning appointments." She grew silent, and for a moment it seemed like she was getting ready to turn him down. "But why Fowler?" she asked finally, still sounding interested. "He's a retired judge. Isn't that a little unusual?"

"It was one of the few things Tami and I agreed on before Brockman got in the way and ordered her not to talk with me about the case. We're splitting Fowler's fees. If he can't work things out, the full-blown custody hearing's set to go in another three weeks before Judge Judith Goldstein in family court. I think you and she are old law school chums."

"If you think that I have some kind of in with Judy, forget about it. She's all business."

"Actually," Nova added, "she seems like a rather thoughtful judge to me. We've had one appearance before her. She ordered our shrink to prepare the supplemental report and had no problem giving me a continuance for the hearing."

"I'll let you in on a little secret known only to us girls," Molly replied. "Judy Goldstein is what guys like you call a ball buster. Hates men with a passion most people reserve for twelve-legged insects." Molly ripped a jagged hunk of bread from the sourdough loaf that had come with her salad as if to emphasize

the point. "It might help if you could find some poor
misguided female who knows you intimately and is
prepared to testify that you're not really the county's
number one sexist."

Nova winced at the prospect of finding a credible
woman to serve as a character witness on his behalf.
Still, he couldn't deny that Molly's suggestion seemed
like a good tactic. "I'll see what I can do."

She gave him a grudging smile, appearing satisfied,
despite her stern tone, that she had agreed to come
to the rescue of an old friend. "Okay, but from now
on I call the shots. No more bonehead moves."

"Aye, aye, Cap'n." Nova returned her smile.

"That includes that middle-aged form of gymnastics
you call your love life."

"I'll be the soul of discretion."

Molly arched a quizzical eyebrow.

"Actually, I haven't had a date in two weeks," Nova
said, as if confessing to an embarrassing personal
failing.

"Keep it up and monkhood will be just around the
corner." She took the divorce file from him and
squeezed it into her briefcase. "I'll call Fowler and
Brockman and tell them I'm on board."

Chapter Three

The Los Angeles headquarters of the Federal Bureau of Investigation was housed in a seventeen-story concrete-and-steel bunker that would have fit right in with Albert Speer's master plan for the new Berlin. Located on busy Wilshire Boulevard near the once trendy Westwood Village section of town, the gray and imperial United States Federal Office Building was also the local base of the CIA and less forbidding public agencies like the Federal Trade Commission, the Peace Corps, and the Passport Office. Its architectural aesthetics notwithstanding, the place was a constant hub of activity. On weekdays it teemed with government officials, harried businesspeople, and bewildered citizens searching for assistance from a disinterested bureaucracy. And on any given weekend, ragtag bands of disgruntled political activists could be found demonstrating on the building's sprawling front lawn, warbling old protest anthems and waving makeshift banners before passing motorists.

Since transferring from the FBI's Seattle branch in the early eighties, Supervisory Special Agent Tony Ross had made the federal building his home. An uncomfortable outsider at first, he had long ago learned to ignore the tumult around him and hone his concentration on the job of putting bad guys behind bars. Handling everything from bank robberies to complex drug-smuggling cases, Ross had worked his way through the ranks, moving from a cramped squad-room cubicle to his own private seventeenth-floor office with a panoramic view of the traffic-snarled 405 freeway. In a world of largely interchangeable G-men, all fighting for promotion, he had carved out a reputation for himself as a cop's cop—one who could talk gigabytes with the computer geeks, DNA samples with the wonks in white lab coats, and surveillance techniques with the stiffs from the graveyard shift.

Among the occasional duties that came with his senior position was the task of fielding media inquiries in the extortion and kidnapping investigations he supervised. A no-nonsense family man noted for his uninhibited tongue and strong conservative views, Ross refused to let his role in the spotlight go to his head. He never pursued interviews, but he never shied away from them either. When called upon, he played the role with the deadpan perfection of a seasoned pro.

Ross was particularly adept at explaining the Bureau's progress on high-profile cases. The trick, he fondly told his underlings, was to convey just enough information to assure the public that the feds had the situation under control, that the "perps" would be found, prosecuted, and punished to the full extent of the law. Revealing anything more, like a detailed description of a crime scene or a suspect's M.O., could jeopardize the integrity of an investigation.

Maintaining a tight lip at this afternoon's hastily called press briefing was particularly easy, but for all the wrong reasons. Ross knew just about zip on the latest crime to come his way—the suspected abduction of a Ninth U.S. Circuit Court of Appeals judge.

Ross also knew that ordinarily the honor of convening the first press conference on a case of such magnitude would fall to the Los Angeles assistant director. But the A.D. was on a rare European vacation, and, even with so little known about the crime, it would have been political suicide for the Bureau to remain silent any longer than it already had. The kidnapping of a federal judge was big news, or soon would be. If the FBI didn't take the initiative in shaping the initial media spin, the media would inevitably learn of the crime and take off in a thousand different directions, portraying the feds as bungling halfwits, enemies of the First Amendment, cover-up artists, or worse. In a singular gesture of confidence, Washington had given Ross a personal green light to proceed not only with the briefing, but to head up the investigation to follow.

With all these concerns and more in mind, the elevator ride to Bureau's spacious first-floor press-briefing room was unusually fraught with anxiety. As Ross stepped to the walnut-veneer podium, with the great seal of the United States plastered on the wall behind him and a row of TV floodlights in front of him, he grimaced from the latest flare-up of the peptic ulcer that in his lighter moments he sarcastically called his "little buddy."

He cleared his throat and began. "Ladies and gentlemen, Lawrence Tanner, senior judge of the Ninth Circuit Court of Appeals, has not been seen for five days. Upon completion of routine preliminary inquiries, the Federal Bureau of Investigation has decided to treat the incident as a probable kidnapping. We are in the process of establishing a joint task force with state and local officials, and we are confident that we will find the perpetrators of this crime. In the meantime, we ask anyone with knowledge of Judge Tanner's whereabouts to contact the FBI. A recent photograph of the judge will be distributed to the media along with the telephone hotline members of the public can call to relay information."

Ross poured himself a glass of water, then added, "I'll take some brief questions."

"Have you identified any suspects?" came the obvious inquiry from an eager young female TV reporter.

"We're looking into various possibilities," Ross replied vaguely. "We prefer to say nothing more at the present time so as to prevent leaks of confidential information."

"Judge Tanner is a staunch, old-school liberal," another reporter chimed in. The reporter's casual dress and scraggly hair identified him as a stringer for the local "alternative" throwaway paper, the *South Coast Inquirer*. "Is there any indication that the abduction is politically motivated?"

"We have no evidence of that," Ross answered dismissively and pointed at another scribe whose hand was held aloft.

"When did the abduction occur?"

"Judge Tanner was last seen leaving the federal courthouse in Pasadena Friday evening. He had planned to take the following Monday off to run some personal errands and was due back at the courthouse early Tuesday morning, but he did not appear."

"Why did you wait until this afternoon to announce that he was missing?"

"We wanted to contact the judge's many professional and personal associates to confirm that he was indeed missing and not ill. We hope that we are mistaken, but at this time we cannot rule out foul play and in fact suspect it."

Figuratively speaking, Topanga Canyon was about as far away from Ross' press conference as you could get without leaving Los Angeles County. For David

Nova, taking the Topanga Canyon Boulevard exit off
the Hollywood Freeway always meant that he was
leaving the legal rat race behind for the solace of the
rugged open-hill country that sat like a land develop-
er's dream between the Pacific Ocean and the posh
Malibu Colony to the south and the suburban nightmare of the San Fernando Valley to the north.

Were it not for Nova's general preference for A.M.
news radio, he might not have learned of the press
conference until the eleven o'clock news or until he
scanned the front-page headlines of tomorrow's *Times*.
His spirits buoyed by Molly's decision to take on his
custody case, Nova had knocked off work early, intending to phone Jamie at her summer camp. He was
on his way home in his steel-gray Lexus sedan, channel-
surfing the dial, when a live bulletin from the FBI field
office broke over the air.

"And there you have it," correspondent Marta Sua-
rez announced, "Special Agent Anthony Ross of the
FBI has disclosed shocking news of the kidnapping of
federal appeals judge Lawrence Tanner. As one of the
journalists gathered at this afternoon's press conference hinted, there is speculation the abduction may
be politically inspired. Judge Tanner is known as one
of the leading liberal activists on the federal bench,
and sources close to the Ninth Circuit Court of Appeals confirm that the judge has received death threats
in the past from right-wing paramilitary organizations.
As yet, however, the FBI has identified no suspects."

"Son of a bitch," Nova muttered to himself. "The
old lech probably had a coronary fucking one of his
law clerks."

Nova hastily switched the radio of his Lexus to an
F.M. rock-music station and turned up the volume.
He already had enough problems on his mind without
sharing in the travails of the larger world. The sounds

of John Hiatt filled the Lexus. A few Grateful Dead, U-2, and Counting Crows tracks followed. In another ten minutes, with a Bruce Springsteen oldie ringing in his ears, Nova was near the summit of Topanga Canyon Boulevard, operating on auto pilot as he negotiated the last of the tight switchback turns that led to the driveway of his home.

For the past ten years, home for David Nova had been a sprawling three-bedroom hillside rancher he and Tami had purchased when she was pregnant with Jamie. Back then she was still a dedicated journalist and he was still an idealistic lawyer arguably on the rise. Though it came with a leaky roof and plumbing that backed up in heavy winter rains, the home's backyard was a major selling point. Large enough for a small horse stable, it featured a flagstone patio overlooking a boulder-strewn arroyo lined with pine and pepper trees that stretched untouched by human hands all the way to the freeway. Nova and Tami fixed the roof, installed new copper pipes, and built a small corral for a Shetland pony they bought for Jamie's fifth birthday. They also shared many a boozy evening under the stars cavorting on the patio chaise longues after Jamie had been put to bed.

It was hard to recall when or why the initial chinks in the marriage first appeared. Like many other professional couples, he and Tami had been so wrapped up in their separate careers, they didn't see the distance they had put between themselves until the gulf was too large to cross. The resulting separation, and now the divorce, was inevitable. As if to signify just how things had changed, the old corral now stood empty (Jamie having outgrown the pony), the chaise longues had rusted to the point where they had to be hauled off to the local landfill, and the roof had started to leak again over the living room fireplace last winter. Only the copper pipes, with their ninety-nine-year guarantee against blockage and corrosion, seemed to withstand the sea changes.

Nova pulled his Lexus into the two-car garage, taking care to leave a wide berth between the luxury sedan and the 1964 Chevy Impala convertible that sat in the other bay. He had purchased the Chevy after his separation from Tami at a car auction at the Pomona Fairplex, and had spent much of his free time since then plying the skills he had learned from his father, restoring the car to near-mint condition. Apart from the Saturday afternoons he spent with Jamie and the nighttime trysts he shared with various and sundry ladies of horizontal recreation, working on the old car was one of the few activities in which he found any satisfaction.

Nova gave the Chevy the once-over, making sure no unsightly pools of motor oil had collected beneath it and no scratches had somehow gone undetected on its two-tone blue-and-white painted body. Then he gathered up his briefcase and opened the interior door that led to the laundry room. From there he made his way into the kitchen, pausing only to pour himself a stiff Scotch on ice, before crossing through the living room and into his study, where he parked himself in the high-backed leather swivel chair behind his desk. He glanced at his watch and saw, to his relief, that it was just five o'clock. There was enough time to reach Jamie before the camp counselors gave the order for "lights out" at eight-thirty Eastern time.

It took some insisting with the elderly woman who answered his call, but after a long wait Nova had his daughter on the line.

"Daddy!" Jamie exclaimed. "I didn't expect you to call until the weekend. How are you? I hope you're feeling better."

It was just like Jamie, always thinking first of how others were feeling before saying anything about herself. Nova was constantly baffled and impressed by her capacity for empathy, a trait neither he nor Tami had passed on to her. "I'm fine, honey, just fine. How are you?"

"I'm having so much fun. This is the greatest camp. We go swimming and horseback riding every day. We play softball, and we're planning a big ten-day camping and canoe trip to the Adirondack mountains next month. There won't be any electricity or radios, and no phones either."

Nova could hear the joy in Jamie's voice. She was still his little girl, but she was growing up so fast it scared him. "That sounds exciting, but I want you to be careful. Make sure you use a life vest and take plenty of sunblock."

"Daddy, I know how to take care of myself."

"I know you do, sweetheart."

"Is anything wrong, Daddy?" Yet another of Jamie's uncanny qualities was her ability to read his moods. "Are you and Mommy getting along any better?"

The one childhood illusion Jamie seemed unable to shake, despite her otherwise grown-up outlook, was the hope that her parents would someday reconcile. "Mommy and I have some problems we still have to work out," he answered vaguely.

"Am I going to stay in New York after the summer or come back to L.A. to live with you? Aunt Barbara says I'm going to stay here."

"We're not sure yet. That's what the court has to decide."

"No matter what happens, I love you both, Daddy. You can tell that to the judge." For the first time since getting on the phone, Jamie sounded a little sad.

"And your mom and I both love you and want only the best for you."

"I know, Daddy. Can you do me a favor?"

"Sure, honey."

"Can you send me my baseball bat, the one you bought me for Little League? I remember how you taught me to swing, but I need my own bat. I think I left it in your backyard, or at Mom's."

Nova canvassed his mind, trying to think when he last saw the aluminum bat. It might have been in the backyard or possibly in the bedroom he still kept made up for Jamie's weekend visits. "I'll look for it," he promised, "and I'll talk to Mom if it's not here."

Nova could hear the uptight woman who had answered his phone call mumble something to his daughter. "Daddy," Jamie said, "I've got to go now. I'll write soon. I love you."

"Love you, too."

Nova replaced the receiver and let his eyes drift across the room. Although his mind was fixed on Jamie and the upcoming custody battle, his gaze settled on an eight-by-ten black-and-white photo sitting in an upright glass frame, gathering dust on top of an old wooden bookshelf. Taken some eighteen years ago, the snapshot showed a beaming David Nova, young and trim, accepting a rolled certificate at an awards luncheon from the honorable Lawrence Tanner. The certificate marked the completion of the two-year clerkship he had served with the judge after graduation from UCLA Law School.

Even now, looking at the photo, he could hear Tanner telling him as he handed over the scroll, that he had landed Nova a plum associate's position in Tanner's old law firm, one of the state's largest. "You have a great future ahead of you, David," Tanner told him. "If there's anything I can do for you, don't hesitate to call."

"Son of a bitch, Larry," Nova muttered under his breath as he studied the photo. "If it wasn't your little pecker that got you into trouble, it must have been your big mouth."

Chapter Four

Was it early evening or daybreak? The thin shafts of light slanting through the edges of the garage door gave no clue. Flat and gray, the light was barely enough to illuminate the hardwood frame of Larry Tanner's bed or the unfinished redwood ceiling overhead. One of the first things Randy had taken from Tanner was his Rolex watch with the glowing green phosphorescent dial. No matter. Tanner had no appointments to keep, no meetings to convene, no lawyers to interrogate from his lofty judicial perch. Except for an occasional bowl of soup or oatmeal or an even less frequent trip up the back stairs, there were no daily events to break the monotony of captivity.

He had been asleep—two, four, eight hours. There was no way of knowing. Awake finally, he rubbed his forehead with his left hand and opened his eyes, letting them drift across the semidarkness. The pain in his bandaged right hand was dull but constant. The IV drip, still inserted in his right forearm, itched. He recognized the solution and the calming effect it had as Demerol, quite probably mixed with an antibiotic. Was it meant to relieve the pain, or to drug him into a perpetual torpor in which he would remain unaware of his surroundings and location? Perhaps the drip served both purposes. He made a mental note to ask his captor. Then slowly, even against his will, he felt his mind wander.

It got hot during the day, and cool at night, but never unbearably so, for which he silently gave thinks. The cool mountain air and the stand of tall pines outside the cabin kept the garage reasonably comfortable in the day. A noisy vertical space heater, positioned at the foot of his bed, maintained the temperature at a constant seventy-two degrees at night, just like the bedroom of his home back in Brentwood.

Several times since the kidnapping Tanner had imagined himself waking up at home, rising as if from a bad dream to prepare for another day at court. Another day filled with stentorian tirades directed at his law clerks. Another afternoon of animated conferences with his fellow judges. Another evening spent hunched over his laptop crafting judicial opinions that would become the law of the land in the nine western states within the jurisdiction of the Ninth Circuit Court of Appeals.

A self-acknowledged workaholic, Tanner had dedicated his life to his career and his career, as he saw matters, to the goal of bettering society, especially the conditions of the poor and underprivileged. Apart from Vera, his longtime administrative assistant, he had no enduring or close personal relationships. He enjoyed the company of women and even at sixty-eight still fancied himself as something of a heart-breaker, but he had never married or sensed a need to pass on his seed to a new generation. Nor, if the truth be told, had he ever been in love. His only true mistress, as a conservative judicial colleague had once quipped, was the law. "You're one of those liberals," his associate observed, "who loves humanity but doesn't give a rat's ass for real people."

At the time Tanner dismissed the jibe as a petty insult uttered by a Reagan appointee steeped in the phony ideology of family values and trapped in a boring marriage, and who was intimidated by Tanner's superior intellect and jealous of his bachelor lifestyle. Only now serious doubts were beginning to surface.

After the pain in his hand and his fear of Randy's machinations for the immediate future, the doubts were what Tanner found worst about captivity. For the first time since he was a college freshman, he was being forced to reflect on his life. Not just on the quality of his legal opinions or how he might have been able to win over an initially dissenting judge to his views on a particular case or how the United States Supreme Court might have reviewed his ruling in another case. He was well used to that kind of reflection and in fact thrived on it.

As long as he kept his mind fixed on his work, he was comfortable with his role in the world. What he dreaded, and yet in the present circumstances could not seem to stop, was the soul-searching kind of reflection that forced him to look inward, to examine the moral balance sheet of his own life, to confront and question his most deeply held assumptions and values. He had written hundreds of legal opinions on every conceivable subject, from civil rights and criminal procedure to environmental protection. All were penned with the arrogance and certitude of a man who saw the world in stark hues of black and white and never second-guessed the correctness of his decisions.

But what good was the law and the power he wielded as a judge if the world was a more dangerous and mean-spirited place today than it was before he had ascended to the bench more than three decades ago? After all the years of issuing judgments *ex cathe-*

dra, affecting the rights and interests of millions of ordinary mortals, what had he really accomplished?

And what of Larry Tanner the person? Did he in truth find spiritual solace in the dispensation of justice, or was he merely on some kind of colossal ego trip, reveling only in his authority, oblivious to any harm he might have caused to those who came out on the losing end of his legal opinions? Was the man behind the black robes and the self-righteous judicial prose as sure and confident as others perceived him, or was he just a husk of man, a mirage, a hypocrite? In the last analysis, wasn't he just as uncaring and insensitive as the big corporations, prison wardens, and government officials who lost case after case before him? For every rapist and drug smuggler whose convictions he had reversed in the name of upholding constitutional rights, wasn't there a woman somewhere whose right to live in safety and without fear had been trampled or a school kid who someday would be hooked on cocaine? No matter whose rights he vindicated as a judge, wasn't there always some party who was victimized by his rulings?

That's what Randy had been telling him. Maybe Randy was right. Maybe Randy was also right when he said that they were two of a kind, men with interlocking destinies, driven and consumed by their pasts. "In the end, we're all called to account," Randy had told him in that cryptic, singsong manner of his. "The death fires inside your own mind will see to that, Larry. I can see them dancin' already behind your eyes."

An incident Tanner hadn't thought of in years came suddenly to mind. Soon after his appointment to the federal bench, he had granted a federal habeas corpus petition filed by a state prisoner convicted of sodomizing an eight-year-old girl. A month or so later, he received a letter from the child's mother. The distraught parent asked how, if the defendant was guilty, could he be given a new trial simply because the police failed to read the defendant his entire *Miranda* rights?

"What about my daughter?" the woman complained. "She's going to have to testify all over again in front of the man who destroyed her childhood and nearly killed her. What will happen if the jury fails to convict without the defendant's confession? Have you thought about what that man might do if he's set free?"

Certain that the woman would not understand his reasoning and that any response would be inappropriate, Tanner had stuck the letter in a file cabinet drawer, where it remained unanswered and ignored. Like God, he mused, the law giveth and the law taketh away. God never explained his actions, so why should he? Only now, after he, too, had become a victim could he understand the woman's anguish and feel her pain.

At the center of the anguish and pain he now felt was another sensation heretofore entirely foreign to Larry Tanner: He felt alone. Not just because he was physically alone, chained to a bedpost in some dank, godforsaken garage. His loneliness transcended such physical discomfort. Like the drug-induced dark realm he now inhabited, his solitude seemed interminable and irredeemable. Struggling to overcome the emptiness, he tried to recall all the judges and lawyers he had known over his career, all the law clerks he had scolded, all the willing women he had bedded. He knew hundreds, perhaps thousands, of people. In a certain sense, his life was filled with people. Still, the only true friend he could count among them was Vera.

Vera became his principal clerk when he was still a state court judge and she was an eager young woman fresh out of business school. A few months later, largely at his urging, they became lovers. Although their physical liaison lasted little more than a year, Vera remained by his side, following him to the federal bench, attending not only to his needs as a judge but, as time wore on, serving as his social secretary with successively younger generations of women. Like Tanner, Vera never married. The torch she carried for him never dimmed. More than any other person, she knew him best and had reason to despise him.

In his dreamlike state Tanner felt a deep desire to make amends, to declare his gratitude and, yes, his love. He lifted his head from his pillow and peered into the vacant room, imagining that he saw Vera's form as it had been—girlish and inviting—thirty years ago. He longed to touch her and take her in his arms. He longed to hear her murmur with pleasure as he unhooked her bra and lifted the elastic waistband of her panties with his probing fingers. "Vera," he said aloud. In his mind, he heard her answer.

"Yes," the female voice shouted. "Yes, baby, oh, yes, yes, yes." She was in a zone, a place beyond space and time, where the only reality was the excitement of Randy inside her and the incomparable pleasure he gave her.

Lying facedown on the living room rug, with the skirt of her business suit hiked high above her waist and her black panty hose pulled down around her ankles, she writhed and moaned as Randy mounted her from the rear for the second time that evening. She had driven to the cabin to insist that Randy release the judge, but as usual had abandoned her concerns and better judgment the second Randy unbuttoned her blouse and drove his tongue into her mouth.

"It will only be a little while longer," he had assured her before the rough sex commenced.

"But he's an old man and he isn't well," she protested. "It's getting dark and he must be scared."

"He's been sleeping like a baby. He never looked as good in his life, and he has no idea where he is. Trust me."

"I never wanted this to happen," she countered. "You shouldn't have brought him here."

"No one knows he's here, and no one ever will. Just leave everything to ol' Randy. I would never do anything to hurt my angel."

Her resolve began to weaken. She gave him an insistent look, which he immediately read as her last line of defense before succumbing to his charms.

"I need my video equipment back," she said, as if changing the subject.

"No problem. I'm done with it." He pulled her closer, flashing a provocative grin that chased all thoughts of Larry Tanner from her mind. "You know you're the only girl for me."

"The only one?" she giggled.

"The only one." He pinched her nipples, making them grow full and erect, and began to bite her neck. Together they sank to the floor.

Cupping his hands around her shoulders, Randy pulled her toward him and slapped into her, penetrating deeper and harder with each advancing thrust. "I want you. I need you."

"You fuck me so good," she cried, reaching yet another climax, her body quivering and rocking under Randy's grip. The entire cabin seemed to reverberate with their panting and shake with their movements.

"You fuck me so good."

Tanner could hear Vera say the words, but he was

unable to touch her. Instead of her soft cheeks, innocent brown eyes, and dewy mouth, his outstretched
hands found only air. In another instant her voice was
gone, replaced by the empty, dark stillness. Even the
thin shafts of light around the garage door had disap-
peared into the void.

Slowly, he felt his mind drift off again. He closed
his eyes. All the pain and all the longing left him as
he yielded to the urge to sleep.

Chapter Five

In a rare moment of concord, David Nova and Tami "Darling" Dawson had selected Ernest Fowler, a retired superior court judge, to mediate their child-custody slugfest. Fowler had offices with the law firm of Browning and Quim. "B.Q.," as legal insiders referred to it, was the bluest of blue-chip outfits, exuding good breeding and button-down deportment from the lowliest grunt of an associate to the most highly paid partner. Founded in the 1890s by a pair of Harvard graduates who had set up shop in downtown Los Angeles, the firm was not only one of the city's oldest but among its most respected.

Although the firm had long ago relocated to the top three floors of one of Century City's concrete and glass skyscrapers, the current management team insisted on retaining the interior decor of an earlier age, if not another continent. From the reception areas to the law clerks' quarters, each floor was appointed with antique furnishings that would have blown the budget of a small hotel chain. Biedermeier desks with Tiffany lamps, colonial-style armoires and client chairs, Regency umbrella stands and Chippendale bookcases with beveled glass shelf covers, were strategically placed throughout. Instead of the usual high-tech treatments, the walls were adorned with the most expensive London wallpaper and heavy oil paintings depicting fox hunts, rolling green country landscapes, and eighteenth-century sea battles. Only the computers and fax machines hinted that the firm was about to enter the twenty-first century.

The desired payoff was invariably achieved: Upon entering the B.Q. domain for the first time, a visitor experienced a refuge from the chaos of the modern era, a place where legal strategies could be plotted with calm, precision, and discretion. Appearances notwithstanding, B.Q. was no less adept than its competitors in the corporate legal jungle at going for the jugular. The lavish furnishings were paid for by a client list that included more than a score of Fortune 500 companies, not to mention many of the West Coast's most powerful CEOs and a top-heavy contingent of entertainment industry players.

Like the antique chairs and desks, Judge Fowler was a perfect fit for the B.Q. image. A celebrated trial jurist, with five *pro tem* stints on the court of appeal, Fowler had had his choice of joining any number of the city's mega firms after stepping down from the bench at age sixty. His decision to affix his name to B.Q.'s embossed letterhead was made partly because of the office's sterling reputation and partly because of the promise of a guaranteed six-figure salary and one half of an equity partner's share in the office's annual profits—a stipend that was easily many times what he had earned as a public servant. The senior partners considered the addition of Fowler to be a good, if expensive, investment.

In the five years since coming aboard, Fowler had been utilized as a fence mender with disgruntled clients, and as the firm's ambassador at bar association and local government functions. He also more than earned his salary by hiring himself out as a rent-a-judge at $350 an hour to wealthy litigants who chose to resolve their legal disputes through private arbitration and mediation, thus bypassing the delays and uncertainties of the regular court system. Like the old E.F. Hutton commercials, when Fowler spoke, people with any sense listened.

David Nova had never appeared before Fowler in court, but he was well acquainted with his reputation for fairness and his ability to forge workable settlements in cases in which other judges saw no possibility for compromise. That was why he had suggested Fowler in the first place. Although Nova held little hope that Fowler would recommend that he be granted primary custody of Jamie, he expected the judge to be equally wary of Tami's plan to take the child out of state. "Move-away" cases, as such matters were known in the family law business, were becoming a hot item with the courts, and most judges treated them with special care. With this in mind, Nova and Molly hoped to use the settlement conference with Fowler to convince Tami that she had just as much to risk as Nova by taking the custody issue to a full-blown hearing in family court. Somewhere between the extremes of total victory and abject defeat, there had to be room for an arrangement that both sides could live with.

With Molly at his side on Thursday morning, Nova stepped off the elevator at the thirtieth floor and pushed open the heavy wooden doors to the B.Q. office. Making his way to the receptionist, he was struck not so much by the over-the-top decor but by how the office reminded him of the firm where he had toiled briefly after completing his clerkship with Larry Tanner before opening his own shop. The familiar smell of money, he told himself under his breath, never changes.

"David Nova and Molly Carpenter to see Judge Fowler," he announced at the reception desk. "We have a nine-thirty mediation session."

The attractive young woman behind the desk smiled easily and brushed a sleek brunette curl from her eyes. "The judge and the others are expecting you. If you'll follow me, I'll take you to the conference room." She stood to lead the way, revealing as she rose a form-fitting black Lycra dress cut at mid thigh and a set of matching high heels that accentuated both her shapely calves and the slimness of her hips.

Nova followed closely behind, unable despite his best efforts to avoid eye contact with the jiggles and wiggles in front of him.

"No drooling," Molly whispered sternly, taking him by the arm the way a home-care nurse might guide an elderly shut-in to the restroom. "We're going to a settlement conference, not a singles bar."

Large enough to accommodate a small U.N. delegation or Louis XIV's entire privy council, the firm's principal conference room featured a wall-to-wall smoked-glass picture window that looked out over the city, affording on clear days a panoramic view that extended to the Palos Verde peninsula and the steel blue waters of the Pacific. At the room's center was the conference table, a monolithic oval of burled walnut buffed to a mirror-like sheen and accented with an equally high-gloss black lacquered marquetry border. It was here that B.Q. conducted its most important depositions, its key case meetings, and partnership confabs. Here the fates of litigants were determined, lives were ruined and rescued, corporations ushered into mergers or bank-ruptcy, and the flow of dollars added to and subtracted from the firm's all-important bottom line.

At the far end of the conference table, nearly dwarfed by the empty seats around them, sat Tami and Thomas Brockman, Esq. Opting for a low-key but businesslike look, Tami was tastefully attired in an unassuming navy suit. Brockman sported the usual pinstripes and multicolored power tie, his male-pattern baldness nonetheless apparent to anyone who cast a careful glance despite a painstaking comb-over.

David and Molly, both sensibly dressed in all-purpose business suits, exchanged uneasy greetings with their adversaries and settled into their seats across the table. A tense silence set in, but before any hostile words could be uttered, Ernest Fowler entered from the opposite end of the room, noisily clearing his throat to announce his presence.

A small man with stooped shoulders and heavy old-geezer trifocals, Fowler took his seat at the head of the table nearest the parties. Placing a yellow legal pad and a small manila file in front of him, he introduced himself, recited the name of the case, and asked for the appearances of counsel, just as he would have in a regular court of law. "I take it you're new to the case, Ms. Carpenter," he said, peering over his glasses.

"I notified your secretary late yesterday that I'd be appearing on behalf of Mr. Nova," Molly answered.

"That's fine. What I have in my file are briefs from Mr. Nova, written while he was still representing himself, and from Mr. Brockman on behalf of Ms. Dawson. I'll use your maiden name, as you have indicated you prefer." Fowler nodded respectfully toward Tami. "I also have received, with the consent of the parties, the supplemental family evaluation ordered by Judge Goldstein, which appears to have been transcribed only within the past two weeks. And while no brief has been submitted by Ms. Carpenter—I assume because she has only recently been retained—I note that

Mr. Nova is an attorney and appears to have laid out his side of the case most adequately."

Fowler placed his hands on the table, interlacing his fingers in a contemplative gesture. "Before we proceed, I want to emphasize that this is a private mediation conference. The parties have requested my services to see if, working together, we might be able to resolve a contested issue of custody regarding their minor child. . . ."

He paused a moment to glance through his file. "Jamie, their ten-year-old daughter. My recommendation, of course, will bind neither the parties nor Judge Goldstein in the event that a settlement cannot be reached. However, I want to assure you that I have carefully reviewed the papers submitted to me and, as noted in the initial cover letter sent to the parties along with my resume, I have extensive judicial experience in the area of family law. Now, with those preliminaries out of the way, I'll hear from counsel, beginning with Mr. Brockman."

One of the first rules of practice a litigator masters is to make a good first impression on the judge. Be aggressive, be contentious, even be a wise guy, but never act as if the proceeding in which you're participating is a waste of time. Not if you hope to achieve a favorable result.

From the grim expression on his face to the nervous way he kept looking at his watch, as if to remind himself of the pressing business he had elsewhere, Brockman seemed to have forgotten the rule. "Your Honor, Ms. Dawson is here today only because, prior to hiring me to represent her interests, she unwittingly signed a written agreement with Mr. Nova to take any dispute regarding custody of their child to private mediation before having the dispute formally resolved in family court. Given my client's impending move to New

York, there is no real room for compromise. Either Mr. Nova voluntarily agrees to let Ms. Dawson take the child with her to New York, or we will ask Judge Goldstein to enter an order to that effect. The family evaluation recommended that custody be awarded to Ms. Dawson, and we're confident Judge Goldstein will follow the evaluation."

With the air of one who has seen every form of legal hardball known to the bar, Fowler sighed softly and shook his head ever so slightly. "It's a rare case where a party cannot benefit from a good-faith effort at settlement. Perhaps in this instance we might proceed more productively if we started at the beginning, with a brief summary of the status of the case."

Fowler looked at Brockman, expecting him to deliver the requested summary. It was Molly, however, who spoke first, seizing both the initiative and the judge's attention in the process. "When Ms. Dawson filed for dissolution approximately two and a half years ago, the parties appeared able to resolve all marital issues, including disposition of property, child support, and child custody. With regard to Jamie, they entered into an order, subsequently issued by Judge Arthur Ferguson—whom I might add retired this year—that they would jointly share physical and legal custody. The marriage was thereafter formally dissolved. However, when Ms. Dawson learned six months ago that her TV show was relocating to New York, she filed an order to show cause, asking Judge Goldstein, to whom the matter was transferred, to award her sole physical custody."

Red-faced and chagrined at being upstaged, Brockman weighed into the conversation, prompted by a pained look from Tami. "The order may have provided for joint physical custody, but in practice Ms. Dawson has had Jamie with her during the week, making sure that she went to school, did her homework, and sustained a normal social life, while Mr. Nova took the child on weekends."

"Not even that," Tami chimed in, directing a set of dagger eyes at Nova. "With all his girlfriends, Sunday afternoons were usually all he could spare for Jamie."

Tami had thrown down the gauntlet. Even as he reminded himself of the importance of retaining his cool, Nova felt himself falling for the bait. "That's not true and you know it. You just can't stand the thought of me having a normal sex life."

"*Normal*? That's not the term I would use." The color rose in Tami's cheeks. "You cheated on me during our marriage, and now you're setting a horrible example for our daughter."

"What about all the crank hang-up phone calls you make to me in the middle of the night? Afraid you might find I'm not alone? You call that behavior normal?" Nova felt Molly's grip tighten on his arm. He struggled to restrain himself from saying more.

Judge Fowler clapped his hands together like an angry schoolteacher. "Ms. Dawson and Mr. Nova, if you'll please allow your attorneys to speak for you, we'll stand a far better chance of making progress."

Fowler and the lawyers spent the next fifteen minutes circumnavigating the rocky shoals of family law. Brockman argued that since his client had actual physical custody of the child, the current case law, as set forth by the state supreme court, favored allowing his client to move to New York with Jamie. "The fact that Jamie is already thriving in summer camp in the Catskills proves she will have no difficulty adjusting to the move."

Molly countered that while Tami might have had actual physical custody in the first months following the couple's separation, the situation had changed as

Tami's TV show became increasingly popular and she became increasingly preoccupied with the demands of stardom. "By the beginning of the summer, when Jamie was sent away to camp, physical custody was being shared on a nearly even basis. There should therefore be no presumption favoring permanent relocation to New York."

Both lawyers conceded that the child was attached to each of her parents and that to spare her emotional trauma, Jamie would not be brought back to California for the custody hearing in front of Judge Goldstein.

Fowler listened intently to the discussion, scribbling a few notes on his legal pad to highlight what he considered each side's most salient points. After a long pause, he chose his words carefully, gazing at Tami and Nova as he spoke. "I am mindful of the fact that the evaluation ordered by Judge Goldstein recommended awarding physical custody to Ms. Dawson. But the evaluation is so closely balanced that any decision remains extremely difficult. What I'd like to do now is confer privately with each party, beginning with Ms. Dawson."

With the ease of one used to decades of office life, the judge pivoted in his swivel chair and reached for the intercom resting on the antique English credenza behind him. "Martha," he said into the earpiece, "I'd like you to escort some of my guests back to reception."

In another instant the young woman in black Lycra arrived to take Nova and Molly to the client-waiting area, where they took up positions on a couch below a flawless reproduction of Joseph Mallord William Turner's *Ulysses Deriding Polyphemus*.

Both Nova and Molly knew from their years of experience not to make too much of Judge Fowler's request to speak with Tami and Brockman alone. Whenever negotiations bogged down, it was standard practice for a seasoned settlement judge to lean on the recalcitrant party, pointing out the pitfalls and hidden dangers to the foot dragger's interests if the case proceeded to trial. Like any crapshoot, sometimes the tactic worked and sometimes it didn't.

"I think it went pretty well in there," Nova offered, picking up the current issue of *Time* and turning to the story on the abduction of Larry Tanner.

Molly raised an eyebrow as if to signal qualified agreement with Nova's assessment of the settlement conference. Her eyes drifted to the kidnapping story. "Unbelievable about Tanner, huh?"

"There's a nut under every manhole in this town."

"What do you think will happen?"

"You mean about Tanner or in there, with Tami?"

Before Molly could clarify her question, the receptionist's phone buzzed again, and Molly and Nova found themselves reentering the conference room.

The disappointed look on Fowler's face was all Nova needed to see to know that the custody issue was going to trial. Tami, seated to the judge's immediate left, was glowering in defiance, her gaze tracking Nova like an animal of prey as he resumed his place at the conference table. Brockman, for his part, was busily packing up his briefcase and primping his combover to prepare for a noon lunch appointment. The morning had come to a close.

"I'm afraid," Fowler announced, "Ms. Dawson and her counsel are most adamant that the issue of custody be decided by Judge Goldstein. For what it's worth, I was going to propose a flexible arrangement, with an initial award of physical custody to Mr. Nova, subject to mandatory review upon completion of the child's next school semester here in Los Angeles. I think both parents are capable of raising the child, but I feel that a move to New York, at this time would not be in the child's best interests. However, all that's so much water under the bridge now."

The judge smiled wanly, reminded everyone that he would forward his bill, and asked the parties to show themselves out.

"Was it all a waste of time?" Nova put the obvious question to Molly as they walked to her car in the underground parking lot after the conference.

"Depends on how you look at it. On the plus side, your ex and Brockman know that a reasonable judge is capable of ruling in your favor. In that sense the conference went about as well as it could have."

"And the minus?"

"Next time they'll be ready for war. And if you think Judith Goldstein's going to be anything like Uncle Ernie up there, take a good look in the mirror and pinch yourself. It's going to take a shitload of preparation, especially on my part, to get her to see things our way."

Nova took Molly by the arm, an expression of sincerity and worry inscribed on his face. For once the trademark Nova cynicism and wisecracking were completely gone. "Look, I realize that bringing you into the case at the last minute was asking a lot. If you want out, I'll understand."

Molly returned his gaze with an earnest expression of her own. "That's not at all what I'm saying. I never desert a client . . . or a friend."

Arriving at her Maxima, she reached into her handbag for her keys, then climbed into the driver's seat and rolled down the window. "Just be ready for anything. They're going to try to portray you as morally unfit to raise Jamie. Remember what I told you about finding one of your lady friends to vouch that you're really the warm fuzzy type?"

"I'm working on it," he lied.

Molly nodded and drove off. As she pulled away, Nova could only wonder what he had done to deserve such loyalty. Was she a sucker for underdogs and sad sacks in general, or just a sucker for him?

Chapter Six

"I don't give a flying fuck how busy your client is," Nova screamed into the phone. After the just-concluded mediation session with Judge Fowler, he was in no mood for any more of the games lawyers play. "The deposition's set for tomorrow morning, and it's going forward this time or I'll move for sanctions against you *and* your client. No more delays. I'm not going to change my plane reservations. Do we have an understanding, Barry?"

"Yeah, yeah, we have an understanding. I'll tell Mr. Brewster to be at my office at nine-thirty, bright and early."

"Your client's lucky I'm not making him fly to L.A. for the depo."

"He knows. I've already told him that. See you tomorrow."

Barry Margolin, the slightly intimidated voice on the other end of the line, was the attorney for Brewster Brothers, Inc., in a products-liability suit Nova had filed in Pasadena on behalf of an Arcadia man who had been painting the second story of his house when he fell off a defective extension ladder made by the company Richard Brewster owned and operated. Brewster's deposition had been postponed twice already, and Nova was determined to get it over with before Margolin could submit another inflated bill to the insurance company that paid him by the hour to defend the manufacturer.

Margolin was also the first among equals, at least for the moment, of the menagerie of attorneys and clients who had left urgent messages with Nova's office that morning. As the pile of "While You Were Out" message memos on Nova's desk attested, missing an entire morning's work was invariably a small disaster for a solo practitioner. Even as he reminded himself that his daughter took top priority, he was forced to wade through the longhand scribblings of Sylvia Gomez, his droll Roseanne lookalike secretary and de facto office manager from East L.A. He took a sip of the convenience-store styrofoam cup of coffee he had purchased on his way back to the office and grimaced as he swallowed and got down to business.

A low-level film studio executive who had been arrested with a half gram of powdered cocaine in the glove box of his Beemer had phoned at nine a.m. to see if Nova had talked the D.A. into placing the exec on diversion so he could attend a drug-counseling program and avoid criminal prosecution. A hysterical Woodland Hills housewife suing a neighbor for tearing down a masonry dividing wall the surveyors insisted was on her property had been served with a cross-complaint for harassment and was threatening to find another lawyer if Nova didn't become more responsive to her needs. An auto pileup on the Pasadena Freeway that had left a teenager with a compound leg fracture was coming up for a status conference. The court clerk had called to remind Nova that the judge expected all discovery issues to be resolved by the time of the conference.

Everyone and his uncle, it seemed, wanted a piece

of Nova's time. His personal life might have been in shambles, but at least business was good. Man's basic inhumanity to man, animated by equal measures of stupidity, negligence, and greed—the leitmotif of every good tort attorney—ensured that Nova would never go hungry.

Knowing that he had more work than he could handle for the rest of the afternoon, Nova buzzed Sylvia to tell her he was not to be disturbed.

"You and Greta Garbo," Sylvia chuckled at Nova's imperious tone.

"Why don't you take one of those long siestas and just let the answering machine take over for a while?" Nova teased back.

"Not a bad idea, but before I do, you might like to know you received another call while you were on the phone with that soft-spoken Mr. Margolin."

"Just write it down and put it on the stack," Nova sighed wearily.

"I don't think Special Agent Ross of the FBI would appreciate that. I told him you'd phone back before two o'clock." She listened as Nova choked down another sip of the now tepid java before leaving on her break.

Tony Ross picked up his phone on the first ring. "Ross," he barked out a single-syllable salutation.

"David Nova returning your call. I assume this is about the Larry Tanner matter." In the back of his mind, Nova had been expecting to hear from the Bureau. The FBI was probably contacting everyone who even so much as shook hands with Tanner in the past.

"Thanks so much for getting back to me," Ross answered, his tone moderating slightly. "You guessed right. There are a few things I'd like to discuss. Our file shows that you once clerked for the judge at the Ninth Circuit."

"That's right, and I'd be happy to help in any way I can. But right now I'm a little swamped."

"I'm not surprised, what with the custody case and all."

Nova's chest tightened and he felt a cramp in the back of his legs. The feds were the best investigators in the business, but this was a remark from deep left field. "How did you know about that?"

"We make it our business to know, but don't get nervous. Your secretary told me earlier that you had been in a custody hearing this morning."

"Well, if it's something we could handle over the phone, I can spare a few minutes now," Nova said, regaining his composure.

"Actually, I prefer to handle this in person."

Nova pulled out his appointment book and shook his head. "How's Saturday morning at my office, say ten o'clock?"

"I'm afraid I can't wait that long. I also need to see you here. With all the late-breaking developments in the case, I can't leave the field office."

Ross waited for a response. Hearing none, he added, "If it's a problem getting over here, I can send a squad car to pick you up."

The guy wasn't going to quit, Nova concluded. Better to give him what he wanted and get it over with than to have a pair of goons scaring the tacos out of Sylvia. "I can be there by four."

"Terrific. We're in the Westwood Federal Building, in case you didn't know. Just take the elevator to the seventeenth floor and ask for me at reception."

Ross sounded placated but still a far cry from friendly as Nova said good-bye.

*   *   *

In the flesh, Tony Ross was no more personable than he was as a disembodied voice on the phone.

Nova was escorted to Ross' corner office by a low-level male functionary in a white oxford shirt and plain blue tie that could have passed inspection for a Mormon mission. He found the special agent hunched over his desk, absorbed in a small mountain of paperwork.

"Thanks for coming," Ross said, extending his hand without rising from his chair. He motioned for Nova to take a seat in the chair across from him, the only one not otherwise occupied by stacks of files and cardboard boxes of varying weights and sizes. From Nova's chair to Ross' desk and the stand of gun-metal gray filing cabinets lining the rear wall, the furnishings bore all the gentle touches of prison industry.

Apart from the framed pictures of Ross' wife and kids on the desktop, about the only items in the entire room that didn't look like they were hewn on the assembly line at Leavenworth was a color TV and VCR set on a portable stand near a floor-to-ceiling bookshelf. Constructed out of particle board with a walnut veneer, the bookshelf contained five rows of three-ring olive green looseleaf binders, stuffed with the last decade's worth of FBI policy and training memos on criminal procedure and an annotated multi-volume copy of Title 18 of the United States Code, setting forth the nation's principal penal laws in dense statutory prose.

"Nice place you have here," Nova remarked with a nod toward the large window, the office's sole permanent amenity, which gave Ross an expansive view of L.A.'s sprawling west side.

"It has its charm." Ross smiled at Nova's sarcasm, a hint of irritation in his eyes. "Of course, we can't afford the wet bars and Danish modern playthings you ambulance chasers have in your offices, but the air conditioning only breaks down once each summer and the heat works in January. For a government employee, I should consider myself lucky."

The guy was one of those cops who obviously had a hard-on for lawyers, Nova thought to himself. "I'm sorry if I sounded flip," he apologized. "It's been a bad day."

"So you said earlier." Ross smiled again, appearing to enjoy Nova's rising level of discomfort.

"I really would like to help in any way I can with Judge Tanner," Nova volunteered, hoping to bring his visit to a quick conclusion.

"You also said that earlier."

"But I'm afraid I have nothing useful to offer. I clerked for Tanner a long time ago, and I haven't seen or spoken to him for at least two years."

"We know that." Ross tapped his fingers on one of the many thick files on his desk. "We've done our homework."

"I also have no idea who would kidnap him."

"I didn't expect you would."

"Then why call me down here? I could have answered any questions about Tanner over the phone."

"I didn't call you down here to talk about the judge."

Nova's eyes widened with a mixture of dread and curiosity at Ross' comment.

"I called you down here to talk about Randy Sturgis."

Ross regarded Nova carefully, noting with particular interest the sudden flush that had come over the attorney's face. "I take it you haven't forgotten the name."

Chapter Seven

"You're saying Randy Sturgis is a suspect?"

"Before I answer any of *your* questions about Sturgis, I want you to answer mine. Fair enough?"

Nova nodded his assent, knowing that protest would get him absolutely nowhere.

Ross took out his pen, preparing to take notes. "Would it be accurate to say that you and Randy didn't exactly have a normal attorney-client relationship?"

"I can only comment on those aspects of our relationship that are a matter of public record," Nova answered stiffly.

"Because of confidentiality?" Ross practically sneered as he uttered the "C" word. Like many law-enforcement lifers, Ross seemed to regard the attorney-client doctrine and large parts of the Bill of Rights as little more than a grab bag of technicalities designed to protect the guilty and obstruct the course of justice.

"That's right. But it's no secret that Sturgis tried to get me removed as his trial lawyer."

"He wanted to represent himself, didn't he?"

"That's what he said."

"He thought he might do better on his own."

"Right again." Nova was growing increasingly annoyed by the special agent's bedside manner. "Is it just me or do you insult all your interview subjects?"

Slightly taken aback by the directness of Nova's complaint, Ross leaned back in his chair. "Sorry. Just tell me about Sturgis' case. I won't say another word."

Ross held his tongue as Nova recalled the complex procedural history of the matter known as *People* v. *Randy William Sturgis:* On an overcast spring evening Sturgis followed Grace Cowley, his sixty-seven-year-old landlady, home from a shopping center. He parked his Buick Skylark down the street from Cowley's Mediterranean-style three-bedroom and waited two hours until the retired schoolteacher turned off the lights and went to bed. Then he slipped on a pair of rubber gloves and broke into Cowley's house through a sliding glass door off the rear patio. Finding Cowley asleep, Sturgis crushed her skull with a cast-iron fireplace poker. After he was certain the old woman had expired, he retrieved a meat cleaver from her kitchen, returned to the bedroom, and attempted to hack off the victim's head. He left after merely severing her neck down to the fourth cervical vertebra.

Had it not been for one of Cowley's neighbors, forty-five-year-old Jill Brennan, who had kept a furtive eye on Sturgis' car, Randy might have gotten away with murder. Although she didn't contact the police until the murder was discovered the next morning, Brennan took down the Skylark's license plate when Sturgis left his vehicle to walk to Cowley's home. Brennan's testimony, combined with the discovery of the rubber gloves and a handful of hairs matching the victim's at Sturgis' apartment, was more than enough to enable the cops to make a quick arrest.

Sturgis was charged with one count of premeditated murder. The statutory special circumstance of "lying in wait" for Cowley also made him eligible for the death penalty under California law.

"So the prosecution had a solid case," Ross interrupted. "How did you get involved?"

"Back in those days I was trying to build up my own firm. I was taking criminal court appointments to help with our cash flow and enhance our reputation."

"What did Sturgis hope to gain by discharging you?"

"Not long before the trial was set to start, he told the judge that I had refused to put on an alibi defense to confirm his innocence, that I wanted him to claim some sort of mental impairment and negotiate a plea to second-degree murder. When the judge told Sturgis that he thought I was one of the better trial attorneys in the county and that I was known for getting along well with criminal defendants"—Nova flashed an ironic grin—"Sturgis brought a *Faretta* motion, seeking the court's permission to represent himself."

"The D.A.'s provided us with copies of the trial transcripts. I haven't read them all, but I remember that part," Ross said. "Sounds like another one of those legal loopholes that make ordinary people want to turn lawyers into lawn fertilizer."

"The name *Faretta*," Nova explained, "comes from the 1975 case of *Faretta* v. *California,* in which the United States Supreme Court held that a criminal defendant has a constitutional right to represent himself. As long as the motion for self-representation is brought in a timely fashion and the defendant is mentally competent, the right is absolute. In Sturgis' case, I convinced the trial judge both that the motion had come too late and that Sturgis suffered from emotional problems that would prevent him from adequately representing himself."

"And then you proceeded to lose the guilt phase of

the case, as well as the special-circumstance finding, just as Sturgis had predicted."

"But I did convince the jury to return a life sentence instead of the death penalty."

"And you did that without putting on Sturgis as a witness at the penalty phase. Why?"

Nova shifted uncomfortably in his seat at the sharpness of Ross' tone. "I can't tell you that."

There was no need to invoke the term confidentiality again. Both men knew the reason for Nova's silence. Nova had agreed to discuss only those aspects of the case which were already a matter of public record, and he wouldn't be intimidated into changing his mind, even by the FBI.

A few uneasy seconds ticked away before Nova felt it was appropriate to continue. "I put on a standard penalty-phase case, emphasizing the sympathetic aspects of Sturgis' early life."

"I know," Ross offered. "Poor Randy was orphaned at age three, after his real mother OD'd on brown Mexican heroin. His adoptive parents, a pair of medical doctors with a joint practice in Pomona, were closet sadists. His adoptive father used to beat and sexually abuse the boy. I've read that part of the transcripts, too."

"His new parents were also closet drug addicts, hooked on prescription painkillers," Nova added. "When his mother was diagnosed with terminal ovarian cancer, his father shot her up with an overdose of Demerol that would have taken down an elephant. Then he took his own life with an equally fatal injection. Sturgis was just sixteen at the time. He found the bodies. Except for a small sum of money, all of his parents' assets went to his stepbrother and assorted charities."

"Forgive me if I don't shed any tears."

"The jury seemed to feel differently. Sturgis had some problems with drugs as a teenager, but as of the time of the Cowley trial he had no prior criminal record. And he had managed to use his small inheritance to put himself through two years of college and get a license as a registered nurse. Whatever disagreements I may have had with Sturgis as a client, he was someone who never got a break in life."

Ross reached into a stack of documents on his desk and pulled out one of the volumes from Sturgis' trial transcripts. "You told the jury that Sturgis killed his landlady," Ross said, flipping to a premarked page, "from an accumulation of stress brought on by years of torment and his landlady's threat to evict him from the apartment he rented from her."

"I suggested that as a possible explanation for the crime in my closing argument of the penalty phase," Nova answered defensively.

"You know what I think?" Ross asked. "I think Sturgis killed Grace Cowley because she was friends with a certain elderly woman who had died of a mysterious drug overdose in the rest home where Sturgis worked. I think Cowley suspected Sturgis had a hand in her friend's death, and she confronted him with her suspicions."

"Sturgis was never charged with any other homicide."

Ross shrugged his shoulders. "You know what else I think? There were two other unexplained deaths from overmedication in another rest home where Sturgis worked before Mrs. Cowley's friend met her end. In all three cases the victims were elderly females, and intravenous injections of Demerol, or some combination of Demerol and Percodan, killed them. I think your ex-client—the man you saved from death row—

is a budding serial killer who gets his jollies from reen-
acting the death of his adoptive mother.''

"I may have saved my client's life, Agent Ross, but
I didn't put him back on the streets.''

"No, Judge Tanner deserves the credit for that.''

Nova had been wondering when Ross would turn
the discussion back to Tanner. He had blown the afternoon driving to Westwood and listening to the special agent. He was becoming concerned now that he'd
blow the evening, too.

Ross, however, was in no particular hurry to let
Nova go. "It took Sturgis years to get a habeas corpus
petition in front of Tanner at the Ninth Circuit," he
continued, "but when he did, that old *Faretta* motion
of his proved to be his ticket to freedom. Tanner
wrote the opinion ordering that Randy be given a
new trial.''

"That's the problem with *Faretta*,'' Nova replied
sympathetically. "No matter how strong the prosecution's evidence is, the defendant gets an automatic reversal if an appellate court thinks the trial judge
should have let him act as his own lawyer.''

"The *problem*,'' Ross corrected, "was that by the
time of Tanner's ruling, Jill Brennan had died in a car
accident. Without her, the prosecution's case became
so iffy and stale that the People offered to let Sturgis
cop a *nolo* plea to voluntary manslaughter and walk
out of court with credit for time served. Even for
someone who insisted he was innocent, the deal was
too good to pass. He was put on parole, but he
skipped out on that three years ago.''

Ross stood abruptly from his desk and walked to
the office window. After a long moment he asked, "It
was all part of a game, wasn't it? Sturgis never wanted
to represent himself at trial. He made the *Faretta* motion to give him a winning argument on appeal in the

event he lost the guilt phase of the trial. He was just a savvy con playing the angles."

Nova dropped his eyes to his chest. "That's more or less what I told Tanner when I ran into him after his decision was issued."

"What did he say?"

"He told me the Constitution was bigger than either my fragile ego or Sturgis as an individual. He knew Sturgis was guilty. He even commented in the opinion he wrote that the crime was among the most depraved he had ever reviewed in his entire career. But Larry truly believed his role as a judge was to follow the law, even if it required him to overturn a murder conviction."

"Damn fool." Ross shook his head. "I had one of my guys run Tanner's judicial voting record on the computer. You know, he's voted to reverse the convictions in over eighty percent of the criminal cases before him on the federal bench."

"Maybe he is a fool, but at least he's a principled one. That's more than you can say for most of us. It's not easy to be an idealist these days."

Ross gave Nova's observation a concurring nod. "And it's not going to be easy to find him either."

"But why would Sturgis kidnap the judge who set him free? Even if he is some kind of serial killer, that doesn't make sense."

Ross walked to the TV set and clicked on the VCR. "To you and me maybe. To Randy Sturgis, well . . . Just keep your eyes on the screen."

It took only a few seconds for Nova to recognize the pale, disheveled figure on the monitor. Seated behind a small clear pine dining table and garbed in green hospital pajamas, the Hon. Lawrence Tanner looked smaller, weaker, and considerably older than

Nova remembered. His right hand was heavily bandaged in a swath of gauze and white first-aid tape. In
his left he held a typewritten statement. As he read
from the single sheet of paper, his eyes shifted between the camera and the prepared text. His face bore
the vacant expression not uncommon to hostages and
kidnap victims of one who had surrendered the last
traces of independent will.

"As my colleagues in the law and the world at large
no doubt know," he began, "I have been abducted.
My kidnapper is a man named Randy Sturgis. He is
a man who was falsely convicted of murder and who
thereafter served a decade of hard time confined like
an animal in an eight-by-ten-foot prison cell.

"He is also a man whom I have grievously wronged.
Although I authored the Ninth Circuit opinion that
led eventually to his release from prison, I wrote—
falsely, gratuitously, and in the most scandalous of
terms—that I believed Sturgis was guilty as charged
but that my ruling was nonetheless required under existing legal precedent. I must also accept responsibility
for causing the decision in that case to be delayed by
over a year. During that time, as I have throughout
my entire career as a judge, I wrote numerous other
opinions and issued many other orders reversing the
convictions of men who had murdered, raped, and mu-
tilated. Unlike Randy Sturgis, these men were guilty
of their crimes and deserved the punishment they
received. . . ."

As Tanner's voice began to trail off, another voice,
slightly bemused but insistent, could be heard in the
background, offering words of encouragement. "Go
on, Larry, you're doin' just fine."

Tanner took a breath and appeared to regain a little
strength. A slight flicker of anger crossed his eyes but
quickly gave way to resignation. "Instead of using the

powers vested in my office to clear the name of an innocent man, I used my authority to place a stain on his name forever.

"Now I am paying for my misdeeds with my captivity and possibly with my life. As I stand before you, I have been convicted of delaying my opinion in the Sturgis case without cause and filling it with lies. This is my confession. My fate now is in your hands."

Nova continued to stare at the screen in stunned disbelief as Tanner's image gave way to a still shot of the dinner table, now empty except for a small brass model of the goddess of justice with her blindfold, sword, and scales.

Ross pressed the pause button on the VCR and remarked, "Looks like your ex-client got mighty pissed at not receiving the usual executive treatment from Tanner."

Moved by the pathetic image of Tanner, Nova was in no mood to disagree. "Randy's appeal to the Ninth Circuit was resubmitted twice, which caused it to be delayed an unusually long time. But Larry can't be blamed for that."

"That's not how Randy sees it," Ross cut in. "Randy not only blames Tanner personally for the delay, but he's livid at the fact that Tanner went out of his way to note that he was a depraved murderer."

Nova raised a hand to his chin and leaned back in his seat. "All of the shrinks who testified at his trial agreed that Sturgis had a colossal ego and was uncommonly sensitive to insults, especially from authority figures."

"The touchy type," Ross cut in again.

"He was the type who always thought he was morally superior and smarter than everyone else. One of the things he told the trial court when he tried to get me off the case was that he wanted to be placed in protective custody, where he would be segregated from the general jail population. He said he couldn't stand being housed with criminals. Everyone in the jail was guilty and getting what they deserved but him."

"You know, the more I think about it," Ross observed, "he kind of makes sense . . . in a warped way, of course. He imagines himself as a straight-arrow law-and-order type wrongly convicted while the guilty are set loose on candy-ass technicalities. He wasn't just looking to get a new trial from Tanner, he was looking for moral vindication. To him, kidnapping Tanner is the ultimate payback, and he's having a helluva good time with it."

"I still don't see what this has to do with me."

Ross gestured toward the TV and hit the remote's play button. "There's more."

On screen, the camera zoomed in for a long close-up of the statue's face, focusing on the blindfold. The same voice that earlier had mouthed encouragement to Tanner broke the silence; only this time the voice was loud and purposeful.

"Afternoon, Agent Ross, or good morning, evening, or whatever it is on your end of the camera. And hello again to you, too, David." The sound of heavy chuckling interrupted the narrative. "I figured that sooner or later Tony—you don't mind if I call you by your given name, do you, Special Agent?—would get around to inviting David to watch our little performance. Please excuse Larry's small mid-confession lapse, but overall I think he did a fine job. I've always said that lawyers and judges make even better actors than movie stars. Anyway, Larry and I have gotten to be pretty good friends now that we're roomies. No secrets on this end. We know all about each other.

"Okay, time to get serious. Here's my proposition: As Larry said, he's been convicted, before the high court of the Honorable Randy Sturgis, of a crime for which the ultimate penalty is death. Kind of reminds you of my case, doesn't it, David?"

Sturgis chuckled again, then resumed the pitch. "As you know, in any capital case there are two phases of trial—the guilt phase, which Larry has already lost, and the penalty, which is about to begin. In the penalty phase the job of the defense is to deliver that winning argument in mitigation of punishment to convince the jury to spare the offender's life. The game is to find that argument.

"I am hereby inviting you to play the game, which, as you might have guessed, has already begun. In the game each of us will play a prescribed role. Agent Ross, your role will be to recruit David, and to serve as the general investigator for the defense. That's quite a role reversal for you, Tony, and I do appreciate the irony. David, you'll play the part of Larry's defense lawyer. I'll be the judge and jury. That's two roles, but I can handle it. Just think, David, you'll be the appointed defense attorney in my courtroom. I trust you appreciate the irony as well.

"Now, there's just one argument, and one argument alone, that can save Larry's life. It can be expressed in a simple sentence or three, depending on how much taxpayer money you want to spend. Anyway, I want your answer printed in the personal section of the *South Coast Inquirer* the Monday after next.

"That's the game. Follow the rules and say the magic words, Larry goes free. Break the rules, refuse to play your roles and, well, let's just say there will be another opening on the court of appeals. And just in case you're thinking, Davey, that you can wriggle out of this appointment, be warned, ol' buddy. I'll know, from the ad you place, if you're in the game. It's essential that you play. It's also essential, fellas,

that you identify Larry as the subject of your ad. You
don't have to mention his full name in the ad. 'Larry
T' or even 'LT' will do. That way I'll be able to spot
the ad, and we'll have a public record—not quite a
trial transcript but a public record all the same—of
our game."

A few silent seconds passed. When Sturgis spoke
again, the bemused country-western twang in his voice
was gone, replaced by a detached, almost melancholy,
timbre. "Did you ever wonder why the face of justice
is blindfolded? I know you lawyers and lawmen say
it's because she has to remain impartial. The Greeks,
who called her Themis, thought so, too. Personally, I
think it's because she's afraid of what she might see
when the game ends and the blindfold is removed."

Ross clicked off the TV and turned to Nova. "In
addition to everything else, our boy's a real scholar.
Any thoughts, *counselor*?"

The emphasis Ross placed on "counselor" sent a
shiver down Nova's legs. "You can't be serious about
involving me in this insanity."

"If you mean Randy's court appointment, no, of
course not." Ross shook his head as he returned to
the seat behind his desk. "But I think you're already
involved, and I would appreciate your assistance and
your full cooperation. If we have to, we're prepared
to run a personal ad in the *Inquirer*. They take ad
orders until ten a.m. Fridays. Counting from tomorrow, we'll have just about a week before our
deadline."

Nova paused to consider Ross' request. As much as
he hated to contemplate what might happen to Tanner, there was no way he was going to throw himself
headlong into the effort to save him. His life was filled
with too much stress and turmoil as it was. Still, he
couldn't just get up and leave either. "In the penalty

phase of a capital case," he said, trying to sound helpful, "the trick to saving the defendant's life is to get
the jury to sympathize with him. You do that by bringing out the hardships and mistreatment he's endured,
and any mental illness he's suffered from that might
possibly lessen his culpability. If everything clicks just
right, you get the jury to identify with the defendant,
to the point where they begin to see themselves in
his shoes."

"And in Tanner's case does anything come to
mind?"

"Tanner and Randy Sturgis are as different as two
human beings could be."

"What about Randy's remark that he'd know from
our personal ad that you were in the game?"

"I have no idea what he means."

"Maybe we should have a look at your old trial
file," Ross suggested. "There might be something
there we could use, something he might have told
you."

Another shiver shot down the backs of Nova's legs.
This time he also felt a sick, sour sensation in his
stomach. "You know I can't do that."

"I could have a warrant issued for it." The menacing edge was back in Ross' voice.

"And I could move to have the warrant quashed.
A lawyer just can't turn over confidential material. It's
not that simple."

For a long moment Nova and Ross remained locked
in a stare-down, taking the measure of each other's
resolve. "Look, I'll think about it," Nova said finally.
"If I can find a way to let you have the file without
violating any ethical canons, I will."

"You do that, and while you're at it, here's something else to chew on." Ross took his eyes off Nova
and fished out another file from the tall stack on his

desk. "We've performed a preliminary analysis, and from the background noises—bird calls and such—we think it was made in some kind of rural setting, but we've no idea where. We also think someone is helping Sturgis. The tape was delivered early this morning by a young Asian kid who said that a black guy dressed in the uniform of a messenger service ran into him on the front steps outside this building. The black guy said he was running behind schedule and gave the kid five bucks to drop off the tape at the front desk."

"You think the black guy's an accomplice?"

"That's possible. He seems to have taken off in a big hurry. I have half a dozen agents in the field right now interviewing every delivery service in Southern California. We think it's even more likely, however, that Sturgis is being helped by a woman." Ross opened the file he had retrieved, removed an eight-by-ten prison photo of Randy Sturgis, and handed it to Nova.

The effects of aging notwithstanding, Nova easily recognized the curly black hair, piercing hazel brown eyes, sharp nose, full lips, and square jaw of his former client.

"Good-looking for a psycho," Ross observed. "I understand he attracted quite a female following among the spectators during his trial."

Nova nodded. "He packed the galleries nearly every day."

"The folks at Folsom also tell me that the women just kept on coming while he was in prison," Ross added. "The guy had even more girlfriends than the Nightstalker."

Ross removed another document from the file. "We've compiled a list of over twenty different women who visited Sturgis at least once in prison." He traced a finger down the document. "Some, like

Jane Semple and Mary Daniels, were just bimbos out for cheap thrills. Others, like this Marjorie Olsen and Jennifer Cox, were phonies who used false IDs." Ross handed the paper to Nova. "Did you know your ex-wife was on the list?"

Tami Dawson's name had been highlighted with a yellow marker just above Marjorie Olsen's. A string of dates next to Tami's entry indicated three prison visits to Folsom in the late eighties and early nineties. "No," Nova replied weakly, unable to lift his eyes from the document. "She wrote a few articles back then for the *Times* on prison groupies, but she never mentioned Sturgis. Not in the articles and not to me."

"Then that's another thing you could help us with. Ask her what she and Randy talked about and whether she's seen him since his prison days."

"Why don't you ask her yourself?"

"We tried that a few hours ago. She told one of my guys to refer any questions to her lawyer."

For the first time since Ross had said hello on the telephone, his demeanor seemed to soften. "I know you think I'm a hard-ass, and I know you think you've got the weight of the world on your shoulders. But I've only got a matter of days, and I need your help. You remember Tanner's bandaged hand? The tip of one of his fingers arrived in the same package with the videotape."

Wincing from Ross' latest disclosure and sensing that the interview had run its course, Nova rose from his seat. Part of him—the young, almost forgotten part that used to revel in fighting for a good cause—was ready to enlist in the FBI's crusade without reservation. The other part, now cautious and older, wanted only to be left alone, to take the next plane for Tahiti or some other far-flung venue where he'd never have to think about Tony Ross, Tami, or Larry Tanner again.

Despite all the conflicting thoughts racing through his mind, "I told you I'll think about it," was all he could manage to say.

Visibly disappointed, Ross pressed the button on his intercom to summon an assistant. "That's not good enough," he said icily, putting down the phone. "We're going to keep a lid on the video, but we'll be going public about Sturgis being our perp. Any way you look at it, it's going to be virtually impossible for you to stay out of this."

And instant later, the junior G-man with the white oxford and blue tie responded to the call and escorted Nova back to the elevator. It was the second time that day Nova had been asked to leave another man's office under less than gracious circumstances. The experience felt bad the first time and even worse now.

Chapter Eight

Nova drove his Lexus out of the Federal Building garage and into the evening rush hour on the 405 freeway, hoping that the long ride home would clear his head. God, how he wished he had never returned that phone call from Ross. But he had returned the call, and he knew that sooner or later Ross would again be breathing down his neck or, worse still, showing up at his home or office with a warrant in his hand and a crew of grim-faced colleagues wearing FBI jackets that looked like varsity team jerseys. Loosening his tie, Nova rolled down the driver's-side window and tuned in a jazz station on the radio. The soothing rhythms of Miles Davis' *Sketches of Spain* helped him to relax, and he began to consider his options.

To his great relief, the farther he traveled from Westwood, the easier it seemed to say no to Agent Ross' extraordinary requests. He wasn't a hero and he had no civic or legal duty to do any more than answer the FBI's questions. He had spent the last two and a half hours doing precisely that. But the idea of becoming more involved in the Tanner kidnapping and turning over the Sturgis trial file was out of the question. Surely Ross knew that and had been bluffing when he threatened to have a warrant issued for the file. Surely the FBI had more promising avenues of investigation than the slim hope that the old file might hold the key to Tanner's release. Although Nova had not seen the file since sending it to storage in what seemed another lifetime, he knew there was nothing in it that even obliquely referred to Tanner or could be used to win the judge's freedom.

Ross' request that he act as the Bureau's liaison with Tami was equally implausible. If Tami's relationship with Sturgis was anything other than professional—a possibility Nova dismissed out of hand—he would be the last one in whom Tami would confide. While he wouldn't mind being a fly on the wall when someone else posed the annoying questions to her, the last thing he needed now, with the custody battle looming, was to give Tami grounds for claiming he was joining the FBI in a campaign to smear and harass her.

By the time Nova reached the Topanga Canyon Boulevard turnoff, he had made up his mind. He would, as he had promised Ross, think about Sturgis and Tanner. That much was, in any case, inevitable. If he came up with anything that might help the feds, he'd pass on his ideas. Beyond that, the FBI would have to do what the taxpayers and Congress created it to do without any overt assistance from him. He would keep his time and attention fixed on the mounting demands of his own life. Thanks to his unscheduled interlude with Agent Ross, he was already falling behind on his legal work, and that was just on his L.A. cases. He also had to be on a seven a.m. flight for San Francisco Friday morning for the deposition of Richard Brewster, and he had hours of preparation to complete before he could even think of stepping on the plane. No matter what Ross or anyone else might think of him, he was not going to jeopardize his prospects of turning the deposition into a big payday.

*   *   *

Nova had in fact been waiting for over six months to tear the heart out of Richard Brewster, and his eagerness to begin the carnage was evident as soon as he opened the doors to the law offices of Barry Margolin at nine-thirty sharp Friday morning. It had been three years since Nova's client, a forty-year-old postal clerk, had fallen off a defective extension ladder manufactured by Brewster's company, sustaining a fractured tibia and broken right collarbone. Ordinarily, such a case would settle in the neighborhood of a hundred grand, taking into account lost wages, hospital bills, and that gleam in the eye of personal-injury lawyers everywhere, pain and suffering. Six months ago, however, Nova had received a phone call that opened up the specter of punitive damages against Brewster. Suddenly the settlement value of the case had taken off like a Fourth of July firecracker.

The phone call was from Tom Wycoff, one of Brewster's disgruntled ex-employees, a hard-bitten former production supervisor who claimed that Brewster knew that a dozen aluminum extension ladders with defective locking devices had been shipped from the company's Bay Area plant to two retail outlets in Los Angeles. Yet despite such knowledge Brewster had refused to recall the flawed products, preferring instead to take his chances on being sued. Ever since Wycoff decided to blow the whistle, Brewster had been hiding in the weeds, prevailing on Margolin to offer up one excuse after another to postpone his deposition. Now the day of reckoning had arrived.

The deposition began in typical fashion in the unassuming conference room Margolin shared with another law firm on the twelfth floor of a no-frills office building in the Financial District. With the court reporter busily pecking away at her transcriber and Margolin sitting a nervous shotgun by his client's side, Nova took the CEO of Brewster Brothers through a predictable litany of questions, establishing, among other matters, that Brewster was the managing partner of the business he and his older brother had founded thirty years ago.

"And you've had occasion to examine the two locking devices on the ladder my client was using at the time of his accident?" Nova asked, moving to the heart of the lawsuit.

Brewster unfolded his hands and adjusted the Windsor knot of his tie, as if checking to ensure he had a proper air supply to get himself through the interrogation. Though only fifty-five, he had the appearance of a man at least ten years older—crow's feet as prominent as war paint at the corners of the eyes, deep furrows etched like creases of rawhide above the brow, a loose flap of turkey wattle sagging beneath the chin that shook from side to side as he spoke.

"Yes, I've examined the locking clips myself and also had it looked at by an independent lab," Brewster answered.

"And those devices are supposed to be riveted to the side rail of the ladder, correct?"

"Yes."

"And in order to make sure the rivets hold up over time, they are supposed to be properly 'headed,' meaning that on the interior surface of the side rail, the rivet has to be flattened and pressed flush against the side rail to prevent slippage."

Brewster nodded.

"But those specifications were not followed in this case, were they?"

"No, they weren't."

"In fact, the rivets on the locking devices in this case were weren't pressed flush against the side rail.

They were loose and eventually they failed. Isn't that correct?"

"That's also true," Brewster admitted.

"And isn't that exactly what happened in this case? Because the rivets were loose, the locking device slipped and broke, and my client fell off his ladder onto the hard concrete beneath him, sustaining serious injuries?"

Before Brewster could reply, Margolin raised his hand in the fashion of a traffic cop, signaling his client to button up. "Objection, that's a compound question, and it also calls for a conclusion." A small man with heavy gold-rim glasses, Margolin had the nitpicking manner of a CPA, an impression made all the more distinct by the pocket calculator he toted to every deposition and inevitably retrieved to cross-check and challenge the damage claims raised by his adversaries.

"I'll gladly rephrase," Nova said testily.

"Then I would interpose a continuing objection, for the record," Margolin said, his right hand still upraised. "Brewster Brothers has already conceded in their answers to your third set of interrogatories that the locking device was defective. This line of questioning is cumulative and designed only to vex and annoy."

"For the record," Nova replied, "I want to hear the words from Mr. Brewster's mouth, even if the question does vex and annoy, just in case I have to read the transcript of this deposition to a jury."

In what was for Margolin a supreme act of spontaneity and concern, the defense lawyer laid a gentle hand on his client's shoulder. In his most accommodating tone he asked to "go off the record."

"This better be good," Nova said, nodding his permission for the court reporter to lift her hands from the keypad.

"Look, we all know why you're here," Margolin said.

"I'm here because Tom Wycoff says he submitted a written memorandum to Mr. Brewster about the defective ladders and Brewster tore the memo up and threw it away." In truth, Nova had no proof there ever was such a memorandum. He had only Wycoff's word. Still, judging from the pale shade of green that had come over Brewster's cheeks and jowls, Nova knew he was on the right track.

"Tom Wycoff is an ungrateful SOB," Brewster said, his voice tremulous with indignation and fatigue. "There was never anything in writing."

"But he alerted you about the ladders all the same," Nova shot back, "and you didn't take any corrective action. Isn't that true, Mr. Brewster?"

"Don't answer that," Margolin shouted, raising his right hand again to reassert control over his flustered client. Directing a pained expression at Nova, he reached inside his jacket and pulled out his calculator. "If you'll agree to call a halt to Mr. Brewster's deposition, we're prepared to settle." He punched in a few keys on the calculator as if to accentuate the bona fides of his position. "Two hundred thousand dollars. It's more than twice what the case is worth."

Only a fool would fail to see that he was in a no-lose situation, and Nova was no fool when money was on the table. He smiled. "Make it four hundred thousand dollars and we have a deal."

Brewster and Margolin exchanged uneasy looks. "Two fifty," Margolin said, expecting a quick acceptance from Nova. Hearing none, he took a hard swallow. "Three hundred thousand, take it or we go to trial."

"I'm not afraid of going to trial," Nova said.

"I never said you were," Margolin replied, "but let's

be reasonable. With all the three-strikes cases in L.A. getting trial priority, it will be another two years before we even get to pick a jury. Who knows where you, me, your client, or Mr. Brewster will be by then?"

Margolin had finally hit on something that just possible might stem his client's financial hemorrhage. The number of criminal defendants facing life terms under the three-strikes statute was increasing all the time. As more and more of the three-time felons demanded jury trials, civil-court judges were being pulled from their personal-injury and contract dockets and recruited to preside over rape, robbery, theft, and drug trials. The net result for law-abiding citizens was supposed to be safer streets. For civil litigants the net result was interminable delay.

"I want a lump-sum settlement," Nova said finally. "No periodic payments. No annuities."

"Done." Margolin extended his hand. "I'll send the release along in about a week."

"I also want a letter of confirmation," Nova added, shaking Margolin's hand. "Today, before I leave."

Margolin's lips arched in an ironic half smile. "I'll get my secretary right on it. It'll take about fifteen minutes, and in the meantime you can make yourself comfortable in here. There's a phone on the credenza if you'd like to make some calls. Dial nine for an outside line." Margolin and Brewster excused themselves, leaving Nova alone to savor the spoils of victory.

Acting like he paid the rent, Nova leaned back in his chair and put his feet up on the conference table. He didn't need a pocket calculator to determine that his share of the booty, after deducting court costs and expert fees, would be close to a hundred grand, the original settlement value of the entire case. With that kind of fee he could afford to upgrade his office computer system, buy a new hot tub for his home, or head off for two weeks of fun in Hawaii. He could even pay Molly the rest of her retainer.

The mere thought of Molly was like a sharp poke in the ribs, bringing his brief celebration to a premature end. Even a six-figure payday would be a hollow triumph if he lost Jamie.

Remembering Molly's oft-repeated advice, he reached into his briefcase for his personal phone book and looked up the business number of Sandy Nash. If he needed a mature, credible female at the custody hearing to testify that he really wasn't womankind's worst nightmare, who could possibly make a stronger impression than his first wife? Their break-up had been amicable and, in a somewhat atypical role reversal, had been caused by her desire to postpone child rearing in favor of pursuing a career in interior design. If anyone could convince Judge Judith Goldstein that Nova valued family above all else, it was Sandy. There was, of course, no guarantee that Sandy would agree to the assignment, or even that she would be in town, but having wrapped up the Brewster depo in record time, Nova had the rest of the afternoon to track her down and if necessary grovel at her feet.

As luck had it, Nova needed only a single attempt to find Sandy. A youthful receptionist answered her phone with the perky salutation "Nash and Associates," and transferred the call without delay.

"Sandy Nash," the familiar voice answered, picking up on the third ring.

"Sandy, this is David." A brief and somewhat uncomfortable silence followed. "Your ex-husband."

"David? What a surprise." She sounded neither pleased nor annoyed, just busy and now understandably distracted. It had been at least three years since she and Nova had seen each other. The contact between them in the interim had been limited to letters and e-mail, occasional phone calls, and an annual exchange of Christmas cards.

"I'm in the Financial District, and I was wondering if you were free for lunch," Nova said cautiously. "I'd love to see you."

"I'd like to see you, too, but you've caught me at a bad time. I have a proposal to get out by five and some important calls to return. David, this is so unexpected. I don't know what to say. Can it wait until tomorrow?"

"I'm afraid it's too important to wait. It's about my daughter. Tami's moving to New York and threatening to take Jamie with her."

Nova could feel Sandy vacillate as she took in his announcement. She knew about his divorce from Tami, but he hadn't told her about the custody squabble.

"You should have called me sooner. I would have cleared my calendar." She sounded firm, even a little put out at his ill-timed attempt to dump his personal problems on her.

Disappointed, Nova was prepared to make the obligatory transition to small talk before saying goodbye when she spoke again. "Look, even I have to eat. There's a coffee bar called Melanie's nearby. It's nothing special, but the cappuccino is good and the salads and sandwiches are fresh. It's right off the intersection of Mission and Spear, not far from the Rincon Center. I could meet you there in a half hour, but I can't stay long."

"As long as you don't mind me talking with my mouth full, that would be perfect. And Sandy, thank you."

"You're welcome. It'll be good to see you again." She sounded like she meant it.

Nova heard Sandy call his name just as he finished paying his cab fare. Stepping onto the curb, he turned and saw her standing by the entrance to Melanie's, her shoulder-length black hair tossing in the blustery afternoon winds that had picked up over the bay. She had on a blue turtleneck sweater, a matching pair of jeans, and an unfastened double-breasted glen plaid jacket that hung loosely from her shoulders. Though nearly forty, she was still fit and trim, long-limbed, with wide blue eyes, just as he remembered, a good-looking woman by any standard.

Nova hurried toward her and, without hesitating, set his briefcase on the pavement and gave her a big affectionate hug. "It's been a long time."

He realized almost immediately from the way her body stiffened at his touch and the way she patted him on the back instead of returning his embrace that a handshake would have been more appropriate. He considered apologizing but thought that doing so would only make the situation more awkward. "Let's eat," he said, pulling away slowly. "My treat."

It took only a few minutes for them to grab a couple of tuna salads and lattés and find a table where the rock'n'roll oldies from the cafe's sound system wouldn't drown out their conversation.

"So, you're looking hale and hearty," she said appraisingly between bites. "Just a little gray around the temples, but otherwise you haven't aged a bit since . . ." She paused to think.

"Three years ago. Joe Ostroff's fiftieth birthday bash in Santa Barbara," he interjected, referring to the memorable shindig thrown by one of their mutual friends. "You drove down for the day."

"That was when you told me you and Tami planned to separate. I never did think you two would last."

"Really?"

Sandy shook her head and smiled. "You made a fine-looking couple and I know you had a few good years together, but she had her sights set on bigger things than being a lawyer's wife. I ought to know. I once felt that way, too." She munched a few more leaves of lettuce, took a slow swallow of her latté, then asked, "So what's ol' Ms. Darling up to now?"

Nova related the blow-by-blow details of the custody battle, beginning with Tami's impending transfer to New York and her hysterical reaction to his dating habits and culminating in Molly's suggestion that he scour the bars and tanning salons for a female friend willing to offer good-character evidence on his behalf.

"Sounds like Molly's grown up to be quite a clever attorney. I remember her from *our* divorce. You set things up so that she was your attorney on paper, but I felt like she represented my interests, too. I'm not sure if you know it, but she spent quite a bit of time talking with me at the time, to make sure I wasn't getting shortchanged."

"She's the best there is, and she's also a friend."

"And she thinks that I'm your witness?"

"Actually, I haven't asked her, but I'm certain she'd agree. Tami would have a much harder time making me out to be unfit to raise Jamie if my first wife was willing to vouch for my better qualities."

Sandy cocked her head to one side and narrowed her eyes. "You mean you want me to testify that behind the womanizing, trash-talking exterior there lurks the heart of a teddy bear who would make a perfect father for a young girl."

"Something like that," Nova laughed. "When it comes to Jamie, I'm a regular Ozzie Nelson—milk and cookies after school, Little League in the spring, dance classes all year round. She wanted to go to Camp Oga-danga in the Catskills this summer, and I just couldn't say no, even though I probably should have."

"The sisters in my old women's group would confiscate my mascara for saying so, but I'm sure you're a damn sight better parent than Tami."

"I'm glad you agree." Nova knew that Sandy had never liked his second wife. Whether it was out of some sort of mutual jealousy or just on general principles, the friction between Sandy and Tami had been palpable the few times they had met in the flesh. "Does that mean you'll testify?"

"Why not? I assume Molly will contact me to go over the questions I'll be asked."

"We'll give you plenty of lead time and pick up your plane fare, of course. I realize you'll be sacrificing valuable time."

"That's very kind, but I can handle the sacrifice." She flagged down a waitress and ordered another latté. "Actually, I've been traveling to L.A. practically every other week for the past two years. I just got back last night from interviewing a wealthy widow in Palos Verdes. I'm sure we can coordinate schedules."

Nova heaved an audible sigh. "I was afraid you'd turn me down or I'd have to roll over and beg. In case you've forgotten, I do a great Irish setter." He curled his hands into doggy paws and stuck out his tongue.

"I should have brought a Frisbee along for you to fetch," she said with mock disappointment. For a few seconds she let herself share an easy laugh with Nova, as if reliving old times. Then just as quickly, she became serious again. "But there's really no need to beg. Let's just say I still enjoy doing the right thing, and in some ways I feel I owe you. It's taken me a long time to realize that you can have a career and a family, too. I'd like to help you and Jamie stay together."

Sandy had been difficult to read ever since she'd answered her phone but never more so than now. At one moment she was oddly distant, the next almost too eager to plunge headlong into a domestic war she could easily avoid. Only now did Nova detect a certain sadness about her as well. "I get the sense that things haven't exactly worked out the way you wanted."

"Hey, I have it pretty good," she said, running a manicured fingertip along the edge of her newly arrived refill of latté. "Business is booming. I have two full-time associates, a secretary, a receptionist, a nice mountain cabin I use as a vacation getaway, and more money than I know what to do with."

"And apart from business?"

"Up and down. I hold my own, but there's no one special." She hesitated, then added, "Well, actually, there was someone, but it's been over for quite some time."

"I'm sorry to hear that."

"Don't be." Sandy glanced nervously at her watch and took a sip of coffee. Nova had the impression she wanted to say more about herself, but for some unstated reason decided to hold back. "If you're looking for someone to feel sorry for, you could start with Judge Tanner."

Nova blinked hard at the mention of Tanner. It was the first time all day anyone had raised the dreaded subject of the kidnapping. "You've heard what's happened?"

"Who hasn't? The radio says the FBI's looking for Randy Sturgis. I nearly fell over when I heard that. He was one of your clients."

"But that was a long time ago. How did you remember?"

Sandy shrugged her shoulders. "How could I forget? That was one of your biggest cases. You must be worried sick about Tanner."

Nova considered Sandy's last comment for a long moment. What he could he say in reply? That he had decided to forget he ever knew Larry? That he had decided to turn his back on the FBI's plea for help and concentrate on his own problems? Sandy would tell him to stick his request for *her* help where the sun didn't shine if he told her the truth.

"The FBI contacted me the other day," he said. "They asked if I'd do a few things for them."

"What kind of things?"

"It's best if I don't go into any details. I'm in a somewhat sensitive situation having represented Sturgis in the past."

"I understand." She gave him a searching look. "But you are going to do what you can? Larry was like a second father to us in the old days. He got you that job after you finished your clerkship. He even performed the ceremony at our wedding. And Vera. This must be killing her. I should give her a call."

"Why don't you leave that to me?" Nova said gently. "I'll tell her you send your best."

"Okay. I'm sure you'll do what's right." She finished the last of her latté and stood. "I should be getting back now. Tell Molly to call anytime."

"It was great seeing you again, and thanks." Nova held out his hand. To his surprise Sandy ignored the proffered handshake. Leaning across the table, she planted a soft kiss on his cheek.

"Be careful, David," she said.

Nova laid a tip on the table and watched her leave. Then he walked to the back of the café and found a pay phone. Within seconds he succeeded in rousing the redoubtable Sylvia Gomez, just back from lunch herself, from her afternoon crossword. He told her to order the Sturgis file from storage. "It's a case I tried a long time ago, before you joined me," he explained. "Tell the storage people it's a rush job. I want the file on my desk by Monday morning."

He wasn't sure if he had made the right decision in ordering up the file or what he might ultimately do with it. The only thing he knew for certain as he stepped outside to hail a cab for the airport was that Sandy would be proud of him. For the time being, that seemed to matter quite a lot.

Chapter Nine

Noah Chamberlain fluffed up the pillows on Mr. Fisher's hospital bed and checked his medication chart. "You need to take two of these every four hours," he said, cradling the back of the frail old man's neck in one hand. Chamberlain used his other hand to give the patient a pair of red and white capsules, then held a cup of water to his lips to help him drink.

The old man swallowed the pills with obvious effort. "Thank you, nurse," he whispered.

Mr. Fisher's daughter, a middle-class woman in her late forties, looked on as her father settled back into bed and closed his eyes. Choking back her emotions, she struggled to stay calm. "Daddy, Nurse Chamberlain is going to take care of you the rest of the evening. I'll be back tomorrow morning."

She leaned over and gave her a father a good-bye kiss on the forehead. Turning to Chamberlain, her tired eyes brimming with tears, she said, "Please don't let him suffer."

"We'll do everything we can to see that's he's as comfortable as possible." Chamberlain laid a gentle hand on the woman's shoulder and walked her into the hallway of the small convalescent hospital. In his crisply pressed white uniform, with his head newly shaved and his goatee neatly trimmed, Chamberlain looked like a black Mr. Clean—broad-faced, unthreatening, strong, and competent.

"Thank you so much," the woman said as she walked to the elevator.

"You're welcome, and please, try to get some rest yourself. Your father's in the last stages of Parkinson's disease, but he's in no immediate danger. He'll still be with us in the morning and for many days thereafter. Of that I'm more than certain." Chamberlain watched the woman board the elevator before resuming his rounds on the third floor of the skilled nursing facility that was the physical, as well as the medical, centerpiece of the Alpine Convalescent Home.

In many ways the evening so far had been indistinguishable from any other Chamberlain had spent in the six months since hiring on at Alpine. The elderly residents of the home's independent-living unit supplied a seemingly endless pool of patients for the skilled nursing facility. And while the nursing facility never seemed to be overcrowded, there was never a time Chamberlain could recall when the facility was less than eighty percent occupied. As he began to walk down the corridor, he ran through the list of patients he had to see before taking his initial break. First, there was Mrs. Jackson, in the room just next door to Mr. Fisher, whose colostomy bag needed to be cleaned and drained twice a day. Then there was Mr. Barker, who had just returned from an acute-care hospital where he had undergone lymph-node surgery; and then there was Mrs. Lapinski, at the end of the hall, who only last weekend suffered the third in a series of disabling strokes in the middle of a canasta game with a group of distressed octagenarian friends.

Although Chamberlain was still regarded as a new hire, he had already become a fixture on the three twelve-hour shifts he worked each week, usually from six p.m. until six the following morning. The elderly patients whose needs he tended found his easygoing manner and wide-ranging skills in dispensing medications and assisting with feeding and bowel functions reassuring and comforting. He always had a smile and words of encouragement for the depressed, a joke or two for those who still had a sense of humor, and, unlike many of the other nurses, who came from the Philippines, Central America, and parts of Asia, he spoke flawless English, an asset the patients appreciated perhaps most of all.

Chamberlain finished ahead of schedule with Mrs. Jackson and had begun adjusting the Demerol solution in Mr. Barker's IV drip when Alba Martinez, the Salvadoran night-shift nurse supervisor, stuck her head into Barker's room. Chamberlain sensed immediately from the serious expression on Alba's normally cheerful round face that something was amiss.

Motioning Chamberlain toward her, Alba spoke in hushed tones so as not to disturb Mr. Barker. "The sheriff's investigator is here. She wants to see you in my office. She's with Ms. Cates."

"I thought they were supposed to call before coming back," Chamberlain protested. "I haven't finished my rounds."

"I don't know why they didn't call in advance, but the point is they're here. I'll finish up for you. I'm sure it's nothing to get excited about."

Chamberlain stepped aside to let Alba inside Barker's room. He knew that the county sheriffs were still in the process of interviewing the nursing staff. He also knew that eventually they would get around to interviewing him. But the fact that the nursing facility's number two administrator was also present without any prior notice and at nine o'clock in the evening was more than a little inconvenient. It was down-right troubling.

Chamberlain stepped into the men's room and washed his face and hands. He had met Cates only once before, during his job interview, and while she clearly had found him sufficiently qualified to hire, he found her aloof, abrupt, and decidedly lacking in personal warmth. At the time he'd thought he had pretty much sized her up as a bean-counting bureau-crat with no life apart from her work and whose ab-sence of social skills was in no way a sign of animosity toward him. Now he wasn't so sure. As far as he had heard, Cates had never accompanied the sheriffs on their other interviews, but then again, the other inter-views had been held in the admin offices downstairs, during normal business hours. Hopefully, there was nothing to get excited about, just as Alba had cautioned.

Chamberlain found Cates in Alba's office, seated behind the supervisor's desk. Dressed in a plain brown business suit, she was a slight woman in her mid-fifties with tinted blond hair blown back off her forehead in a Barbara Walters-style sweep. To her left sat a much younger woman, early to mid-thirties, dressed in a charcoal business suit, with matching dark eyes and a thick head of curly black hair shaped just below the ears in a fashionable wedge cut. Together, they looked like the directors of an employment agency for mid-level professional women out to sign a contract or cut a low-budget commercial for cable TV.

Cates gave Chamberlain a thin-lipped smile of rec-ognition as he entered the office and gestured for him to take a seat in one of the upholstered red client chairs on the other side of the desk. "I'm sorry to pull you away from your duties, nurse, but Ms. Ambrose phoned earlier today and asked if I might be able to arrange for her to speak with you this evening."

"Hi, I'm Janet Ambrose," the younger woman said, extending her hand across the desk. "I'm an investigator with the Riverside County Sheriff's Department."

"Pleased to meet you." Chamberlain took the investigator's hand in his own, noting both how small her hand was in comparison to his and how cold it seemed, as if Ambrose was nervous or anxious in his presence.

"I think we all know why we're here," Cates said impatiently.

"I assume you want to talk about the death of Anita Oglesby," Chamberlain said. "Roughly two weeks ago, if I'm not mistaken." He folded his arms defensively across his chest and wondered if his mounting sense of unease could be detected.

Ambrose nodded and opened the half-inch-thick manila file set in front of her on the desktop. "As you probably know, we've been interviewing all of the nursing personnel who had any contact with Mrs. Oglesby from the time of her admission to the nursing facility to the morning she was discovered to have expired."

"Mrs. Oglesby's family is quite influential in the community," Cates broke in, "and when the coroner's report came back suggesting—and mind you, I emphasize that no conclusion was reached—that she may have been overmedicated, the family insisted that everyone be interviewed."

"Because you only work three nights a week, I've waited until now to speak with you," Ambrose clarified. "If I've caught you by surprise, you have my apologies."

"How can I help you?" Chamberlain asked politely.

"Just tell me, as simply as you can, what kind of contact you had with Mrs. Oglesby."

"Very little, actually. If I recall correctly, Mrs. Oglesby was admitted for nursing care after returning from the hospital. She had her gallbladder removed and was in considerable pain. Most of her care was seen to by the nurses on the day shift. By the time I made my rounds each evening, she had already been fed and bathed. All I did was check the flow on her IV drip and give her pills around midnight."

"Do you recall what medication she was being given?" Ambrose asked.

"Without reviewing the chart, I can't be certain, but to the best of my memory, she was being administered Vancomycin in a saline solution on the IV and Percodan, four times a day, orally, for pain management."

"That's very good," Ambrose said, arching an eyebrow as she scanned Oglesby's nursing record. "The problem, however, is that the autopsy showed that the level of Percodan in Oglesby's system was higher than might be expected. Can you tell us anything at all that might explain why?"

"Anything at all," Cates chimed in, as if rushing to reinforce the importance of Ambrose's question.

Chamberlain stared back indignantly. Why was it that he got along famously with the patients in every hospital he ever worked in, but the administrators never seemed to cut him any slack? "I followed the instructions in the patient's medication chart to the letter. You're not suggesting that I—"

"I'm not suggesting anything," Ambrose interrupted. "These are just routine questions."

"There were at least four other nurses on the floor the night before Mrs. Oglesby expired, and several others still who attended her the previous afternoon," Chamberlain snapped back.

"They've all been asked the same questions."

"Were any of them questioned in the middle of the night, without any advance warning?"

"As a matter of fact, no," Ambrose admitted, "but your name wasn't on the first printout of hospital employees we were given, so I neglected to schedule you for the initial round of interviews."

"That's my fault," Cates said. "I gave the Sheriff's Department an old list."

Chamberlain took a deep breath and directed an accusing stare at Cates. "Is it because I'm black or is it because I'm a man that I haven't been shown the same courtesies as everyone else?"

"I'm sure you take a lot of pride in your work," Cates responded quickly, "but we have to cooperate with the sheriff's investigation. And I assure you this has nothing to do with race or gender. You're not the only male nurse on staff, you know."

"But I am the only black."

"That's true, at least for the present," Cates said grudgingly. The last black nurse employed at Alpine had left Cates with a racial-discrimination lawsuit that the rest home had been forced to settle on less than favorable terms. It was a bitter experience Cates did not want repeated.

The two women exchanged uncomfortable looks, after which Ambrose stood and forced a smile. "Thank you for answering my questions, nurse. If I need to speak with you again, I'll call ahead."

Chamberlain walked out of the office and smoothed away the wrinkles in his uniform. Then he headed down the third-floor corridor in the direction of Mr. Fisher and his other patients. He still had a great deal of work to do before completing his shift.

The old people who lived at the Alpine Convalescent Home were dying every day, he told himself as he stepped inside Mr. Fisher's room. That's why their sons and daughters sent them to the home in the first place—to pass from this earth in peace and dignity and with the least possible inconvenience to their relatives. No matter how the Oglesby investigation proceeded, no one was going to make Noah Chamberlain the scapegoat for a tragedy that sooner or later was bound to happen anyway.

Chapter Ten

There were eight file boxes in all. They were stacked two rows deep by the side of his desk. Together they comprised everything David Nova knew or ever wanted to know about Randy Sturgis—the bound transcripts from Randy's preliminary hearing and trial, the discovery materials turned over by the prosecution, the legal motions Nova had written, the witness statements he had taken, and the reports of his experts. Nova could have begun his review Monday afternoon with any one of the boxes. Instinctively, he reached for the transcript of his closing argument from the penalty phase of the trial.

A full thirteen years had passed, but Nova could still feel the raw tension in the courtroom, the searing dryness in the back of his throat and the rush of adrenaline in the pit of his stomach that hot afternoon. This was it, the grand finale, the end of the line, the last opportunity he would have to address the jury before it retired to decide whether Sturgis would be sentenced to life in prison or condemned to die in the state's gas chamber.

Nova had already lost the guilt phase of the trial, and from where he stood, the evidence on the issue of penalty was so evenly balanced that the final outcome would in all probability be determined by how well the lawyers for each side performed their last act in the courtroom. Not just the words they spoke but their body language and facial expressions would come under the strictest scrutiny. Now as never before, there was no margin for error. To save his client's skin, Nova's closing had to be flawless.

"Ladies and gentlemen," he began, gripping the lectern with both hands as he steadied himself and scanned the faces of the jury for signs of compassion and understanding. "This is the first time in my career that I have had to stand up and plead for the life of another human being. Unlike some lawyers, perhaps, who live to get their names in the newspaper and their faces on TV, this is not a task that I am eager to undertake. To the contrary, it is a task I had hoped I would never have to perform, and it has me scared as I have never been since I was a small boy suffering through the traumas of childhood. Still, I can think of no greater honor."

Nova remembered catching the eye of one juror, a middle-aged black woman who had sat impassively through the entire trial, observing the witnesses and taking in the evidence but never revealing so much as a hint of her own feelings. This time, however, the woman looked straight at him and seemed to offer the faintest nod of empathy.

Whether what he saw was real or imagined, he took heart from the woman's gesture. As every veteran trial attorney knows, forging an emotional connection with just one juror can make all the difference in the outcome of a case. The woman appeared to appreciate Nova's openness about his own fears and anxieties. Maybe she was just as scared as he by the unbearable responsibilities the legal system had assigned to each of them in the trial. If so, it was a bond Nova was determined to strengthen as the day wore on.

"Every attorney who enters this profession driven by ideals rather than a desire for money or power imagines himself or herself one day arriving at a moment such as this, when they have to summon all their skill and courage to see that justice is served," he said, resuming his closing. "Justice, ladies and gentlemen, is what we all seek this afternoon, a form of justice that each of us can live with for the rest of our lives.

"But what does it mean to do justice in a case like this? You already have found the defendant, Randy Sturgis, guilty of first-degree murder with special circumstances. And while I may disagree with that verdict, I will raise no quarrel with it today."

Nova paused a moment to cast a glance at Sturgis, who sat quietly at the defense table, dressed in a long-sleeve button-down shirt and dress slacks, his hands folded loosely on his lap, his dark hair neatly combed, his eyes fixed on the great seal of the state of California above the judge's bench. Although Sturgis had refused to take the stand in his own behalf during the penalty portion of the trial, he seemed peaceful, even contemplative, now.

"What I plan to do this afternoon, ladies and gentlemen, is simple: I'm going to implore you to reach the conclusion that even if my client has taken a life without cause or provocation, justice will not be served by a verdict that commands his life to be taken as well."

Under California law, the jury in a death-penalty case is required to decide whether the defendant should live or die by balancing and weighing the "factors in aggravation and mitigation" set forth in Section 190.3 of the state's penal code. The prosecutor, in her closing argument, predictably had emphasized the factor that pointed most strongly in favor of a death sentence—the brutal circumstances of the crime, the murder of sixty-seven-year-old Grace Cowley. As the prosecutor repeatedly reminded the jury in her closing, Cowley had been bludgeoned to death and her neck nearly severed by a man who had invaded her home. Surprised by an intruder of superior strength and size, the old woman never had a chance to survive, much less say her final good-byes to her loved ones.

"The only proper verdict in this case," the prosecutor had argued, "is a death verdict. Don't show Mr. Sturgis any more mercy than he gave Mrs. Cowley." In the eyes of the prosecution, Randy Sturgis was something less than human, a biological mistake, that should be eradicated for the safety of the community and the memory of his victim.

To counter such a powerful pitch for retribution, Nova had to turn the jury around, to get it to appreciate, and if possible to feel, the tragedy in Sturgis' background—the unspeakable mistreatment he had endured as a child, the unending pain and anguish he had known as an adult. If Nova succeeded in doing that, he could humanize Sturgis in the jury's eyes. He could move the jury to conclude that killing Sturgis would simply be another crime. It was one thing to extinguish a monster; it was something altogether different to take the life of another person, even one who had himself committed murder.

Step by step, Nova summarized the testimony in mitigation he had elicited from defense witnesses during the penalty phase of the trial: the retired family doctor who had discovered during a routine physical exam, that young Randy, then a child of eight, suffered from rectal bleeding and who benignly attributed the condition to overvigorous bowel movements; Sturgis' half brother, ten years his senior and now deceased, who had admitted that he knew his father had sodomized Randy on at least one occasion; the grade-school teachers who had testified that despite being withdrawn Randy was a good student; the hospital administrator who had hired Randy for his first nursing job, who told the jury that Randy had always performed his duties with professionalism and courtesy.

And then there was Dr. Irving Horowitz, whose testimony had enabled Nova to tie together the diverse threads of the defense's case in mitigation into a coherent whole. A board-certified psychiatrist who ran a private substance-abuse recovery clinic in Encino, Horowitz had testified in dozens of criminal trials. He was recommended to Nova by none other than Larry Tanner, who considered him the best forensic mental health expert in the business.

Given the needle tracks found on the inside of Sturgis' thighs at the time of his arrest, the referral to Horowitz was a natural. However, Horowitz did more than confirm Sturgis' addiction to street drugs, painkillers and hypnotics. He diagnosed the defendant as suffering from a bipolar mood disorder, which made him expansive, hyperactive, and voluble during his manic phases and withdrawn, paranoid, desperate, and confrontational in his depressed periods, especially when subjected to extreme stress.

"Dr. Horowitz hasn't offered you an excuse for the crime Mr. Sturgis has committed," Nova told the jury, "but he has given you an explanation. Faced with the prospect of being evicted from his home, and suffering from a very real and painful psychological disorder, Mr. Sturgis took the life of another person. You now face the enormous task of determining whether Mr. Sturgis should die for that crime. In doing so, you must ask yourselves whether a man who was orphaned at a tender age only to endure unspeakable degradations as a child deserves your mercy."

Although the transcripts did not reflect it, Nova remembered pausing at just that moment, as much to catch his breath as to search the faces of the jury once more. Confident that he was hitting all the right notes, he continued, gesturing at Sturgis, who remained motionless at the counsel table, staring uncomfortably in the general direction of the judge. "This is a man, ladies and gentlemen, who has never before been arrested or previously committed an act of violence against another human being. He is not some kind of predator who has spent his life harming others. It only takes a moment or two to commit a heinous act, such as the murder of Grace Cowley. But as horrible as that crime was, it cannot erase a lifetime spent obeying the law.

"Given the totality of the evidence that you have heard throughout this trial, doesn't Mr. Sturgis deserve your compassion just as much as he has earned your condemnation? I submit to you that he does, and I implore you to return a verdict of life imprisonment. In a case such as this, nothing of value will be gained by adding Mr. Sturgis' death to Mrs. Cowley's. For a man who has already lived through a lifetime of punishment, a sentence of life behind bars surely will be punishment enough."

As Nova completed his rereading of the penalty-phase argument, he knew he wasn't just revisiting an old trial. He was revisiting both the high and low points of his entire legal career. The high point was attained when the jury came back into court the next day and announced its verdict of life imprisonment. Never before and never since had Nova been as eloquent or persuasive in court. Never before or since had he used his God-given gifts as an advocate to save a life.

The low point, ironically, was reached at the same time. Only two persons—Nova and Sturgis—could appreciate the irony. Only they understood that the penalty-phase victory was purchased in large part with a lie.

Nova lifted the box containing his research notes and witness interviews from the trial to his desk and opened it. It took only a few seconds to find the small manila envelope that contained the audiotape of his interview with Sturgis at the Los Angeles County Jail, conducted before the penalty phase of the trial.

Nova retrieved the tape and held it to the light, studying it the way an arson investigator might scrutinize traces of an accelerant at a fire scene. He thought about slicing the tape to ribbons and throwing it in the trash can, something he could, and perhaps should, have done years ago. Only he and Sturgis knew about the tape, he told himself, and if Sturgis ever mentioned it, Nova could always claim it never existed. No one would take Sturgis' word over his. With the recording gone, Nova would have little to fear from turning the entire file over to the FBI. A lot of messy problems could be avoided. Or would they?

In order to bring the tape recorder into the county jail interview room, Nova had to obtain permission from the deputy sheriffs on duty. If they were ever tracked down, would they remember the tape? Had they made a written record of the permission they had given to him? Would the written record have been preserved all these years?

The more Nova contemplated the issue, the question of what to do became less clear. If his old law firm was still in business, he could have grabbed one of his former partners for a confidential conference.

From time to time even the best attorneys needed a second opinion to put matters in perspective, especially when their personal interests were at stake. But as a solo practitioner, Nova had no such luxury. He did, however, have a friend and a lawyer in Molly. Putting down the tape, he reached for the phone and punched in the private line to Molly's office.

"Something's come up," he announced even before Molly could finish saying hello. "We've got to talk."

"That's what people usually do on the phone," she replied, sounding a little annoyed at his abrupt manner. She glanced at the clock on her desk and noted that it was a quarter past five. She saw her plans to make it to the gym by six evaporating with the passing seconds. "I'm listening."

"I have a problem."

"Who doesn't? I just got out of an all-day deposition with an Armenian interpreter who must have picked up her court certification at Kmart. I'm still not sure if the person I deposed was the plaintiff's wife, his cousin, or his girlfriend. I may have to get a court order to take the damn thing all over again."

"Well, if it would make you feel any better, I also have some good news," Nova said, recalling that he had yet to tell Molly about Sandy.

Molly sighed audibly. "I'm sorry to sound like such a bitch. It's just that my secretary's gone and I have no one else to whine to. Why don't you start with the good stuff?"

"I've found a woman to testify at the custody hearing."

"That really is good news. Who's the lucky lady?"

"Sandy."

"Your first wife?" Molly hurried to answer her own question before Nova could. "A very interesting choice. I would have suggested her myself, but I never thought she'd be willing."

Molly took notes as Nova filled her in on his re-union with Sandy. "I guess that old Nova charm really means something," she said when he was done. "I'll ring Sandy first thing tomorrow and work out a battle plan. Now, what else is on your mind?"

"This is still attorney-client, right?"

"That's the general idea. My lips are sealed."

"You've heard that the feds are looking for my old client Randy Sturgis?"

"Me and the rest of humanity. I even saw your name mentioned in the *Times*. I guess you weren't available for comment when the reporter called your office. Most lawyers would kill for a page one quote."

"The last thing I need right now is publicity."

Molly hesitated, as if anticipating some truly dreadful news. "You're not going to tell me that Sturgis has contacted you, are you, David?"

"No, but Special Agent Anthony Ross of the FBI has. He wants my old trial file."

"That's crazy. The file's confidential."

"That's exactly what I told Ross, but he's threatened to serve me with a search warrant."

"Why does he want the file?"

Nova took a deep breath. "To answer your question I'm going to have to tell you things the FBI hasn't made public yet. Are you sure you want to know?"

"If you want my advice, David, I'm going to have to know."

Slowly, and sparing only a few details, Nova told her about the videotape Sturgis had sent to the FBI and Randy's bizarre "appointment" of Nova as Tanner's defense lawyer. "Ross suspects that the file might contain information that would help the feds find Sturgis."

"Where's the file now, David?"

"Right in front of me. I had it pulled from storage."

"And does it contain anything that might help the FBI?"

"No, not that I can see."

"Then what's the problem? Chances are, Ross was bluffing. He must have a million other things to do than go on a fishing expedition through your files. But just in case he's not bluffing, my advice is to stick to your principles. If Ross gets a warrant and tosses your office, we'll slap him with a civil rights complaint that will net you more than double the money you're paying me for the custody hearing."

"I don't want to wait to file a lawsuit. There's something in the file I don't want Ross or anyone else to get their hands on."

"What's that?"

"A tape recording I made of an interview with Sturgis at the county jail before the penalty phase of his trial."

"You tape-recorded an interview with your own client? Why?" Her voice resonated with incredulity. Not a single member of Nova's old firm, including Molly, knew about the taping.

"Because he refused to testify at the penalty phase, and I wanted proof, in case the jury returned a death verdict, that it was his decision and not mine that he stay off the stand. I know it sounds stupid, but at the time I thought it was the only way I could cover myself in case the prick tried to argue on appeal that he was denied effective assistance of counsel for not being called to testify."

"So you wanted Sturgis to declare, on tape, that he wouldn't testify on his own behalf?"

"That was the plan."

"Did you get what you wanted?"

"Yes and no. Sturgis was still incensed that the judge had denied his *Faretta* motion at the guilt phase. He thought the only reason he was convicted was because I blew the case. He told me that if I called him to the stand at the penalty phase, he would tell the jury the truth."

She grew silent and took a breath, then asked, "What truth?"

"That in addition to Mrs. Cowley, he had killed three other people—all elderly women—in rest homes he worked in as a nurse. He overdosed each of them with painkillers. He said that they were old and sick, and ready to die anyway. They reminded him of his mother, who also died from an overdose of painkillers."

"And the prosecution didn't have that information?"

"They knew about the deaths of the patients, but there was never any evidence to tie them to Sturgis."

"So Sturgis was prepared to sabotage his own case?"

"He said he wasn't interested in spending the rest of his life in prison, and that sooner or later he'd get his conviction overturned anyway. He told me that he'd keep his mouth shut during the penalty phase if I kept him off the stand, but that if I didn't, he'd tell all. He was playing mind games with me, almost like he was setting me up for something down the road."

"I'm sorry," she interrupted, "but it sounds to me like he was trying to cut a deal with you. He would get to keep his honor by not participating in the penalty phase, and in return you'd get to put on your case without disruption. I'm not saying it was right, but under the circumstances his position kind of made sense. You couldn't have called him as a witness after you learned about the other homicides anyway, not if you wanted to avoid a death verdict."

Molly's observations, as usual, were dead on the

mark. Short of suborning perjury there was no way Nova could have put Sturgis on the stand during the penalty phase and either kept him from voluntarily disclosing the prior killings or shielded him from a probing cross-examination into every aspect of his past. That much had been clear at the time of the trial, and it remained so now.

What troubled Nova, however, was Molly's comment about Sturgis offering him a deal. To a neutral third-party listening to the tape, it might very well seem as though Sturgis had attempted to strike some kind of underhanded deal to subvert the integrity of the penalty portion of the trial. The problem was that it might also seem as though he had taken the deal. As Sturgis' lawyer, Nova had an ethical obligation to put on the best case he possibly could on behalf of his client. He also had an ethical duty not to intentionally mislead the court or the jury. The potentially conflicting obligations were separated by a fine line that sometimes became blurred during the course of a high-stakes criminal trial. The idea that a trial was an unalloyed search for truth, in which the advocates simply let the chips fall, was a fantasy akin to childhood beliefs in Santa Claus and the Easter Bunny. Above all else, the lawyers wanted to win.

"Aside from the Cowley murder," Nova said, still turning Molly's remark over in his mind, "Sturgis had no criminal record. He knew that I would hammer hard on that fact with the witnesses and in my closing argument, and that's exactly what I did."

"But you were only arguing the evidence. There's nothing wrong with that. Anything Sturgis told you was protected from disclosure by the attorney-client doctrine, just like our conversation right now."

"I wish I could see it that way," Nova said pensively. "But I just reread the transcript of my closing argument, and I did much more than simply argue the absence of any prior convictions. I told the jury flat-out that Sturgis had never committed a prior act of violence. I also brought a formal motion *in limine* before the penalty phase to prevent the People from making any mention of the rest-home deaths. I built my whole penalty case on the claim that the Cowley murder was an isolated act. Two of the jurors told me after the trial that they voted for a life sentence because they believed me. Maybe I just got carried away, but I'm afraid I might have crossed the line."

"Okay, even assuming that you went a little over-board, who besides you and Sturgis knows that you crossed the line?"

"No one, but Ross is already suspicious. He knows about the three rest-home patients, and he's already decided Sturgis killed them. The way I see it, if Ross ever gets a hold of the tape . . ."

"He'll try to make you look like a slime ball who withheld evidence that would have sent a killer to death row and prevented the kidnapping of a federal judge years later. But he'll never succeed, because your interview with Sturgis is still privileged."

"What if the feds arrest Sturgis and, just to fuck me over, he decides to waive the privilege? He'd be taking himself down with me, but he's just crazy enough to do it."

Molly tapped the fingers of her free hand lightly on her desk as she took in Nova's question. The attorney-client privilege was one of the most ironclad bars to the disclosure of incriminating statements known to the law, but the privilege was designed to protect the client, and the client was always free to waive its protections. "In that case you might face some serious questions from the state bar."

"Not to mention what the press would do if they

ever found out about the tape," Nova added. "It would be like finding a tape of O.J. confessing to his lawyers that he killed Ron and Nicole. Their careers would be over and so would mine. I'd never be able to keep a straight face in another trial court. And I don't think anyone would bail *me* out with a fat book contract. At my age, I wouldn't want to have to find a real job to support myself."

"You're letting your imagination get the best of you, David. There's no reason for Ross or anyone else to get hold of the tape."

"Are you suggesting I throw the tape away?"

"No." She paused, as if contemplating the depth of Nova's dilemma. "But you could give the tape to me."

A few seconds ticked away as Molly's offer registered. "There's nothing wrong in having your lawyer review an item from one of your old files," she continued. "If you're served with a warrant, I'll ask for an in-camera hearing with the issuing magistrate to have the tape suppressed. Chances are, Ross will never lay his hands on the tape. How's that for a solution?"

"I don't know what to say," Nova answered. "It sounds better than anything I've come up with, but I don't want you to get sucked into this mess."

"I'd make the same offer for any client, David," she insisted, "and so would you."

"Maybe you're right."

"Look, you don't have to decide right now. Sleep on it. We'll talk again."

"Okay." Nova sensed that she expected him to say good-bye now, but he hadn't finished all he wanted to say. "The flip side, though, is that I'd really like to help the feds find Larry, if I didn't run the risk of screwing myself in the process. When I left Ross' office, I thought I'd just walk away. Now I'd feel like a worm if I did."

Nova told Molly about his promise to Sandy—that he'd pay his respects to Tanner's old clerk, Vera. He also thought about telling her of Ross' request that he question Tami about Sturgis, but he held himself back at the last moment. He knew, without asking, that Molly would have a meltdown if she thought he might do anything to antagonize Tami on the eve of their hearing.

Molly listened patiently to Nova's laments, but when she spoke again there was a new strain in her voice. Nova read it either as a sign of exasperation or fatigue.

"It's only natural that you'd want to help," she said, "but it's the FBI's job to find Tanner, not yours. If seeing Vera would make you feel better, fine, by all means go and see her. But as far as the rest of it goes, my advice is to stay as far away as you can from Ross and this whole business with Sturgis. You're a forty-five-year-old lawyer, David, with a one-person office and a custody trial coming up. This is no time to play hero. And in any event, you told me yourself that you have no information that could help the FBI. So what's the point of feeling bad?"

Molly's lecturing tone reminded him of the way his mother used to upbraid him back in high school for driving his father's car too fast and wearing his hair too long. "Maybe I just like beating up on myself." He chuckled at the situation.

"Now, that's a subject for your shrink or your priest, not your lawyer." She returned the laugh. "But I'm serious about the tape."

"I know, and I appreciate the offer." Nova said good-bye and hung up the receiver. He put the audio-tape back in its manila envelope, slipped the envelope into the inside pocket of his sports coat, and packed his briefcase for the drive home to Topanga.

*   *   *

Nova passed the night restlessly, tossing in bed as the muscles of his jaw and upper back tightened like high-tension wires. Waiting in vain for sleep, he debated what to do with the audiotape. Molly's offer was a godsend, a gesture of friendship as well as a clever legal tactic. He could never repay her for the offer, but he also knew he would never accept it. If Ross came looking for his files, the last thing he would want would be to drag Molly into a battle with the feds. She was already doing more than enough to salvage the final third of his life. If it came down to it, he'd hire some stranger to represent him or square off alone against Ross.

In the meantime, he'd lay low and tend to his own affairs, just as Molly had advised. Or would he? He wondered again if there wasn't some safe way he could contribute to the hunt for Tanner without jeopardizing his own interests. But each time he asked the question he drew another blank. He felt impotent and cowardly for thinking only of himself. Then he thought again of his promise to Sandy. Under the circumstances, maybe consoling Vera was the best he could do—to show someone who had once shown him great kindness a little concern and comfort at her time of need. At least that would be something positive.

Realizing that sleep would not come without a little pharmaceutical assistance, he dragged himself into the bathroom at two a.m. to look for an old vial of prescription sleeping pills one of his lady friends had left behind. He switched on the bathroom light and stared at himself in the mirror. There he was, much as Molly had described him, an aging, heavy-lidded over-the-hill attorney, with an expanding middle and worry lines in his forehead. Time and gravity were finally beginning to take their toll. Before he could ruminate further, however, the phone rang.

Annoyed at the intrusion, he hurried back into the bedroom and picked up the receiver. The silence on the other end was, for him, a dead giveaway. "Tami," he said sharply, "I'm in no mood for this. You've got to stop these calls." Irritated that his complaints elicited no response, he added, "I'm going to see that Judge Goldstein understands just how sick you really are. You need help, Tami, lots and lots of help."

Randy Sturgis hung up the receiver a split second after Nova had clicked off on his end. Smiling broadly, he poured himself another shot of tequila, opened the small plastic vial lying on the kitchen counter, and quickly downed two large red-and-white gelatin capsules. Then he strolled into the living room and walked out onto the cabin's redwood deck. The Big and Little Dippers, Orion, and all the other constellations were in their proper places, he noted, staring at the night sky. The universe was secure, and David Nova sounded like a man on the verge of an emotional crack-up. Everything, he told himself, was going according to plan.

Chapter Eleven

"I'm sorry, but Ms. Fletcher isn't in today. Would you like to leave a message?"

Nova didn't recognize the voice on the phone, but then there was no particular reason he should have. The federal court was always hiring new office help, constantly replacing the deadwood, and it had been a long time since he had tried to contact Vera through Judge Tanner's chambers. There was also a good deal of static over his car phone, which caused the voice on the other end to break up in mid-sentence as he maneuvered his Lexus through the morning traffic on the 101 freeway enroute to downtown.

"Who am I speaking to?" Nova asked.

"Louise Davis."

"You must be with central staff," Nova said, guessing that Ms. Davis was one of the newer hires assigned to service the general needs of the appellate bench rather than being assigned to work for any particular judge. "Louise, this is David Nova. I used to clerk for Judge Tanner, a long time ago, and I wanted to reach Vera. Is she out sick, or on vacation?"

"I'm sorry, but I can't give out that information."

"Can you tell me, then, if Vera will be back tomorrow?"

"I really don't know, sir. You'll either have to try back or leave a message."

Ms. Davis had been trained well in the art of the stonewall, Nova thought. If only Sylvia Gomez, his own clerk, were as tight-lipped, he'd have at least five less annoying phone calls a week. Still, the fact that Davis didn't know when Vera was expected back could only mean that she had called in sick, or was on some kind of stress leave related to Tanner's kidnapping. Either way, she was probably at home.

"Just tell her I called," Nova said as he hung up. With no appointments scheduled until the late afternoon, he flashed his turn signal and pulled into the exit lane for the 134 freeway and the green and white GLENDALE/PASADENA sign. Even in rush-hour conditions it would take no more than a half hour to drive to Vera's home.

Thinking it advisable to call ahead, he punched in Vera's number on the car phone. He listened as her phone rang—two, five, ten times with no answer. Maybe she had gone to the doctor or was out shopping. It was odd, however, that her answering machine didn't pick up. As far as he could recall, Vera always kept her answering machine on when she went out. Having a fully functional phone recorder was one of the requisites for being Tanner's chief administrative clerk. Even if you were on vacation out of the country, you were expected to check for His Honor's commands and wishes at least once a day. Feeling a slight but mounting sense of concern, Nova drove on.

Although he couldn't remember the last time he had driven to her home, he had not forgotten the directions or the well-earned reputation Vera had garnered for fastidious housekeeping. Like many single working women of her generation, Vera had been extremely frugal. Combining the earnings from her clerkship with a small bequest from her father, she had managed to purchase an attractive Spanish-style three-bedroom with whitewashed stucco walls and a red-tile roof in the foothills above New York Avenue. Over the years property values in the racially mixed neighborhood north of Pasadena, known as Altadena, had more than doubled, and though her home was one of the more modest on her block, Vera always made it a point to keep her front lawn meticulously trimmed and her flower beds, which always sported a rainbow of roses, daylilies, agapanthus, and other perennials, in showcase form.

But despite the obvious energy which went into such upkeep, Nova always had felt slightly depressed whenever he visited, mostly on court business but occasionally for dinner or an afternoon lunch on the back patio. There was a sense of loneliness that pervaded the place, almost as if the house had been purchased with the expectation, or at least the hope, that it might one day become the base for a happy family. But from the living room to the two spare bedrooms that Vera kept made up for company that rarely came, the house seemed practically uninhabited. Only the kitchen and the small den where Vera read and watched TV showed the wear and tear of continual use.

Nova found a parking space in front of Vera's home and walked down the red brick path to the front door. He rang the bell and waited. To his great relief, within a matter of seconds he heard the sound of light footsteps treading on the terra-cotta tiles of the entrance room. A moment later the bolt lock was released and the door pulled back a crack, restrained by a heavy steel safety chain. A pair of anxious brown eyes peered out from over the chain.

"Vera, is that you?" Nova asked. "It's David."

"Thank goodness. I was afraid you might be another reporter." She let out a deep sigh, unfastened the safety chain, and took a long, discerning look at Nova. "Well, don't just stand there in your suit and tie like some real estate agent looking for an easy sale. Come on in."

Vera led Nova into the kitchen and beckoned him to take a seat on one of the benches of the small built-in breakfast nook. "I was just about to have my second cup," she said, reaching for the tempered glass pot below the automatic coffee maker on an adjacent counter. "There's enough for another if you'd like a cup. It's pure Colombian."

Nova accepted a steaming mug and smiled at Vera, surprised and pleased at her unexpected perkiness. As she settled onto the bench across from him, dressed in a pink shortsleeve cotton-knit pullover and denim skirt, Vera looked anything but ill. To the contrary, with her straight brown hair tied back in a ponytail and her milky white skin still remarkably firm and unblemished, she looked the picture of health, at least ten years younger than her sixty years. Although just a shade over five feet, she was still slender, and still carried herself with a dancer's physical grace, a trait she had acquired from studying ballet as a young woman.

Her changeless qualities were immediately evident to Nova. Despite the passage of time he felt entirely at ease in her presence, almost as if she were still a regular part of his life. Of all the people he had met and worked with at the court of appeal, she was perhaps the only one he really considered a friend. As a young attorney, still wet behind the ears in the ways of the law, he had found her to be a constant source of reassurance and sympathy. There were times when the stress of toiling for Tanner nearly had driven him to tender an early resignation. Time and again Vera had taken him aside to deliver the kind of heart-to-hearts mothers reserve for their sons. She had acted then out of nothing more than the undisguised desire to see him finish his clerkship and embark on a prosperous legal career. He felt he owed her at least the same kind of solicitude and concern for the pain he knew she now felt.

"I tried to reach you at the courthouse," he said, "but a certain Ms. Davis told me you were out. I was afraid you were sick."

"I *am* sick," she answered wryly.

"About Larry?"

"About Larry mostly. About the FBI, too, asking me questions like they thought I might somehow be involved in Larry's disappearance. And I'm sick up to here"—she lifted her left hand above her head for emphasis—"of those writers from the *Times,* the *Daily News,* and the TV stations. I came home one night and found three of them camped on my doorstep. The phone's been ringing off the hook. I even got one of those deep breathers late last night."

"The same thing's been happening to me, but on a much reduced scale," he explained sympathetically. "When the press smells a story, they're like sharks. Is that why you turned your answering machine off? I tried calling about a half hour ago and it didn't pick up."

"I'm sorry. I guess I just wanted a little peace, and I had no idea you'd be calling." She furrowed her brow. "It must be at least a couple of years since we last spoke."

"I know," he said, "I've been pretty wrapped up in some personal problems." He wanted to apologize further for letting their friendship lapse, but was afraid she would consider the gesture hollow.

"Larry told me about the divorce."

"That's surprising, I wonder how he knew."

"Oh, you know how word of personal strife makes the rounds in the legal world. Lawyers always seem to live for other people's misery. Anyway, how's it going?"

"We have a custody hearing coming up week after next. It could be ugly."

"I'm sorry to hear that." She reached into her skirt pocket and pulled out a pack of Virginia Slims. "You don't mind, do you?" She lit up without waiting for an answer. "I hope everything works out for you in your case."

"Thanks, but I didn't come out here for you to console me." Nova gazed at her with concern. In all the years he'd known Vera, he'd never seen her smoke. A drink after work, some wine with dinner, but never a cigarette. "I understand how much Larry means to you."

"That just might be what makes me sickest of all."

"There's a joint task force assigned to the case. I'm sure they're doing everything possible to find him."

"I know." She inhaled thoughtfully and blew a gray plume of smoke into the center of the kitchen. "But that's not what I mean."

Nova looked at her quizzically. "What, then?"

"Please don't get me wrong. It breaks me up inside to think of Larry tied up in some dark room somewhere. But do you know how long I've been with that man?"

"Twenty, thirty years," he guessed.

"It will be thirty-two years this October. That's longer than most successful marriages."

"Is that what's bothering you, that Larry never asked you to marry?"

"When I first came to work with him back in state

court, I was just twenty-eight. I was young. I was pretty and I thought I had a career as a dancer. The idea of spending the rest of my life as a clerk never entered my mind." She took another puff, then doused the cigarette in a glass ashtray she kept with the salt and pepper shakers at the end of the breakfast table just below the double-hung window that looked over the garden on the side of her yard. The sunlight slanting through the parted curtains played across Vera's face, causing the tears that had begun to well in the corners of her eyes to glisten. The perkiness was gone now, replaced by the sadness Nova had expected to find on the way over.

"It's no secret that we became lovers," she resumed in a subdued voice. "Everyone knew about us, and I was never ashamed or embarrassed. I suppose, all things considered, our affair—if that's how I should refer to it—lasted longer than I had a right to expect. I was the closest thing Larry Tanner ever had to a wife. That's for sure. It's just that I never stopped caring, and I never stopped hoping, even after he began to chase younger women, that we might settle down together someday. It's funny how it takes some kind of disaster; like this kidnapping, to make you realize just what a fool you've been."

"He took you for granted," Nova offered gently. "But then he took everyone for granted, one way or another. The law clerks used to joke about it."

"He always worked you guys pretty hard. Each new staff attorney got the same treatment. No such thing as an eight-hour day." She managed a bemused smile.

"And he never apologized for it."

"No, but he always said, David, that you were one of his favorites. As hardheaded and as incommunicative as he was, I could tell he thought you were something special."

"And you must know that in his own way, he thought you were special, too."

She nodded almost imperceptibly. "I didn't even get a chance to say good-bye. I left the courthouse early the day he was abducted. Ever since, I've been wondering if I had been there, typing his opinions, going over his schedule, or even fixing the knot in his tie, maybe he would have left the building just a few minutes later and none of this would have happened."

Nova reached across the table and took her hands in his. Her hands were small, much like Tami's, but they were also strong and capable. They were the hands of a woman who never had the money or the inclination to hire others to shop, clean, or perform any other of life's mundane chores for her. "The worst thing you can do is play the what-if game."

"I just know he isn't coming back."

"No, you don't," he said, slowly releasing her hands. "He's a fighter. He'll pull through."

"That's funny," she said, cocking her head to one side. "That's exactly what Dr. Horowitz said." She forced another smile and fought back the tears.

"Irving Horowitz?"

"He called last night to see how I was getting along. He even asked me out for lunch, but I took a rain check."

"Larry recommended Horowitz to me as an expert witness for the Sturgis trial."

"I know. He and Irving were good friends when they were younger. We used to double-date in the old days. Larry even considered recusing himself from Sturgis' appeal because of their friendship."

Horowitz and Tanner were contemporaries stamped from the same mold. Both grew up poor in big cities back East. Both resettled in California as young men, and each rose to the top of their professions through a combination of self-reliance, pugnacity, and hard work. Nova knew that Tanner and Horowitz were acquainted, but not that they had ever been close. Hearing that they were didn't particularly surprise him. The bit about the recusal, however, did. Since Horowitz had been a penalty-phase witness and Sturgis' appeal had dealt exclusively with his conviction at the guilt phase of his trial, the appeal did not require Tanner to review or pass judgment on Horowitz's testimony in any way.

"But why would the fact of their friendship cause Larry to consider recusing himself?" Nova asked.

Vera nervously fished out another Virginia Slim. For a moment it seemed as though she was unwilling to look at him. "Because he was also one of Irving's patients, and he was afraid that fact might somehow come out if he kept the case."

"When did he come under Horowitz's care?"

"When he was still a relatively new judge on the federal district court." Vera's voice took on a flat affect, as if she were confessing to a secret she had pledged never to reveal. "Long before you met him on the Ninth Circuit. I guess you didn't know it, but Larry was an alcoholic."

"I always wondered why he never drank," Nova said. "I just assumed he was one of those people who just didn't like the stuff."

"Oh, he liked it, all right," Vera sighed. "Scotch on the rocks, dry martinis, white wine. You name it. For the most part, though, he was one of those very private, after-hours kind of drunks. To his colleagues on the court, he seemed like nothing more than an ordinary social drinker. At first he thought it wasn't a problem. Then he thought he could quit on his own. Finally, when he realized he needed help, he saved up his vacation time and told the presiding judge he was taking time off to go to Europe. He went to Irving's clinic instead. Except for me, nobody outside the clinic ever knew he became an inpatient. Later, he just told his friends he'd given up drinking to lose weight."

She turned away toward the window and began to sob. "Larry would be furious with me for telling you all this. But you know what? I'm too exhausted to care anymore."

Nova walked over to her. "I don't think Larry would be furious in the least," he said, sliding onto the bench beside her and placing his arms around her. "If he had any brains at all, he'd consider himself lucky to have had someone like you in his life. I know I would." He stroked Vera's hair and held her until her sobbing subsided.

Back in his Lexus Nova felt the anger well up inside him as he turned the situation over in his mind. "There's just one argument, and one argument alone, that can save Larry's life," Sturgis had warned in the videotape sent to the FBI. Find the winning argument and win the game. Fail, and Larry dies. It was a simple proposition, and thoroughly insane.

Perhaps even crazier, from Nova's perspective, was the notion, as he pulled away from Vera's home, that he was finally and indisputably in the game. To quit and go home now, with Vera's mournful image on his conscience, was unthinkable, even for the most hardened of cynics. There were, he quickly reminded himself, only three days left before the deadline Sturgis had set for placing the personal ad in the *South Coast Inquirer*.

He glanced at the digital clock on the dashboard of his Lexus. It was eleven. If he hurried, he might be able to catch Dr. Horowitz at his Encino clinic by noon.

Chapter Twelve

In all of Los Angeles County there was perhaps no better place for Dr. Horowitz to have founded his substance-abuse clinic than Encino. Located at the western end of the San Fernando Valley, between the Ventura Freeway to the north and the Santa Monica Mountains to the south, Encino was an upscale, uniquely Southern California conclave of trendy shopping malls, flashy foreign cars, exclusive country clubs, and sprawling ranch-style housing tracts. Renowned as the site of Michael Jackson's boyhood home and as the spawning ground of the airheaded "Valley Girl" caricature, the community offered both close proximity to the movie studios and easy freeway access to L.A.'s affluent west side. And while it had long since lost the country ambience that first had attracted Angelenos seeking refuge from big-city crime and overcrowding, Encino remained on the eve of the new millennium an island of material comfort and relative safety.

For Irv Horowitz, Encino had proven to be a terrific place to grow filthy rich, tending to the needs of those who had taken to booze and drugs to cope with the vicissitudes of modern life. Taking advantage of attractive real estate prices and lending rates in the mid

1960s, Horowitz had purchased a twenty-acre parcel of rolling hills near the Encino Reservoir. Two years later, with the initial construction of his residential treatment center completed, he left his Beverly Hills psychiatric practice behind for a new beginning in the Valley.

After a slow start, the Horowitz Clinic grew to become one of the Golden State's most exclusive recovery facilities, catering mostly to wealthy alcoholics and prescription-pill abusers from the entertainment industry and the legal community. A second residential complex was built in the mid seventies, together with an indoor/outdoor swimming pool and spa complex, lighted red clay tennis courts, three oversized putting greens, and a state-of-the-art golf driving range. For patients able to afford its hefty price tag, Horowitz's Haven, as it was affectionately known in the burn-out biz, was both a place to get well and a five-star resort all rolled into one.

In addition to providing its clientele with the latest and most effective therapies, the clinic made its top-flight staff of treating therapists, M.D.'s, and nurses available to provide medical-legal consultations and expert testimony on behalf of patients whose addictions had gotten them into legal problems. Occasionally, the clinic's doctors would even agree to consult as court-appointed experts in high-profile criminal cases involving non-clinic patients.

Dr. Horowitz thought such forensic ventures were good for the clinic's reputation and was particularly enamored of the courtroom. He had taught classes on law and psychiatry at USC law school, Tanner's alma mater, and he seemed to enjoy not only the theoretical aspects of litigation but the actual experience of butting heads with prosecutors bent on debunking his opinions before a jury. Even though the court-funded rates he received for such work were less than half what he charged privately, he had eagerly accepted Nova's invitation to work on the Sturgis trial over a decade earlier, terming Randy one of the most challenging specimens he had ever been called upon to examine.

Unlike the bureaucratic runaround Nova had encountered on calling the federal court for Vera, the clinic's receptionist put him through directly to Dr. Horowitz himself, interrupting a three-city conference call in the process. The mere mention of Larry Tanner and the kidnapping was all Nova needed to secure the promise of an immediate audience with the doctor.

Satisfied that the remainder of his morning would be well spent, Nova put his car phone back on its jack and continued down the 101 freeway, cruising past Burbank, Studio City, Sherman Oaks, and sundry other garden spots of suburban culture. As he drove deeper into the Valley, the temperature rose steadily, climbing past the ninety-degree mark en route to a predicted high in the low hundreds. Along with the rising temperature came the dreaded Valley smog. Although it was only late morning, a carpet of searing gray pollutants had already begun to settle upon the Valley floor. Wondering whether the air-quality board would declare a third-stage alert by the end of the day, Nova cranked up the air conditioning, filling the interior of his Lexus with a steady blast of recirculated cool air. Smog, air conditioning, and the automobile. In the Valley, he mused, they were like the chicken and the egg.

At the outskirts of Encino, he took the exit for the reservoir, then headed for Havenhurst Avenue and drove south, past the Jackson family compound and the nearby cottage that Clark Gable and Carol Lombard once had called home. In another few minutes he was turning down the winding black-topped driveway to the clinic's reception building.

Not much had changed since his last visit prior to the penalty phase of the Sturgis trial, he thought as he made his way. The same old overgrown California pepper trees, perfectly adapted to the harsh and dry Valley summers, lined either side of the driveway. Their gnarled, leafy branches arched together high overhead to provide a shaded canopy under the unrelenting sun. Farther in the distance, stands of cactus, palm, and eucalyptus trees dotted the rolling green lawns that a time-controlled, full-purpose sprinkler system kept looking like lushly hydrated parkland even in the midday heat.

Nova parked his Lexus in the bilevel lot adjacent to the reception building and walked inside the hall. A pleasant-looking female receptionist dressed in a cotton floral top and a long, tapered skirt cut at midcalf greeted him with a friendly smile and escorted him upstairs. No waiting. No questions.

Dr. Horowitz had his office on the second floor of the reception hall in a corner suite overlooking the low-rise, horseshoe-shaped new residential complex and the free-form pool and rose gardens that adorned the complex's central courtyard. Nova found him seated behind a big desk of blanched teak, reviewing an old manila file that contained the records from Tanner's stay at the clinic.

"I figured that if it involved Larry, it had to be urgent," Horowitz said as he rose and extended his hand to Nova. A round little man in his mid-sixties, Horowitz stood no more than five feet six, with a pink bulbous nose and a thick shock of snow white hair wreathing an otherwise bald crown. Good-natured and affable, his face was creased with deep smile lines, giving him an uncanny resemblance to the lovable old pirate Mr. Smythe from the Disney cartoon production of Peter Pan whenever he laughed and his ample belly shook.

Nova apologized for the interruption and promised not to take up any more of the doctor's time than was necessary. "As I said on the phone, I've come because of Randy Sturgis," he explained.

"Has he sent some kind of ransom note?"

"Not exactly," Nova answered, taking a seat at the foot of Horowitz's desk. "He's sent a videotape, inviting the FBI and me to play some perverse little game to save Larry's life."

"What kind of game?" Horowitz asked in an almost clinical tone.

"He's appointed himself as the presiding judge in his own courtroom and has found Larry guilty of the capital crime of delaying the opinion that eventually led to his release from prison while rushing to reverse the convictions of other less deserving convicts. We only have a few days left to dig into Larry's background and find something—an experience, a character trait, some kind of past behavior, at this point we really have no way of knowing—that Larry and Sturgis share in common, which might mitigate Larry's crime and prompt Sturgis to spare his life. We're supposed to publish our findings in the personal ad section of the *South Coast Inquirer*."

Horowitz stroked his face with the pudgy fingers of his right hand as he took in Nova's startling news. "But why come to me?"

"Because you once examined Sturgis at my request."

"But that was a very long time ago. The Department of Corrections must have evaluated him half a dozen times since then."

"And because you once also treated Larry."

Horowitz gave Nova a look of surprise.

"Vera told me this morning," Nova answered, responding to what he knew would have been Horowitz's next question.

"How can I help?" Horowitz asked instead.

"You can fill me in on the particulars of Larry's stay here."

Nova noticed the color rising in the doctor's face. Sensing Horowitz's discomfort with his request, he thought back to his own reservations about releasing the Sturgis trial file to the FBI. The two situations weren't really comparable, he told himself quickly. He wasn't the FBI, and he wasn't going to ask Horowitz to release Larry's files, only to discuss his treatment. And he was prepared to do that entirely off the record. There was no danger, either, of the doctor being reported to the state medical board for a breach of patient confidentiality.

"I know that Larry's medical records are private," Nova said, "but under the circumstances, I think he would want you to tell me. Look, I wasn't even supposed to tell anyone about the demands Sturgis has made, but I figured you'd have a right to know about them if I was going to ask you to talk about Larry. I wouldn't have come here if I didn't think it absolutely necessary."

Horowitz pursed his lips like an investor considering a risky new stock venture. "There's not that much to tell, I'm afraid," he said after a few moments of contemplation. "And it was quite a while ago, at any rate. Larry came here shortly before his nomination to the court of appeal," he said, leafing through the file in front of him.

"Was his problem confined to alcohol?"

Horowitz nodded thoughtfully. "Larry had a special

weakness for Scotch and Jack Daniel's. He'd been bat-
tling the problem all his adult life. Both his parents
had been alcoholics. His older brother, too. Like them,
he was very good at concealing his addiction. He
rarely drank at lunch or with other judges, and when
he did he managed to do so with surprising moderation. At night, alone, it was a different story."

Nova knew that Tanner's father, a heavy smoker,
had succumbed to lung cancer while still a relatively
young man, in his fifties. The judge's mother had died
about a decade later, from a stroke, while she was
residing in Larry's Brentwood home. He had never
heard about the history of alcoholism. "Larry never
talked much about his family," he said. "I think it was
Vera, in fact, who told me how they passed away. The
only way I knew he had a sibling was that the brother
was mentioned in an old profile of Larry published in
a legal newspaper. I read it before I went to work for
him at the court of appeal."

"I'm not surprised," Horowitz remarked. "Larry
has always been a very public man but a very private
person. Ben was Larry's only sibling. He was seven
years older. A dentist, as I recall. They were never
close. I've run into him a few times over the years.
The last I heard he had a stroke and was living at
a convalescent home up near Idylwild. The Alpine
Convalescent Home, I believe it's called. It's funny,
though, now that I think about it, but in some ways
Larry and Ben were very much alike."

"How so?" Nova asked, jotting down the name of
the rest home on a piece of scrap paper.

"Like Larry, Ben seemed stubborn, single-minded,
and driven to succeed. He had a nice home in the
Palisades, and like Larry, he was a bachelor. They
both seemed to be afraid of long-term emotional com-
mitments, as my contemporary female colleagues

would say." Horowitz chuckled softly at the last reference.

"What prompted Larry to seek treatment?"

Horowitz took another moment to collect his thoughts. "With most people the decision is made for health reasons, or because their family or working lives are falling apart. With Larry, I think, it was mostly ambition. He was in the running for a spot on the Ninth Circuit and was terribly concerned that his secret could get out and become an issue in the confirmation process."

"Was there anything special about Larry's treatment here?"

"Not really. He went through the standard four-week residential program of individual and group therapy and physical conditioning. We also put him on a special high-protein diet. Then we followed that up with another four weeks of outpatient counseling, twice a week, in the evenings. When he completed the program, he looked great, and, according to what he told me at least, he felt better than he had in years."

"Did he have any visitors while he stayed here?"

"Actually, we discourage visiting. It tends to interfere with patient recovery. Larry, however, insisted that Vera be allowed to visit him, to keep him apprised of the goings-on at court. I think I saw her here a few times. I don't think she stayed very long. Because it was Larry, I never raised a fuss."

Nova raised his right hand to his forehead and gently massaged his temples. Except for a single piece of wheat toast, he hadn't eaten all day. He was already hungry when he arrived at the clinic, and now he was beginning to get a headache, too. Fearing that he would learn little more about Tanner from Horowitz than he had already learned from Vera, he decided to shift the discussion to Sturgis. "What do you think Randy Sturgis really wants?"

Horowitz shrugged his thick shoulders. "Only Sturgis knows for sure, of course, but this is no ordinary kidnapping. If he's not after money, I'd say he's looking for some kind of personal vindication. Perhaps by publishing something very humiliating to Larry, he hopes to show that those who run the justice system are either corrupt or, at the very least, no better than he is. And while he may have used the term 'mitigation' in articulating his proposition, he may have something very different in mind from what you or I or a trial jury might understand by that term."

"Why do you suppose he's come right out and identified himself as Larry's kidnapper? Does he expect or want to get caught?"

"Randy Sturgis is a manic depressive. If, as is probable, his condition has deteriorated over the years, he may be riding right now on a manic high so strong that he thinks of himself as being invulnerable."

"And why has he chosen to involve me in his game?"

"That's an easy one," Horowitz answered with an ironic grin. "He no doubt blames you for his initial conviction, and he wants to make sure you share the blame for Larry's death if you fail to find the right answer to his game. I'm sure it all hangs together from his point of view."

"I thought you might say that." Nova stood, disappointment and resignation registered on his face. "Thanks again for your time," he said. He shook the doctor's hand, excused himself, and began to head for the door.

"You know, you used to be a little more dogged in the old days," Horowitz called out from behind his desk.

"Is that just a comment on my advancing age, or did you have something specific in mind?" Nova asked, halting his progress across the floor and turning to face Horowitz.

"You never asked me about my relationship with Larry after he completed his outpatient program."

"Is there something I should know?"

"I think so." Horowitz motioned Nova back to his seat. "When Larry was a patient here, there was a young black man working on our staff as a nurse's aide. I fired him not long after Larry left us for stealing medical equipment. The young man went on to file a discrimination complaint against me with the EEOC. About a year after that he suddenly dropped the complaint."

"Why?"

"He called me on the phone one afternoon and said that he didn't need to pursue the lawsuit, that he had gotten a new job working for Judge Tanner."

"Did you ever ask Larry about the kid?"

"Of course. But Larry just laughed and said he'd never seen the kid outside of the clinic. After that, whenever I raised the issue, Larry always changed the subject."

"What was the kid's name?"

"Andrew Marsh. Bright kid, but such a waste." An ear-to-ear scowl settled across Horowitz's face. "The last I heard he was serving a life term for a drug-related murder."

Horowitz gazed at Nova for a moment, as if he expected to field a few follow-up questions. When it became clear there would be no more queries, he added with some concern, "You look tired and hungry, David. I can appreciate what you're going through. If you'd like, I could have one of my gals order up some lunch."

Nova politely declined the doctor's offer with a wave of his right hand. "My secretary's probably ready to send out a search party for me. I'll grab a bite back at my office." He gave Horowitz his thanks again and stood to leave, this time for real.

Chapter Thirteen

There was no need to send out a search party. Nova found the party waiting for him the moment he stepped off the elevator outside his office. With his leather-tooled briefcase gripped tightly in his clenched right fist, he walked quickly past a group of onlookers from other firms who had stepped into the corridor to observe the afternoon's excitement. He felt his heart sink into his stomach as he locked eyes with a clean-shaven, heavyset man in his late twenties standing sentry at his office door, partially obscuring the small sign that read, DAVID NOVA, ATTORNEY AT LAW. Despite the summer heat, the man was wearing the traditional blue windbreaker with the trademark bright gold block letters: FBI.

"I'm sorry, sir, but this office is the subject of a government search," the man announced like a Marine Corps private on assignment in occupied territory as Nova slowly approached. "Members of the public aren't permitted to enter."

"I'm not a member of the public," Nova snapped back. "I'm David Nova, and this is my office." He retrieved his wallet from his back pants pocket and held his driver's license and California state bar card in front of the man's face. "I assume you have a warrant." He waited a split second for an answer, then added, "Well, are you going to let me in, or do I have to phone my attorney?"

The young agent examined Nova's documents. Satisfied that Nova wasn't a foreign agent or a terrorist, he opened the office door and stepped aside. "Just don't touch anything, sir. I believe Special Agent Ross is inside and that he has a copy of the search warrant for you."

To Nova's relief and surprise, the office looked relatively intact. There were no desk drawers open in the reception area, no files strewn about the floor, no soft cushions slit open or furniture overturned. Following her usual afternoon routine, Sylvia Gomez was seated behind her desk, working away at her word processor as if playing host to the FBI was part of her job description. Only the tense, tight-lipped expression on Sylvia's face gave any hint that the office had been violated by the most powerful law enforcement agency in the country.

"The action's all in your office," Sylvia said nervously, without waiting for Nova to ask what had happened. "They got here about forty-five minutes ago. I've rescheduled your two afternoon appointments. I've reset Mr. Solomon for Monday and—"

"We can go over that later," Nova interrupted. "But thanks for the quick thinking." A lot of secretaries would have panicked under the circumstances, he told himself as he walked through the reception area and past the vacant conference room en route to his interior office.

Inside his office, another two agents, also dressed in the blue windbreakers, were busily packing up the nine file boxes from the Sturgis case and loading them onto two steel hand trucks. The agents had undoubtedly spent the past three-quarters of an hour inventorying the contents of the boxes and making sure there were no other Sturgis files in the room. Neither made eye contact with Nova as he stood at the door, scrutinizing their handiwork, and neither said a word. Apparently acting on instructions, they were content to leave the talking to Tony Ross.

Nova diverted his gaze from the trial boxes to Ross, who had been standing behind Nova's desk, supervising the operation.

"I hope the feds will pick up the tab for the punitive damages you're going to have to cough up after I sue your ass for this," Nova said. He walked over to the foot of his desk and took a seat on an upholstered red client chair.

"I don't think it will come to that," Ross said, reaching into the inside pocket of his gray sports coat and pulling out a thick multipage document stapled together in the upper left corner and neatly creased down the center. "It's your copy of the search warrant issued by federal magistrate Robert Harding this morning. There are at least thirty pages, including my affidavit and the exhibits. I'll wait for you to read through it if you'd like."

Nova took the document from Ross. He glanced quickly at the word WARRANT printed in capital letters atop the first page, then tossed the packet dismissively on his desk. There would be time enough to pore over the fine print later. For now, he wanted a little quality time alone with Ross.

Nova waited for Ross's subordinates to vacate the office, then said, "You must be pretty fucking desperate to come out here. I told you before, there's nothing in the files that could possibly help you. This is one of the most irresponsible invasions of privacy and client confidentiality I've ever seen."

"Save the big words for your lawsuit, if you can

find anyone foolish enough to represent you," Ross retorted. "We've done nothing illegal or irresponsible here. In fact, I would have been derelict in my duties if I hadn't pressed for a warrant." He placed his hands on the back of the armchair behind Nova's desk. "Mind if I sit?"

Nova nodded his grudging permission. He watched as Ross settled into the seat he normally occupied.

"You don't have any attorney-client privilege in the Sturgis files anymore," Ross continued. "It's been waived."

"Bullshit," Nova shot back instinctively. "There isn't a court in this state that will back you up on that, and you know it."

Ross flashed the closest thing to a shit-eating grin that Nova had ever seen on the face of a law enforcement officer. Despite a full afternoon's growth of heavy dark stubble on his face and the gravity of the situation, the special agent looked like a man who knew he held the upper hand, pleased and relaxed at the way he had outfoxed a clever adversary.

"I've already told you to read over the warrant," Ross said, "but since you don't seem to be in a reading mood, I'd suggest, at the very least, that you look at the last three pages." He gestured toward the warrant packet Nova had thrown on the desktop.

Nova picked up the packet and quickly leafed through it to the last three pages. The third-to-last page contained a photocopy of an envelope addressed in longhand to Agent Ross at the Bureau's Westwood headquarters. The envelope was postmarked from L.A. on Saturday. The last two pages contained the payoff: a handwritten letter scripted in black ink with a ballpoint pen on lined sheets of spiral notebook paper, which had arrived in Ross' mailbox along with the accompanying envelope.

Dear Agent Ross,

As with any creative endeavor—be it a movie, a novel, a legal brief, or an argument to a jury—there's always something you wished you included in your presentation but for whatever reason—time pressures, a late lunch, distribution headaches, a date with the executioner—you inadvertently neglected to say. The same is true, unfortunately, of my little video. I flat-out forgot to give you your best clue.

Now, I know that you and David—I assume you'll share this little epistle with Davey as soon as possible—are very resourceful and that you'll scour the four corners looking for the right words to place in that personal for the Inquirer. But, and I say this with all due respect, I think you need a little push in the right direction, just to get you oriented and properly motivated. I'm sure that Larry would agree, but right now he's what they say in the professional world, "away from his desk." Actually, he's asleep at the moment, and he's just fine . . . for now.

Anyway, here's your hint: Start with my old trial file and work back from there. I realize it's not much, but I wouldn't want to give the game away without giving you boys a chance to show your stuff. You probably don't have much time left, so I'll let you get right to work. Larry and I have gotten to be very good pals over the last few days. It's amazing how much two people can learn about each other in such a short time.

And just in case you're worried about those pesky legal technicalities, what with my file being subject to various privileges and all, I hereby renounce—knowingly, voluntarily, and

*I would contend, intelligently—any claim of
attorney-client privilege in my old trial file.*

    *Remember, fellas, ol' Larry's been convicted of
high crimes and misdemeanors. What you're
looking for is that argument, or combination of
arguments, in mitigation of punishment that
might preserve his golden years. I look forward
to your answer.*

                Have fun.

The main body of the letter was followed by Randy's
signature in longhand, and a freehand rendering of
the goddess of justice, replete with her scales and
blindfold. The word TANNER was written just above
one of the scales, which was evenly balanced against
the other, atop of which was placed a question mark.
Two teardrops trickled from behind Justice's blindfold. Though crude, the quality of the drawing revealed a certain measure of skill. Like many long-term
prisoners, Nova thought, Sturgis must have spent a
fair part of his considerable free time behind bars perfecting the elementary techniques of pen-and-ink
illustration.

If Nova had taken up Dr. Horowitz on his offer of
lunch, he might very well have launched a half-
digested brisket or corned beef sandwich right on his
lap as he placed the warrant packet back on his desk.
This was his office, but he felt ill and entirely out of
control. For the first time in recent memory, he flashed
back in earnest to one of the many "lessons in life"
that his gray-haired Sicilian grandmother had tried to
drum into his prepubescent head: *If you worry long
and hard enough about something awful, it will surely
come to pass.*

"The crazy old crow may just have been right," he

said silently to himself. Struggling to turn his attention back to Ross, he added aloud, "I assume you've analyzed the handwriting and checked the original for prints."

"The letter arrived at the regional office yesterday. Whatever else you might think about us, our lab techs are no fools. It's Randy's writing, and his finger and palm prints are all over the notebook pages and the envelope. There's also another set of prints, which we think belong to the postal worker who delivered the envelope."

Ross folded his hands against his chest, like a poker player intent on bluffing or upping the ante. "I must admit I was a little surprised to find the files stacked up so neatly next to your desk. I was afraid you'd have them tucked away somewhere dark and lonely."

"I had the files returned from storage. You're not the only one interested in helping Tanner." There was an undisguised anger in Nova's voice. It was bad enough that Ross had violated his inner sanctum, but what ticked Nova off just as much was the agent's morally superior tone.

"As I told you before," Ross said, sounding sincere and even a little conciliatory, "we'd be only too happy to have your help."

"And as I said before, you must be pretty desperate to spend what little time you have left raiding my office."

Ross heaved a deep sigh and regarded Nova carefully. "You're right about that, counsel. We *are* desperate. I've got a fully staffed joint task force on this case, and we've saturated the media with photos of Sturgis, from the time he was on trial to ones taken just before his release from prison. In the last forty-eight hours we've followed up at least twelve alleged sightings, from Eureka to San Diego. All we've come up with is hot air. To tell you the truth, I wasn't even going to bother with the personal ad for the *Inquirer*, but given the lack of other leads, the ad might be our best hope. So when Randy's letter arrived, I had no choice but to come back to you."

"With a warrant," Nova said stiffly.

"With or without a warrant, we're still on the same side in this."

Nova took some time to consider the olive branch Ross seemed to be showing him. Slowly, he felt his anger subside. "There's nothing in the files that will help us in placing the ad, at least not directly."

"What about indirectly?"

"I've just come from Irving Horowitz's clinic in Encino."

"I was wondering where you'd gotten to. Your secretary said you had gone to see Vera Fletcher, but that was early in the morning."

"Vera told me that Tanner was once a patient at the clinic. He went there before he was nominated to the Ninth Circuit to dry out from alcohol abuse."

"And Horowitz was the doctor you used at the penalty stage of Randy's trial." Ross paused to ponder the connection. "So, in a sense, Tanner and Sturgis had the same shrink. You think that's what Sturgis wants us to print in the ad—that Tanner is an alcoholic who went to the same doctor as a man convicted of murder?"

"I think what Randy really wants is to have us print the most humiliating details of Tanner's personal life we can find," Nova offered, conveying Dr. Horowitz's insight without revealing that he had told the doctor about Randy's proposal. "When you think about it, that's what defense attorneys do at the penalty phase of a capital case. The more abuse and humiliation the defendant suffered in the past, the more deserving he is of mercy in the present, and the less responsible he is for the crimes he's committed. That's the approach I took at Randy's trial, and it worked."

Nova stood and walked to the window. Outside, the streets were already beginning to swell with traffic. Even up on the eighth floor of the building, the sounds of car horns and squealing brakes could be heard as the afternoon exodus from downtown commenced. The gridlock and the oppressive temperatures made for an inordinate number of edgy drivers. Still, in another two or three hours the inner city would be deserted, except for the cops and the bedraggled legions of homeless people who spent the night holed up in cardboard shanties on the sidewalks and freeway underpasses.

"I think the alcoholism is a start," Nova said, "but I doubt it's all Randy has in mind."

"Are you just guessing or do you know more?"

"A bit of both, actually." He turned to face Ross, but was silent.

Ross cleared his throat like an impatient schoolteacher. "I'm all ears," he said.

"I want my files back, and I don't want you making any copies."

Ross grimaced and shook his head. "If the files are as clean as you say, we'll have them back to you in a few days. That's the best I can do. Now, what else do you know?"

"There's someone else you need to check out: a guy named Andrew Marsh. He's doing hard time somewhere in the state system for murder one."

Ross unfolded a small notepad and began to scribble away as Nova related the bizarre information Dr. Horowitz had given him on Marsh and Tanner. "I'll run a check on the guy tonight," he said when Nova had finished. "If he's still alive, it shouldn't be too hard to set up an interview for early tomorrow."

Looking satisfied with the new lead he had been given, Ross got up and walked over to Nova. The two men met in the middle of the room. "I'd like to see you at my office tomorrow morning by seven-thirty—no, make that seven," Ross said.

Nova felt another sick and sour sensation shoot through his midsection. "What for?"

"You know both Tanner and Sturgis a lot better than I do. I want you to come with me when we talk to Marsh. I don't want to have to chase you down later and hear you tell me about all the questions I forgot to ask him."

"Okay," Nova said, half surprised by Ross' request and half relieved that Ross now regarded him as an ally, and an important one at that.

"Be ready to fly," the agent added.

Nova escorted Ross out into the hallway and watched as the agent stepped onto the elevator. Back in his inner office, when he was certain Ross had left the building, he reached into the inside pocket of his sports coat and pulled out the small manila envelope containing the audiotape of his old jailhouse interview with Sturgis. Back in the old days, before the business with Tanner's kidnapping and his custody case had turned his world upside down, he would never have worn the same jacket two days in a row. Both his personal habits and his mental agility were clearly slipping.

He walked over to his desk, picked up the search warrant packet, and placed both the packet and the tape in his briefcase. Then he buzzed Sylvia and instructed her to cancel his appointments for the remainder of the week.

Chapter Fourteen

At nine-thirty sharp, Randy Sturgis parked his old Chevy Impala two doors down from the Aquino Pharmacy. In his wallet he carried a forged prescription for sixty capsules of Percodan and another sixty of Dalmane. If things went smoothly, he would have the prescription filled inside of an hour.

In the three years since he had skipped parole, he had learned that there were certain keys to obtaining controlled substances like Percodan and Dalmane without a valid prescription. The first was knowing how to obtain blank "triplicate" prescription forms and up-to-date DEA numbers for the physicians whose triplicate forms you acquired. Fortunately, that was never too big a problem for someone with direct ties, whether through friends or employment, to doctors or hospitals, or for someone skilled in the methods of commercial burglaries.

The second was learning how to forge the physician's handwriting on the blanks. That, too, was never much of a hassle, given the illegible penmanship of the healing profession. Few, if any, busy pharmacists would stop to examine whether all the "t's" in a particular script were crossed in exactly the same manner or whether all the "i's" were always dotted the same way.

The trickiest part was finding enough pharmacies to spread the bogus 'scrips around. The greatest danger of getting caught came from using the same drugstore too often, particularly when the kind of drug or the quantity prescribed was likely to raise questions about whether the patient really wanted the goodies for recreational, rather than medical, reasons. If a pharmacist doubted the bona fides of a prescription, he was duty-bound to reject it. Failing to do so could cost the pharmacist his license or even result in criminal prosecution.

Over the years Randy had also learned that in some matters he had to be patient. It wasn't enough to know how to obtain and fill out blank prescription forms. To acquire a steady supply of the painkillers and hypnotics he desired, he knew he would often have to wait for an appropriate cooling-off period to ensure that the physicians he stole from did not report the thefts of their prescription blanks.

The forged 'scrip he now carried in his wallet had been pilfered six months earlier in a late-night burglary of a small medical group on the outskirts of Idyl-wild. The rip-off was one of several burglaries of medical offices he had perpetrated during his time on the lam, and it had netted him prescription blanks for five different doctors. He also had found the DEA numbers for three of the five doctors jotted down on a yellow Post-It note under a desk calendar by the phones behind the reception counter. Medical offices, as he had long known, rarely maintained tight security over either prescription tablets or doctors' DEA numbers.

Randy had waited a month after the last burglary to make an appointment with Dr. Lincoln Albright, one of the medical group's doctors whose DEA numbers he had obtained. Using one of several fake driver's licenses he had purchased in downtown L.A. from one of the Latino community's many underground immigration runners, he signed the medical group's appointment log under the name of James Barlow, feigning flu-like symptoms of congestion, headaches, and a sore throat. The act enabled him to score a prescription, filled out in Albright's virtually indecipherable hand, for antibiotics and a powerful decongestant.

Five months later, after he had spent hours perfecting his imitation of Albright's handwriting, Randy decided it was time for the doctor to issue another prescription. All that remained was for Randy to select the right drugstore.

After giving the matter considerable thought, he believed he had chosen a promising candidate in Aquino Drugs. Located on the corner of a modest strip mall just off state highway 74 in the small farming community of Hemet, twenty miles east of Idylwild, Aquino Drugs was a small sole proprietorship. The store was owned and operated by Rosalee Aquino, a first-generation Filipino immigrant who had come to the United States as a teenager in the 1960s, paid for her education by working nights as a secretary, and had never married.

In the last month Randy had made two incidental purchases of chewing gum and Tylenol at Aquino's, and he had spent the better part of an hour one afternoon watching the store's customers come and go from the front seat of his Chevy across the street. Such advance planning was time-consuming but necessary. It also gave him great confidence that Aquino's had been a good choice.

Although he had never spoken directly with Rosalee, he had heard her conversing with other customers. In a way, he actually felt he knew her, or at least the social type she represented. To his twisted way of thinking, immigrant pharmacists like Rosalee were the easiest marks for phony prescriptions. As a group, they were easier to fool, concerned only with making a buck, and less scrupulous about legalities than their native-born counterparts. Still another plus that Aquino Drugs had going for it was the fact that it stayed open weeknights until eleven, long after the clothing boutiques and the donut shop that also operated out of the strip mall had closed.

Randy waited for a young couple to leave the pharmacy before making his own entrance at nine forty-five. Once inside, his initial impression was that he could not have picked a better time to transact business. There was only one person on duty—Rosalee herself. He spotted her busily filling out forms behind the counter that separated the prescription drugs from the non-prescription items that filled the shelves in the front section of the store.

"May I help you?" Rosalee asked as Randy stood in front of her at the counter.

Randy handed over the phone prescription. "I'd like to have this filled as soon as possible. I don't mind waiting."

Rosalee studied the form and seemed to hesitate. A skeptical expression settled over her face, her eyebrows arching, her thin lips pursing like two tightly drawn strings.

"Is there a problem?" Randy asked.

Rosalee took her eyes off the script and fixed them on Randy. "This is quite a large order, sir. It would be better if you came back in the morning." She sounded polite but firm, patient yet reproving. It was also clear she hadn't noticed him before in the store. To her Randy was a perfect stranger.

"I can't wait until tomorrow," Randy said. In a show of consternation, he turned his face to the wall, contemplating what to say next. A surge of adrenaline shot down the back of his legs as he gazed at a video surveillance camera mounted high on the wall, above a bank of light switches. The camera was angled directly at the counter, perfectly positioned to capture the interactions between the pharmacist and her customers. He had seen the camera before, on one of his earlier visits to the store, but had been careful to stay out of its range.

"I need my medication tonight," he said angrily. "I have two pinched nerves in my back and I have trouble sleeping."

Rosalee shook her head and handed the prescription back to him. She had delicate but capable hands, not unlike his mother's. "I'm afraid you'll have to come back tomorrow. With such a large quantity I'm going to have to verify the prescription with Dr. Albright's office in the morning. Please, try to understand. You'll either have to come back in the morning or have the prescription filled elsewhere."

Randy stuffed the 'scrip in his pants pocket and stalked off. "Fucking bitch," he muttered under his breath. Rosalee wasn't at all like the smiling, accommodating foreigner he had anticipated. To the contrary, she was officious and demeaning. People like her were taking over the country, ruining it with their ostentatious cars and large extended multigenerational families. He hated them and their clipped, open-voweled accents.

Back outside, Randy slipped behind the wheel of his Chevy, started up the engine, and pulled out of the parking lot.

He had two choices now. The first was to drive back up the mountain without delay. He had left Larry sedated and chained to his bedpost in the garage. The sooner he returned to check up on him, the better. If he went that route, however, he would be taking a chance that Rosalee might decide on her own to call Albright's office in the morning, just to see if his prescription had in fact been valid. Judging from their brief encounter and the way she had scrutinized the form, she seemed the type to take it upon herself to report a suspected violation of the Health and Safety Code, as the collection of state statutes governing the dispensation of controlled substances was known.

Randy began to inventory the disquieting possibilities in his head. If Rosalee did decide to call Albright. If the pharmacy's video camera had captured him on tape. If he had left any fingerprints in the store that could be matched to his image on the video. Then all the pains he had taken to create a new identity for himself would be severely compromised. He could not allow that to happen.

The other option was simple. He could find a dark, secluded parking place and make sure that Rosalee never made another phone call, to Albright or anyone else. Another half hour or so would bring Larry no further harm.

Never one to leave anything to chance, Randy pulled the Chevy to the curb a block and a half away from the strip mall, under a big, leafy oak tree on a residential side street. Exiting, he walked to the rear of the car, opened the trunk, and removed a pair of latex surgical gloves from a small canvas bag, together with an old cloth wash rag. He slipped the gloves on his hands, stuffed the rag in his rear pocket, and slowly made his way back to the strip mall on foot.

He had been careful, he reminded himself as he

walked, not to have touched anything earlier inside the pharmacy. A simple swipe with the washcloth of the steel handle on either side of the front door would be all that was required to remove any trace of his prints. The surgical gloves would ensure that anything he contacted from this point forward would yield no clues of his presence.

Still busy with her paperwork, Rosalee cast only a fleeting glance at Randy as he reentered the store and walked to the prescription counter. Outwardly, she seemed only slightly annoyed to see him again. She had taken no notice of the surgical gloves on his hands as he had approached, and now that he was at the counter, with his hands held at his waist, the gloves were below her immediate line of sight.

"Yes? Is there something you forgot, sir?" she asked.

"I have a sty in my left eye. I need something for it." Randy leaned forward slightly as he spoke, inviting her with the movement of his own body and his eyes opened wide to examine the malady.

Rosalee hesitated, then slowly leaned toward Randy to make the inspection. She was still tilting her head forward when her left cheekbone and the delicate bridge of her nose were shattered by a vicious blow from Randy's tightly clenched right fist. The punch was delivered with such force, speed, and surprise, she had no chance to avoid it or defend herself. She crumpled to the floor behind the counter like a rag doll, losing consciousness as she fell.

The impact of the punch caused only a transitory shooting pain in Randy's right wrist. He shook it off and stepped quickly to the bank of light switches mounted on the wall below the surveillance camera. After a few seconds of fumbling, he located the switches for the overhead lights in the front section of the store and turned them off. Only the lights in the rear section remained on, creating the impression that the store had closed for the evening.

Moving behind the counter, he kneeled beside Rosalee. A thin ribbon of blood trickled from her nose, collecting in a rust-colored pool in the hollow between her lower lip and chin. There was also a small depression in the bridge of her nose left by the large proximal knuckle of his middle finger. The bruises were only just beginning to swell and color, but they were already obvious and disfiguring. Yet somehow, to Randy, she looked peaceful and serene, almost as if she were thankful that he had come along to relieve her of the tedium of her nightly routine.

Still kneeling on the floor, Randy slid behind Rosalee and lifted her head and neck onto his lap. Drawing on his knowledge of anatomy and his experience with Grace Cowley, he cupped his right hand under her chin and across her left cheek and wrapped his left in the opposite direction around her forehead. One sharp and violent twist was all he needed to sever her spinal cord from the occiput, precisely at the C-1 vertebrum. It was as simple as breaking kindling wood. Knowing that death had come to Rosalee instantly, he lowered her head to the floor, turning it gently to one side on the carpet and shutting her dark, lifeless eyes as he began to rise.

It was then that he noticed his image—back to the camera—on the small TV monitor set atop an inexpensive VCR unit on a shelf below the pharmaceutical counter. Realizing that Rosalee's assault had been captured on tape, he turned to face the surveillance camera. Like a kid caught on TV at a baseball game, he flashed a broad grin and a thumbs-up sign. Then he reached for the VCR, popped out the videotape that it held, and stuffed the cassette into one of the

large paper bags the pharmacy used to package purchased items for its customers. He had never before
been filmed performing an ultimate act of retribution,
and he was greatly excited by the prospects the video
opened up. He and Larry would have a high old time
watching reruns and instant replays of the sucker
punch that had felled Rosalee, and the chiropractic
"adjustment" that had ended her pain in this world
and sent her off with a running start to the next.

Working now against the clock, he hurried into the
back room, where the supplies of prescription drugs
were kept. He helped himself to a big plastic jar of
Dalmane, an ampule of liquid Demerol, a bottle of
Diazepam, and smaller containers of a half dozen
other assorted pills he had no time to inspect. Stuffing
them all into the large paper bag, he felt like a kid
out on the town for Halloween. In another two minutes, he was out the front door, with his bundle of
goodies tucked securely under his right arm, setting a
brisk but controlled pace back to his Chevy.

All in all, it had been a most remarkable night, he
told himself as he pulled away from the curb. Even
without stopping to examine the booty he had liber-
ated from the pharmacy, he knew he had come away
with perhaps a six-month supply of some of his favorite painkillers and other drugs. And thanks to his
strong hands and quick thinking, his work had gone
undetected. Of that he was certain.

The only thing he'd forgotten was to say the words.
He uttered them now, aloud, just above the hum of
the engine:

> *"About, about, in reel and rout*
> *The death fires danced at night."*

Chapter Fifteen

Nova had visited the state prison at Folsom only twice before, both times as a young up-and-coming attorney in the years immediately preceding his representation of Randy Sturgis. Like many criminal defense lawyers, he hated prisons and the perceived injustices they stood for. Folsom he hated with a special reverence born of fear and respect.

Next to San Quentin, Folsom Prison was California's oldest and most renowned state pen, celebrated in song by Johnny Cash and used as a backdrop by Hollywood in at least a half dozen sweaty convict movies. Located in the dry, rolling hills east of Sacramento, the prison had opened its doors as an earthly kind of hell in 1880. Over the next fifty-seven years, until San Quentin's gas chamber established its monopoly on capital punishment in the Golden State, it was the site of ninety-two public hangings and living conditions so deplorable they earned the institution the sobriquet of "the end of the world." Although the gallows were eventually mothballed and conditions upgraded more or less to twentieth-century standards, the institution continued to thrive, hosting an increasingly multicultural powder keg of many of the state's most violent career criminals, drawn from the ranks of street and prison gangs like the Mexican Mafia, the Crips and the Bloods, various Asian crime syndicates, and the Aryan Brotherhood.

It wasn't just the junkyard dog reputation of its inmate population that gave Folsom its unique signature but its architecture as well. The prison's old wing had been designed to instill a sense of resignation and obedience in new arrivals. Resembling a medieval fortress, the original section was protected by great perimeter walls of rough-cut rock hewn from a nearby quarry that inmate chain gangs had worked through the late 1940s, conical-shaped gun turrets, and a multi-ton cast-iron gate hanging from a forbidding Gothic arch at the main entrance. A newer maximum-security, low-rise campus-style wing, built of concrete and steel and equipped with the latest internal-surveillance technology, was added in the 1980s to relieve overcrowding and provide the badly outnumbered guards with additional means of monitoring and controlling the behavior of their charges.

For those sentenced to hard time at Folsom, life was a constant Darwinian struggle. For visitors the prison presented a different set of problems. Though officially welcome, civilians were shown few courtesies by the staff, many of whom seemed to regard outsiders as either potential threats to the always fragile institutional order or merely as nuisances whose concerns were entitled to priority somewhere between coffee breaks and an afternoon workout in the prison gym.

The last time Nova had graced the gates of Folsom Prison, he had to be placed on a two-day waiting list to see a client who had been convicted of voluntary manslaughter for squeezing three shots from a .22-caliber pistol into the brain of his wife's younger and better-looking lover. Once at the prison he was required to fill out a two-page visitors slip, submit to a pat-down search, and cool his heels for a good hour in a sterile waiting room not unlike a crowded public hospital reception area. Then he was herded on a correctional department bus that took him to the new visitors center. Jam-packed nearly to the point of standing-room with the wives, kids, and giggling girlfriends of the inmates, the bus was the only means of transportation allowed for civilians inside the prison. Walking from one building to another was strictly forbidden on penalty of immediate arrest and prosecution.

It was amazing, Nova thought as he and Tony Ross landed at Sacramento Airport early Wednesday morning, how a badge could open the doors of even so intractable a bureaucracy as Folsom. From the moment they stepped off their plane to their arrival at the prison, he and Ross were treated as though they controlled the swing votes that would determine the size of next year's prison budget. The warden sent his personal assistant, a third-year correctional officer, to meet them at the airport and drive them through the main gate, no questions asked. After a brief chin wag and coffee with the warden himself in the main administration building, they were escorted to a small conference room down the hall and asked politely to take seats at the neatly polished California oak conference table. Two minutes later, the doors to the room opened, and a black inmate, manacled at the wrists and ankles and with a guard on each arm, was escorted inside.

The guards deposited the inmate in a chair at the head of the table, and introduced him as Andrew Marsh. Responding to Ross' instructions, they removed his shackles and excused themselves from the room.

Marsh took a moment to rub the dark marks left by the cuffs on his wrists, then shot a long, unsmiling look at his company. A trim six-footer, with his head and face freshly shaved and his chest and arms pumped to unnatural proportions by long bench-pressing sessions in the exercise yard, Marsh looked in his prison blues considerably younger than a man in his mid-forties. Only the deep, wedge-shaped furrows between his eyes, the product of more than two decades of coping with the exigencies of life as a caged animal, bespoke his true age.

"I'm special Agent Anthony Ross of the Federal Bureau of Investigation, and this is attorney David Nova," Ross announced formally, without bothering to offer a handshake. "I think you know why we're here."

"Shit, I hardly had time to finish my Sugar Smacks when they told me I'd be coming to the admin building this morning. I feel like a regular cel-eb-ri-tae." Marsh flashed a wide grin, pleased with himself at the little linguistic flourish he had delivered in the face of the dour G-man. "But you all got nothin' on me, and I ain't got nothin' to give to you. Still, the change of scenery is appreciated."

Marsh leaned back in his chair and studied the landscape paintings on the walls. Although the paintings were little more than the kind of inexpensive reproductions found in coffee shops and dental offices throughout the state—scenes of waterfalls, towering mountain peaks, a portrait of the world-famous Half-Dome rock overlooking the valley in Yosemite National Park—Marsh seemed almost transfixed by the natural beauty and unbounded freedom they suggested.

"When was the last time you heard from Randy Sturgis?" Ross asked sharply, emphasizing with his tone that he was unprepared to put up with the usual dance.

"Let's see, now," Marsh said, raising his right hand thoughtfully to his chin. "Was that the rotary meeting last Wednesday or golf at the club on Sunday? I've left my Day-Runner at the office, so I can't be sure."

"Look, I know you think there's nothing to be gained by talking to us, but maybe you're wrong," Nova interrupted. He cast a sidelong glance at Ross that seemed to say, "You fucked up the intros. It's my turn now."

"How's that?" Marsh asked. He sounded skeptical but curious.

"You're in for murder one, twenty-five to life?"

"Twenty-seven, counting the gun use."

"Parole's always possible," Nova said. "A little letter of cooperation from the FBI would come in handy at your next release hearing."

Marsh smiled. The glare from the overhead lights reflected off his bald dome as he shook his head. "Ain't no way I'm getting out of here before I turn sixty-five, or I'm smoked before then. It don't matter who I cooperate with."

"Well, what about a single cell?" Nova suggested, looking at Ross for backup. "After all these years, that would seem like a real luxury. Maybe we could help out with something along those lines."

"I already have my own cell," Marsh replied stiffly. "Had it for the last six months, since my roomie got hisself stabbed in the neck."

"Then maybe we can make sure you get a new roomie real quick," Ross said, breaking back into the discussion. "If I tell the warden you stiffed us, he'll have your belongings packed up before you're sent back upstairs. How does the idea of a four-man cell

with a group of young cokeheads sound? I'm not in
the mood for prison bullshit today."

Marsh tapped his feet lightly on the floor and bit
his lower lip, as if reconsidering the situation. If there
was one thing the older and more mature cons like
Marsh hated, it was being shut in with a bunch of
disrespectful, loud, rap-addled druggies. "Sounds like
maybe I should answer your questions. But I ain't
seen or heard from Randy Sturgis since he walked out
of here over three years ago. All I know is what I
hear, that he jacked the judge who set him free. Kind
of cold, if you ask me."

"How well did you know Sturgis?" Ross asked.

Marsh stopped to think. "We was in the same cell
block for the better part of a decade. For a white
dude, we got along pretty good. He sure knew his
legal shit. Helped me with a writ petition and did a
real fine job. I didn't win, but then, most of us don't."

"Did he ever talk about his own case?" Nova asked.

Marsh smiled at Nova, coyly arching an eyebrow as
if he was about to broach an embarrassing subject.
"He talked about how his trial lawyer screwed him. I
guess he meant you."

"You mean he maintained that he was innocent,"
Nova said.

"We're all innocent in here, Mr. Nova," Marsh answered with a laugh. "But Randy was a little different
from the rest."

"How so?"

"He really believed it, and he was ready to mess
with anyone who said they doubted him. I saw him
take out at least two Mexicans who called him a liar.
Dude had a mean temper, and he could fight when he
wanted to. He had a special thing for the Hispanics
and Asians. Thought they had no right to be in this

country. Used to get right in their faces and call 'em wetbacks and slanty-eyed gooks."

"What about Judge Tanner, did he ever talk about him?" Nova asked.

"All the time, after he learned that Tanner was going to hear his writ. At first he had nothing but high praise for the man. He was the judge who was going to set the record straight once and for all. He wasn't afraid to butt heads with the politicians, you know, that kind of crap. Then, when he finally got his decision, and he read how the judge was releasing him only on a technicality, not because he was an innocent man . . . why, I don't think I ever saw Randy so mad."

Ross grimaced like a man choking on his own bile. "Wasn't Randy happy that he won?" he asked angrily.

"That's what I asked him," Marsh responded. "But Randy was one of a kind. It wasn't enough for him to get out of prison. He wanted complete absolution. He said he felt betrayed, personally and deeply betrayed. Sounded to me at times like he was talking 'bout his own father rather than some federal judge. But, then, who am I to pass judgment on how another man feels, especially when that man walked hisself right out of Folsom Prison, and I'm still here."

"Did you ever tell Randy that you knew Tanner personally?" Ross asked.

Marsh pushed himself away from the table and folded his arms against his chest. "Who says I did?"

"Dr. Irving Horowitz, you scumbag," Ross answered, wagging a menacing forefinger at Marsh. "Remember what I told you about the bullshit, the four-man cell?"

"You guys are really sharp," Marsh, said, taking a deep breath. "Yes, I knew the judge for a brief time. I guess you might say I was his personal supplier."

"You sold drugs to Larry Tanner?" Nova asked.

"Dr. Horowitz used to prescribe various painkillers, sleeping aids, and such for his patients, to take the edge off while they tried to give up the drink. I was just a nurse's assistant, but I knew the routine pretty well, and I could spot someone who loved the pills from around the corner. After they sent Larry home and I got my sorry ass fired, him and me kind of made a little arrangement. I stole a bunch of pills—Valium, Demerol, what have you, about a six-month supply— on my way out. Instead of shopping them on the street, I sold them to him."

"Was this just a one-time thing?" Nova asked.

"Well, like I said, I thought the judge had a real sweet tooth and that he'd provide me with some kind of permanent cash flow. Lord knows, I needed it. But when I went back to sell him more, he told me his secretary flushed all the candy down the toilet, and that he didn't want no more. He was determined to clean hisself up. He thanked me for my help and of- fered me fifty dollars for my time. Can you believe that, fifty dollars?"

"Sounds like you thought he was ripping you off," Ross commented.

"I told him I couldn't be bought off for no fifty dollars," Marsh said indignantly. "I said there must be a lot of newspapers would be interested in learning how a judge who just left the Horowitz Clinic was buying street drugs. I asked for five grand to keep my mouth shut. I settled for two."

Marsh shrugged his shoulders. "So he Jewed me down. I guess I'm just an old softie at heart."

"You ever tell your little story to Randy?" Ross inquired.

"Now and again. He ate up every word, like a little kid hearing about the three little pigs."

"What about Randy's girlfriends?" Ross asked. "He ever talk to you about them?"

"Not much. In addition to being a stand-up scholar, Randy thought of hisself as a gentleman. I knew he had a lot of ladies, and was always going off to the visitor center. Only one I can remember him bragging about, though, was that reporter lady. I even saw her once with him at the center. They seemed to get on real good."

Nova balled his right hand into a fist as he took in Marsh's remarks. "That reporter lady was my wife, you son of a bitch."

"I know," Marsh said apologetically. "But, hey, I'm only answering your questions, man. If you've got a bone to pick, it's with Randy, not me."

"What did Randy say about the reporter?" Ross asked.

"Only that she turned out to be real sweet, not at all like the bitch he thought at first."

"That's all?"

Marsh shrugged his shoulders again. "That's about it."

Ross glanced at Nova, preparing to yield the floor. Seeing that Nova was still wrapped up in his private rage, he concluded that it was time to send Andrew Marsh back to his cell block. "Thank you for your time, Andrew," he said. "You've been a bigger help than you might realize. I'll have my secretary type up a letter of cooperation for your file. It might come in handy someday."

"Appreciate it," Marsh replied.

"By the way, just so my letter can sound like I know a little something about your case, who was it that you whacked way back when?"

"A young punk trying to steal my stash. It was self-defense all the way."

"That's what they all say, isn't it?" Ross asked rhetorically. "And the punk's name?"

Marsh took a hard swallow before answering, "Noah. Noah Chamberlain."

"Like the man from the Bible and the famous basketball player," Ross remarked. "Interesting combination. Has a nice ring to it, especially for a dead guy."

Chapter Sixteen

"Welcome back," Tami shouted above the applause of the studio audience. "For those of you who have just joined our special Thursday morning edition of *O Darling!*, today's topic is 'Married With Hormones: What would you do for sex if your husband was too pooped to pop?'"

Skipping lightly up the three steps to the stage, she turned to the camera and flashed that Emmy-aspiring smile. "You heard earlier from Dr. Joyce Allen, certified marriage and family counselor. Now it's time to meet our guests."

The curtain parted slowly, revealing three middle-aged white women, all well dressed and properly groomed, seated in the plush upholstered red chairs Tami had taken lightly to calling the "hot seats."

"Why don't we start with you, Nancy?" Tami said, sliding gracefully to the side of the slightly overweight brunette to the left of the stage. "Nancy is an accounts-receivable secretary at a San Gabriel car dealership," Tami commented, reading from a pair of three-by-five cards pulled from her suit pocket.

"She writes, and I quote," Tami added, mugging for the camera with raised eyebrows, and drawing the usual anticipatory chorus of catcalls from the audience, " 'For over twenty years of marriage, our sex life was always steady but never sensational, kind of like an old reliable Chrysler. Mostly we made love when he wanted to and on his terms, in ninety-second bursts that seemed just right for him and which left me with plenty of time to finish my crossword puzzles before turning off the lights. The problem is, I guess, that when my husband hit forty-five, the old reliable Chrysler couldn't even seem to release its parking brake anymore. I, on the other hand, felt hornier than a teenager at a drive-in movie. I'm not sure that I could ever go back to a Chrysler, even if it got an entirely new transmission.'

"Well, if a Chrysler wouldn't do," Tami asked, "how did you solve—and I use that term advisedly—your transportation problems?"

The audience murmured with expectation as Nancy wriggled in her seat, obviously more nervous than she had anticipated being in front of the TV cameras. "Look, don't get me wrong, I'm no slut. But women have biological urges, too, just like guys. We just tend to get ours a little later in life, that's all. I was a virgin when we got married."

Nancy's mention of the "V" word provoked another round of laughter and boos from the audience. "So you started sleeping around," Tami prodded, shushing the crowd with an upraised palm. "How did it start, or should I say, with whom did it start?"

"His name was Carlos, and he was a salesman at the dealership," Nancy answered.

"A younger man?" Tami inquired, sounding like one of Nancy's gossipy girlfriends.

"Much." A deep red blush rose in Nancy's cheeks.

"How much?" Tami prodded.

"He was about twenty-five when we first got together. I suppose that made him two years older than my oldest child."

"Didn't you feel a little odd taking up with someone like that?"

Nancy tilted her head to one side, like a supermarket customer debating whether to purchase ground chuck or splurge for sirloin. "Only at first."

"So how did you get together?"

"In the backseat of his new four-wheel-drive Explorer. It was a tight fit." She flashed a playful smile, finally growing comfortable with her role as a source of amusement. The audience tittered with appreciation. "The leather seats and the stereo CD player helped to get me in the mood. I felt like I was back in high school. Only this time I knew what I was doing, and I got off more times than the guy I was with. A lot more."

"I'm sure you did. And how long did this relationship last?"

"With Carlos, about three months. We'd sneak away from the showroom sometimes at lunch, and occasionally we'd work late, usually at his place. Eventually, he was transferred to another dealership, and our relationship petered out, you might say."

"Interesting choice of words," Tami commented, staring into the camera, her jaw dropping in mock astonishment. "And after Carlos, how many others were there?"

Nancy wriggled her nose, as if jump-starting her memory. "Four or five, not counting Andre."

"Andre?"

"He's the instructor of my over-forties aerobics class."

"And why shouldn't we count him?"

"He's still trying to decide if he likes boys or girls better."

"I see. That must be quite a problem, or quite a challenge, I'm not sure." Tami chuckled softly at her own joke. "But seriously, was all this running around motivated simply by the desire to hop in the sack, or was there some other reason?"

"To be quite honest, it wasn't just about sex. I think I just needed some kind of jolt to get me out of the middle-aged routine I'd fallen into."

"And what kind of effect did your extracurricular activities have on your marriage?"

"My marriage ended," Nancy said matter-of-factly. "The divorce became final about six months ago. I'm not sure if my affairs caused our marriage to end," she added after a moment's reflection and with surprising thoughtfulness, "or if, like Dr. Allen suggested, the marriage was already falling apart when I started to have my flings."

"Did you ever try counseling with someone like Dr. Allen?"

"Not really. Jim—that's my ex—didn't believe in counselors, and after he found out about me, I don't think there was any way he would have taken me back."

"Sounds like you passed up an important opportunity," Tami said, adopting a lecturing tone. "You gave up your marriage for the backseat of a four-wheel-drive vehicle. Seems like a big waste, if you ask me. When you really stop to think about it, there's nothing more sacred than marriage and a family. Isn't that right, folks?" The studio audience responded to Tami's query with a loud roar of approval.

"What a load of horseshit," Nova said just loud enough to hear himself talk. And yet she sounded like she meant every word. As Nova stood backstage watching Tami perform, it was almost possible for him, too, to believe she meant it. Almost, but not quite.

The truth was that when her own marriage hit the skids, Tami had reacted to his suggestion that they try counseling the way most people respond to getting sued. For her, counseling was a personal affront, a threat to her integrity, her pocketbook, and her privacy. Counseling was something that might be beneficial for people who didn't know their own minds, but it was utterly superfluous for someone who did. After weeks of prodding and pleading, she consented to attend only a few ineffectual sessions, with a matronly female therapist not unlike Dr. Allen, but only on condition that they be scheduled around her increasingly hectic TV and personal-appearance calendar and that she be permitted to bring her cell phone along. Although she agreed to put the phone away after receiving two calls in their first meeting—one from a casting agent who thought she might be interested in taking a gambit into film and the other from her hairstylist in Bel Air—the effort was doomed from the start and proved to be an abysmal failure.

Hearing Tami invoke the efficacy of counseling, Nova could only laugh at the mess his own life had become. He could practically imagine himself out there in one of Tami's "hot seats," the butt of jokes, whispers, and jeers, disclosing the sorry details of his private life alongside the other losers on the show. They could call his episode, "Married to a TV Juggernaut: What happens when your wife loves her Nielsens more than she loves you?"

Even Ross had warned him to stay away from Tami. On their flight back to L.A., he gave him a regular fatherly heart-to-heart. With the information on Tanner's alcohol and drug abuse, they had all they needed, he maintained, for the *South Coast Inquirer* personal. And given the way Nova had reacted to Andrew Marsh, Ross felt there was nothing to be gained by having him contact Tami.

"Any guy would be pissed by what Marsh had to say," Ross had counseled. "Hell, I know I would be. But now's not the time to go picking a fight, not with that custody hearing of yours pending." By the time they touched down at LAX, Ross was sounding uncannily like Molly, cautioning against any rash actions, advising him to keep his mind focused exclusively on bringing his daughter back to California. He even gave Nova his unlisted home phone number just in case he needed a strong male shoulder to cry on.

"It's like a little story I tell all the rookie agents in my squad," Ross had told him, warming to the opportunity of imparting a little personal lore. "When I was first starting out back in Seattle, I nabbed a guy who'd kidnapped and raped a retarded ten-year-old girl. Imagine that, a retarded kid. The scumbag who took her was thirty-five and a three-time felon." Ross' voice took on an angry edge as he recalled the particulars.

"I thought that nothing in this world would have given me greater personal satisfaction than to beat the living crap out of the creep. I was thoroughly convinced I'd get away with it, too, that I could make it look like the guy took a spill down a flight of stairs or got hit by a swinging door. It took an older partner to sit me down and talk me out of it. 'When you see the sonofabitch convicted in court and led off to jail to serve a life term, you'll be glad you didn't do anything to give some bleeding-heart judge a chance to dismiss the case,' he told me. And you know something? Although I always regretted that I didn't rip the scumbag's heart right out through his throat, I knew my partner was right.

"It's the same in your situation. You don't want to

do anything to let your ex-wife or her lawyers argue that you're harassing her on the eve of the hearing."

It was sound advice and well intended. Nova spent a sleepless night mulling it over before deciding to disregard it. The fact that Tami had a morning taping, and that he still had a few sympathetic contacts at the TV studio that he knew would let him backstage, made the decision easy. He had no intention of picking a fight, but he had to know the truth.

Back on stage, Nancy's five minutes of fame and derision had passed into daytime TV history. Tami had moved on to introduce her other guests: Susie, a nurse practitioner whose fifty-year-old husband had become so exhausted from her sexual demands that he actually ordered her to seek satisfaction with other partners; and Brenda, whose husband had taken exactly the opposite tack, threatening to hire a contract killer if she took up with another man. Both women took their spouses' admonitions literally. Susie slept with two surgeons and an anesthesiologist inside a month while Brenda left her husband to settle down with another woman.

Tami took each of her new guests through the routine interrogations, exploring the demise of their marital lives and the sexual urges, fantasies, and escapades that ultimately resulted in separation and divorce. Then, after fielding a few bemused questions from the studio audience, she put another episode in the books, reminding her viewers that the *O Darling!* show would be relocating to New York in the fall, with a power-packed lineup of programs dedicated to exploring the "issues that affect our daily lives, the issues that other shows are too afraid to touch, too timid to talk about, and too cautious to confront." She blew a big kiss into the camera and, along with the studio audience, waved a big good-bye.

* * *

"If you expect me to act surprised, you're going to be very disappointed," Tami snapped at Nova as she made her way toward him behind the curtain. "I saw you after the first commercial break. Who the hell let you back here?" In her double-breasted green wool crepe pantsuit, with her hair newly clipped just below the ears and the muscles of her face and neck stretched with anger, she looked like an enraged leprechaun.

"I don't think that's important," he replied. Knowing that anyone he mentioned would have their walking papers by the end of the day, he wasn't about to name names. "We need to talk."

The determined look on his face told her that he wasn't going to leave without a struggle. With all the technicians and today's guests still milling around, a public squabble was to be avoided at all costs. "Okay," she said finally, "but not here. I'll give you five minutes in my dressing room. And it had better be important. My lawyer's warned you about coming here."

"Your lawyer and just about everyone else I know," he answered, returning her icy stare with one of his own.

About the size of a small bedroom, Tami's dressing room was surprisingly utilitarian in its furnishings and decor. A small hair salon swivel chair stood in the room's center, where Tami received the finishing touches on her coiffure, lipstick, and blush before stepping in front of the cameras. An inexpensive white-lacquered vanity with a brightly lit mirror and a tray loaded with cosmetics, combs, and hair spray occupied most of one wall, while an oversized closet with two sliding wooden doors occupied the full length

of another. Except for a few framed pictures of Tami
and Jamie, and the name tag on the door outside,
there was nothing specific that identified the room as
the inner sanctum of TV's newest talk-show sensation.

"This isn't about lawyers, and it isn't even about
Jamie," Nova said tersely as she closed the door behind them. "I know you saw Randy Sturgis when he
was in prison. I need to know why, and I'm not leaving
until I do."

Tami brought her hands to her hips and cocked her
head to one side. "Honestly, David, if this is about
the disappearance of that judge, you really are wasting
your time . . . and mine, too, if that matters at all
to you."

"But you did see Sturgis, and you knew he was a
client of mine from before our marriage."

"It was for that series I wrote for the *Times* on
prison groupies. Even you could have guessed that."

Nova shook his head, unable to suppress a sarcastic
laugh as she spoke.

"You might think the series was a laugh, but it
helped get me where I am today. I've already done
one show on the subject out here, and I'm planning
another for New York in October. With all the crime
and prison construction going on in this country, it's
a hot topic."

"But why Sturgis?"

"Because of you." She waited for the irritation to
register on his face before continuing. "You used to
talk about him all the time. You said that you were
amazed by all the women who had visited him in jail
and in prison. I thought it would be helpful if I interviewed him. He agreed to talk if I promised to keep
his name out of my stories and not to speak to any
of his girlfriends. He gave me what we call 'background and color,' nothing more."

"But why didn't you tell me?"

"That was another of his conditions. That and the fact that I knew you'd overreact if you found out I had gone to see him. Just like you are now."

"How many times did you see him?"

"Three, maybe four."

"That's an awful lot of visits just to pick his brain about prison groupies."

Tami considered Nova's accusatory tone for a few seconds before replying. "He was a very fascinating man, but then I guess you already know that. He wasn't at all like the other inmates I interviewed in prison."

"Sounds like you got to know him pretty well."

"It was just talk, David. He just liked to talk to me."

"What about, besides his groupies?"

"A lot of things. History, politics, the news. He thought of himself as some kind of deep social thinker. But he especially liked to talk about families. Not just his family, but the *idea* of family. He used to say there was nothing that revealed more about a man's individual character than the character of his family. I think he felt a deep sadness at never having married and at not having kids. I think his lady friends must have sensed that sadness. I think it's what drew them to him. At one point I thought I'd do an exclusive on him, but I could never coax him into it."

"Did you ever tell him about Jamie?"

"He asked once if I had any children, and I told him we had a daughter. Nothing more than that."

"You're sure?"

She took a seat on the stool in front of her mirror and began to wipe the stage makeup from her face. "If you think there was anything even vaguely romantic between us, or that I've seen or heard from him since he got out of jail, you're even more desperate than you look. It's not like I was fucking him in the ladies' room."

She glanced at her watch, then added, "Now, really, David, I have more productive things to do with my time, and I'm sure you do, too."

She pointed at the door and watched through the mirror as he left.

Chapter Seventeen

Ben Tanner sat on the balcony of his second-story apartment, studying the flock of bluejays that had begun to stir in the Douglas fir and juniper trees on the nearby forest hillside. It was nearly six o'clock, and as another hot summer day wound down toward dusk, Ben knew the jays would soon descend to the ground and start hopping comically through the thick grass and dead pine needles—like tiny feathered men on pogo sticks—in search of their evening meals. The jays would squawk and fight among themselves for the small morsels of sustenance the forest floor offered. Occasionally, other birds native to the San Jacinto Mountains—mostly black-throated warblers and crows—would also join in the fracas, and the thin mountain air would echo with their cries. And then the anarchy would end, like clockwork, with the setting of the sun.

Observing the birds' evening ritual through a pair of high-powered binoculars was one of the few bright spots in Ben's daily routine at the Alpine Convalescent Home. In the early days of his residence at the home, when the effects of a stroke had left him bound to a wheelchair, he frequently needed one of the nursing attendants to take him out on the balcony. With their services always in great demand, the attendants often arrived too late to take him out before sunset, or returned too early to wheel him back to bed or to plunk him in front of the TV before the birds had concluded their performance. Now, after three years of intensive therapy, he was able to ambulate on his own, albeit with the aid of a four-pronged steel safety cane and with an emergency beeper clipped to the waistband of his pants.

A highly successful orthodontist by trade, Ben had never been a particularly gregarious person. He had a quick temper and a sharp tongue, which he rarely hesitated to use. Other than meals at the cafeteria and an infrequent game of hearts or checkers at the recreation center, he rarely socialized with the other residents of the home. The balcony was his window on the world, his place to relax, his place to forget, if only briefly, that he was a bitter old man well into the process of dying alone.

Unmarried and childless, Ben rarely received visitors. Apart from Melinda, the hygienist who had worked for him in the years just before his retirement, the only visitor he'd had in the last six months was that earnest young woman from the FBI. She had come to learn if he had seen or heard from his brother, Larry.

A trim, healthy specimen in her early thirties, the agent was the first female law enforcement official Ben had ever spoken to at any length. Including coffee, which she fixed right there in his kitchen, she must have spent a solid hour with him. She asked a lot of questions about both Larry and himself: When did he last see Larry? Were he and his brother especially close? Did they contact each other in times of trouble? Did Larry have any particular enemies who might want to hurt him?

Ben had tried to answer the agent's questions as

best he could, but he was having a hard time keeping his mind from wandering. In addition to taking a heavy toll on his body, the stroke had left him with intermittent memory loss. Sometimes—like today—his mind was as sharp as ever. Other times—like the day the FBI came calling—his mind felt sluggish and frozen, like an antique car engine on an icy February morning.

Although he had heard about his brother's abduction on the news, it took nearly twenty minutes before he was able to recall either the kidnapping or the fact that the FBI had launched a national manhunt for Larry. By then the young agent had concluded that her visit had largely been a waste of time. She confirmed that Ben knew nothing that might assist the Bureau and spent the last minutes of their time together inquiring about the quality of care at Alpine and whether the institution might be a suitable place for the agent's elderly mother, who was in the midst of weighing the always difficult pros and cons of selling the house she had lived in for over forty years and moving to a nursing home.

Because he was seated comfortably in his favorite wooden deck chair and preoccupied by the avian parade beyond his balcony, it took five long rings of his doorbell before Ben realized that he had another visitor this evening. Irritated by the interruption, he rose with some effort and shuffled inside the apartment and across his living room. "Hold your horses," he yelled as he walked. "You'll wear out the buzzer. I'll be right there."

Never having met Ben, Nova had no idea what to expect as the door was slowly pulled open. He knew that Ben would be in his seventies, but he was unprepared for the frail, rheumy-eyed figure who blinked nervously at him from the other side of the threshold.

Unlike Larry, who even in his salad days had never stood above five feet seven, the elder Tanner brother must have been a six footer in his prime.

"Dr. Tanner, I'm David Nova. I used to clerk for your brother at the Ninth Circuit," he said, extending his hand and attempting a reassuring smile. "May I come in and talk for a few minutes?"

"If you're with the FBI, I already spoke with that gal the other day. I told her I didn't know anything," Ben answered gruffly.

"I'm not with the FBI. But I am helping them. I won't be more than a few minutes." After leaving Tami at the TV studio, it had taken Nova the remainder of the afternoon to find the rest home, and another fifteen minutes to persuade the staff to admit him to the residential living quarters. He was tired and hungry, but he sensed that anything less than his most congenial demeanor would likely cause Ben to slam the door on him.

Ben's pale face wrinkled into a long frown as he took a step back to let Nova enter. "Okay, but you'll have to come on out to the balcony. I'm watching my birds."

Declining Nova's offer of help, Ben made his way back out to the balcony and settled again into his desk chair. Raising the binoculars to his eyes, he invited Nova with a nod of his head to pull up another chair. "You see that big fella out there?" he said, lifting an arm covered with brown liver spots and pointing in the distance at a group of bluejays Nova could hear but hadn't a prayer of seeing with the naked eye. "He's the king of the hill. When he spots something to eat, all the others run for cover. Sparrows, warblers, even crows."

"I'm afraid I can't quite make him out. It's too far," Nova replied.

"Here, have a look through these." Ben passed the glasses to Nova, who lifted them to his eyes and dialed the lenses into focus.

"I see a bunch of bluejays," Nova said. "Is that what you mean?"

"Jays, warblers, sparrows, crows, even a red-tailed hawk or two. I come out here every night to watch 'em feed." For the first time since opening the door, Ben grinned, revealing a set of pearly porcelain crowns that any orthodontist would be proud of. "Not too exciting, but for an old fart like me, it beats pulling teeth."

"I've always been fond of the mountains myself. I used to camp a lot." Nova took a deep breath of pine-scented air to show his appreciation, then handed the binoculars back to Ben. "Mind if we talk a little about Larry?"

"I told the gal I haven't seen him. I may not have had all my marbles that afternoon, but that was the truth."

"I'm sure it was. But I didn't drive all the way out here to ask you that."

Ben took the binoculars and turned to face Nova, as if to give him permission to continue.

"I understand that you and Larry were never the best of friends. Would you mind telling me why?"

Ben raised a withered hand to his chin. "That's a tough question. Do you want the long answer or the short?"

"I haven't got time for anything but the economy version, I'm afraid."

"Well, you worked for him. You ought to know."

"Know what?"

"That he was one stuck-up sonofabitch."

"A lot of people felt that way. Me, too, sometimes."

Sensing Ben's reticence to elaborate, he added, "Still, I think he's a good man at heart."

Ben lowered the binoculars again. A pained and disagreeable expression flashed across his face, causing his lips and eyes to narrow at the same time.

"Why do you dislike your brother so much?" Nova asked.

"Who said I disliked him?"

"Dr. Horowitz for one."

"You went to see Irv? What's that charlatan got to do with all this?"

"We're trying to negotiate with the man who kidnapped Larry. Dr. Horowitz was someone who knew your brother well, and we thought he might be able to help us understand both Larry and the man who abducted him a little better."

"Did he help?"

"I'm not sure. He told me that Larry once had a problem with alcohol. He said you did, too."

"A lot of people have problems with drink. Mine helped cause the stroke that put me here. Having a problem doesn't necessarily make a person bad."

"I quite agree. But you still haven't told me why you have such hard feelings toward your brother." Nova gave Ben another friendly smile, hoping to encourage an honest answer.

Ben seemed to drift off with Nova's question, as if moving through some kind of a cerebral cloud. Emerging after a long pause, he turned to Nova and said, "It was Larry's drinking that killed my mother."

"How?"

"Not long after my father died, Larry and I had a big fight over who would look after Mother when she became too old to live on her own. We never did reach a final agreement, but for a time she went to live with him. She died one night from a brain hemorrhage while he was passed out in a bedroom down the hall."

"And you blame him for that?"

"If he had checked up on her, like he was supposed to, he could have called an ambulance on time. When he found her the next morning, she was already cold."

"I think Larry might have a different explanation for what happened, and in any event, I'm sure he feels terrible about it. But to hold a grudge against him for all these years, it doesn't seem right."

"Sometimes your grudges are all you have to keep you going," Ben snarled.

"But he's your brother, after all."

"In name only, young man," Ben replied, raising his voice several decibels. "The truth is that Larry Tanner isn't really my brother."

Ben struggled to his feet, his body quivering with resentment as he spat out the words. "His father was unknown, could have been any one of a dozen aimless drifters. His real mother was some little floozy, a second cousin to my dad. She came to stay with us back in Pittsburgh during the Depression.

"Life was hard for everyone then. My father was out of work, and Larry's birth mother didn't receive regular medical care. The baby came early and she had a home birth, with a midwife. Then two weeks later she took off with another man and was never heard from again. My parents raised Larry as their own. They even got a doctor to fill out a birth certificate for him in our family's name."

"Did Larry know?"

"My folks told him after we moved out here, when he was in his twenties. That was a big mistake. Despite all they did for him, he said he felt betrayed." Ben took a hard, bitter swallow. "Betrayed, my ass. Letting my mother die was his way of getting revenge."

Excited beyond his physical limits, Ben paused to take a breath and steady himself. The fatigue on his face showed the toll the interview was taking, but he was determined to finish his say. "All of this 'great man' stuff you read about Larry in the papers is a crock, as far as I'm concerned."

Slowly, he lowered himself back into his seat, waving off another helping hand from Nova. "I think you know now why I have no love for my brother."

"Yes, I think I do." Nova could also see why there was no love lost on Larry's end as well, but he chose to keep that observation to himself.

Nova tried to squeeze a little more information from Ben about Larry's mother, but the old man was either too exhausted or too cantankerous to cooperate any further. After a few parting pleasantries about the charms of the forest and the mountain sunsets, he thanked Ben for his time and let him get back to his binoculars and birds.

Every family has a few skeletons or dirty underwear buried in their closets, Nova thought as he made his way down the stairs and into the lobby of the residence center. In Larry Tanner's case, the closets were just a little more deeply hidden and their contents more explosive.

There was, however, an upside to Larry's dirty laundry. The more Nova reflected on the story about Larry's real mother abandoning him, together with his later drug and alcohol abuse, the more the whole package reminded him of exactly the kind of mitigating "hardship" evidence a defense lawyer puts on during the penalty phase of a death-penalty trial to save a convicted client's life. Even someone with sawdust between his ears also could see that the story bore more than a passing similarity to the hardship evidence that Nova once had offered on behalf of Randy Sturgis. The hardship approach had worked back then to convince a jury of twelve strangers to spare Randy's life. Maybe it would work again. It was Randy now, of course, who had to be convinced to spare Larry. And while there was no way of knowing if he really had found the evidence Randy had in mind, or even if Randy would honor his promise to free Larry, Nova nonetheless felt encouraged by what he had discovered.

By the time he pushed open the lobby doors, he was thoroughly absorbed in composing a first draft of the *South Coast Inquirer* personal—so much so that he took no notice either of the male African-American nurse who walked right past him, nearly brushing up against his shoulder, or the black-and-white plastic name tag pinned to the nurse's uniform.

The name tag read: NOAH CHAMBERLAIN.

Chapter Eighteen

With only hours to go before the ad deadline, there was no time to stand on formalities. Although it was after nine by the time Nova got back to L.A., and Tony Ross had already left his office for the night, Nova couldn't wait for tomorrow to finalize the *South Coast Inquirer* personal. He pulled out the unlisted number Ross had given him, took his car phone in hand, and dialed the special agent at home.

The receiver was picked up by one of Ross' kids. "Hello, Piazza residence. Mike's not in right now, he's out hitting home runs for the Dodgers." Judging from his voice and the way he giggled, the kid was still several baseball seasons away from being old enough to hit a slow curve. "Would you care to leave a message, or would you like to speak with someone in the Ross family?" the kid asked in a more well-behaved tone.

Nova asked to speak with "Mr. Ross," and waited as the child went to find his dad. As he waited, he could hear the sounds of evening TV in the background and the excited play of other children. Like most kids in the summertime, the Ross children stayed up way past their normal bedtimes, often entertaining friends for evening videos, pizza, and sleep-overs. Tonight there were no less than six kids—Ross' three plus a pal for each—wreaking havoc in the family's recreation room.

Nova tried to keep his thoughts fixed on Tanner and Sturgis, but the noisy commotion reminded him of the pajama parties he sometimes hosted for Jamie and her girlfriends. Almost unconsciously, he found himself drifting back to Jamie's parties with a special kind of fondness he had never shown while they were actually happening. In truth, he had always regarded his daughter's parties and the temporary upheaval they caused with the kind of trepidation small, defenseless countries reserve for invading armies. They were something he had to endure out of love for Jamie and his obligations as a parent. Now, listening to the Ross children at play, he remembered how Jamie also loved to laugh and sing with her friends, how free and happy she was just to be with them, how oblivious she was to the minor annoyances her little celebrations created. He wondered sadly if he would ever get to see his daughter that way again.

"Ross," the deep voice boomed into the receiver, jolting Nova back from his misgivings.

"We need to talk," Nova said.

"Can it wait till tomorrow morning? I'm supposed to play a game of Risk with a gang of twelve-year-olds. They've been looking forward to it all day." Ross paused a moment, then asked, "Is it urgent?"

There was a trace of disappointment in Ross' tone, as if he, too, had been looking forward to the game. Despite the circumstances, Nova felt bad about interrupting a night of family fun. "It's about the *Inquirer* personal."

"I figured that, but I'm way ahead of you. I wrote out a draft myself and faxed a copy to your office this afternoon. I talked about Larry's drug and alcohol problems. I expected to hear back from you, but I guess you weren't in."

Nova explained that he had seen both Tami and Ben Tanner. "Whatever you've written, it's not going to be enough. I could try to explain things now, but I think it would be better if we talked in person."

Ross listened intently before agreeing to uproot himself from the benevolent domestic anarchy around him. "Give me an hour. I'll meet you at the field office. If you get there before me, tell the night-shift guys you're there to see me. They'll let you inside and even fetch you a cup of coffee."

"Tony, I'm sorry to take you away from your family," Nova said before hanging up.

"Don't sweat it," Ross replied. "They're used to it."

Nova found a coffee shop in West L.A. to catch a quick club sandwich and write down the thoughts for the *Inquirer* ad that he'd been rehearsing in his head since leaving the Alpine Convalescent Home. By the time he stepped off the elevator on the seventeenth floor of the Federal Building on Wilshire Boulevard, there was no need to tell the night-shift crew much of anything. The mere mention of his name got him a royal escort directly to Ross' office. He found Ross waiting for him, seated behind his desk, pawing his way through a fist-size stack of phone messages. Dressed casually in a striped shortsleeve button-down shirt and a pair of khaki twills, the special agent looked very much like a man who had been dragged back to work against his will.

"Look at these, would you?" Ross said with a trace of irritation, holding up a bunch of pink While-U-Were-Out sheets. "When I first joined the Bureau, I thought I'd spend all my time catching bad guys. There's everything here from bills for the water cooler and that joke of a computer guy we've hired to an urgent message from the widow of one of our senior agents who died last year. She's what you might politely call a little disturbed and lonely. She's having trouble again with strange men supposedly stalking her at the mall. Wants me to personally investigate the situation. And I can't just throw the message away, or in one of her more rational half hours she'll make up some story and file a complaint against me."

He laid the messages aside and rubbed the fatigue from his eyes. "Now, what's so important it couldn't wait? I thought we had all the information we needed for the personal."

"It turns out that Larry Tanner was abandoned by his real mother just after birth."

Ross furrowed his brow and gave Nova a look of surprise and disbelief. "But he gave the eulogy at his mother's funeral. We found a copy of a prepared speech in one of the filing cabinets at his home. We also sent an agent out to talk to his brother in that rest home near Idylwild. There's been no indication that Tanner was adopted."

"He wasn't," Nova interrupted. "His real mother left him when he was only a few weeks old, but there never were any formal adoption proceedings. The Tanners were relatives who took Larry in and had a phony birth certificate issued for him. It's a long story." Nova gave Ross a capsule sketch of the Tanner family tree and Mrs. Tanner's alleged demise, then added, "His brother, Ben, blames Larry for causing his mother's death."

"So you think our ad should say that Larry Tanner killed his mother?"

"Not exactly." Nova reached into the breast pocket of his sports coat to retrieve the draft he had penned at the coffee shop. "It's a little long, but it's all there," he said, handing the paper to Ross.

"That shouldn't be a problem. We've reserved twice as much space with the *Inquirer* as we thought we'd ever need. The same gal who interviewed Ben Tanner worked out a deal with the paper. They think she's going to place some kind of coded message for a friend. Actually, the way she explained things to me, the paper doesn't give a damn what it prints in its personals so long as they get paid on time. You should see some of the stuff they have in here." He pointed at a copy of the *Inquirer* lying on his desk. "I never knew there were so many earth mothers out there searching for lost blond Adonises."

Turning his attention to the note, Ross strained to make out Nova's handwriting. Lawyers and doctors, he thought to himself, invariably had the penmanship of eight-year-olds. Finally, the chicken scratch came into focus:

LT has been convicted and must pay for his crimes. The question is how. Abandoned by a mother he never knew, he grew up a stranger in a family he thought was his own. Deceived and alone, he took to drugs and alcohol. Yet despite his crimes, he must be spared. The death fires dance. Can they show mercy, too?

"I get the first part," Ross said, still scrutinizing the note. "But I'm not sure I like saying Tanner's been convicted and has to pay for his crimes. Then again, I suppose we have to play along with Randy if this thing has any chance of working."

"That's right."

"Okay, but the last two sentences. What are they, some kind of inside joke?"

"The part about the death fires is a reference to a poem," Nova answered.

"A poem?"

"The first two lines from one of the verses of *The Rime of the Ancient Mariner*, by Samuel Taylor Coleridge." Nova noticed the uncomprehending look on Ross' face. "He was one of the great English poets of the romantic school. He lived in the late eighteenth and early nineteenth centuries."

"And what the hell does that have to do with the Honorable Lawrence Tanner?"

"It doesn't have anything to do with Larry." Ross' uncomprehending expression had metamorphosed to one of impatience, prompting Nova to add quickly, "It has to do with Sturgis. His father, the doctor who adopted him and later molested him, made Randy memorize the poem as a school boy. He used to lock him in a closet whenever Randy missed a verse or complained. The part about the death fires comes from a stanza in the middle of the poem."

"How does the verse go?"

"I looked it up again the other night." Nova cleared his throat, then recited in his best English Lit class voice:

> *"About, about, in reel and rout,*
> *The death fires danced at night;*
> *The water, like a witch's oil,*
> *Burnt green, and blue and white."*

"Maybe I'm not as literary as you and Randy, but I still don't get it," Ross said.

"When Randy was a kid, he had nightmares about that verse. He became obsessed with the image of the death fires. He told me that the poem echoed inside his head just before he snapped and killed Grace Cowley."

"But why do we have to put the poem in the personal ad?"

"Do you still have Randy's videotape?"

"Of course."

"I'd like you to play it."

Ross hesitated an instant, then stood and walked to one of the gun-metal filing cabinets lining the wall to the right of his desk. It took only a few seconds for him to retrieve the tape and another few to pop it into the VCR, which, along with the color TV to which it was connected, still stood tucked away in the corner of the office like abandoned home electronics equipment.

"If you don't mind, I'd like to have the remote," Nova said, reaching out his hand.

Ross grudgingly turned over the controls, and Nova began to fast-forward through the tape until the video monitor focused closely on the small statue of the blindfolded goddess of justice. "I think it was right about here," Nova said, pushing the play button.

The voice of Randy Sturgis filled the office, deadly serious and animated by the trademark Southern twang he liked to feign when he was having fun and felt in control. "Now, there's just one argument, and one argument alone, that can save Larry's life. It can be expressed in a simple sentence or three, depending on how much taxpayer money you want to spend. Anyway, I want your answer printed in the personal section of the *South Coast Inquirer* the Monday after next.

"That's the game. Follow the rules and say the magic words, Larry goes free. Break the rules, refuse to play your roles and, well, let's just say there will be another opening on the court of appeals. And just in case you're thinking, Davey, that you can wriggle

out of this appointment, be warned, ol' buddy. I'll
know, from the ad you place, if you're in the game.''

Nova clicked off the tape and turned to Ross. "I'm
the only person Randy's ever told about the Coleridge
poem. He'll know I'm in the game if he sees the reference in the ad.''

"That's funny," Ross said, his lips curling in a skeptical half smile. "I don't remember reading any notes
about a poem in your trial file.'' There was a slight
accusatory edge in Ross' tone, as though his cop's
sense of paranoia had suddenly been kick-started
again by Nova's revelation.

"I didn't take any notes," Nova answered abruptly.
"It was something he told me in jail the day before
the start of the penalty phase of the trial. I've never
told anyone about it until now.'' Nova stopped short
again of telling Ross about the audiotape he had
made. Whether he had made the right decision in removing the tape from the Sturgis file in the first place
would always be debatable. He had, in fact, been second-guessing himself ever since he first slipped the cassette into his sports jacket. But to disclose the
existence of the tape now, after the FBI had obtained
a warrant for the entire file, was unthinkable. At best,
it would utterly destroy the trust he had built up with
Ross. At worst, it could earn him an indictment for
obstruction of justice.

"And you've remembered what Sturgis told you all
these years?'' Ross asked harshly.

There was no question now that Ross was changing
before Nova's eyes. In the space of no more than
thirty seconds, he had gone from being Nova's good
buddy to sounding like a disbelieving cop about to
launch into a new round of interrogation. "That's
right," Nova answered. "It's not every day that a cli-

ent tells you something like that. I don't think I'll ever forget it."

"I guess not," Ross said, nodding in agreement. A few seconds passed before he added, "I've been through the file pretty thoroughly, and I have to agree with you that there's nothing in there relevant to this business with Tanner."

"Does that mean I can have the file back?" Nova asked. He tried not to show the relief he felt that Ross had elected not to press the issue of the poem.

"Let's wait until after Monday, when the *Inquirer* hits the stands. If the file still looks clean, I'll have it delivered back to your office."

Ross read through the ad copy one more time, then lifted his eyes to Nova. "Okay. I have to admit it's better than anything I came up with. I'll have it typed up and taken over to the paper early tomorrow." He heaved a sigh of frustration and shifted his gaze back to the unfinished paperwork on his desk. "Unless Randy does something to give himself away between now and Monday, about all we can do is wait."

"And hope that Randy makes good on his word," Nova said, rising from his seat and preparing to say good-bye.

"That's not exactly something I'd bet the farm on. Still, you did a good job and I appreciate it. I had my doubts about you at first." A forgiving smile that seemed to say, "Let's be friends again," slowly spread across the special agent's face.

"I hadn't noticed," Nova said, returning the smile but still wary that Ross might revert to his menacing mode at any moment.

Following Nova's lead, Ross stood up and offered to walk his guest back to the elevator. "So, on a personal level, if you don't mind me prying, how did your visit with Tami go?" he asked in an affable tone as they crossed the squad room and made their way into the seventeenth-floor corridor.

"There were the usual daggers and barbs," Nova answered, "but I kept my cool."

"That's good. I don't envy you going through that custody case. It must be hell, especially after all the years you lived together as a family." Ross paused as Nova pushed the down elevator button before continuing, "How long did you say you and Tami have been separated?"

"I didn't, but it's been about three years."

The muscles in Ross' face seemed to tense ever so slightly. For an instant it seemed like he wanted to say more but confined himself to a final "thank you," a manly handshake that inflicted a moderate amount of unintended pain, and an admonition to drive safely on the way home.

It didn't take an advanced degree in abnormal psychology for Nova to figure out what Ross was thinking. He and Tami had separated at roughly the same time Randy Sturgis had dropped from sight. In the mind of a perpetually suspicious FBI agent convinced that Randy wasn't acting alone, that kind of timing might be seen as more of a clue than a mere coincidence.

Chapter Nineteen

"It's just my second day back at work," Vera said, voicing a mild demurral. "I've been reassigned to another judge, and I have a stack of mail to sort through and some overdue memos to type. So I guess I'd better take a rain check, but I'm very pleased that you called and it's good to be back."

It was great to hear Vera sounding so strong, even if she was turning down his offer of lunch at the bistro of her choice in nearby Old Pasadena. Nova had phoned Vera as much out of a desire to check up on her emotional state as out of his own need for company as he waited for news on Tanner. He had tried reaching both Sandy and Molly, but in both cases had gotten only their secretaries. Vera was the next logical choice and, in some ways, the person to whom he felt most drawn to under the circumstances.

The *South Coast Inquirer* had hit the stands as scheduled Monday morning with the ad copy he had drafted occupying a prominent place in the personals section. After picking up a copy of the paper, he had spent most of the Monday at his office, catching up on his mail and waiting for Ross or one of his underlings to call with the hoped-for bulletin that Larry had been released alive. But the call never came, and

Nova's calls to the FBI were met with polite but curt assurances that he was the first civilian on the Bureau's contact list. He'd learn of the judge's fate, he was told, as soon as the feds did. It was now Tuesday morning and there was still no word.

"What about a cup of coffee?" Nova persisted before Vera could say good-bye. "Say around two, two-thirty? I know how you love a double cappuccino."

"I don't know," she vacillated.

"Oh, come on. You're entitled to two coffee breaks a day by law. Besides, by the time I get there, half the judges will be out playing golf, and the other half will be asleep in their swivel chairs. We'll be out and back in half an hour."

She laughed at Nova's persistence. "Okay, but you've got to promise to stick around long enough to say hello to some of the old clericals you haven't seen in years. They'd never forgive me for not bringing you by."

"The return of the prodigal," he quipped. "It's a deal."

Nova spent the next three hours drafting a set of interrogatories for a new multiple-vehicle freeway collision case that had the potential to bring him another six-figure contingency fee. Normally with such a lucrative matter under scrutiny, he would have spent the better part of the day working up his discovery plan and lining up the doctors and accident-reconstructionist experts he would need to prepare the case for settlement or trial. But even the lure of another easy payday wasn't enough to hold his interest. Having thrown himself headlong into the quest to save Tanner, he found it impossible to take his mind off his former boss. By twelve-thirty, he'd had enough. He scribbled a hasty note to Sylvia Gomez that he was gone for the day and headed out to Pasadena early.

*   *   *

The Ninth Circuit Court of Appeals had relocated its southern California branch from downtown L.A. to the fringes of Old Pasadena in the mid-eighties. The eastward move not only relieved overcrowding in the downtown federal courthouse, where the circuit had shared space with its judicial underlings in the district trial courts, but it also rewarded the circuit judges with a working environment better suited to the contemplative nature of the appellate process. Gone were the crime, noise, and curbside destitution of the legions of homeless people who had made the inner city their stomping grounds. Housed in a refurbished turn-of-the-century army administration office, the newly christened appellate courthouse afforded its judicial tenants inspiring vistas of the San Gabriel Mountains, the Rose Bowl, and the Arroyo Seco—the dry and rugged mountain water bed that sliced through the western end of Pasadena, where the local horse, hiking, and archery sets pursued their recreational passions under eternally sun-kissed skies. It also placed the circuit court and its staff within walking distance of the culinary delights of Old Pasadena for quick noontime conferences, birthday celebrations, and after-work libations at the numerous happy hours hosted by an ever expanding array of upscale bars and eateries that had turned the historic center of Pasadena into one of the trendiest shopping districts in Southern California.

Although Nova had completed his Ninth Circuit clerkship before the relocation, he was no stranger to the new courthouse. He had argued a half dozen appeals in its third-floor courtrooms and, at least in the years immediately following his clerkship, he had visited there often with Vera and Tanner in their fifth-floor offices. Heading north on the Pasadena Freeway from downtown, Nova found the traffic unusually light and pulled into the courthouse parking lot at one o'clock. He was an hour early, he knew, but Vera would just have to put up with him.

The sight of three squad cars from the local police department outside the courthouse entrance was the first sign that something was wrong. Although located within the confines of the Pasadena city limits, the court was a federal installation under the jurisdiction of the U.S. Marshal's office. It wasn't unusual to see federal law enforcement vehicles parked around the building, but if the Pasadena cops were there, it could only mean that the feds had called for some kind of quick backup.

Hurrying past the squad cars, Nova walked into the lobby and up to the metal-detection booth stationed just inside. He began to place his car keys and spare change on one of the small black plastic trays at the side of the booth before passing through when his progress was halted by the upraised palms of two deputy U.S. marshals dressed in official black blazers and neatly pressed khaki pants.

"I'm sorry, sir, but the courthouse is temporarily restricted to permanent staff only," the older-looking of the two deputies said.

"Why? What's happened?" Nova asked excitedly.

"There's been an incident. We can't say anything more at this time. You'll have to come back later. I'm sorry for the inconvenience."

"Look, I'm here to see Vera Fletcher," Nova persisted. "She's Judge Tanner's clerk. Does this have anything to do with the judge?"

"Are you here with the media?" the other deputy cut in, sounding as though he anticipated an imminent onslaught from the fifth estate.

Before Nova could answer, a grim-faced young

woman with short, neatly clipped blond hair and a sensible but no-frills houndstooth jacket approached the deputies from the interior of the lobby. "It's okay," she said firmly. "Let him through."

"I'm Gaylin Forbes, FBI," the young woman said, extending a strong athletic hand after Nova had passed the test for hidden weapons. "You must be Mr. Nova. I tried calling your office about fifteen minutes ago," she added as they walked to the elevators and stepped inside an idle compartment.

"What's happened to Larry?" Nova asked as the doors closed behind them. The elevator began to climb to the fifth floor.

Gaylin Forbes blinked hard and dipped her eyes. "I think we were chumps to believe that Randy Sturgis would play by the rules. The judge is dead."

At the fifth floor, Forbes led Nova off the elevator and down the hallway to Tanner's chambers. There Nova found Tony Ross and a small forensics squad, including two emissaries from the coroner's office, engaged in what appeared to be the end stages of a crime-scene investigation. Except for Ross, who was busy wrapping up a phone call, the attention of all concerned seemed to be focused on a large cardboard box resting atop a steel hospital-style cart that could only have come from the coroner. One of the men gathered about the cart held a flash camera in his hand, while another was packing up a fingerprint kit.

"You must have some kind of intuition," Ross said, turning to face Nova as he hung up the phone. "I've only been here for forty minutes myself."

"What happened?" Nova asked.

"He's dead. That's all that really matters." Ross' deep-set eyes never had looked more troubled or defeated.

"But how? And why are *you* here?"

Without waiting for an answer, Nova took a few quick steps toward the hospital cart. Ross reached out to try to pull him back, but it was too late. "I guess you deserve to know," Ross said flatly, yielding to what had by then become inevitable. He signaled the coroner's men to step aside. "I hope you have a strong stomach."

Nova recoiled at what he saw, like a man who had been hit with a taser gun. The few dead bodies he had glimpsed firsthand in his life, as a child at Catholic funerals, had all been carefully washed, dressed to the nines, and looked merely asleep. Even his withered Sicilian grandmother, steeped in embalming fluid, had seemed in her casket to be at peace both with herself and the cosmos to which she had returned. All of the deceased he'd seen shared still another vital characteristic—physically, they were intact. Not so now.

The head of the Honorable Lawrence Tanner, stuffed inside a large Zip-lock plastic bag and still cradled in protective styrofoam lining, stared back at him like a crude rubber Halloween mask, at once horrifying and mournful, terrible and unreal. The head had been severed just below the Adam's apple. Discolored shreds of collapsed veins and arteries, entwined in sinews of brownish-red connective tissue and muscle, protruded below the cleavage. The judge's once defiant eyes, now milky, soft, and nearly colorless with the advancing effects of putrefaction, had been pinned open with duct tape, giving the head a haunted look of permanent surprise.

"It was delivered here around eleven-thirty pretty much as you're looking at it," Ross continued in a monotone, "in an ordinary cardboard box packed with dry ice, which we've removed." As he spoke, he gripped Nova supportively by the right arm. "The package was addressed to Vera Fletcher. She thought it was a box of law books and opened it on top of Tanner's desk."

Fighting off a powerful urge to vomit, Nova said nothing. The image of Vera innocently prying the box open and peering inside flashed through his mind. At least *he'd* received some forewarning.

"Looks like Randy used a chain saw," Ross added. "The break in the skin's a little jagged, but the spinal cord was severed cleanly, just like a small tree branch. We're pretty sure the decapitation occurred postmortem. We've taken some photos, dusted the box and the wrapping paper it came with for prints. We'll be doing tissue, blood, and fiber studies later, the usual workup."

"And the rest of the body?" Nova asked weakly.

"No idea," Ross said. "Come on, we'll get a cup of coffee. You look like you could use one. We can talk."

Nova retreated to Tanner's desk. "Thanks, but I'll be okay. Where's Vera now?"

"She's in the employee lounge down the hall," Gaylin Forbes said, breaking into the conversation from her position at the open doorway. "I think they've called in a doctor. She was pretty shaken up, as you might imagine."

"I'd like to see her if that would be all right," Nova said.

Ross nodded in approval.

For someone who had just suffered the fright of a lifetime, Vera looked remarkably calm, seated upright on an oversized green couch in the lounge. Wrapped in a blanket to ward off shock, she was cradling a cup of hot tea, as the doctor Gaylin Forbes had mentioned stood by taking her blood pressure. A group of female clericals was gathered around Vera, uttering words of comfort and reassurance.

"A hundred and forty over ninety," the doctor, a young intern from nearby Huntington Memorial Hospital, intoned, releasing the cuff from Vera's right arm. "That's slightly higher than normal but pretty good, considering what you've been through. I'll write you a prescription for something that will keep you settled."

Nova recognized two of the clerks seated nearest to Vera as women who had already attained senior typist status when he was on the court. The women greeted him with muted surprise and cleared room for him to sit down on the couch.

"You got here early," Vera commented wryly, directing her gaze at Nova. "Too bad I'm going to have to break our date."

Looking at Vera, it was impossible for Nova to tell if she was just putting up a brave front, which would crumble the moment she was left alone, or if, like many shock victims, the full import of what she had seen had yet to register. Nova reached out and took her small left hand in his. "I'm so sorry," he said.

"I know," she sighed. "He may have been a sonofabitch, but he didn't deserve to die like this." One of the women—a plump fifty-five-year-old named Irene—put a tender arm around Vera, as if to emphasize that there was no need to say more. Vera smiled appreciatively at her colleague, then turned back to Nova. "What kind of animal would do a thing like this?"

"The kind that should have spent the rest of his days in a cage," Nova answered softly. His observation met with a chorus of approval from the gathering.

"In a way, you might say that Larry brought this upon himself," Vera added with a note of irony. "He wrote the opinion that set Randy Sturgis free."

"You can't fault Larry," Nova replied. "He was just following the law."

Vera sighed again and cocked her head to one side,

like someone recalling a distant and elusive memory. "He was always following the law, a man of principle to the end." She sounded angry and sarcastic, and for a moment it seemed that she was going to burst into tears. Yet somehow, whether out of fear of letting herself go or because she had already done most of her grieving in anticipation of Larry's demise, she held her emotions in check. Nova wondered at the inner strength of this tiny woman who had devoted most of her adult life to a man who had relied upon her to keep his professional affairs in order but done little else than take her for granted. As the afternoon wore on, a steady stream of court employees filed into the lounge to pay their respects. Finally, at a quarter past three, Nova said his good-byes, offering up a long hug and a solemn promise to stay in touch.

By the time Nova left the courthouse, both Ross and Gaylin Forbes had returned to the FBI's headquarters in Westwood. The coroner's men and the awful box containing Larry's head were also gone. By early tomorrow, Nova told himself as he took the elevator back to the lobby, the Ninth Circuit would again be open for business as usual. The larger world, minus one distinguished appellate judge, would limp along, too, in its customary pattern of barely contained chaos.

Lacking anywhere specific to go, Nova climbed into his Lexus and drove into the early rush-hour traffic on the 134 freeway. Taking an inventory of his own state of mind, he felt an uncomfortable mixture of numbness, anger, and relief. Coming on the heels of Larry's senseless death, and the failure of his own efforts to save him, the numbness and anger were easy to comprehend. The odd sense of relief came from the realization that the mad game Sturgis had inveighed him to join was finally over. Above all, he felt the need to unburden himself.

He tried again to reach Molly and Sandy by phone. This time Molly's receptionist told him she was gone for the day, taking a deposition in Century City. Sandy's assistant reported that her boss was out of town. Like a loyal employee, she wouldn't divulge where her boss had gone. She promised, however, to tell Sandy of David's need to talk as soon as she called in for messages. "In fact, Ms. Nash should be calling in very soon," she assured Nova. "She usually checks in late afternoons when she's traveling."

When Nova's car phone came to life around four-fifteen, he was traveling west on the Ventura freeway in heavy traffic, en route to the turnoff for the Topanga Canyon off-ramp. Keeping his gaze trained on the road, he picked up the receiver, fully expecting to hear Sandy's voice. The voice he heard, however, belonged to Gaylin Forbes.

"Mr. Nova?" Forbes inquired. "This is Gaylin Forbes from the Bureau. Your secretary gave me your car phone number."

"Is there something I can do for you?" Nova asked. "I'm expecting another call."

"Agent Ross asked me to call. He'd like you to swing by the office if it's not too much trouble. He said it was important."

"Can it wait until tomorrow?" After all he had been through, another visit to the FBI wasn't high on his list of priorities.

"I'm afraid not, sir."

"What could possibly be so important that it couldn't wait another sixteen hours? I could make it over early tomorrow morning."

"We have someone in custody, Mr. Nova. Agent Ross would like you to take a look at him."

"You're not telling me that you've arrested Randy Sturgis, are you?" In his excitement Nova took his eyes off the freeway and nearly rear-ended the late-model pickup in front of him.

"No, but we've picked up the man who delivered the package to the court."

"It may take me a while," Nova said, glancing at his dashboard clock, "but I'll be there as soon as possible."

Chapter Twenty

"I tell you before," the portly little man dressed in the blue uniform protested in a thick Mexican accent. "I don't know nothing about the package. I just a delivery man. I take it to the courthouse."

"But you didn't get a receipt," Ross barked back. "You're supposed to fill out a delivery sheet and get a signature and a receipt, no?"

"That's true, but the black guy, he say he in a hurry and he give me an extra fifty dollars. Just like I tell you."

"Tell me again." Ross sat down in the steel-frame chair across from the man and folded his arms expectantly.

With Gaylin Forbes leading the way, Nova took a seat in the observation booth in the basement of the Wilshire Federal Building just as the nerve-racked Mexican-American delivery driver was about to give Ross his answer. Shielded by the one-way mirror that separated the booth from the adjacent interrogation room, Nova could neither be seen nor heard by the driver or Ross.

The delivery man began to sweat profusely, his hands and shoulders shaking with tension. "Okay," he said weakly. "I work for the company—Miguel's Crosstown Express—four, five years now, ever since I get my green card. I never break the company rules before. Never."

"Cut the crap, Mr. Hernandez," Ross shot back. "Your boss just told me on the phone that you've delivered packages on your own before. He said he's warned you many times to shape up or ship out."

Hernandez bowed his head, like a man who had stumbled into a trap of his own making. "Okay, okay, you are right, of course," he replied. "But what am I to do? So now and then I make a little extra on the side. The boss, Miguel, he always make a profit. He has five delivery vans now. I only have one car—a 1985 Chevy, with bald tires. And I have a family."

"So do I." Ross directed a cold stare at the man. "Now, where did the black guy approach you?"

"In the parking lot outside the office. I was just about to leave for my morning deliveries. He came up and knocked on the window of my van."

"And what did he say?"

"He had this package under his arm. He say his boss was a lawyer who needed it taken to the court in Pasadena. He say it was heavy and that it contain law books."

"What did you say?"

"I tole him I have to go to the office and have an order form filled out. That's when he give me the fifty dollars and said he didn't have no time to wait. I thought about it for a minute. Then I say okay, and he leave. The package was sealed. I never look inside it, I swear." Hernandez gave Ross a look filled with fear and remorse. "I still don't know what I did that was so wrong. You never tell me what was inside the package. Look, I agree to tell you all I know. I want to go home now."

Ross ignored the man's pleas. "What did the black man look like?"

Hernandez shrugged and raised his arms, palms up in a pleading gesture. He was sweating even more profusely than before, and the armpits of his work shirt were stained dark with perspiration. "He was a big man, about six feet and strong. His hair was short, normal-looking for a black man. I think he had a little beard, but I'm not sure. He seemed like a regular working person. I don't know what else to tell you. I don't know one black person from the other."

"Had you ever seen him before?"

"No. Never." Hernandez shook his head from side to side to emphasize the good-faith nature of his answer.

"And what about Vera Fletcher, whose name was written on the package. Have you ever seen her?"

"No. She just a name on a package to me. I take the package to the court, like the address say. I leave it with the guys in the garage. That's all. Honest."

Ross grew silent and gave Hernandez a long, appraising stare, designed as much to prolong the man's agony as it was to put the fear of God in him lest he refuse to cooperate in the future. "All right. I'm going to let you go. But I don't want you taking any trips below the border. If you do, that green card of yours won't be worth the plastic it's printed on. I'll have an agent take you back to work."

Hernandez thanked the Almighty and Ross in that order and buried his head in his hands as Ross left the room.

Ross met Nova a few seconds later inside the observation booth and thanked him for coming. "Did you get a good look at the driver?"

"Right down to his clammy palms," Nova answered.

"Ever see him before?"

"No."

"I didn't think you would, but I couldn't pass up the opportunity to give you a chance to ID him." Ross sounded more tired than disappointed at Nova's answer. "One of the mail clerks at the courthouse garage remembered the van the guy was driving. His boss was only too willing to make the driver available to talk to us."

"Is that why you called me back here?" Nova asked.

"Partly," Ross answered. "There's something else I'd like you to see."

Ross led Nova down the hall and into a large windowless chamber about twice the size of a blue-chip law-firm's main conference room. A long wood-veneer service counter spanned the width of the room, separating it into two sections. Beyond the counter, in the larger of the two sections, the room was filled with a phalanx of heavy steel filing cabinets and wall-to-ceiling shelves stacked with cardboard boxes marked up with the names and case numbers of ongoing investigations. Although Nova had never set foot in the place, he recognized it instantly as an evidence-collection center.

Ross stepped behind the counter and unlocked one of the filing cabinets. Reaching into the top drawer of the cabinet, he pulled out a manila folder and walked back to Nova. "We found this note in another Ziplock baggie taped to the bottom of the box Sturgis sent to court," he said, slipping on a pair of latex gloves and removing from the folder a plain sheet of photocopy paper with double-spaced typing on it. He unfolded the paper carefully and placed it atop the counter.

Nova leaned over and passed his eyes across the page:

I thought it was about time the judge got back to his office. All those taxpayer dollars being wasted on his unscheduled vacation are an outrage. Goddamn lazy government employees, you've really got to keep an eye on them. Please keep Larry in a cool dark place.

Ciao.

P.S. Congratulations to Agent Ross and David Nova on winning the game! That part about the death fires was especially on the money. Poignant and nostalgic at the same time. Unfortunately, Larry couldn't stand the stress and excitement. Being on trial really takes it out of you. But then, you already know that, don't you, David . . . or do you?

Yours Truly, Randy S

The note was signed in longhand with a triumphant Cyrillic flourish on the closing S.

"Any idea what the creep means by the last sentence?" Ross asked. Once again, without advance warning, there was a hint of suspicion in Ross' tone, as though he felt that Sturgis might be addressing Nova in some kind of code only the two of them would comprehend.

Nova read the note once more and stared back at Ross. "Just another potshot at my lawyering skills, I suppose. I wouldn't read too much into it."

"Yeah, that's what I think, too," Ross said quickly. "Still, it could be a reference to your custody hearing, assuming, of course, that someone's told Sturgis about it."

"Someone like Tami, you mean," Nova replied, shaking his head at the long shot Ross was floating. "I doubt it."

Ross thought for a moment, as if reconsidering his hunch. "You're probably right. Sorry I mentioned it. It's just that we don't have a hell of a lot to work with right now."

"No offense taken," Nova said reassuringly. "I understand how frustrating this case must be for you." Nova watched Ross return the letter to its evidence folder, then asked, "But what about Vera? Why did Sturgis address the package to her?"

Ross thought for a moment and shrugged. "Randy could have gotten the name of Tanner's administrative clerk just by calling the court, or Larry could have told him about her. He said in the video that he and Larry had gotten to be good friends. As for his reason for sending the package to her, it might have been his way of being cute, or he might have thought it was the only way he could have gotten the package through the mail room. They've been screening everything addressed specifically to Tanner."

"I guess we'll have to wait until Randy decides to enlighten us on that one," Nova said. "Well, at least Vera seems to have weathered the shock about as well as anyone could have."

"A remarkably strong woman," Ross replied agreeably. "Still, I'm going to ask the county sheriffs in her neighborhood to keep an eye on her home for a few days just in case."

Ross thanked Nova again for all his help and escorted him out of the evidence room. "Oh, by the way," he said when they had reached the basement elevator, "it looks like we're going to have to hang on to that old trial file of yours a little while longer. Some of my more technically inclined colleagues think it might be helpful in developing a better personality profile on Randy. It's all part of the usual workup we do on serial killers."

"What do *you* think?" Nova asked, masking his dismay at the thought of Ross' buddies spending long nights combing through the file.

Ross took a deep breath. "Me? I think we have about as much chance of catching this guy any time soon as we had of bringing the Unabomber in before his brother blew the whistle on him."

Nova uttered a few parting words of encouragement and stepped into the waiting elevator. Despite his concerns over the Bureau's decision to retain his trial file, the curious sense of relief he had felt earlier in the afternoon began to return. Unlike Ross, who would remain tethered to Randy Sturgis until one of them died or justice was done, he was now free to get on with the next phase of his life. For the moment at least, that seemed almost comforting.

Chapter Twenty-one

News of Larry Tanner's return to court in a cheap cardboard box hit the papers and TV with a vengeance. The judge's homicide was the lead story on Court TV, the local stations, and the *L.A. Times* for three days running. Then, slowly, the incident faded to page three and then to the metro section of the *Times*, with only brief and intermittent coverage on the eleven o'clock news. Finally, like other contemporary tales of man's inhumanity to man, the story faded altogether, replaced in the headlines by an outbreak of fresh bloodletting in the Middle East, a new spate of airline accidents nationally, and a series of brutal rape-homicides in Boyle Heights that had the local cops completely baffled and a coalition of attention-seeking Hispanic political groups hollering for the police chief's *cojones* on a silver platter.

For Nova, however, the unspeakable image of Tanner's death would never completely fade. Unlike the media, which simply moved on to the next atrocity, he had to make a conscious effort to push it from his mind. Even then, he was only somewhat successful. The sense of closure he thought he had found with Larry's passing proved to be short-lived. His sleep was disrupted by nightmares, his waking hours by the chill-

ing thought that Sturgis might have told Larry about
the other murders he'd committed, and that he had
also admitted his guilt long ago to Nova, in a taped
jailhouse interview. How Larry might have reacted to
such revelations—with anger, dread, surprise, or some
unspeakable combination—Nova would never know.
Nor would he ever know if in his final hours Larry
came to regard himself as a fool for granting Randy's
writ petition and releasing him from prison. When the
end was at hand, had he admitted that he had been
duped by his own principles and rigid faith in the law,
or had he stood by his decision to release Sturgis and
take his principles unshaken to the next world?

Then there was the way Larry had died. Perhaps he
had perished from a heart attack or just sheer stress,
as Sturgis claimed, or perhaps Sturgis had played a
more hands-on role in his demise. Even the FBI remained uncertain. Worst of all for Nova was the guilt
he felt as the lawyer who had saved Sturgis from the
gas chamber, only to set in motion the unforeseeable
string of events that led to Randy's release from
prison and culminated in Larry's abduction.

Even Molly, with all her persuasive powers, couldn't
convince him that he bore no responsibility for Tanner's death. Lost in a fog of second-guessing and self-
doubt, Nova seemed impervious to her pep talks.
Even more important, he was dangerously disengaged
from the critical strategy sessions they held on the eve
of the custody hearing. He postponed one session in
order to complete an impromptu phone call to Jamie
and cut short another in order to meet a filing deadline he had all but forgotten in one of his most important civil cases. And on those occasions when he was
available to Molly, he was often too distracted and
tired to be of much help in assisting her to prepare for
the cross-examination of Tami's anticipated witnesses.

In the end, ironically, it took another judge—the Honorable Judith Elaine Goldstein and the power she wielded over his future—to bring him fully back to the present.

Unlike many superior court judges, who viewed stints in family court as the judicial equivalent of janitorial work, Judith Goldstein regarded domestic relations as the cutting edge of the law. While other aspiring jurists had their eyes set on plum civil trial appointments or even higher offices, she had no intention of putting in for reassignment. "It is in family court, and only in family court," she once declared in a formal speech before the state's largest women's bar association conference, "that the playing field in the battle of the sexes is leveled so that women have a fighting chance to receive the law's promise of equal protection."

Her activist leanings notwithstanding, Judge Goldstein was no mental midget, either. She was a cum laude graduate from Stanford and a former law-review editor at the University of California's Boalt Hall at Berkeley. She knew the law and expected the lawyers who presented cases in front of her to be no less well versed. And while she had a clear track record in custody cases of leaning in favor of the right of mothers, her primary concern was always, as the law required, in crafting orders that advanced the best interests of the children. This meant that on occasion, when the evidence so warranted, she had no compunction about yanking physical custody from a deadbeat mom and sending the kids home to live with dad.

Physically, too, Goldstein was an imposing specimen, standing just over six feet tall in her queen-size panty hose. Thin and lanky, with unusually large hands and deep furrows between the eyes, she gave the impression, even in her loose-fitting black robes, of being a person of boundless energy and concentration. A crown of thick wavy brownish-gray hair pulled back in a tight French twist and a pair of oversized tortoise-shell glasses completed a look that was designed to underscore the no-nonsense approach she took to the bench.

Arriving early on a Tuesday morning for the first day of the custody hearing, Nova took a seat in the gallery, waiting for Molly, Tami, and Brockman to show up for an in-chambers conference scheduled for ten-thirty. Although the conference would be little more than a formality, designed primarily to clarify the evidentiary issues and the scope of the testimony that would commence in the afternoon, Nova wanted an opportunity to assess the judge's mood as she disposed of the preliminary matters on her calendar.

By all appearances, "Judge Judy," as one unfortunate unrepresented petitioner addressed Her Honor, was in rare form. The petitioner, a rough-looking electrician from Highland Park, was appearing *in pro per* to contest a contempt order his ex-spouse had requested for non-payment of child support. Judge Goldstein firmly rebuked him for the disrespectful title with which he had addressed her. Then she promptly ordered him to pay up all past arrearages forthwith or to bring his toothbrush to his next court appearance, which she set for two weeks hence. "You'll need the toothbrush for the thirty days you'll be spending in jail," she chastised, bringing down her gavel and calling the remaining cases on her docket.

The judge was decidedly more benevolent with the other four preliminary matters, all of which involved uncontested modifications to prior decrees and, in one case, a jointly requested continuance for a trial date. With her morning agenda cleared, she turned to her clerk, knitted her brow, and gave a slight nod of her head. By that time Nova had been joined by Molly, while Tami and Tom Brockman had taken up positions in the gallery's opposite aisle.

"*Dawson* v. *Nova*," the clerk announced dutifully. "The parties may step forward."

Judge Goldstein waited for the litigants and their lawyers to approach the counsel tables and state their appearances. "I'll see the parties and their lawyers in chambers," she announced for the record, bringing her gavel down again and leading the way into the suite of interior offices the judges referred to as their chambers.

Like most judges, Judith Goldstein's chamber reflected a little of both her private and professional personas. The wall behind her large mahogany-stained desk was plastered with the usual assortment of law degrees and bar association awards. The desk itself was stacked high with open case files, sharing space with framed photographs of her elderly parents on vacation in Hawaii and her two sisters, one a prominent managing attorney with the local legal aid society, the other a happily married housewife from Sherman Oaks. Since Goldstein was unmarried herself, there were no pictures of the judge's spouse or kids. By far the most atypical feature of the office, however, was the tall wooden bookshelf to the left of the desk, packed with colorful stuffed animals, bright plastic action figures, and children's books, ranging from Berenstein Bears stories to Mother Goose rhymes.

"I examine a lot of children in here," Goldstein said, nodding toward the bookshelf after the parties had taken seats in the client chairs in front of her. "The toys help them to relax." She took a moment

to survey the small gathering in front of her, Brockman and Nova outfitted in expensive pinstripes; Tami
and Molly, at opposite ends of the height spectrum,
in sober but finally tailored business suits, respectively.

"Let's see," Goldstein resumed, opening the court
file. "This matter is here on Ms. Dawson's OSC for a
modification of the present joint-custody order."

"Ms. Dawson is moving to New York, Your
Honor," Brockman broke in. "That's where the child
is now, at summer camp in the Catskills."

"I can read, counsel," Goldstein snapped back, lifting her eyes abruptly from the file. She removed her
glasses and cleared her throat. "As I was going to say,
since we're here on an OSC rather than an initial custody determination, the court has broad discretion
both to control the order of proof and to limit testimony. In fact, I could decide the matter strictly on
the basis of the written declarations that have been
submitted with the moving and responding papers. I
take it that the settlement conference before Judge
Fowler was to little avail."

Molly and Brockman answered in the affirmative
and exchanged uneasy looks. They also promised to
stipulate, wherever possible, to the admission of sworn
written declarations from potential witnesses in lieu of
live testimony, in order to expedite the proceedings.

"I appreciate that," Goldstein replied. "And, in
view of the seriousness of the issue at hand, I do not
intend to limit either party to the mere use of declarations. I've cleared my calendar and can give you three,
perhaps four days of court time at the outside, including this afternoon. Is the child going to testify?"

"No, Your Honor," Brockman answered, "both
parties have agreed that it would be best if their
daughter were not forced to testify, unless, of course,
you determine otherwise."

"My foremost interest, counsel, is to protect the child. If you're prepared to present a thorough case without the child, that suits me just fine," Goldstein said. "Is the petitioner prepared to proceed?"

"Yes, Your Honor, we have three witnesses for this afternoon," Brockman replied.

"Then I'll see you back in court at one-thirty. My clerk will escort you out." Goldstein returned her gaze to the case file. "It's nice to see you again, Ms. Carpenter," she added without diverting her eyes. "I understand your practice is going quite well."

"Yes, Your Honor, it is, thank you." Molly gave Nova a Mona Lisa smile on their way out, a discreet lawyer's substitute for a thumbs-up signal. Maybe, Nova thought with a small measure of relief, there was something to the old girls' network, after all.

After a long lunch at a nearby coffee shop, Nova and Molly returned to court, and the case of *Dawson v. Nova* was finally called to order. Since custody cases were exempted by statute from the general rule requiring trials to be held in public, Judge Goldstein ordered the courtroom to be cleared of witnesses and spectators. "I'll hear the petitioner's opening statement at this time," she said from the bench, training her eyes on Tom Brockman.

Brockman took a few steps to the lectern that divided the counsel tables and checked his notes. "If it pleases the court," he began, "there is no more difficult decision that a family court must decide than the issue of which parent to award with primary custody when one of the parents must, for economic reasons, move out of state. Approximately three years ago Ms. Dawson and Mr. Nova separated, and in due course they were later divorced. They are here today because Ms. Dawson, who this court knows is a TV personality, is being transferred to New York City. Her new assignment is slated to begin the first week of September."

Brockman segued into a rather long summary of the procedural history of the case, beginning with the initial divorce petition Tami had filed six months after the separation and ending with the new OSC that had brought the parties before Judge Goldstein. "As Your Honor knows, of course, the standard which governs this case, and all others, is the best interests of the child. While Ms. Dawson wishes to cast no unwarranted aspersions on the character of her former spouse, we will show—through both expert and lay testimony—that their ten-year-old daughter's interests would clearly be best served by awarding primary physical custody to the mother and, in the process, approving the move to New York."

Goldstein directed a critical gaze at Brockman as he concluded his opening statement. "Let me get absolutely clear on this," she said, poker-faced and solemn. "Are you going to claim that Mr. Nova is unfit to raise his daughter?"

Brockman took a step back from the podium and cast a quick glance at Tami. A slight blush rose in Tami's cheeks. She took a deep breath and pulled herself to an exaggeratedly upright posture in her chair in a show of hurt pride and self-righteousness. "What we will show, Your Honor," Brockman answered, "is that Mr. Nova has an attitude toward the opposite sex, and an overly active sexual appetite, that not only destroyed his marriage, but would create an unwholesome atmosphere for a little girl to grow up in. We think that's quite relevant to the issue before us."

"So do I," the judge mused, "but my decision must be based on proof, not accusation. Ms. Carpenter, will

I be hearing from you now, or would you prefer to reserve your opening?"

"We prefer to reserve," Molly answered. "However, I do appreciate Your Honor's good judgment in declining to pin a scarlet letter on my client's chest prematurely."

Goldstein grumbled a few pointed warnings about the need for all sides to maintain proper courtroom etiquette and directed Brockman to proceed. The petitioner called her first witness, Jennifer Sawyer.

An attractive woman in her late thirties, with thick shoulder-length auburn hair and pale blue eyes, Sawyer was led into the courtroom by Goldstein's bailiff. Visibly displeased at being dragged into someone else's nasty business, she took her seat on the witness stand without looking directly at either Tami or Nova.

The court clerk swore Sawyer in and turned her over to Brockman, who quickly took the witness through a litany of standard introductory questions. Growing more comfortable with each inquiry, Sawyer told the court that she was a thirty-eight-year-old real estate salesperson with a new home in the San Fernando Valley community of Sherman Oaks. She was divorced, and had sole physical custody of her only child, a ten-year-old girl.

"Do you know the parties in this proceeding?" Brockman asked, gripping the lectern with both hands as he moved into the heart of his direct examination.

Sawyer cast a sweeping glance at Tami and Nova seated at their respective tables. "Yes, I'm acquainted with both of them, particularly Mr. Nova."

"Can you tell the court where and when you met Mr. Nova?"

"I met him three summers ago at the first practice of my daughter's peewee baseball league in the Topanga Canyon area where we used to live. Mr. Nova's daughter, Jamie, and my little girl, Kirsten, went to the same elementary school and were selected for the same T-ball team."

"And how did you get to know Mr. Nova?"

"He was one of the assistant coaches on the team, and one of his jobs at the practices was to work with the kids who didn't have a lot of prior experience playing baseball."

"Like your daughter?"

"Yes, and like his daughter, too. He would take the less experienced kids off to one side of the field and give them special instruction on the fundamentals, like hitting and throwing."

Sawyer dipped her eyes for a moment, as if she was about to make a troubling confession. "I was already separated from my husband at the time. He had moved out of state, and I didn't know a thing about baseball myself. Girls of my generation didn't play a lot of sports. But things are different today, and I wanted Kirsten to have the opportunities for athletics that I didn't. So I made it a point to enroll her in Little League and take her to the practices and games."

"And at some point, did you and Mr. Nova speak to each other?"

"After practices Mr. Nova made a point of talking with parents like me about the team and the progress that the kids were making in learning the fundamentals. I remember telling him at the beginning of the season that I was a single mom and that I wasn't much help with baseball."

"How did he respond?"

"He said he would keep that in mind and give my daughter a little extra attention."

"And at some point did the conversation between the two of you take a more personal direction?"

"Yes." Sawyer clenched her teeth and for the first time since entering the courtroom looked directly at Nova. "After one of our games the team was having a snack of pizza and sodas. Mr. Nova came up and started talking about Kirsten getting an important hit in the game. We started laughing about how excited the kids got when they won the game, like they were in the pennant race or the World Series. Then, out of the blue, he asked me out to the movies."

"How did you react?"

"I lowered my voice and walked him away from the picnic tables where our kids were eating. Then I asked him about his wife." Sawyer blinked hard, reliving the event all over again in her mind. "He told me that he and Tami had recently separated, and that they had agreed it was all right for them to see other people. He knew that I was raising Kirsten by myself, and he said Jamie was going to be spending the night at his house and that he had a baby-sitter who could take care of Kirsten, too."

"And what did you say?"

"I was a little flabbergasted. I really didn't know what to say."

"Did you accept?"

"Yes, I did. I brought Kirsten over to his house at around seven, if I recall things accurately, and we went out."

"Did you continue to see Mr. Nova socially after that?"

"We continued to date for most of the remainder of the summer."

Brockman cleared his throat and adjusted the knot of his tie. "And at some point did the relationship become serious?" The witness, Tami, and Nova seemed to wriggle in their chairs simultaneously as Brockman completed the question.

"If you're asking whether we became sexual partners," Sawyer answered, "yes, I'm afraid we did. We spent nights at each other's houses, and we even went away to a mineral springs resort in San Luis Obispo, just the two of us, one weekend."

"What caused your relationship to end?"

It took Sawyer to a few long seconds to frame her answer. "David," she used Nova's first name, "was the first man I had gone to bed with since I separated from my husband, and as far as I know I was also his first relationship after Tami. I'm not used to jumping in the sack after dinner and the latest Demi Moore movie. I wanted a relationship. I wanted a commitment, and . . ."

"He didn't?" Brockman prodded.

"He said he wasn't sure what kind of commitment he could give me. It sounded like such a line." Sawyer laughed softly to herself. "We met one morning at a coffee shop—Kirsten and Jamie were still at a sleepover party from the night before. I even remember what each of us was wearing. I had on a pair of cutoff shorts and a shortsleeve white blouse. It was a warm day. He had on a pair of tight jeans and new cowboy boots."

As Sawyer related her tale of woman scorned, Nova leaned over to Molly and whispered, "What the hell do my boots have to do with anything?"

"It's her way of saying she thought you were a stud muffin, you big lug," Molly whispered back, drawing an admonitory stare from the judge.

"That's when he told me he wanted more time for things to develop between us," Sawyer continued from the stand. "He just wasn't ready for anything more permanent."

"And what was so wrong with that?" Brockman asked, feigning incredulity.

"It wasn't just me that I was concerned about," the witness answered, "but the girls. Kirsten and Jamie had just been through marital separations. They knew David and I were seeing each other, and they were starting to ask questions." Sawyer began to wring her hands, and color rose in her cheeks. "I didn't think it was very good for Kirsten that her mother was sleeping with her baseball coach, unless, of course, David was willing to make a commitment. I told David that the arrangement couldn't be any good for Jamie, either. Both girls needed positive role models in their lives, especially in their parents."

"What did he say?"

Judge Goldstein overruled a halfhearted hearsay objection from Molly, and directed Sawyer to answer. "He said that Jamie and Kirsten were just little girls, and that I was projecting my own anxieties on to them. He wanted things to continue just as they were. He failed entirely to credit my comments or concerns with any merit."

"Is that why the relationship ended?"

"From my point of view," Sawyer replied, sounding more and more like a witness whose closing comments had been carefully rehearsed, "our relationship ended because David turned out to be a man who didn't understand me, my daughter, *his* daughter, or women in general."

Sawyer's last comment brought Molly springing out of her chair. "Objection, Your Honor," she shouted. "The witness may be permitted to state how she personally feels about my client, but she has not been qualified to speak on behalf of womankind."

"That's quite true," Judge Goldstein mused. "However, there's no jury here either to be misled or unduly impressed by such testimony. The witness' last remark will stand, and I will give it the weight to which it is entitled after all of the evidence is received."

Knowing that he had scored heavily with his first witness, Brockman announced he had no further questions and passed Ms. Sawyer on to Molly.

"You became quite fond of my client, didn't you?" Molly began, walking swiftly to the lectern.

"For a time," Sawyer answered tersely.

"And you liked the way he treated your daughter and the other kids on the baseball team, did you not?"

"That's true."

"Mr. Nova was kind and gentle with the kids?"

"I have no complaints with Mr. Nova's approach to coaching peewee baseball. He was very good at that."

"Your complaint is with his approach to personal relationships?"

"Yes." Sawyer nodded.

"And it is your testimony, is it not, that my client did not understand you, your daughter, or women in general, that he was insensitive to your needs and concerns?"

"Yes." Sawyer sounded firm but wary of the direction Molly was heading. She also seemed to be tiring.

Molly exchanged a glance with Nova, giving him just the hint of an encouraging smile. Of all the women on Brockman's list of potential witnesses, Sawyer was perhaps the one for which Molly was most prepared. Despite his other preoccupations, Nova had taken the better part of an afternoon briefing Molly on the tawdry details of his affair with the witness. "Then perhaps you can explain to the court," Molly asked, turning back to Sawyer, "why it was that after you broke things off with my client, you wrote him a letter asking to get back together?"

Sawyer flashed a expression of quiet panic and looked at Brockman for help. Brockman, however, could offer only a feeble relevance objection, which was promptly overruled. "The question goes to the witness' credibility and bias," Her Honor intoned.

Left to fend for herself, Sawyer bit her lower lip. "I remember writing David a letter, but I can't recall exactly what I said."

Molly's eyes widened as Sawyer's resolve began to wane. "Oh, come now, Ms. Sawyer. This is the letter where you said you were sorry for breaking up, and for saying all those nasty things, and that Mr. Nova was the kindest, most understanding man you or your daughter had ever met. How could you forget?"

"It's been a long time," the witness stammered.

"Would you like me to show you a copy of the letter?" Molly asked, walking back to the counsel table.

As Molly lifted up her briefcase to the table, Nova scribbled a hasty note on the legal pad in front of him and quickly handed it to Molly. Without bothering to read it, Molly folded the note and stuffed it inside the pocket of her jacket.

"Yes, it's true I wrote those things," Sawyer added hastily, even before Molly had completed the task of opening her briefcase. "At the time I was very lonely, and confused. I thought there might still be a chance for David and me."

"That's quite understandable," Molly said in a conciliatory tone. Satisfied, she closed her briefcase and returned to the lectern. "But all that talk about Mr. Nova not being a good role model and not understanding women, that wasn't really what you thought during the period you were seeing him, was it?"

Sawyer closed her eyes and took a deep breath. "I suppose that at times I did feel that way, and at other times I didn't."

"And yet today, under questioning by Mr. Brockman, you were able to recall only the negative impressions you had formed about Mr. Nova, is that right?"

"I'm just here to answer questions, not to take sides," Sawyer answered defensively.

"Then answer this," Molly said, pausing to give her inquiry added weight. "You're still very bitter toward my client because he declined to accept your offer of reconciliation, aren't you?"

"I felt very foolish after I wrote that letter," Sawyer said. "I still do." The witness' eyes began to tear up under the strain of cross-examination. "Maybe I am bitter, but I have a right to be."

Molly looked at her notes and then at Nova. "No further questions," she announced, and returned to the counsel table. Now that Jennifer Sawyer's credibility had been severely compromised, there was no point in prolonging her agony on the stand.

Undaunted by his lead witness's slow collapse under cross-examination, Brockman spent the rest of the afternoon hammering away at the theme of Nova's irredeemable womanizing. Although Brockman informed the court that there were several other jilted women he could have called to testify, he announced that he had decided, "in view of the time pressures facing the court," to limit his presentation for the remainder of the day to two live witnesses.

The first, Teri Beale, was a curvaceous legal secretary Nova had met at a Friday afternoon office party hosted by an old attorney friend. Succumbing to a little too much champagne and tequila, Ms. Beale agreed to accompany Nova home for the evening, where, after some music and a nightcap, the inevitable occurred. She and Nova continued to date for two months before he stopped calling, and she finally came around to taking the hint that their affair was history.

Molly disposed of Beale quickly on cross, establishing that she never had been introduced to Jamie and extracting the concession that her relationship with Nova had been at all times one of consenting adults. "All things considered," Molly said to Nova in a hushed voice during a short recess after Beale had been excused, "she didn't hurt us much, apart from proving that you're a charter member of the Four F Club." She smiled at Nova and shook her head. "Find 'em, feel 'em, fuck 'em, and forget 'em. Sooner or later we're going to have to give you a makeover."

The day's final witness, Alice Tompkins, came close to providing Molly with the opening she was looking for. Unlike Jennifer Sawyer and Teri Beale, Alice was one of Nova's peers. A junior partner in a well-respected Century City law firm, with a six-figure annual income, she was his equal, if not more so, both professionally and intellectually. She was also Nova's last flame and the one with whom he had shared the longest relationship since his separation from Tami. Brockman's purpose in subpoenaing Tompkins was to show that over the past three years Nova had changed little in his attitude toward women and remained as incapable as ever of forming a lasting relationship. Once a horndog, always a horndog.

Like her counterparts, Tompkins was less than pleased at being dragged into the custody battle. As a lawyer long used to questioning others, however, she kept her testimony particularly well focused and somewhat guarded. Brockman took her through a crisp direct, establishing that she and David had met at a deposition in her office on a multi-party civil case and had begun dating shortly thereafter. They continued to see each other for about five months, "on a mutually monogamous basis." During her time with David she got to know Jamie, whom she saw with some regularity at Nova's home and on weekend outings to local parks and the zoo. She considered her a bright and well-adjusted child, but she also believed that Jamie resented her and, "for that matter, all of the women her father had dated since parting from her mother. In time," Tompkins added, "I thought Jamie would grow to accept me, but the situation became more and more uncomfortable. The decision to break things off between David and me was David's, but I also agreed it was for the best."

Molly's cross picked up exactly where Brockman's direct had ended, but with three times the intensity. "Your breakup with Mr. Nova didn't just come about by way of a slow attrition, did it?" she asked with a discernible edge in her voice.

"I'm not sure I understand the question," Tompkins answered defensively.

"In fact, there was a specific incident that precipitated the breakup, wasn't there?"

Tompkins replied in he affirmative, and Molly continued, "Jamie overheard you and David making love late one night and almost walked in on you, didn't she?"

Tompkins paused to consider her answer. Nova had promised that he would keep the incident strictly between them, and it was apparent from the way Brockman and Tami had pitched forward in their seats that until now he had kept his word. But this was a custody battle, the legal equivalent of war.

"We thought she was asleep, but it turned out that she was having a bad dream," Tompkins said, her fair complexion reddening with embarrassment. "We were both surprised. The lock to David's door was broken, but he managed to reach the door just before Jamie opened it. He got dressed, walked Jamie back to her room, and stayed with her until she went back to sleep."

"And the next morning, and for several days after that, David urged that the three of you—he, Jamie and you—sit down together and talk about your feelings and your differences?"

"Yes, he did."

"And you declined, didn't you?"

Tompkins cocked her head to one side and furrowed her brow. "I guess I had already decided that our relationship wasn't working out. I just wasn't ready to invest the emotional energy needed to forge a bond with David's daughter."

"And that's why David ended your relationship, wasn't it?"

"In his life Jamie was number one, and I would always be a distant second."

"I'll take that for a yes," Molly said, wrapping up her cross-examination on another high note. She hadn't exactly succeeded in showing that Nova was a candidate for a remake of *Father Knows Best*, but the look of surprise on Judge Goldstein's face was sufficient to tell her that she was making progress.

On redirect, Brockman tried to exploit the late-night incident as yet another sign of Nova's unfitness, but the afternoon was growing late and Judge Goldstein let it be known that she had heard more than enough on the subject. "It's already four-thirty, Mr. Brockman, and I intend to adjourn for the day," she announced with a show of irritation from on high. "I do hope you'll have something different for me tomorrow. This isn't a TV talk show, after all." She directed a stern gaze at both counsel tables and descended from the bench.

Molly and Nova waited for Brockman and Tami to leave the courtroom before making their own exit. Like any litigant, Nova was anxious to discuss the case and obtain Molly's assessment of their prospects. "You did a great job," he said as they pushed open the oversized double wooden doors of the courtroom and walked slowly down the public corridor outside en route to the elevator. "But you took a pretty big risk with that letter Jennifer Sawyer sent to me, don't you think?"

"What risk?"

"You didn't even read my note."

"Oh, that." Molly stopped and reached into her coat pocket with her free hand to retrieve the still uninspected sheet of lined legal paper. "Here," she said, handing the sheet back to Nova, "you read it to me."

Nova unfolded the note and read. "I threw the letter away. You don't have a copy to show the witness." The cramped, nearly illegible scrawl betrayed the urgency with which the missive had been penned.

Molly gave Nova a long, discerning look and heaved an exasperated sigh. "I knew that, and you knew that, but Jennifer Sawyer didn't. The way I see things, we're going to have to take a few risks if we have any chance of convincing Judy that you have a heart and mind as big and reliable as your dick." A slow smile spread across her lips as she took in the worry and doubt inscribed on his face. "But all in all, I think we managed to even the playing field a little today."

She gave him a pat on the back like an old fraternity buddy. "Go home and get some rest, and keep your thoughts pure."

Chapter Twenty-two

It was five o'clock by the time Nova climbed into his Lexus and picked up his car phone in the parking lot across the street from the courthouse. Although he had planned on making a quick trip back to his office to catch up on his own cases, he succeeded in rousing his secretary from the enigmas of her afternoon cross-words, and was relieved to learn that it had been a slow day.

"Only six calls in all," Sylvia Gomez told him, finishing up the last of her tea. "Three from lawyers confirming depos for next week, one from *West Law* about your subscription—it's behind again, surprise, surprise—one hang-up, and one from a reporter who wanted to know if you were going to come back here today after your custody hearing. He said he wanted to interview you. I told him I had no idea and that there was no way you were going to talk to anyone but your own lawyer about the case."

"Must have been someone from a sleazy tabloid," Nova replied.

"I don't know. He hung up before I could get his name. Sounded pretty nasty, though."

In the absence of any urgent business to command his attention, Nova was free to follow Molly's advice and drive home. He maneuvered the Lexus through the rush-hour traffic filling the surface streets, and plotted a course to the Pacific Coast Highway, eventually squeezing into the crowded column of cars, their brakes lights forming a river of red as they twisted their way toward the Malibu Colony and the turnoff for Topanga Canyon Boulevard that would, in due time, deliver Nova to his doorstep.

As he crept forward, he had plenty of time to think about the hearing. The day had gone well, as Molly had remarked, no doubt about it. Each time Brockman had tried to portray him as a middle-aged skirt chaser, she had managed to turn the tide, impeaching his spurned ex-lovers, drawing out the inconsistencies in their stories and making Nova seem—what were the right words?—like a normal single heterosexual male who valued the well-being of his daughter above all else. That might not be enough to carry the hearing, especially in front of an icicle like Judith Goldstein, but it was a strong start in the right direction.

Far more than anything that had transpired in court, Nova was annoyed by the call from the tabloid reporter seeking an after-work confessional. It wasn't that the call came as a total surprise. The custody dispute had garnered a small mention in *Variety* some weeks ago, and given Tami's ascending media star, it was only natural that some bottom-dwelling scribe would want to dish up the usual smut to advance his own reputation at the expense of the truth. Then again, maybe Tami had already talked to the bottom dweller, and he was merely calling back to get Nova's side of the story. Who knows what she might have said. When she was angry, as she was now, she was capable of saying just about anything. Nova mulled over the possibilities without reaching any particular conclusions until he pulled into his driveway at a little after six.

Like most residences in the rustic canyon, Nova's ranch-style home had an old-fashioned black metal mailbox mounted on a wooden post just outside the front gate. Noticing that the small red flag on the box had been raised, Nova exited the Lexus and walked back to the street to collect the postman's offerings. Among the bills, catalogues, and other inconsequential flyers from local supermarkets and home-and-garden supply houses was a thick nine-by-twelve envelope with a postmark from a small town in the Catskills. Both his address and the return were scripted in neat and legible juvenile handwriting that he immediately recognized as Jamie's.

Nova retrieved his briefcase from the Lexus and, with the mail tucked under one arm, unlocked the front door to his house and hurried into his study. He threw his sports coat onto the sofa along the far wall and settled into the swivel chair behind his desk, propping his feet up for comfort. Then he carefully sliced open the top fold of the envelope with the Swiss army knife he kept in the middle desk drawer and let the letter's contents spill into his hands.

There were ten color snapshots in all, accompanied by a four-page handwritten note on blue stationery bearing Jamie's name, imprinted and centered at the top in stylish black cursive script. Nova remembered ordering the paper and matching envelopes for her from a stationery shop downtown. He was pleased to see that she was making good use of the gift.

"Dear Dad," the letter began, "Everything at camp is still just as much fun as the last time we talked, except, maybe, that it rains a lot more out here than back home. We've even gotten a couple of thunderstorms, with lightning and hail!! But even then there's lots to do inside with arts and crafts, playing board games, listening to CDS, going to play rehearsal

(we're putting on a version of *Twelfth Night*), telling
scary stories, and watching old movies in the big old
barn the camp has converted into an assembly hall."

Jamie's mention of the word "home" brought a lump
to Nova's throat. L.A. was the only home Jamie had
ever known, but her use of the term was probably more
a force of habit than an intentional comment on the
major changes in her life that loomed only a few months
ahead. He pushed the thought aside and read on.

"To give you an idea of what a typical day is like,
we finish breakfast by eight, then it's off to horseback
riding, archery, hiking, or some other fun activity until
lunch. Afternoons are spent playing sports, mostly
baseball or swimming. We do our water sports either
in the camp pool or at the lake nearby. The lake is
real clean, and has a sandy beach for sunbathing and
picnics. The local people come there to fish and water
ski. By the way, one of the girls in my cabin has
loaned me her baseball bat, so if you haven't already
sent my bat from Little League, I can do without it.
The girl's name is Dorothy, and she's way cool. She's
from New York and goes to the same school Mom
wants to send me to in the fall."

Nova took his eyes off the letter and let his thoughts
drift. Jamie had asked about her bat several weeks
ago, and he hadn't even bothered to look for it. If
only for an instant, he felt like a neglectful parent who
had let his kid down.

Returning to the letter, he was surprised by the sudden shift in Jamie's tone. "I know I'm supposed to be
a little kid, Dad," she wrote, no longer sounding like a
ten-year-old kid with freckles and pigtails, "but I still
don't know how I feel about moving back here for good.
I love you and Mom very much, and just wish that we
could be a family again. Mom told me before I left for

camp that as you grow up, you have to get used to changes. I know that's true but it's still hard.

"I've taken a lot of pictures with the camera Mom bought me, and thought you'd like to have some. We start our trip to the Adirondacks next week. I'll take some pictures there, and I'll send you some more from camp, too . . . real soon. Until then, I hope you're happier than you seemed when I left for camp. Know that I will always love you." The letter was signed with age-appropriate triple Xs and Os and Jamie's name in a longhand style matching almost exactly the script on the letterhead.

Nova placed the letter on top of his desk and flipped through the snapshots. It had only been a month, but Jamie looked much older, especially in the photos of her playing ball and sharing sandwiches and soft drinks with a gang of other girls on a golden summer afternoon at what had to be the lake Jamie had mentioned. His little girl was growing up, and she looked happy, secure, and independent.

Nova, for his part, felt a mix of emotions—pride at how smart, caring, and poised Jamie was turning out to be; sadness, at moments bordering on panic, at the very real possibility that from this point forward, he would no long be able to experience Jamie's life directly but would do so only secondhand, through letters and photos like the ones he had just received.

After a quick tuna melt and a cold Carta Blanca, he dashed off a reply to Jamie on his computer. He told her how much he appreciated her letter and the photos, and how he remembered, back when he was a kid growing up in New Jersey, the rains that would break up the teeming heat and humidity of summers on the East Coast. "I remember my nana saying when I was just five or six that thunder was God's way of reminding people that he was up there watching us.

She was always saying things like that. Little beliefs she picked up from the old country. I don't know if she really believed them, or if she was just trying to frighten me and my sister so that we would grow up to be good adults. Speaking of rain, I don't think we've gotten a drop back here since last winter. The weather bureau says we could be in for another drought. I'm going to have to make sure the back hillside is trimmed to minimize the fire dangers by the time the Santa Ana winds kick in next fall."

Nova added a little more small talk about how he was going to start a new exercise program, and even join a softball league "for old guys." Then he passed to the custody hearing, knowing that Jamie would regard a letter in which he failed to mention the crucial subject as evasive or even phony.

Your mom and I are now in court, asking a judge if she should be allowed to keep you in New York, or whether you should live here with me. The court hearing should last about a week. In fact, by the time you get this letter, the hearing will likely be over. But whatever the judge decides, you have absolutely nothing to worry about. You will still have two parents who love you very much, and I'm sure the judge will rule that you'll be able to spend lots of time, during vacations and the summer, with the parent who isn't awarded custody during the school year. No matter what happens, you'll always have a home here with me. I'll keep your bedroom just the way you like it, and we'll be able to talk any time you want.

Your mom was right when she told you that growing up involves getting used to changes in

*your life. Sometimes it helps to ask if the changes
are necessary, but sometimes, like now, when
you can't avoid the changes, the best thing to do
is accept them, and even make them work to
your advantage. I know that you can do that, and
as always, I will be ready to help you in any
way I can.*

Nova promised to write again soon. "And changes
or no changes, you'll always be my little pumpkinface," he said in closing, invoking the special term
of endearment he had used in tender moments with
Jamie since she was tiny.

"Little pumpkinface," Randy said aloud, chuckling
above the commercials broadcast over the all-news
station on his car radio. "I like that."

Ever since Tanner's death Randy had adopted a
somewhat lower profile, and he felt that he still had
a lot of catching up to do if the rest of his plans were
ever to be realized. He had waited until after eleven
before making the drive from Tami's beachfront home
in Malibu to Nova's place in Topanga, timing his trav-
els with the silver-plated pocket stopwatch, with the
engraving of a giant steam locomotive on the back,
that he had inherited from his adoptive father. With
the traffic light and the roads dry and clear, the trip
had taken less than a half hour. That was a good sign,
better than even he had anticipated.

The fact that the red flag had been raised on Nova's
street-front mailbox was also a good sign, an unexpected bonus. Like many other Topanga residents,
Nova apparently used his mailbox not only to receive
incoming missives but to deposit outgoing mail as well.
Short of eavesdropping on phone calls, Randy be-

lieved there was no better way to plumb the depths of someone else's soul than to read their most personal thoughts. He had no way of knowing, of course, that Nova had a curbside mailbox, much less that there would be a letter to his daughter inside the box. This was, after all, his first visit to the Nova estate. But there it was, mailbox, letter, and all.

He felt as never before that he understood his former attorney, the nature of his anxieties and fears, the fragility of his pathetic hopes and dreams. Outside of his little girl, there really wasn't much to Nova's life. And despite the reassuring tone of his letter, Nova remained a man on the edge, just like Randy himself. Perhaps even more so. Just how far would Nova go if he really thought he'd lose the child? Of what aberrant acts of aggression, impulse, and irrationality was he capable if pushed just the right way? These were weighty questions, but ones that could only be answered in the fullness of time, and only with the right kind of preparation. Contingency and chance, Randy told himself, had brought him together with David Nova, but Ol' Randy was in the driver's seat now, literally and figuratively.

From his vantage point at the top of the narrow mountain road, Randy could see the lights of Nova's front and back porches. The air was still and filled with the scent of dry pine, eucalyptus, and sage. With the aid of a pair of high-powered binoculars purchased only that morning, the outline of the property looked clear and simple: two main entrances, front and rear, and probably a third, leading from the attached garage to the kitchen or a possibly a laundry room. There were no visible signs of a home-protection system, and the louvered windows on either side of the home seemed like easy pickings. Still, there was no reason to act hastily. He had learned the virtues of patience through his stultifying years in prison. He was not going to forget them now.

Randy waited on the hilltop until the news bulletin he had heard an hour earlier came over the radio once more. "Sheriffs in Riverside County," the anchorman announced in the same modulated voice with which he had delivered the last weather update only a few seconds earlier, "have reported lifting a fingerprint from the front door of a Hemet pharmacy that the FBI crime lab in Washington believes belongs to Randy Sturgis, the suspected kidnapper and killer of Ninth Circuit court of appeals judge Lawrence Tanner. The proprietor of the pharmacy, Rosalee Aquino, was brutally murdered as she prepared to close her store for the night. Authorities are not prepared to charge Sturgis with the Aquino homicide, too, but that possibility is now under active investigation by a joint local, state, and federal task force. Sturgis, a forty-six-year-old former nurse, is still at large and considered extremely dangerous."

Leaving the fingerprint behind was a mistake, the only real one he had made so far. He made a silent vow to redouble his efforts not to make another. He opened the glove box of his old Chevy and retrieved a brand-new tube of aloe vera lotion. He unscrewed the cap and proceeded to rub the lotion gently over his sunburned forearms. Spending too much time in direct sunlight was bad for his skin, he reminded himself. Health was a gift; he had to be more careful about that, too.

Satisfied that the night had been well spent, he stuffed Nova's letter and the tube of aloe vera inside the glove box, started up the engine, and slowly made his way down the canyon. Only an occasional mournful howl from one of the neighborhood canines echoing off the canyon walls gave any notice of his presence.

Chapter Twenty-three

"How could you!" Tami shouted. "What could you possibly have thought you'd gain?" Her blue eyes flickered with indignation, and the color rose in her cheeks, nearly matching the fever red of the silk blouse she wore under her snug double-breasted black blazer. The ligaments of her normally delicate neck added to the show of pique, stretching into unladylike sinewy cords as she yelled and balled her tiny right hand into a menacing fist. For an instant it almost seemed as though she might try to strike him.

The court clerk and the stenographer lifted their heads in unison from their styrofoam cups of morning coffee and danishes to gauge the severity of the ruckus. As they located the commotion's source, their lips curled into bemused half grins. They exchanged knowing looks and then quickly returned to their breakfasts. To less seasoned observers of the human condition under self-inflicted stress, the altercation might have seemed like the opening salvo of World War III. To them it was just another domestic show-down, predictable in its volatility, slightly titillating perhaps in its content, but ultimately unremarkable. "Been there, done that," the expressions on their faces seemed to say.

"I don't know what you're talking about," Nova snapped back. The early morning broadside had taken him completely by surprise. The fact that he had offered such fair-minded comments about Tami in his letter to Jamie only made the attack seem all the more vicious. He was in no mood to be trading insults, but he was more than capable of matching his ex-wife's decibel level. "You should save your outrage for the witness stand. It doesn't impress me."

"I don't think this is the time," Brockman cut in, gingerly inserting his heavyset frame between Tami and Nova like a nervous referee at an out-of-control hockey game. "I'm sure Ms. Carpenter agrees," he added, looking to Molly for collegial support.

"Oh, I don't know. I kind of enjoy a good blood-curdling scream before nine a.m. Gets the heart pumping and the juices flowing." Molly blinked hard in Brockman's face and gave him an astonished smile. "How about trying a little client control, Tom? Sometimes it really works."

Brockman nodded in assent and led Tami by the arm across the gallery to her place at the petitioner's counsel table in the interior of the courtroom.

"You really have no idea what she was squawking about?" Molly asked sotto voce as she and Nova took their seats at the opposing table.

"I got a letter from Jamie yesterday, asking about the hearing," Nova replied. "Tami probably got one, too. Maybe she didn't like what Jamie had to say. Apart from that, your guess is as good as mine."

Further speculation about the cause of Tami's histrionics was immediately tabled upon Judge Goldstein's entrance. "I understand that we've had a little verbal calisthenics," Her Honor remarked as she deposited her rangy torso on the bench and adjusted the position of her chair to secure much needed leg room. "Now that our exercise period is over, I expect everyone to proceed like grown-ups, or reasonable facsimiles." She let a cold stare settle on Tami and Nova. "Are we ready to proceed?"

"We are, your Honor," Brockman answered. He and Molly spent the next twenty minutes hammering out evidentiary stipulations regarding such matters as the introduction of Jamie's school records, and affidavits from the principal of her new school in Manhattan and from Tami's sister. After some initial disagreement over the weight to be given to the documents, the lawyers concurred that they could be received into evidence without the necessity of live testimony. Brockman then proceeded to call his witness for the morning session, Dr. Margaret Engstrom.

A slender woman in her late forties, with straight brown hair cut just above the shoulders and a pleasant smile that always put others at ease, Dr. Engstrom was a longtime member of the panel of psychiatric evaluators the family court relied on to furnish recommendations in child-custody disputes for a set fee paid by the parties. She was also a board-certified marriage and family therapist, and had a thriving private practice in addition to the cases she handled on referral from the court. "In this case," she explained in response to one of Brockman's opening questions, "I was privately retained by the parties rather than brought into the case through the court's psychiatric office."

"Did that make any difference in the way you approached your evaluation?"

Engstrom considered the question. "Substantively, the approach is the same. However, for financial reasons the amount of time I can devote to a matter referred by the court is limited."

"So if the parties can afford to hire you independently, as they did here, you can prepare a more thorough report?"

"That's often the case."

"And would you say that the report and recommendation you've prepared in this case are particularly thorough?"

Engstrom furrowed her brow. "I'd like to think so." With the court's permission, the witness summarized the history of her involvement in the case, explaining that she had been jointly retained by the parties roughly two and a half years ago, at the direction of the lawyers who had represented them in their original dissolution action. "Joint evaluations are quite common in custody cases," she explained.

"And that's what was done here?" Judge Goldstein broke in, intending to move the examination along.

"Yes. I conducted rather extensive interviews with both Ms. Dawson, Mr. Nova, and Jamie. I spoke to the child's teachers and visited both parents' homes. The interviews are summarized in the report I filed with the court at the time of the initial dissolution. As you know, I recommended that Jamie's parents be given joint legal and physical custody, meaning that, pending any significant change in family circumstances, they be permitted to work out the everyday details of how many days per week, or month, the child would spend with one parent as opposed to the other."

"Both parents seemed equally fit?" the judge asked, not willing as yet to turn the Q&A back to the lawyers.

"Each seemed fully committed to the child's well-being."

"But now the family circumstances have changed, haven't they?" Brockman asked, resuming his interrogator's role.

"Move-away cases like this are the most troubling for any evaluator, because they force us to make decisions that in an ideal world might be best avoided."

Engstrom interlaced her hands and tented her forefingers contemplatively at her lips before continuing. "For the most part, there's just no middle ground. In this case, placing Jamie's interests first, but bearing in mind the rights and feelings of her parents, I have recommended that the child be permitted to move to New York, and that she return to California to spend vacations and perhaps the summer with her father."

"And how did you arrive at this conclusion?"

"Although I had less time than I might have wanted to spend, what with the urgent nature of the move-away petition, I managed to re-interview the parents and Jamie, before she left for summer camp."

The doctor opened the thick work file she had taken to the witness stand and began to leaf through it. "Basically, I concluded that of the two parents, Ms. Dawson was in a better position to provide Jamie with a normal, everyday family life right now than Mr. Nova. Any way you look at the situation, however, the child is going to experience a difficult period of adjustment, so it's important for her to have as stable a home life as possible."

"What does Jamie have to say about her mother's move to New York?" Brockman asked next.

The question was a critical one, and Engstrom stopped to contemplate her answer. "As might be expected, Jamie would like parents to get back together, but she is a very mature child for her age and she understands that won't happen. She also understands that the purpose of this proceeding is to decide whether she will go to New York with her mother or stay with her father in Los Angeles. She absolutely refuses, however, to choose one parent over the other, and her parents—to their credit—have decided not to put her through the ordeal of coming to court and being forced to make a choice. Jamie has indicated that she will go along with whatever recommendation the court makes on the issue, and I am confident that she will."

"And is the custody recommendation that you have made in favor of Ms. Dawson clear and unequivocal?"

"It's clear, all right," Engstrom answered. However, before Brockman could utter the words, "Nothing further," she added, "But I'm not entirely comfortable calling the recommendation unequivocal."

Brockman could feel the reproachful eyes of Judge Goldstein descend upon him, exhorting him to invite the witness to elaborate lest she be forced to jump into the examination again and do it for him. "And why is that?" Brockman inquired, gazing back at Goldstein, small beads of perspiration forming on his forehead.

"A lot has changed for this family. The parents not only are divorced and living apart, but their relationship has become quite acrimonious. Where once there was an effort to compromise and cooperate, there is now suspicion and resentment on both sides. All of this has weighed on Jamie. My recommendation on custody, however, still stands."

After moving for the formal introduction into evidence of the doctor's original and supplemental written evaluations, Brockman thanked the doctor for her candor and quickly passed her on for cross-examination.

Molly stood for a moment at the lectern. Normally, this was the time in a trial when, as a litigator, she bared her teeth and tore into the flanks of her opponent's expert witness like a hungry beast on the scent of fresh meat. For a variety of reasons, however, Dr. Engstrom presented an elusive target. First, there was the fact that the good doctor had been jointly retained. Although she had come out in favor of Tami, there was no point in portraying her as a forensic whore out to sell her expertise to the highest bidder. Then there was the balanced nature of her opinion and the thoughtful manner of its presentation. She was a middle-of-the-road professional, who performed her job with care and respect for everyone involved. Nor was anything to be gained by assailing her credentials. Margaret Engstrom might not have been mistaken as one of Freud's great protégées, but she was a far cry from being a self-help psychobabbler.

Lacking any easy means of impeachment, Molly elected to zoom in on the "family circumstances" that served as the basis for Engstrom's recommendation. "Now, doctor," she began, "both Mr. Nova and Ms. Dawson are single, are they not?"

"Yes, of course," Engstrom answered. "Neither has remarried or formed a strong permanent relationship with another partner since the divorce."

"And they both have very demanding jobs that often require them to be away from home for lengthy periods of time."

"That's also true. But overall, Ms. Dawson still is in a better position to offer Jamie a more complete family environment."

"How is that?"

"Well, for one thing, her sister Barbara also resides in New York. It's my understanding that Barbara is married, with a teenage daughter of her own, and that Jamie is very close both to her cousin and her aunt. In fact, Ms. Dawson has signed a lease for an apartment in the same building as her sister. Mr. Nova has no comparable living arrangement here. His sister lives in Florida, and he has no family here."

"And yet isn't it true," Molly attempted to counter,

"that during the spring of this year, while Ms. Dawson was engaged in negotiations with her TV network for the move to New York, Jamie resided primarily with Mr. Nova?"

Engstrom nodded in agreement but with a skeptical expression on her face that gave advance warning that the agreement came with an important qualification. "I believe she spent slightly more time with her father, but that was at Mr. Nova's insistence, and even then, it's my understanding that he had to sign Jamie up for extended after-school care on the weekdays she spent with him."

"What about nannies or housekeepers?" Judge Goldstein interrupted, sounding slightly concerned at the mention of after-school care. "Were any available to either party?"

"That's another area I covered in my interviews, Your Honor," Engstrom answered agreeably. "Ms. Dawson has had the same housekeeper, on a live-in basis, since well before the dissolution. The housekeeper is quite fond of the child, and that fondness is mutual, from what I gather. According to Mr. Nova'"—she diverted her eyes momentarily to her file—"he has a cleaning service come to his home once a week. Here again, the more fully developed family setting has been provided by the mother."

Molly and Nova shared a quick look of frustration. Dr. Engstrom had defended her position effectively. It was time to change the subject.

"You don't consider it a sign of bad parenting, do you, that Mr. Nova has had relationships with other women since the dissolution?" The question was a bit of a gamble, coming on the heels of the lack of progress Molly had made with her earlier queries. If Engstrom replied that she, too, considered Nova's romantic liaisons inappropriate, Molly would be left with no alternative but to pursue an even more risky strategy of attempting to portray the doctor as a man hater or a prude. If Engstrom went the other way, however, her testimony would undercut Brockman's argument that Nova's womanizing made him unfit to assume custody of his daughter.

Engstrom tried to keep from smiling, as though she had been waiting for precisely that question all morning. "No, I don't consider Mr. Nova's dating as a sign of bad parenting," she said, giving Molly the opening she was hoping for. "And on this point I part company from the petitioner, who still feels very aggrieved by her ex-husband's success with other women. On the other hand, I don't consider Mr. Nova's dating to be a particular plus for his daughter either."

"But as far as you are aware, Mr. Nova has handled his dating interests with discretion, is that right?"

"Yes."

Feeling encouraged by the doctor's response, Molly decided to press ahead. "And I also assume, Doctor, that you have no quarrel with the line of work Mr. Nova is in, insofar as being a role model for his child is concerned."

"Of course not. Some of my best friends are lawyers," the doctor quipped, bringing a snicker to the lips of the court stenographer.

"And what about Ms. Dawson's TV show, have you ever seen it?"

Tami's back stiffened with the increasing harshness of Molly's tone, prompting Brockman to lay a reassuring hand on her arm.

"I have."

"And you are aware that the program often deals with provocative and sexually explicit subjects?"

"I am."

Molly took a step back from the lectern. She

stroked her chin with the fingers of her right hand for a second or two, as if uncertain of her next move, then fired off a verbal dart that was destined to nick a nerve. "Do you think that Ms. Dawson's role as a purveyor of that kind of sleazy entertainment is a particular plus for Jamie?"

The question had barely been asked when Brockman jumped out of his chair, arms waving, voice raised. "Objection. Argumentative and irrelevant."

Following her counsel's lead, Tami joined in the uproar. "That's really low, David," she yelled in her best stage voice, turning a face etched with exaggerated hurt and pain toward Nova. "First you have that reporter from the *Herald* call me at home, and now this."

"So that's what was bothering you earlier," Nova shot back, oblivious to Judge Goldstein's admonitions that order be restored. "That reporter called me, too, but I didn't talk to him and I most certainly didn't tell him to call you."

"You expect me to believe that?" Tami asked. Leaning toward him, almost to the point of tumbling out of her chair, she delivered her words more in the form of a challenge than a question.

Rather than take the bait, Nova turned his eyes away in disgust. Before he could turn them back, Molly had rejoined him at the counsel table, whispering words of calm while Brockman did the same with Tami. Then, as suddenly as the outburst had arisen, the parties and their counsel grew deadly silent, like a class full of contrite kindergartners who knew that they had misbehaved and would now have to face their teacher's wrath.

"You're going to have to slug that one out over lunch," Judge Goldstein said, pounding her gavel three times to make certain she had everyone's attention. "I'm going to sustain Mr. Brockman's objection, and then I intend to excuse Dr. Engstrom from this proceeding. I trust both sides have concluded their examination."

Brockman and Molly offered no objection, and the judge returned her gavel to its customary reclining position atop the bench. "We'll begin this afternoon with a small act of charity in the form of thousand-dollar donations to the county treasurer," Goldstein intoned as she prepared to adjourn the morning session. "I'm going to fine each of you, lawyers and litigants alike, as a sanction for your performances. Next time you act out in that fashion, you'll need bail money." She gave the assembled throng a sarcastic smile and descended from the bench, wishing "bon appetit" to all.

Chapter Twenty-four

"I like my tuna sandwiches with plenty of mayo. Just like Mother used to make."

Randy inspected Vera's progress with his lunch, making sure she was supplying just the right mix of ingredients, all the way down to the wafer-thin slices of tomato and the carefully rinsed leaves of Romaine lettuce with their spines cut away with surgical precision. Then he parked himself on one of the wooden benches of the breakfast nook in her kitchen and leaned back, propping his hands behind his neck and emitting a long, deep sigh of satisfaction.

"I'm really sorry about your mouth," he said a moment later, gesturing with a raised right forefinger toward the strip of shiny gray duct tape he had plastered across Vera's face and around the back of her neck. "I just can't take the chance that you might scream. You understand, I'm sure. Anyway, I'm one of those people who likes the sound of his own voice, so I don't mind keeping up your end of the conversation for you."

He laughed at his little joke and went on talking as she scooped a heaping tablespoon of mayonnaise into a large white ceramic bowl filled with canned chunk-style albacore. "I guess you think I owe you some kind of explanation."

She turned toward him and stared. She had been using a sharp, serrated kitchen knife to prepare the sandwiches, and it was still in her hand. Another set of knives, some considerably larger and no doubt just as sharp, was within easy reach, housed in a multi-slot polished hardwood block.

"If you're thinking what I'm thinking 'bout them knives," he said with a big smile, "I'd forget it. 'Ol Randy's learned a thing or two 'bout defending himself over the years. Up in the big house, he had to square off against more than a few of them big bucks with blood in their eyes and homemade shanks honed like razors in their paws."

He reached inside his long-sleeve, lightweight cotton jacket and nonchalantly removed a small-caliber pistol. "Besides, little mister equalizer here," he said, cradling the gun in his hand, "is always ready should the need arise. Not that I expect any trouble." He gave her a searching look and slipped the weapon back into its leather shoulder holster.

Vera laid the carving knife down on the food-preparation counter in front of her, placed one of the tuna sandwiches on a blue china plate, and carried it to him.

"Milk, please," he said after taking his first bite. "If you have any Hershey's, I'd appreciate it."

Vera returned to the fridge. As it happened, she had an old squeeze bottle of syrup she kept on hand for the gourmet french vanilla ice cream she often treated herself to. She poured Randy a tall glass of milk and stirred in a generous amount of chocolate. She handed him the glass and walked back to the counter, unsure of what to do next, her hands trembling with fear.

"Ah, just like Mom's," he remarked with contentment, wiping away a lactose mustache after downing three thirsty swallows. "Sit down, Vera," he said, pointing at the empty bench across from him. "I don't like eating alone." Both his tone and body language told her that he was on the verge of becoming annoyed. Acceding to his instructions, she slid onto the bench but tried not to engage his eyes.

"Now, about that explanation. Bet you're wondering how I knew you were home, and how I got in." He took another bite of his sandwich and grinned from ear to ear. "You see, I figured that after I sent Larry back to court, the police would keep a little eye out for your home for a while. My hunch was that the local sheriffs would draw primary responsibility for that kind of grunt work, seeing as how you live out here in Altadena. The feds have got more important stuff to take care of than to wait on the slim possibility that I might have been fool enough to show up any time soon."

She took a deep, anxious breath, and he added, "Oh, I can tell I hit that one on the money. I went away for a little while myself, and I thought that when I got back, the surveillance team would be reassigned, what with nothing happening and all, or that you'd even have gotten tired of seeing cop cars around and asked them to disappear yourself. Am I right?"

He grinned again and reached across the table, causing her to flinch and lift her arms defensively. Brushing her small upraised palms aside, he took her face in his right hand and gently but firmly turned it toward him so he could gaze directly at her. "You know I'm right. People can't hide the truth from me." She lowered her eyes and slowly pulled away as he released his grip.

"The gal who answered the phone at the court didn't want to talk at first, but I told her I was one of your cousins. She softened up some and said that you had retired," he added between bites, "or maybe that you were just on another leave of absence. I forget her exact words. Anyway, I drove out here this morning and waited until I saw you leave for the grocery store. Bet you didn't see me follow you. Then I waited until you went into the store, and I hightailed it back here."

He paused to look around the kitchen, like a real estate broker appraising a property for a potential quick sale. "You have a real nice place here, but if I were you I'd get rid of the French doors." He turned around and nodded his head toward the rear of the room, letting his gaze settle on the double wood-and-glass doors that led out to a flagstone backyard patio. "They're no match for ol' Randy." He shook his head. "And no security system, either. Just like David Nova. You know, he doesn't have one either. Some people just like to take chances, I suppose."

He saw a flicker pass across her eyes at the mention of Nova's name, and took the reaction as a sign of interest. "Oh, I've been out to Davey's house in Topanga, too, though I can't say I helped myself inside. It was late and dark, and, if you must know, I wasn't ready."

He wiped his mouth and carried his plate back to the sink before returning to his seat at the breakfast nook. "I guess that makes us like one big family. A typical American family of four, just like I used to have. You and Larry, me and David. More nuclear than an A-bomb."

He stopped to think, as if reconsidering his last statement, or as though he had become lost in some kind of personal reflection. "Well, maybe that's a little too Freudian," he said finally, "or would it be more Jungian? I'm never too clear on all the nuances. Still, there's no denying that I once counted on Larry." He gave her another long, searching look. "I know you counted on him, too. He told me. He let us both down."

As he had sounded on the videotape he had sent to the FBI, Randy's voice was suddenly shorn of the veneer of jocularity he had maintained up until now. No longer the jester, he seemed deadly serious, even sad. "Do you know what it's like to be locked up for years on end?"

He canvassed her face for the answer she could not voice, but he was able to discern little beyond dread and disbelief. "It's like living with a festering sore that never heals. The pain starts in the hollow of your stomach and burns its way through every nerve ending in your body. It follows you through the concrete exercise yards enclosed with barbed wire, the eight-by-ten cells with the steel wash basins and exposed toilets, the cell mates that cry in their sleep and piss on their sheets, the mess-hall food that isn't fit for a cockroach, the body-cavity searches, the gang rapes on the weaker inmates. No matter how many girlfriends come and visit, you spend each and every day waiting and planning, planning and hoping that something might happen to give you back your freedom and your dignity as a human being."

He clenched his right hand into a fist and brought it down crashing on the breakfast nook. The table wobbled from the blow, and the still unfinished glass of chocolate milk tumbled onto the floor, shattering into tiny shards on impact. Vera jumped back instinctively, nearly banging her head on the wall behind her, but she kept her eyes trained on Randy.

"For me," Randy resumed, his voice beginning to quake, "Larry was that hope. I lost my trial and all my appeals. Then, when I learned that Larry was on the Ninth Circuit panel that would hear my habeas petition, I knew my break had come. I read every published opinion in the field of criminal law that Larry ever wrote."

He smiled appreciatively and lifted his eyes to the ceiling as though gazing heavenward. "You probably typed each one of them, so you know what I mean when I say that he was the one judge who really seemed to care about people like me. Other judges might make a lot of noise about the constitution and the Bill of Rights, but the Honorable Lawrence Tanner understood that the system can make a victim out of anyone."

He leaned forward until he was close enough to smell her anxiety. "And then I waited. I waited until I received the decision." He reached inside his jacket, next to the shoulder holster where he kept his gun, and retrieved a photocopy of the Ninth Circuit opinion issued in his case. "This disgraceful collection of words and phrases.

"Four lousy pages," he announced, hastily unfolding the document and spreading it on the table. The opinion was divided into two parts. The first discussed the denial of the *Faretta* motion Randy had brought before his state court trial to relieve David Nova as his counsel and to represent himself. The second offered a brief but gruesome summary of the home-invasion murder and partial decapitation of Grace Cowley.

"This is what really galls me," Randy barked, flipping to the final page. Pointing at a passage underscored in red ink, he read from the opinion:

"Despite the depravity of the crime and the overwhelming evidence of guilt, the case law and the Constitution mandate that the petitioner's conviction be overturned. The court reaches this conclusion with reluctance and misgivings, mindful of society's paramount interest in eliminating the kind of predatory aggression that all too

*frequently places innocent victims at mortal
risk in their own homes. We are confident, however, that on retrial, the state will again prevail,
and this time on a record free from prejudicial
error."*

Randy shook his head and stared at the words, almost as if he had just read them for the first time and
expected them to change in response to his disapproval. "Can you imagine how I felt when I saw this?
There isn't another case in which Larry dressed down
a man who had been unfairly convicted. He lumped
me together with the common scum. He humiliated
me for all the world to see, just like my father did
when I was a kid."

He picked up the opinion and shook it angrily in
the air. "I had to make Larry understand how that
felt—what it's like to have your freedom and dignity
taken away and to place your hopes for deliverance
in the hands of someone else, only to be let down.
Like my father before him, I had to make Larry
humble."

His tirade completed, Randy grew silent. Slowly the
trademark sly grin spread back across his face. "In the
end I think Larry learned his lesson, but by then,
well . . . you know the rest." He looked at the spilled
milk and broken glass littering the floor, shook his
head and laughed softly. "Sorry about the mess. I'm
kind of the emotional type."

From behind the duct tape Vera tried to speak. The
sounds she made were indistinct and muted, and she
quickly tired of the effort. Under Randy's watchful
gaze she reached across the table for the memo pad
and pencil she kept for preparing grocery lists, and
scribbled a note. "What did you do to your father?"

Randy stared at the note and studied it long and hard. Was she truly interested or simply stalling for time? Her question took him by surprise and at the same time intrigued him. He couldn't ever recall anyone asking it before, not once. Not even the police back in his hometown. Could it be that this stranger, this frail little aging bundle of wrinkled flesh and porous bone named Vera Fletcher, sensed the truth? "You really want to know?" he asked.

She nodded her head.

"I killed him."

"But," she scribbled another hasty note, "I thought you found your parents dead."

"I see you've read the transcripts from my trial. That's what Davey told my jury. Even he doesn't know what really happened."

She raised an eyebrow, encouraging him to elaborate.

Randy leaned back and trained his eyes at the clock on the wall just above Vera's head. When he spoke again he did so with a flat affect, clinical and distant, almost as if he were telling a story about someone else. "My mother had been sick for months with ovarian cancer. She was dying. I came home one night late just after my father had injected her with an overdose of Demerol. I found him in their bedroom putting the syringe away. He saw me and told me to leave.

"I went downstairs and loaded up an old shotgun my father kept in the garage and brought it back to his bedroom. Then I placed it against his head as he was undressing, cocked it to the ready, and ordered him to inject himself with a dose of Demerol or I'd squeeze both barrels into the back of his skull. He hesitated a while and tried to talk me down, but after what he'd done to me, he knew that I meant business."

Randy curled the left corner of his lips and lowered

his eyes to hers. There was pain and hurt in his face, but he fought his way past them. "He used to say that I was his bad seed, and that I deserved all the abuse I got. He said it all the time. Of course, I wasn't his seed at all. I never knew my real parents. I made him apologize, and I watched as the poison entered his veins. My only regret was that my stepbrother wasn't there. I would have humbled him, too.

"That's about the size of it," he continued in a lighter vein, " 'cept that I filled up another syringe and injected my father with a second dose myself, after he fell asleep. Just to make sure. The cops never found the other syringe, and they never doubted my story that I found them just the way they died, in bed together, her in her cotton-print nightgown, him in his undershirt and slacks. It went into the books as a murder-suicide, the kind of thing that happens from time to time."

Vera flipped the pages of her pad and tried to finish another note, writing this time in large block letters: "WHY DID YOU CHANGE YOUR S—"

Before she could complete her question, Randy laid a hand on hers, removing the pencil in the process. "No more," he said calmly. "You know too much already."

She tried to speak again, more urgently than before, but with the same ineffectual result. She began to point to her waist and then to the door leading to the hallway, raising her eyebrows and making a soft honking sound from behind the duct tape.

"I was never much good at charades," Randy said in amusement, following her hand motions with his eyes. "Here, I'll let you write just one more note, but this is positively the last one." He handed her back the pencil.

Vera flipped the page and wrote: "I have to use the bathroom."

Randy chuckled loudly as he studied her script. "Nature has a funny habit of intruding at the wrong times, I guess. Okay, but you're gonna have to leave the door open just a crack. I'm sorry, but them's the rules."

He accompanied her out of the kitchen, down the hall, and into her bedroom, where he picked up a copy of the morning edition of the *L.A. Times* from the nightstand next to her bed. He rolled the paper into a thick scroll and wedged it against the doorjamb as Vera entered the bathroom. The paper left an open shaft of several inches as Vera closed the door behind her.

"You can turn on the water if you're nervous," he shouted through the crack. "It's a little trick my mom taught me." He waited at the door until he heard the sound of the running tap, then returned to her bed and picked up a copy of *Prevention* from the nightstand. "My girlfriend has a subscription to this one, too," he said as he began to leaf through a health and fitness story entitled "Nutritional Strategies for a New Century."

He became so engrossed in the article's discussion of tofu as an antidote for hot flashes that he was barely able to rise to a standing position as Vera emerged running from the bathroom. She came toward him recklessly, abandoning both hope and fear, flinging her slight frame forward, slashing the air with the exposed straight-edged razor Larry had left behind several years earlier. The duct tape, now partially peeled away, had left a garish red band across the lower third of her face. Through it she screamed, "I won't let you kill me."

Still gripping the magazine in his left hand, he raised

it to ward off the razor. Despite his advantages in size and strength, she grazed him lightly across the large knuckle of his hand. More unnerved than injured, he stepped forward and drove his right fist crushing into her sternum. She collapsed to the rug, gasping for air.

Randy stood over her, wrapping his injured hand with a white handkerchief pulled from the breast pocket of his jacket. This wasn't how things were supposed to go, he told himself. Still, there was little danger that anyone had heard her screams. A quick peek through the bedroom curtains confirmed that the neighborhood remained calm, completely unaware of his presence.

Deciding that the time had come, he removed a feather pillow from the bed and lowered it onto her face. She struggled briefly against his weight, but quickly succumbed, losing consciousness inside ninety seconds. Satisfied with his handiwork, he lifted her up and placed her gently on the bed, where he undressed her, removing her shoes and jeans as well as her blouse. After a brief search of her closet, he returned with a cotton-print nightgown and, with the skills he had mastered as a nurse, slipped it over her shoulders and smoothed it down over her waist and thighs. Then he reached for the hypodermic and the vial of clear liquid he had stuffed inside his jacket pocket several hours earlier.

"I have a poem I think you'll like," he said as he inserted the needle into her forearm, filling a prominent vein with a lethal dose of pure Demerol. When he was certain the deed had been completed, he retrieved the straight-edged razor from the floor, folded it up, and placed it in his right hip pocket. It would make a nice souvenir. "All in a day's work," he told himself as he left the house through the rear door, and it wasn't even one o'clock.

Chapter Twenty-five

Calm and poised, Tami began her testimony as if the morning uproar had never happened. Brimming with confidence, she had her stage face on, her luxuriant blond mane meticulously groomed, her blue eyes radiant and alive, as though she were facing the floodlights and delivering a confessional to an audience of devoted fans.

Responding in short, measured replies to Brockman's businesslike questioning, she explained that she had met Nova while she was still employed as an investigative reporter with the *Los Angeles Times*. "I was assigned to cover one of David's civil trials—he was representing a city councilman accused of sexual harassment. We started dating after the jury came back with a defense verdict, and he asked me to marry him six months later."

"That was eleven years ago?" Brockman asked for clarification.

"Give or take a month or two. Jamie was born the following year, in the spring. David and I lived together in a home in Topanga Canyon before our separation."

"And during the time you lived under the same

roof, what kind of husband and father was Mr. Nova?"

The question was both obvious and routine, but was nonetheless loaded with explosive potential. Nova fixed his gaze on Tami, anxious to see if she would use the opportunity to launch another direct assault on his character. To his considerable surprise, she opted for continued moderation.

"At least in the early years, David was kind, supportive, loving, and loyal," she answered, brushing a wayward strand of hair off her forehead. "We were a dual-career family, and he tolerated that much better than most men I know."

"Did something happen to change how you felt about him as a father and a husband?"

"Our relationship hit the skids, you might say, almost from the moment my TV career began."

"How did your career begin?"

Judge Goldstein grimaced at what she thought might turn into a lengthy tangent. "Briefly, if you don't mind, Ms. Dawson," she admonished.

"Because of my work with the *Times,* I became a regular guest on a local public-affairs talk show aired by one of the network affiliates," Tami answered, affecting an air of fond recollection, as if recounting her rise to stardom in a cozy chin-wag with Barbara Walters. "It was kind of a fluke, but shortly thereafter I subbed in for the show's host after he came down with a serious illness. One thing led to another, and one of the producers told me he was looking for a fresh female face to head a new syndicated evening talk show. I auditioned. The ratings were solid, and I haven't looked back since, as they say in the trade."

"How did Mr. Nova react to your career change?"

Tami hesitated. A frown spread across her heretofore cheerful face as she seemed to contemplate the distasteful memory. "He acted like a man who thought his wife was being unfaithful."

"What specifically did he do?"

"He began calling the studio, interrupting meetings and tapings. When I had to travel, he would sulk for days on end, give me the cold shoulder when I returned. He became highly critical and insulting about my shows and the way I dressed. The more popular I became, the more angry and condescending he got. I just don't think he could handle the fact that his wife made more money and had a more high-powered position than he did. Finally, I just couldn't take it anymore. We agreed to try marriage counseling, and when that didn't work, I moved to Malibu."

"Your Honor." Molly stood to raise her first objection of the afternoon. "This is a custody hearing. The issue here isn't whether Mr. Nova was an ideal husband, or why the parties filed for divorce. Counsel's questions are not relevant."

"You point is well taken, counsel," Judge Goldstein replied. "Nonetheless, I think that the relationship between the parties has some bearing on the custody issue, and where it would be best for the child to live. I do believe, however, that I've heard enough in this area for the time being. It's time to move on." She directed a stern gaze at Brockman.

"Yes, Your Honor, I quite agree," Brockman replied. Turning back to Tami, he asked, "How did Mr. Nova's changed attitude affect his relationship with your daughter?"

Tami paused for a moment, giving the impression of someone who wanted her answer to be absolutely accurate and fair. "David remained kind and caring with our daughter, but he began almost immediately to see other women, and I had some misgivings about that—especially when he hooked up with Jennifer

Sawyer, the woman who testified earlier in this hearing."

"And why was that so significant?"

"Well, apart from the fact that Jennifer's daughter was good friends with Jamie, David and I were still in counseling when their affair began." For the first time that afternoon she looked wounded and aggrieved. "We were talking with our therapist about trying to get back together, and here he was hitting on one of the moms from his peewee baseball team. And he did it behind my back. I didn't even know until Jamie told me. Can you imagine how I felt?" Her eyes began to moisten, and for a moment she was unable to continue.

"Did Jamie ever say anything to you about how she felt about her father's behavior?"

"She told me her father's behavior made her feel sad, that she wished we could still be one happy family together. That's the first time I began to wonder if David was in, all respects having a good influence on our daughter."

"And yet you agreed, did you not, to share legal and physical custody of Jamie after your divorce?"

Withdrawing a blue lace handkerchief from the inside breast pocket of her jacket, she began to daub her eyes. "I believed it was very important for Jamie to have a full relationship with her father. She loves him very much. So I spoke with David and told him how I felt about his relationship with Jennifer. I told him I thought it was indiscreet."

"How did he react?"

"He told me he agreed, and he said the affair was already over. So I agreed to joint custody."

"Did any of his affairs, subsequent to the divorce, concern you?"

"Of course, but I tolerated them, and I never tried

to modify our custody arrangement until I learned that my show was relocating to New York this fall."

"Why do you think that Jamie would be better off going to live with you than she would be staying here with Mr. Nova?"

This was the million-dollar question everyone had been waiting for, and Tami took a deep breath before delivering her well-prepared answer. "First of all, I think that between David and me, I am in a far better position to understand and respond to the emotional needs of a ten-year-old girl. I think I provide a strong role model for her and that I will continue to do so as Jamie gets older. Beyond that, I'm in a superior position to provide Jamie with a family environment than David."

"In what ways?"

"I've taken out a lease on a very nice apartment in the same building where my sister lives. Jamie is very close with both her aunt and her cousin Emily, who is a few years older. So she'll have an extended family-support system already in place. She's made new friends at summer camp, and her new school is prepared to welcome her with open arms. And I intend to spend more time at home than I've been able to the last few months while the plans to relocate my TV show were being finalized."

"Do you and Jamie have any special activities that you enjoy doing together."

Looking more and more like a woman in her element, Tami broke into a warm and easy smile. "There are so many things. We enjoy shopping and talking, decorating the house for birthdays and holidays. A lot of 'girl' things like that. I've also gotten her started on dance and piano, and I make it a point to read with her almost every night, even when I'm busy at the studio."

"I take it when it comes to Jamie, you place a high value on the continuity of care, is that right?" Brockman directed a surreptitious glance at Molly, as if the question were a prelude to a new and unexpected angle of attack.

"I most certainly do. That's why I've employed the same housekeeper for practically all of Jamie's life. Yolanda—my housekeeper and, I might add, my friend—is like a grandmother to my daughter. She's lived with us ever since the separation, and I never have to worry about the quality of Jamie's care when I'm away."

"But what's going to happen with Yolanda when you move?" Palms and eyebrows raised, Brockman had the countenance of a worried uncle.

"That's a good question," Tami answered with a smile. "I've asked Yolanda to move back with me, and it's my understanding that David has asked her to come live with him if he's awarded custody."

Nova leaned in close to Molly as Tami finished her response. "I meant to tell you," he whispered. "I guess I should have known it would come up." Molly shook her head and sighed, but said nothing.

"I'm still waiting for a definite answer," Tami added. "Yolanda is from Guatemala and has family members both here and on the East Coast. I'm certain I have the inside track on persuading her to come to New York. She'd have her own room, and both she and Jamie would love to remain together." She sounded confident but neither smug nor threatening.

"I'd like to shift subjects somewhat at this point, Ms. Dawson," Brockman said next in a conversational tone. After allowing ample time for his announcement to register, he asked, "How did Mr. Nova react when you informed him that you were moving to New York and intended to take Jamie with you?"

"He told me that there was no way he would ever permit that without a fight, even if it meant he had to ruin me."

"Did he explain what he meant by that term, 'ruin'?"

Tami straightened up in her seat in a demonstration of seriousness. "No, and I didn't ask, either."

"And yet Mr. Nova allowed Jamie to spend the summer back East?"

"That was something he had agreed to before the decision to relocate the show was made. Jamie was really counting on it, and to David's credit, he kept his promise."

"Has Mr. Nova engaged in any kind of hostile behavior toward you in recent months?"

The question brought another rise out of Molly. "Unless counsel can connect any alleged behavior on the part of my client to his fitness as a parent, the question is irrelevant."

"I'm sorry, I disagree," Judge Goldstein responded, summarily overruling the objection.

"I'm not quite sure where to begin," Tami answered, appearing to search her recollection. "He's accused me repeatedly, and once or twice in front of Jamie, of making late-night hang-up calls to his house."

"What kind of calls?"

"He says I call him to see if he's sleeping with anyone." She shook her head in a show of disgust.

"Are you saying that you've never made any hang-up calls to Mr. Nova?"

"Apart from one or two where I may have inadvertently dialed the wrong number out of habit, no. Yet David adamantly insists that I have. I don't know if one of his other girlfriends is playing pranks, or if the accusations are just his way of embarrassing me or turning Jamie against me."

"Has he done anything else to upset you?"

Tami mulled over the question. "Well, there was the matter of the tabloid reporter who called me at home about this hearing."

"We've heard enough about that already, I should think," Judge Goldstein interrupted before Tami could elaborate. "If there's anything else, however, let's have it."

"I wasn't going to bring this up, but I think it's important," Tami replied haltingly. "David came to the studio a few weeks ago, practically interrupting a show, to accuse me of having a relationship with the man who kidnapped and killed that federal judge."

"Are you referring to Judge Tanner?" Goldstein asked. Wide-eyed and incredulous, she sounded startled right down to the hem of her robes by Tami's revelation.

"David told me that the FBI thought the kidnapper might be receiving help from a woman. He made it sound like both the FBI and he thought I might be that woman."

"Is there any truth to the allegation?" Brockman inquired, resuming control of the examination.

"The allegation is completely absurd," Tami answered firmly, "and I seriously doubt anyone connected to law enforcement places any credence in it. I interviewed the kidnapper in prison a long time ago, when we were still married, in connection with some stories I wrote for the *Times* on women who fall in love with convicts. I won an award for the articles, I might add."

"Didn't Mr. Nova already know that you had interviewed the man?" Brockman asked.

"No, I never told him. The man was once David's client. I was afraid David would be angry with me."

"How did it feel to have that kind of accusation dropped on you in the middle of work?"

Tami blinked hard and took a breath. "It upset me greatly. I couldn't help but think that David was trying to stress me out to gain an advantage for this hearing."

"Tell the court, if you will, Ms. Dawson, what kind of custody arrangement you believe would be in the best interests of your child in view of your impending move to New York."

"I don't think there's any question that Jamie's best interests would be served by coming with me. As for David, I believe that for all his shortcomings, it's important for him to have a continuing personal relationship with Jamie."

She stopped to think, perhaps to give added weight and fairness to her words, perhaps to create the false impression that her answer was anything but calculated and well rehearsed. "I would be willing to have her fly back to Los Angeles for vacations and part of the summer, provided that David sets aside ample quality time to spend with her."

Brockman thanked Tami. "That's all I have for Ms. Dawson, Your Honor. The petitioner rests." He gave the court a respectful nod and returned to his seat.

Like Dr. Engstrom before her, Tami had done a superlative job, even-handed and persuasive, on direct. Drawing on the performance skills she had honed as the new sweetheart of talk TV, she had conveyed all the key emotions—loving and warm, hurt and vulnerable, stern and determined at all the appropriate junctures. Unlike Engstrom, however, she presented a broad target for cross. There was also no reason for Molly to treat her with the kind of kid gloves she had reserved for the doctor. This could be, Molly thought as she walked to the lectern, her last best chance to alter the outcome of the hearing. It was time to knock the halo off Tami's golden locks and expose her for the self-centered bitch she was.

After extracting some mild concessions about how happy and well rounded Jamie's young life had been in Los Angeles, Molly served up a zinger that sounded like a declaration of war. "This move to New York," she asked, locking on Tami's eyes the way a boxer tries to stare down an opponent before a fight, "it isn't about protecting Jamie's best interests, is it? It's about advancing yours."

Despite all the time she had invested preparing for the hearing, and all the years she had spent on TV learning to think on her feet, the question made Tami visibly uncomfortable. Shifting her gaze from Brockman to Goldstein and then back to Molly, she crossed her arms and hugged her chest. "I don't think there's any conflict between Jamie's interests and mine," she answered after a short pause.

"So whatever is best for your career also is best for Jamie, is that what you're saying?" Molly stepped up the pressure.

"Well, to a certain extent, I think that's true," Tami answered haltingly, wary that she might be following Molly blindly into some kind of lawyer's trap. "I am her mother, after all. But I'm mindful that Jamie's her own person."

"And you're mindful also that Jamie will have to leave her friends and her school behind and undergo a difficult adjustment to life in New York, are you not?"

"Jamie is a very resourceful girl, Ms. Carpenter. I'm sure she'll adjust just fine. And besides, she would have to undergo an even more difficult life change if she stayed behind in L.A. with her father while I relocated without her."

"But wouldn't you agree that Jamie would be better off if you had decided not to relocate and your daughter were not faced with an adjustment that everyone concerned believes will cause her pain and anxiety?"

Tami unfolded her arms and placed her hands, palms down, on her lap. She was settling in, adjusting somewhat to Molly's combative style. "Perhaps, but the decision to move my show has been made, and one way or the other, Jamie's life is going to change."

"Whose decision, exactly, was it to relocate the show?"

"The producers and the network," Tami answered quickly. "The thinking was that we had pretty much mined our base of stories in Southern California and needed some fresh input that could only come from moving back East."

"And what input did you have in that decision?"

"It wasn't my decision to make."

"Are you telling this court that the star of *O Darling!* wasn't consulted in advance about moving her show three thousand miles away from the only home her ten-year-old daughter had ever known?"

Realizing she had overstated her position, Tami looked to Brockman for help. Responding to her silent plea, Brockman stood, objecting loudly that the question was argumentative. The protest, however, was promptly overruled.

"I'll allow the question," Goldstein declared from the bench. "However, I would caution you, Ms. Carpenter, to modulate your tone. "This isn't *Perry Mason.*" At Goldstein's direction, the court reporter read back the question.

Tami reluctantly answered, "Of course I was consulted."

"And you didn't raise any objections to the proposed move, did you?"

"No, I did not."

"And that's because you thought the move would be good for your ratings and good for your career, true?"

The questions had come full circle. Flustered and beginning to weary, Tami looked like a person who had been outfoxed by a superior adversary. "I never once thought that the move would hurt Jamie, and I would never have agreed to it if I thought she would be hurt."

"Is that because you were thinking only of yourself?" Molly asked icily.

Tami was spared the necessity of replying by the intervention of Judge Goldstein, who advised Molly that her point had been made, and to move on to another subject.

Complying with the court's directive, Molly flipped a page in her legal pad, and offered a weak apology. "On direct examination," she asked, locking eyes again with Tami, "you stated that you thought you were a good role model for your daughter."

"That's very true."

"Tell us, if you would, then, how often you take your daughter to the studio to watch you work."

"On occasion, when the subject matter is appropriate."

"What kinds of subjects would that be?" Molly raised her eyebrows in a gesture of expectation and incredulity.

"We've had shows on overcoming physical handicaps. I took her to view the taping of one of those, dealing with blind people who have achieved success in the professions. I also remember taking her with me when we did a program about gifted children who have skipped grades in school and what effect that had on their social development."

"Let's see," Molly said, flipping over another page of her legal pad. "I've obtained a printout of a list of your shows from the past year. There are some pretty catchy titles: 'Brotherly love: What happens to a family when two brothers fall in love?' 'I was a teenage call girl.' 'Do drugs really make your sex life hotter: meet six addicts who swear they do.'"

"Is there a question pending?" Brockman interrupted, rising again to his feet.

Judge Goldstein gazed expectantly at Molly.

"Yes, there is," Molly replied. "How can anyone who makes a living peddling this kind of trash call herself a role model to a little girl?"

"That's totally improper, Your Honor," Brockman cried out.

The question, however, had sparked a fire in Tami. With color rising in her cheeks, she pitched forward in her seat, tilting her head toward the bench. "If you don't mind, Your Honor, I'd like to answer Ms. Carpenter's question."

Receiving Goldstein's permission, she continued, "It's quite true that we deal with some very adult and racy topics on the show. But the subjects we discuss, and the people we invite on stage to share their experiences, are real. No one likes subjects like incest or drug abuse, but they are part of the fabric of this society. So what if we dress up the topics with a little humor and make them entertaining? No one gets hurt, and in the end people come away with a greater understanding and appreciation of important topics that other TV shows ignore. We reach millions of people each day. And no one has ever pretended—me least of all—that our programming in general is suitable for children."

Tami sank back into her seat, satisfied with her efforts at self-defense. "If what I do makes me an inappropriate role model, then so be it. But by the same token, I don't think I'd want Jamie tagging along with her father to court very often to hear the kinds of gruesome tales people tell in trials every day of the week."

"Tit for tat, Ms. Carpenter," Goldstein interjected. Drawing back the left cuff of her black robe, she lowered her eyes to the digital readout of the sensible Seiko strapped around her bony wrist. "It's four o'clock, and once again time to move on."

"Just one more area, and I'll be through," Molly promised. Glancing back at Tami, she hurried to put the finishing touches on her cross. Quickly, she forced the admission that Tami might have "overreacted" when she accused David of conspiring with the tabloid reporter to disturb her at home. She also moved Tami to acknowledge, "on further reflection," that she might have made as many as a half dozen hang-up calls to David's home, "either by mistake or to make sure that David was really at home on nights Jamie was sleeping at Topanga."

"And with regard to the man accused of kidnapping Judge Tanner," Molly asked, her voice rising as she hit the home stretch, "you also acknowledge that you visited with this same man while he was in prison in order to obtain background information on a series of articles you wrote for the *Times*."

"Yes, I do," Tami answered forthrightly, like a tried and true member of the press. "He agreed to speak with me only on condition that I refrain from mentioning him in the stories."

"How many times did you meet with him for this background information?"

Tami twisted her lips to one side, as if trying hard to recall. "I don't know. It was a long time ago."

"More than once?"

"Yes, but I really can't say how many times."

"More than a half dozen?" When Tami failed to reply, Molly refused to let up. "Less than a half dozen? More than two?"

"Definitely more than two," Tami replied, color rising again in her face. "Probably three or four."

"Did you meet with any other prisoners you interviewed for your stories that many times?"

"No, I don't believe so."

"And you never told Mr. Nova that you were meeting with this prisoner, even though you were still married at the time?"

"That's correct."

Molly took a half step back from the lectern and raised her right hand to her chin. "Let me see, now . . . You've told us you might have overreacted to the call you received from the reporter; you've acknowledged that you might have made a half dozen hang-up calls to my client; and you recall meeting with the kidnapper of a federal judge three or four times. In light of all that, is it still your contention that my client, in questioning you about the hang-up calls and your involvement with this prisoner, was trying to harass you in order to gain an advantage in this hearing?"

"It was the *way* he confronted me," Tami answered, sounding aggrieved. "He came onto the TV set and all but accused me of having an affair with the kidnapper."

"You don't think David had a right to know what you were doing with this man in state prison?"

Tami pulled herself to an upright posture and tossed the hair off her eyes with a flick of her head. "No. Frankly, I don't."

"And yet," Molly countered, "you feel it's perfectly appropriate to parade all of David's relationships before this court like so much dirty laundry, don't you?"

"Objection, argumentative," Brockman exclaimed as Tami did a slow boil on the stand.

"Withdrawn, Your Honor," Molly snapped back, sparing herself the tedium of another lecture on courtroom protocol from her adversary. "I think we've made our point sufficiently." She looked at Nova and offered him a cunning half smile. Though the odds were still against them, they remained in the hunt.

That was the good news. The bad was that Tami had weathered her storm on the stand. While she had tripped and stumbled in spots, there was no denying that she had shown Jamie would be well looked after in New York.

Chapter Twenty-six

Even for a man who spent half his waking hours railing against the world and everyone in it, Ben Tanner was having a rough evening. He knew that under the terms of his contract with the Alpine Convalescent Home, he was subject to daily visits from nurses and attendants, and that the visits might occur at virtually any time of the day. He was used to the way his caregivers would poke and prod him in the most embarrassing places, take his pulse, listen to his heart, and occasionally insist on walking away with specimens of urine and blood. But he had given strict instructions to the management that he was never to be disturbed on his balcony at sunset. "That balcony's my safe haven," he had told the staff in one of his more demanding moments. Now management had violated his last refuge.

"Jesus Christ," Ben complained, "can't you people find a better time for this?"

"You can go back to watching your birds in just a minute, sir," Nurse Chamberlain replied, "as soon as I finish taking your blood pressure." Chamberlain walked to the side of Ben's deck chair. He adjusted the cuff around Ben's withered left arm and began pumping. "One-eighty over one-twenty," he commented grimly when the reading was finished. "I'm going to recommend that your doctor increase your medication."

"Do whatever the hell you like," Ben growled back. "I'm so full of synthetic substances, my piss has permanently turned green." His torture over, he raised his binoculars to his eyes, searching for a last glimpse of his favorite jays and warblers.

Chamberlain chuckled in spite of Ben's show of pique. "Of all the patients I tend here, I think I'm going to miss you the most."

Startled by Chamberlain's announcement, Ben dropped his field glasses in his lap and turned to face the nurse. "I'm sorry to hear that, Noah," he said in what passed for him as a friendly tone. "You're not like all the other jackasses around here. You know how to mind your own business."

Chamberlain smiled broadly. "I'm glad you appreciate that."

"What's the matter?" Ben asked, not ready to let the nurse go. "Get into an argument with Ms. Cates?"

Chamberlain gave Ben a curious look.

"The woman's a harpie," Ben continued. "I don't know how she ever got to run a hospital. Hates anyone who has a mind of their own, too, from what I can tell. They're a lot of people like that these days."

"It's nothing to do with Ms. Cates. I just think it's time for me to move on," Chamberlain said, without really answering Ben's question. He finished packing up his medical equipment and laid a comforting hand on Ben's shoulder. "It's been good to know you, sir. I'm sorry about what happened to your brother."

"The world's become an ugly place, Noah," Ben said, his head shaking involuntarily as he spoke. "But some might say Larry got what was coming to him.

He always loved to throw his weight around. Live by the sword, die by it, they say."

"Try not to upset yourself," Chamberlain said as he stepped from the balcony into Ben's apartment. "I'll lock the door on my way out."

"There's just one other thing, Noah," Ben called out after the nurse. "Don't ever get old. You either wind up getting done in like Larry, or you end up like me, talking nonsense to people like you and the FBI."

"We have to hit her where it hurts, even if it gets ugly," Molly insisted between bites of her antipasto. The selection of a pricey Italian restaurant—one of the trendy new bistros lining the east side of Ocean Avenue in the heart of Santa Monica—was her idea. A little dinner confab to review Tami's testimony, then a good night's sleep. When it came time to put on their side of the custody case Thursday morning, they'd be ready to roar.

"It already is ugly," Nova said, taking a breather from his starter of fried calamari. His tone said it all. He was tiring of the courtroom combat.

As his words hung in the air, Nova gazed idly out the front window across the street to the Promenade— the grassy, palm tree-lined pedestrian thoroughfare built on the bluffs overlooking the Pacific. Groups of gray-haired, stoop-shouldered senior citizens had gathered on the walkway's wooden benches and around cement card tables, feeding the pigeons, plying their luck at pinochle and canasta, trading the latest news about who was scheduled for surgery or a visit from the grandkids. Clustered within easy panhandling distance of the old folks, ragtag collections of homeless people had staked out strategic spots under the palms. Some were actively begging, holding up styrofoam cups for alms from passersby. Others were stretched out on dingy, threadbare blankets, catching a few fitful minutes of sleep before nightfall. Still others were seated cross-legged or simply standing, staring blankly off into space as if locked in deep meditation, their weathered faces, soiled clothing, and worn shoes offering mute testimony to the unremitting hardness of their lives.

An occasional pair of brightly clad joggers, outfitted in the latest running shoes and leisure wear, bounced across the scene, conscious of the elderly and the down-and-outers around them only as physical obstacles to be avoided in the greater pursuit of flatter abs and tighter glutes. Farther in the distance, the ocean was littered with the fiberglass boards and wet-suited bodies of suntanned surfers. They bobbed in the waves like schools of frolicking black seals. Above them all, the sun had begun its diurnal plunge into the sea, throwing pastel streaks of pink, yellow, orange, and blue across the low-slung summertime clouds hugging the horizon.

Molly took a moment to assess Nova's mood. *Anywhere but here,* his face seemed to say. Such wistfulness was always a bad sign for a litigator in the midst of a hotly contested trial. "You think I was too hard on Tami, don't you?" she asked.

"Maybe a little at the end."

"Really?" She laid down her fork and dabbed her mouth with a white cloth napkin. "I thought I was pretty darn restrained, considering the hatchet job they did on you with your ex-girlfriends." She gave him another searching look. "David, you didn't hire me to play patty-cake."

"I know," he conceded.

"Then buck up," she said before he could do any more whining. She smiled, not like a lawyer trying to encourage the flagging spirits of a client, but as a friend. "The way I see it, three witnesses—that's all we need—and we're on to closing argument. Judy's losing her patience, and we don't want to rile her any more than she already is. If we have to offer anything else, we can do it by declaration."

"Sounds like a plan," Nova replied after considering the matter for a few seconds.

"We'll start with Janet Simpson, Tami's old assistant. Then you'll take the stand. I expect an award-winning performance." Molly took another bite of food. "Then we'll end with Sandy. She's promised to make it to court by the afternoon. If all goes well . . ." She raised her eyebrows and cocked her head. "Your biggest worry come September could be finding a carpool for Jamie's daily commute to school."

Nova nodded in agreement, and they drank on it, Molly lifting a glass of expensive Napa charddonay, and Nova emptying the last of a double shot of his preferred single-malt Scotch.

Chapter Twenty-seven

If Molly's goal was to "hit Tami where it hurts," she was right on target the following morning. After a brief but stinging opening statement, in which she promised to "unmask" the real Tami Dawson, she commenced her case in chief with the ideal leadoff witness in Janet Simpson. With the possible exception of Nova, Simpson was the one adult who knew Tami best, from the inside out. She was also more than willing to testify under oath that underneath the perky, socially conscious image Tami projected, the host of the *O Darling!* show was a cold and calculating narcissist with no loyalties except to herself.

A plump, slightly overweight woman in her mid-forties, Simpson was the polar opposite of her former boss, and not just in girth. Whereas Tami was blond and bubbly, Janet was dark-haired and reserved. Whereas Tami sought the limelight, Simpson was content to aid the career of a rising star from the shadows, seeking nothing more than a competitive salary and a little well-deserved recognition.

"We were like sisters," Simpson told the court after explaining that she had been Tami's personal assistant for three TV seasons until she was abruptly dismissed from Tami's service two months ago. "We did everything together, from shopping for new clothes to crying on each other's shoulders."

Molly established that Simpson also had gotten to know Jamie well through her friendship with Tami, and that over the years she had observed Tami's interactions with her daughter both at the TV studio and at home. Then she asked, "How did Tami treat Jamie when the three of you were together?"

"It would depend," Simpson answered, warming to the opportunity to tell all.

"On what?"

Simpson stared coolly at Tami, and answered, "On whether she had more important things happening at the moment. Tami always came first."

Goldstein overruled an objection from Brockman, and Simpson continued, "I was frequently asked to fill in for Tami at school functions, like class plays or ballet recitals when Tami had to cancel to make meetings with producers or other important people from the network. When they managed to get together, however, she got along fairly well with her daughter, provided that her cell phone was in good working order."

"Can you give us an example?" Molly prodded.

Simpson thought for a moment. "I remember a time when the three of us went out to lunch at the Beverly Center. We were planning on a movie Jamie was dying to see. Tami got a call from New York during dessert and left me with the kid before her coffee had gotten cold. Things like that seemed to happen pretty regularly."

"Speaking of New York," Molly interrupted, "did Tami ever tell you how she felt the move back East would affect her daughter?"

Simpson shifted in her seat and looked again at Tami, who returned an icy gaze. "About six months ago, right after the idea of relocating the show was raised, Tami told me she wasn't sure how Jamie would react to moving. She said that Jamie had her friends and her school and had never lived anywhere else but Los Angeles."

"How did you respond?"

"I told her that the move wasn't set in stone and that if she felt it was wrong, she should speak up. The network would understand her concerns. I guess I came off pretty strong in suggesting that she think about the move carefully before giving her approval."

"And what did Tami say in response?"

Simpson cocked her head to one side. "She thought about my remarks for a few seconds and frowned, as if she felt I wasn't being supportive. Then she said—and you can quote me on this because I'll never forget her tone, it was so dismissive of Jamie—'The move is my chance to go truly national. I'm not going to pass it up. Jamie will just have to adjust, and that's all there is to it.'"

"In other words, the move—as Tami saw matters—was in her interests, not Jamie's?"

"That's right."

"Did your relationship with Ms. Dawson change after you had this conversation?"

"The conversation was the beginning of the end for me," Simpson answered as if she had been waiting all morning for the question. "It was like Tami thought I was being unfaithful to her. After that I couldn't do anything right. Eventually, Tami even accused me of conspiring with her ex-husband to undermine her relationship with Jamie. That's when I got my walking papers."

"Have you conspired with Mr. Nova?" Molly asked, adopting a tone of incredulity.

"No. When he contacted me and asked me to testify

in his custody case, I agreed to go to court and tell the truth, which is what I've done."

Satisfied with Simpson's candor, Molly yielded the lectern to Brockman.

"Why were you fired from the *O Darling!* show?" Brockman asked tersely. Both the timbre of his voice and the way he tensed his shoulders indicated that he was out to attack the witness's credibility rather than contest any of the specific points she had made on direct examination.

"The reason given to me was that I had become inattentive to my duties." Simpson delivered her answer with a sarcastic lift of the eyebrows.

"Let's see," Brockman said, studying the legal pad in front of him. "You missed three meetings with Ms. Dawson inside a single month and failed to give her phone messages from no less than two advertising sponsors and her New York agent. You were also late for the taping of two shows. Isn't that so?"

Simpson gritted her teeth. "My mother was in the hospital. I was distracted."

"But not distracted enough to have retained a lawyer for the purpose of filing a wrongful-termination lawsuit against the TV station and Ms. Dawson, I take it," Brockman chided.

"I have my rights," Simpson shot back. "I'm just protecting my interests. That's what the legal system is for, isn't it?"

"Indeed it," Brockman replied. "And did it ever occur to you that the interests of my client in seeking to advance her career—when all the pros and cons were weighed and considered—might be quite in harmony with the best interests of her daughter?"

"I can only testify from my own personal perspective," Simpson answered defiantly.

"From the perspective of an employee embittered

at being fired and losing a six-figure salary, you mean," Brockman said, directing a smug smile at Judge Goldstein. "Ms. Dawson has nothing further for this witness."

Judge Goldstein excused Simpson and waited for her to exit the courtroom before asking Molly to call her next witness.

"Your Honor," Molly said without getting up, "the respondent will take the stand himself at this time." Leaning over to Nova, she whispered, "Remember . . . short and sweet, just like we talked about it. You're a witness now, not a lawyer." Together, they rose to take their respective places.

As Nova walked slowly to the witness box, he felt his heart flutter. This was what he and every lawyer he knew called "showtime." Only this time he wasn't just orchestrating the show. He was the show.

It was one thing to question a witness from the safety of a lectern or seated comfortably behind a counsel table. In his two decades as an advocate Nova had examined, coaxed, cajoled, and grilled enough witnesses to fill the population rolls of a small town. Exposing the underbellies of his fellow citizens, probing their laudable and despicable attributes, watching them cringe as they fielded his inquiries, was second nature to him, something he did day in and day out like getting out of bed in the morning and brushing his teeth before turning out the lights at night.

Never in his career, however, had he ever been called to the stand himself. After all the years he had spent as a lawyer seeking to control the ebb and flow of a trial, the prospect of being sworn in to answer someone else's questions—even Molly's—left him unnerved. The role of a good trial lawyer was always proactive, prepared to fire when ready, to go for the jugular if necessary. The role of a witness was essen-

tially reactive, to remain calm, deliberate, and above
all, to appear truthful. Like a novice in any field, Nova
was about to enter uncharted waters, uncertain of his
abilities, anxious at the thought that a single mistimed
answer or misspoken word could be enough to change
the outcome of the proceeding.

Even the view from the witness stand was a new
and unsettling experience. Instead of the accustomed
frontal vista of Judge Goldstein he had enjoyed from
the counsel table, he now had a side angle, and a far
closer one at that, of Her Honor's long, rectangular
face and upper torso. Seated no more than three feet
away, he could discern the first light brown age spots
that had sprouted on her forehead and the backs of
her hands, and the old blue sapphire sorority ring she
wore on the fourth finger of her left hand. The new
perspective also forced him to choose consciously
whether to look directly at Tami or to keep his eyes
fixed on Molly. Either way, he knew that Brockman—
and in all likelihood Tami, too—would have their eyes
locked on him, seeking out the slightest sign of weakness, eager to take advantage of any mistake he
might make.

"Mr. Nova," Molly began, "I'm not going to waste
any more of your precious time, or the court's or that
of the petitioner or her counsel than is absolutely necessary. I trust that's agreeable to you?"

"Of course," Nova answered, wondering when the
butterflies in his stomach would disappear.

"What I'd like you to tell the court, as succinctly as
you can, is this: Why do you think your daughter's
best interests would be served by having her remain
in Los Angeles with you rather than relocating with
Ms. Dawson to New York?"

Nova turned away from Molly and let his gaze meet
Tami's. He tried to assess, as best he could, the strain

in each of them. Molly certainly had wasted no time getting to the core of the matter. He took a hard swallow, then mouthed the words straight from the heart, trying to sound firm and full of resolve but without being hurtful. "The most fundamental reason I can think of is that I love Jamie. I can't imagine anyone loving her more."

"Including your ex-wife?"

Brockman interposed a well-timed objection, but Goldstein signaled with a wave of her hand that she wanted to hear the answer. "The question calls for the witness's opinion," she ruled, "but I think he has a sufficient basis for it."

"Yes, I include my ex-wife in that statement," Nova replied, looking back at Molly.

Molly took a half step away from the lectern and crossed her arms, adopting a skeptical pose. "After hearing the petitioner and her witnesses testify, how can you feel that way?"

"Because there is nothing in this world more important to me than my daughter's welfare and happiness."

"Are you saying that Jamie's mother doesn't care about her welfare and happiness, too?" But for the fact that Molly was questioning her own client, the tone of her query—impatient and demanding—sounded very much like the opening salvo of a heated cross-examination.

Subjecting one's own witness to sharp questioning was a technique Nova had often used himself as an advocate. Designed to force the witness to defend his statements and positions and to take the sting out of opposing counsel's subsequent interrogation, it was often a persuasive tactic that paid big dividends with judges and juries. Molly had given him no hint in their prep sessions, however, that she planned on using the approach with him. Being on the receiving end of a

clever trial attorney's maneuver was another new experience that left Nova visibly uncomfortable.

"No, that's not what I'm saying," Nova answered.

"Are you saying that Tami only cares about herself,
as Janet Simpson told us?"

"No, not exactly, although I think there are some
definite problems in that area."

"Then what exactly do you mean, Mr. Nova? Why
should this court look upon you as a more suitable
parent to have primary physical custody over Jamie
than Ms. Dawson?"

Nova rubbed the tension from his face and took a
breath. Even as he told himself to stay cool and objec-
tive, he felt overcome with emotion. "All my adult
life, what I wanted most—more than a successful career, more than a big home or an expensive car—was
a family." He stopped, trying to collect himself but
with little success. "That was the reason my initial
marriage ended. My first wife didn't want to have children. We parted amicably. Then I met Tami."

"And she wanted children?" Molly asked, determined to keep Nova from digressing.

Nova stopped again. Despite the stakes involved,
and the opportunity he now had to deliver a knockout
blow to Tami, he wanted desperately to avoid causing
her any unnecessary pain. "At first she did," he said,
"or at least that's what she told me."

"Did something happen to change her mind?"

"Nothing in particular. Soon after we were married,
she told me she wanted to wait. As it turned out,
Tami's pregnancy with Jamie was unplanned."

"Were the two of you happy that she became
pregnant?"

Nova lifted a hand to his chin and stared at Tami.
Avoiding his eyes, Tami dipped her head, her hands

resting on the counsel table, clasped together, as if in prayer.

"I had to talk her out of terminating the pregnancy." He had never before revealed the fact that Jamie might never have entered this world if not for his active intervention. The story was part of the past that he had always intended to keep dead and buried. Yet here he was, telling the tale. The words tumbled out of his mouth almost involuntarily. He was unable to pull them back or mitigate their sting.

"You mean she wanted to have an abortion?" Molly asked, ratcheting up the volume in her voice, adroitly covering her own surprise at the disclosure.

"She said that she could always get pregnant later, that she wasn't sure she was ready for motherhood. I think she was just afraid." To his shock and surprise, his eyes began to moisten as he recalled the details. Tough guys don't cry, he tried to remind himself as he struggled for composure.

"How did you manage to talk her out of the abortion?"

"I told her she wasn't alone in this, that the pregnancy was ours. I promised to take care of the baby's needs at night, to change her and feed her whenever Tami felt too tired or was too busy."

"Did you keep your promises?"

"I was the one who walked the floor with Jamie whenever she woke up crying and needed to be held. I also took the lion's share of responsibility for arranging Jamie's medical appointments when she was an infant and a toddler."

"During the years that you and Ms. Dawson lived together before your separation, was Tami a good mother to your child?"

"I think she became a good mother over time," Nova answered thoughtfully. "And for a good while the three of us—Tami, Jamie, and me—were just the kind of happy family I wanted."

"Whose idea was it to separate?"

"Hers. She was also the one who suggested counseling, I might add, but insisted that we live apart nonetheless. She first raised the subject of separation about a year after she launched her TV career, after it had become clear that she was going to have a new career."

"What was the problem with that?"

Nova pulled on his tie, looking a little uncomfortable. "She said that I was holding her back. It seemed to me, after a while, that she was beginning to lose interest in me as a husband. We talked less. Our sex life—which was once very good—stagnated and then stopped altogether."

Molly's eyes darted over to Brockman, daring him to raise an objection. Seeing that her adversary was prepared to let Nova say his piece, she continued, "Did you and Tami ever discuss the possibility of having another child?"

Nova nodded. "She made it clear she wanted no more children. To my way of thinking, that was one of the reasons she wanted out of the marriage."

"Is that what she told you?"

"No. She said that I was holding her back, impeding her professional progress. Things along those lines."

"Were you holding her back?"

Nova chose his words carefully. "I didn't think so at the time, but from her point of view, maybe I was. For me, family always came first."

"I appreciate Mr. Nova's perspective," Judge Goldstein cut in, "but we've heard this line of testimony already. It's time to move."

Heeding Her Honor's admonition, Molly spent the remainder of her direct detailing the activities Nova liked to share with his daughter. Besides schoolwork and sports, Nova testified that he and Jamie had taken up an interest in camping, both in the nearby San Gabriel Mountains and the Santa Ynez range outside of Santa Barbara, where they had gone together last summer.

On the subject of his alleged womanizing, Nova conceded he had a healthy sexual appetite but insisted he never let Jamie's interests take a backseat to his dating. On the issue of Tami's annoying phone calls, he insisted that his account of their frequency was accurate. He also insisted that he brought the matter to Tami's attention not to harass her but to simply to get her to stop and to encourage her to "get on with her own life while he got on with his."

On the question of Randy Sturgis, too, his intent was not to embarrass his ex-wife but to act as a buffer between her and the FBI, which had wanted to question her about her prison visits. "Maybe I came off a little strong, but I was just trying to help," he said. "I was shocked when I learned that Tami actually had seen this man in state prison."

"And how did learning that make you feel about Tami?" Molly asked.

"It was like I didn't really know her," Nova replied softly. "Like I never really knew her."

Molly thanked her client and returned to her seat, wearing a satisfied grin she only halfheartedly tried to conceal.

Like Molly's direct, Brockman's cross was crisp and to the point. "Mr. Nova," he began, "these sexual liaisons you've had, beginning with the one while you were still engaged in marriage counseling, how many of them have there been over the past three years?"

"I've never counted," Nova answered stiffly.

"Well, we've heard from three women in this proceeding, but there were more, true?"

"Yes."

"More than six?" Brockman took Nova's hesitation as an affirmative response. "More than ten? More than a dozen? Tell me when to stop."

"More than six," Nova said, fumbling to save face.

"Okay, more than six. Let's leave it at that," Brockman said, affecting a phony air of affability. "Do you really think that exposing your ten-year-old daughter to that kind of behavior is a good idea?"

"I don't think that Jamie is *exposed* to any kind of behavior, counsel," Nova answered sharply. He lurched forward in his seat for an instant and clenched his right fist, as though preparing to take the battle onto a more physical plane. Realizing the foolhardiness of such a gesture, he sank back against the upholstered back of his chair but still was unable to relax.

Pleased that he had evoked a display of anger in the witness, Brockman turned up the heat. "Still, you would agree, would you not, that your behavior can hardly be good for Jamie? She is, after all, old enough to know her father has had brief relationships with a large number of—excuse me, more than six—other women in the past three years."

"If you're asking whether I think of myself as an ideal father," Nova retorted, "I don't. But Jamie always has come first with me."

"So we've heard," Brockman said, enjoying the verbal sparring. "And we've also heard how much you care for your daughter. You would be very hurt, I take it, if this court granted the petitioner's request for primary custody."

"Yes, I would."

"And yet this hearing isn't about your feelings and

interests, is it? It's about the best interests of your daughter."

"Your Honor," Molly objected, coming finally to Nova's rescue. "Counsel surely knows that a parent's feelings are relevant to the issue of custody. If Mr. Brockman has a legitimate point to make, I wish he'd get on with it. Otherwise, he's simply badgering my client."

"My point, Mr. Nova, is this . . ." Brockman added without waiting for a ruling from Judge Goldstein. "Your daughter is now ten years old. She's no longer a toddler but is becoming a young woman. Are you prepared to tell this court that you can provide a better life for her in Los Angeles than your wife can in New York?"

"Counsel," Nova answered, his voice again edged with anger, "I'm prepared to do anything necessary to meet Jamie's needs."

"But you're a single man. You live alone. You're employed full-time. You have no local relatives. You don't even have a full-time housekeeper to look after Jamie while you're away from home. True?"

"That's true," Nova conceded, "but I've asked our old housekeeper if she would consider moving in with me if Jamie stays in L.A. She used to stay with us in Topanga before Tami moved out."

"That would be Ms. Dawson's present house-keeper, Yolanda?"

"Yolanda Ortega," Nova answered. "It would mean a lot to my daughter, and to me, if Yolanda agreed to move in with us."

"Has Yolanda given you an answer?"

"She's promised to get back to me, but no, as of now she hasn't."

The toes of Nova's right foot had gone numb from sitting so long. He wriggled them and crossed his legs, trying to restore his circulation as he braced for the next set of questions.

The next questions never came. Brockman exchanged a catlike glance with Tami, then lifted his eyes to the bench. "I have nothing further of this witness," he announced.

Judge Goldstein dropped her pen and removed her glasses as she ordered the hearing into recess for the remainder of the morning. The surprise etched on her face at what seemed the premature termination of Brockman's cross-examination was also reflected on Molly's face.

No one, however, was more surprised, or relieved, than Nova. His ordeal over, Nova stepped from the stand. By the time he reached the counsel table, the feeling in his toes had returned. His entire body, in fact, felt lighter and more buoyant than at any time in the past six weeks.

Chapter Twenty-eight

"If this was a jury trial, there wouldn't have been a dry eye in the house," Molly chortled over lunch at the courthouse cafeteria. "I never knew you were such a sensitive type. And the part about the abortion. That was brilliant." She took a bite of her salad. "I assume it's true."

"Of course it's true," Nova answered sharply. "You don't think I'd make something like that up, do you?" He stared at her in wonder. This hearing was possibly the most painful event he had ever endured, but Molly was positively enjoying herself, as though she were cheering on her favorite player at an NBA playoff game. Lawyers had a reputation for being perverse, for making their living and getting their kicks off the misery of others. As a trial lawyer himself, he had always thought the reputation was exaggerated. Now, as a witness and a client, he was beginning to see things in a different light.

"Well, I'm glad at least you're having a good time," he said with a touch of sarcasm before she could answer his question.

"What's the matter?" she objected. "I think you did a great job on the stand. So what if I have a little fun along the way?"

"Sorry, it's just that I can't see this as just another chess match. It's too personal."

"Look, if I was out of line, I apologize," she said. Before she could offer any more words of contrition, she looked up abruptly from her food. "We've got company," she said, rising to her feet and extending her hand.

Nova pivoted in his seat, turning just in time to see the warm, friendly smile stretching across Sandy Nash's face.

"Right on time," Molly said, shaking Sandy's hand. "I trust your flight went well."

"Yes, thanks. I flew in last night, actually, and I'm here until tomorrow afternoon, all on business." Sandy said. "I've already been to two business meetings, and even landed another major account. So now I'm all yours." She slid in at the table next to Nova.

"Then we're all having a good day," Molly added brightly.

"Thank you for coming," Nova broke in, his eyes resting on Sandy's, and then, as discreetly as he could manage, drifting to her shoulders and down her torso. She was wearing a finely tailored dark blue business suit, with a silky gray blouse and a strand of large Mexican silver beads around her neck. Trim and well toned, she looked even better than she had in San Francisco.

"My pleasure," she answered, tossing her thick black hair off her forehead with a graceful shake of her head. "I'm glad to help." She let her gaze rest on Nova.

"If you don't mind," Molly said, clearing her throat to make sure she had their attention, "I think it would be a good idea for us girls to go over Sandy's testimony. David," she said, nodding at Nova like a busy mother hen, "you're nearly finished with your daily cheeseburger. Why don't you take a little elevator ride while Sandy and I talk?"

"Sounds like a good idea," Nova replied agreeably. He stood up to leave. As he carried his tray back to the cafeteria's bussing station, he could hear Molly quipping: "I'm in the process of turning Davey into a saint, and I think he's becoming a little embarrassed."

It was funny, Nova thought to himself, how two women who hadn't seen each other in years could get along so well. Molly had never called him "Davey" to his face, not once in all the time he'd known her. Yet here they were, talking about him in endearing, even intimate terms, like two sorority sisters trading tidbits about a new hunk on campus. Maybe he *was* getting embarrassed.

The canonization of Saint David, which, from Molly's point of view, had begun that morning, continued with Sandy's testimony. Molly took Sandy through a brisk introduction, having her explain that she was unmarried, a resident of Mill Valley in Marin County north of San Francisco, a graduate of the prestigious Rhode Island School of Design, and the sole proprietor of one of the Bay Area's most successful boutique interior-design firms.

"And you are acquainted with Mr. Nova, the respondent in this proceeding?"

"He's my ex-husband," she answered, looking first at Nova and then at Tami, whose stiff back and tight-lipped countenance seemed to indicate that she viewed Sandy's appearance at the hearing as a personal insult.

"And what is your current relationship with Mr. Nova?"

"We were divorced a little over twelve years ago, but we've stayed friends, mostly through phone calls and letters. We've also visited occasionally, when he was in the Bay Area or I was down here." After a moment's hesitation Sandy added, "David asked me to testify at this hearing."

"Did you agree to testify voluntarily, or are you here in response to a subpoena?"

"There's been no subpoena," Sandy answered calmly. "I'm here because I want to be."

"But why would someone with a business to run in San Francisco want to come all the way to L.A. to testify in a child-custody hearing?"

Sandy looked directly at Nova. "Because I know how much David's daughter means to him."

"How do you know that, Ms. Nash?"

"Because every time I've spoken with David over the past ten years, the first and last words out of his mouth are about Jamie. Although I've only met Jamie once—about five years ago at David's office here in L.A.—I've heard so much about her that I almost feel we're related."

"What sorts of things has David told you about Jamie?"

Sandy pursed her lips. "I've heard about her progress in school, her first trip to the zoo, the time she learned how to swim, her piano lessons, her tonsillectomy. You name it, David's one of those type-A proud dads. He's even sent me a photo or two." She opened her handbag and pulled out her wallet, displaying a color snapshot of Nova and Jamie taken on a brilliant summer day in front of one of the whale tanks at Sea World in San Diego. "I'm a sucker for Shamu." She put the picture away, but not before eliciting an amused smile from Judge Goldstein.

Molly allowed the brief interlude of levity to pass, then asked in her most serious tone, "Do you have any children of your own, Ms. Nash?"

"No, I don't," Sandy answered. There was a register of sadness in her voice, and some of the luster was gone from her bright blue eyes. "I had an ectopic pregnancy which ruptured one of my fallopian tubes. It's unlikely I ever will have children."

"I'm sorry to hear that." After a suitable pause, Molly moved to the heart of Sandy's testimony. "Did the issue of having children factor in your divorce from Mr. Nova?"

"Very much so. You might say that was the reason for our breakup."

At Molly's request, Sandy elaborated, "I guess I was one of those women who thought that children and careers didn't mix. I saw how my mother sacrificed everything to raise me and my brothers and sisters. When David and I were married, my older sister already had two girls, and she was following along the same path as Mom. I was just starting out in the design business, and I wanted something different for myself."

"I take it that David wanted children?"

Sandy bowed her head ever so slightly. "Very much so. He loved to baby-sit for my sister's kids. I could tell he was really hooked on having a family."

"So hooked that it caused a divorce?"

"I wanted to be fair, both to David and myself. After a while I just thought he'd be happier finding someone else who felt the same way he did about children. We parted on good terms, and we've stayed that way ever since. Our divorce was uncontested in all respects."

"And I handled the divorce for Mr. Nova, didn't I?" Molly asked, sparking a raised eyebrow from the bench.

"Yes, you were an associate in David's law firm at the time."

"The someone else that Mr. Nova eventually found," Molly said, shifting the focus of her examination, "was Ms. Dawson. Can you tell us what kind of contact you've had with her over the years?"

"Apart from today, I've only seen her in person twice before, both times at parties in Los Angeles. Before I relocated to the Bay Area, David and I still had pretty much the same group of friends, so we sometimes bumped into each other on social occasions."

"How did Ms. Dawson treat you on those occasions?"

For only the second time that morning, Sandy let her gaze fall on Tami. Purposely, she left it stay there as she delivered her answer. "She was cool, abrupt, and mildly insulting. I don't think she approved of my continuing friendship with David. It seemed to me like she was jealous, like she was afraid there might still be something romantic between us."

"During your marriage to Mr. Nova, did he ever make you jealous by running around with other women?"

"Never," Sandy answered firmly. "That's not to say that he never noticed other women, but I never worried about him cheating. Our sex life was very active and very satisfying."

"Has Mr. Nova ever told you about his sex life since separating from Ms. Dawson?"

"Not in any detail, but I gather he's remained active." Sandy struggled to keep a straight face, trying to couch her language in listener-friendly terms. "David is a man who likes women. He likes sex."

"Does that make him a sexist, in your opinion?"

"Some people might see him that way, and in a very superficial sense they might be right. Maybe I'm not a politically correct person, but that's not how I see him."

"How do you see him?"

Sandy reflected a moment. "I think he enjoys, and needs, the company of women more than most men, and not just physically but for companionship, too. I wouldn't expect that to change over time, and, more importantly, I wouldn't expect that to interfere in his relationship with Jamie. I don't think the woman's been born yet who could take Jamie's place in David's heart."

Molly spent the next minute and a half defeating Brockman's motion to strike Sandy's final comment, then returned to Nova's side at the counsel table. "Home stretch, Davey," she chortled under her breath. "I can't imagine why she ever let you get away."

The subject of Sandy's affections was also very much on Brockman's mind as he launched his cross-examination. "It would appear from your testimony thus far, Ms. Nash," he said, resting his left forearm casually on the lectern, "that you regret your divorce from Mr. Nova. Is that true?"

"That's hard to say. It's been many years since David and I were together," Sandy answered. "We've gone our separate ways, and have built very different lives." Her voice clear and confident, Sandy showed no signs of distress at the prospect of being grilled by Tami's hired gun. "What I can say, however, is that I was very young, stubborn, and naive when our marriage ended. I no longer believe that women are faced with an either-or choice, pitting family interests against careers."

"So you've mellowed with age?"

"You might say that. We all tend to change with time. If we're lucky, we also mellow."

"But one of the things that hasn't changed with time is your fondness for Mr. Nova. True?"

"I still number David among my close friends," Sandy answered matter-of-factly. "That's why I agreed to testify on his behalf, if that's what you're implying."

"Let me see if I understand, then," Brockman said, crossing his arms and raising his thick right forefinger to his lips. "You're unmarried, you're unlikely to be able to bear children, and you're still quite fond of your ex-husband. Is it possible, Ms. Nash, that you agreed to testify in this hearing, hoping that favorable testimony might win your way back into Mr. Nova's heart for a second chance at romance, or even marriage? After all, you're both available and still relatively young and attractive."

Molly was shouting her objections before Sandy could muster a reply. "If counsel wants to play matchmaker, I suggest he take out an ad in the lonely hearts section of the personals. For the time being, however, he should be admonished for badgering the witness."

Judge Goldstein sympathized with Molly and instructed Brockman to soften his tone, but otherwise overruled the protest. "The question goes to bias and is clearly relevant. The witness may answer."

Slightly flustered but maintaining her cool, Sandy replied, "Actually, the possibility of getting back with David hadn't crossed my mind until you mentioned it, Mr. Brockman. And I'm truly flattered to hear you think I'm still relatively young and attractive." She paused, enjoying the embarrassed blush that began to rise on Brockman's cheeks. "But to return to a question you asked earlier, if I had to live my life with David all over again, I think I would have found a way to balance my desire for a rewarding career with what I now see as a missed opportunity for children and a family of my own."

Despite the similarities they shared as successful career women, the contrast at that moment between Sandy and Tami, in their sharply different attitudes toward life in general and Nova in particular, could not have been greater. Realizing that he was unlikely to come out the winner in any head-to-head comparison between the two women, Brockman directed the remainder of his cross to less volatile matters. He established, among a litany of other items, that Sandy had never heard Nova complain about Tami's parenting skills and had never heard him say she was a bad mother. Nor had she ever heard him say that Jamie would not adjust well to life in New York with Tami and her extended family. It was Nova, Sandy conceded, who would have to make the more difficult personal adjustment if Jamie was permitted to relocate. And so Brockman's cross-examination closed, not exactly with a whimper but hardly with the bang that he had hoped for at its outset.

Molly waited for Sandy to leave the courtroom before completing the remainder of her case, offering a handful of additional declarations into evidence. These included two more accounts of mistreatment from disgruntled former employees of the *O Darling!* show, and a pair of handwritten statements from Jamie's young classmates, proclaiming how sorry they would be to see their good friend leave.

Judge Goldstein heaved a sign of satisfaction at the end of another working day and gaveled the hearing into recess. "I'll receive closing arguments from counsel tomorrow," she announced, stepping from the bench. "Please keep them brief and to the point."

All things considered, it had been a big day for Nova.

Chapter Twenty-nine

There was only one thing Nova had to do before dragging himself home for what promised to be a long, restless night. He had to thank Sandy. In fact, both he and Molly had to convey their appreciation. They caught up to her, as per Molly's lunch-hour request, in the courthouse cafeteria, where she was nursing a cup of English breakfast tea at a corner table. Apart from a single middle-aged woman wolfing down a tuna melt and fries like it was her first meal in a week and two well-dressed lawyers debating the ups and downs of their day in court, Sandy was the only patron left in the drab eatery as it prepared to close for the day.

"Thanks for waiting," Molly said as she and Nova hurried to her table. "I just wanted to tell you how much you helped our case. We're very grateful."

"You really think I made a difference?" Sandy asked, putting the paperback she had been sifting through back into her purse. Although she looked tired, a sunny smile spread across her face.

"Molly thinks our chances now are about even money," Nova remarked, joining the conversation and sliding into the seat across from Sandy while Molly remained standing in the uncomfortable posture of the odd man out. "That's a ninety-degree turn from where we started." He reached across the table and took her hand, holding it gently between both of his as he continued in heartfelt tones. "I hardly think I deserve the effort you gave, and I don't know if I can ever return the favor. No matter how things turn out, I won't forget this."

Taking Sandy's hand, though done spontaneously and out of gratitude, brought on an awkward silence. It was the kind of gesture that easily could have been misconstrued as patronizing or even as the first step of a calculated come-on. But if Sandy took any offense at Nova's forwardness, she didn't show it. She made no attempt to pull away or divert her eyes.

On the other side of the big room, several white-uniformed Spanish-speaking workers were well into their evening clean-up routine, stacking the cafeteria's cheap steel-frame dining chairs before giving the worn white institutional linoleum floor tiles at their feet their end-of-the-day scrub down. Nova released Sandy's hand as the mop-and-bucket brigade approached. Like a trio of nervous spies intent on synchronizing their movements, he, Sandy, and Molly turned their wristwatches skyward at precisely the same instant.

"It's four-thirty," Sandy announced, nervously clearing her throat, "I probably should be getting back to my hotel. I've got a few calls to make."

"And I should be getting back to my office," Molly concurred. "The last time I talked to my secretary, she said she had a pile of messages thicker than a deck of cards. I've still got to prepare my closing argument for tomorrow." Turning to Sandy, she asked, "Can I call you a cab? We'll pick up the fare, of course."

"I think we can do more than that," Nova offered in the spirit of doing his attorney one better. "I'd be glad to give you a lift. I don't have an argument to prepare, and I don't charge by the quarter mile."

"You're sure it's no problem?" Sandy asked, rising from the table before a wet mop could graze the soles of her shoes. "I'm at the Regency downtown."

"No problem at all," Nova answered agreeably.

Molly gave them each a bemused grin, as if recalling the irony of her remarks about Tom Brockman's penchant for matchmaking. "Well, I guess the two of you have that covered. Have a good night, and thanks again."

The Regency Hotel occupied a prominent perch on Grand Avenue at the crest of downtown L.A.'s newly reborn Bunker Hill section. Once the city's most elegant residential enclave, where the renowned Angel's Flight open-air cable car lifted pedestrians along the district's steep eastern slope past rows of brightly painted Victorian mansions, the Hill had gone the way of most of downtown after the Great Depression. The old mansions had been divided up into cheap rooming houses, and the Angel's Flight dismantled and mothballed as money and the people who knew how to spend it deserted the inner city.

Beginning in the mid-sixties, however, the area had embarked on a slow and fitful turnaround. It had taken more than three decades, but by the late nineties the new look was nearly complete. The rooming houses had been torn down and replaced by a thicket of sleek steel-and-glass office towers, subterranean shopping centers, expensive restaurants, and the new Museum of Contemporary Art. Even a Disneylandish replica of the Angel's Flight had been constructed to draw in the tourists, raise a little revenue for the city, and create the illusion of continuity to the Hill's nostalgic past.

Although Nova had never stayed at the Regency, he had attended several conferences at the hotel since it had opened its doors as a popular business gathering ground. Located within a few minutes of his office, the hotel was a convenient and comfortable spot to stow out-of-town experts during trial and an easy place to conduct settlement negotiations with opposing counsel over lunch. Nova always found the waiters courteous and the food to his liking. The lavish lobby was a bit over the top, with its vaulted beamed ceiling, mottled red and white marble colonnades, antique settees and overstuffed sofas, and original artwork—displayed by agreement with a local gallery—but the overall effect was tasteful and gave the Regency a distinctly European flavor.

"Every time I come here," Nova told Sandy after leaving his Lexus with the valet, "I have a fleeting feeling that I'm in Paris or Rome. Then I hear someone talk about the Dodgers, the smog, or the murder rate, and I realize my passport's still in the top drawer of my dresser."

"You were always like that," Sandy replied with a knowing smile and a look of mild amusement. "I remember you saying the same thing about the Windsor Hotel on the west side, when we went there for breakfast. You used to say how you felt you were back in the Jolly Old noshing on bangers and eggs."

"You have an amazing memory. I'd nearly forgotten. You know, they tore the Windsor down last year." Nova sounded positively wistful as he thought about the huge Sunday morning breakfasts he and Sandy liked to consume in the early days of their marriage at the rundown English-style inn.

"I don't know about this place, though," Sandy continued, taking in the Regency's ambience of studied elegance. "With all the East L.A. accents floating around among the maids and bellhops, it's more like Mexico City. The Zona Rosa, of course," she added agreeably, referring to the international heart of the Mexican capital, where she and Nova once spent an Easter holiday feasting on continental cuisine each evening and making love until the early hours of the morning. Travel and sex had always been two of the bright spots of their lives together. But then they were both young and eager in those distant days, full of hope for the future, at the peak of their physical powers.

Even after all the years, there was no denying he still found Sandy arousing. But oddly enough, particularly with the unintended head start Brockman had furnished him and the fact that he hadn't been laid in more than a month, sex wasn't really on Nova's mind. What he wanted most from Sandy, other than to convey his thanks—which he had already done nearly to the point of becoming annoying—was just a little human contact, someone to pass a little time with and help keep his mind off tomorrow. He had been feeling that way—needy and vulnerable—a lot lately, ever since Tanner's murder, but never more so than now. Adversity was either making him weak or more sensitive. Maybe, he told himself as they entered the hotel lobby and headed for the happy-hour crowd gathering in the first-floor lounge, the courtroom makeover Molly had given him as the warm-and-fuzzy type was actually starting to take hold.

On the long drive over from Santa Monica, he and Sandy had agreed to share a drink and nothing more. Not wishing to overstay his welcome, he had left the subjects of dinner or anything thereafter unmentioned. Sandy might not have had any other plans, but she looked tired and drained from her trip, and the last thing he wanted was to give the wrong impression that he was out to return her kindness with one of his patented rolls in the hay. Even with nothing more definite waiting for him than a couple of stiff single malts, he felt content.

Like the Regency's other amenities, Berenger's, the hotel's dimly lit main watering hole, was richly appointed, with dark walnut-stained wainscoting, textured olive green wallpaper accented by black-framed lithographs of New York and London street scenes, and brightly polished brass table lamps in every booth. Its clientele, drawn from the hotel's guests and the local business and legal communities, was always well dressed and free-spending. They came for the hors d'oeuvres of petite quiches and sausage calzones, and they came for the uncommonly wide range of libations that made Berenger's oversized rectangular full-service bar an immediate Los Angeles landmark. Whether they were serious drinkers or the more social variety, thirsty customers knew they could find virtually any form of liquid poison their palates desired, from half-priced happy-hour pints of Budweiser to rare French brandies selling for up to three hundred dollars a snifter.

Sandy and Nova squeezed their way into the crowd and made their way to the bar. Nova ordered a stiff single malt for himself and a gin and tonic for Sandy. With the decibel level pushed upward by the standing-room-only conditions, it was difficult to have a conversation in a normal tone of voice. Keeping things bland and impersonal, they stuck mostly to workaday subjects. Nova told her that, apart from the trial he recently had lost to Molly, the law biz had been lucrative, and he managed to learn that roughly a third of Sandy's clients were in Southern California, primarily in places like Brentwood and Beverly Hills but in outlying venues, too.

"I get most of my business on referrals," Sandy said, practically shouting to be heard. "You'd be surprised how many rich housewives there are with money to burn. Once they hear you're terrific, there's no end to what they'll do to hire you. The woman I'm seeing tomorrow agreed to pick me up here, drive me out to Bel Air, and then to the airport for my return flight."

"Just the opposite of practicing law," Nova replied, hoisting the last of his drink and ordering a refill. "Most of my clients would drop me like a sack of nails if they thought they would get more money with some other shyster."

His cynicism seemed to catch her by surprise. "Your regard for the legal profession seems to have declined," she said with a slight twist of the lips.

Nova shrugged his shoulders. "Beats working for a living, and it pays better, too."

He was prepared to elaborate, but their attention was diverted by a loud, sloppy tête-à-tête between two dark-suited middle-aged white guys well into their third or fourth rounds of martinis. "So I told her, you can have the house and the Mercedes," the taller of the two complained between sips. "Just leave me the condo and my old Honda. So you know what the bitch did? She gave the keys to the Honda to her new boyfriend—Mario, the only CPA in Southern California with more hair oil than tax forms—and the schmuck ran smack into a telephone pole. With all my legal fees and the alimony I'll be paying, I'll be lucky to afford an Escort."

"Sometimes I think marriage is nothing more than an endurance contest," the shorter man replied philosophically, poking a stubby forefinger into the chest of his companion. "The last spouse standing gets to hang the other's photo on the wall to throw darts at and blame the rain on."

Nova turned away from the inebriated duo and shook his head. "This guy must be reading my thoughts." He began to scout the room for a better venue. From out of the corner of his eye, he saw a twentysomething couple laying down a tip before exiting from a booth. "Let's go for it," he said pointing at the couple. They arrived at the now vacant booth just ahead of a group of Asian businessmen who had the same idea of securing a quieter sanctuary.

"Finally, I can hear the sound of my own voice," Nova said, sliding onto the upholstered bench across from Sandy. "You know, you never did tell me about that guy you were seeing," he said, referring to the relationship Sandy had mentioned on his most recent visit with her in San Francisco.

"There's not much to tell, I'm afraid," Sandy said, pausing while their waitress arrived with Nova's refill and began clearing away the dishes and glasses the last occupants of the booth had left behind. "What would you like to know?"

"Well, what kind of a guy was he? What does he do for a living? What does he look like? I assume he has two eyes, a nose, a mouth . . ."

"Yeah, he has all the normal facial features, ears too," Sandy said, showing a little stiffness at Nova's questions.

"But in other ways he was some kind of deviant, is that what I'm hearing?"

Sandy's face reddened a little and she began to laugh at the same time. "He's into computers," she said, hesitating as if choosing what details to reveal and what information to keep private. "Sales and programming."

"So, it just didn't pan out?" Nova asked, working on the refill.

"I got pregnant."

Suddenly, Sandy sounded sad and serious. Her mood swing caused Nova to wipe the smile from his face. "You're referring to the ectopic pregnancy you mentioned in court?"

She nodded slowly. "The pregnancy surprised both of us. This time I wanted a baby; he didn't. In the end it didn't matter." Determined not to let the memory overcome her, she added quickly, "But that was several years ago; it's way past me now."

"For what it's worth, I'm really sorry," Nova offered. "Sometimes life just plain sucks." He waited for what he thought was an appropriate moment of silence before changing the subject. "Speaking of bad breaks, I wonder how Vera is. I hear that she retired from the court, but I haven't spoken to her in weeks." He looked at Sandy, a new spark of interest in his eyes. "Why don't we give her a call? I'm sure she'd get a kick to hear from both of us together."

Sandy bit her lower lip and crossed her legs, nervously swinging the ankle of her top leg under the table. "I'm sure she would, but she isn't home. I phoned her last week, and she told me she was planning a little trip to Baja."

"Then good for her," Nova answered, hoisting his glass to his mouth.

They spent another ten minutes finishing their drinks, discussing Jamie and her summer camp, Sandy's plans to put her vacation cabin on the market, and generally avoiding the issue of what the remainder of the night might hold for them. Finally, Sandy announced that her Bel Air client would be picking her up at seven-thirty tomorrow morning. "She's one of those health nuts, has her own personal exercise trainer, and every Nordic track that was ever made." Then, delivering the clincher, she added, "I really should be getting up to my room to review the plans for her first floor. They're very detailed, and the woman's extremely difficult to please."

"Sounds like it," Nova said, laying down a small bundle of bills for the drinks and tip before rising to his feet. Feeling mildly disappointed, he took Sandy by the arm and began to escort her through the bar. Though the dinner hour had already arrived, the place was even more crowded than before. Running a gauntlet of couples, trios, and quartets packing mixed drinks and appetizers in their hands, they inched their way back to the spot where the two inebriated middle-aged white guys they had overheard earlier were still heatedly decrying the institution of matrimony. Just as they were about to pass, the pudgy one lifted his right arm in a sweeping grand gesture to accent yet another boozy insight filled with learning and wit.

Narrowly avoiding a direct collision with the man's swinging martini glass, Sandy leaned in close to Nova. Reacting with equal speed, Nova pulled her closer still until they were face to face, their eyes and mouths no more than inches apart, like a couple on a date gliding through the crest of a slow one on the dance floor. He could see the tiny flecks of black pigment in her blue eyes and the wetness of her lips. He could feel her breath, soft and warm, on his cheek. For just an instant he thought to press his mouth against hers. Would she mind? His instincts told him she wanted as much, that she even expected it and might be disappointed at a failure of nerve.

Before he could resolve the issue for himself, the pudgy drunk stepped in and decided it for him. "Jeez, I'm sorry, lady," he apologized, sticking his flushed face within nuzzling range, filling their senses with an overwhelming odor of stale vermouth. "My friend and I got a little carried away."

Sandy and Nova declined the man's conciliatory

offer of a drink and finally navigated a path back to the lobby and the elevators that led to the upstairs guest rooms.

"Is it okay if I call you?" Nova asked as the lift arrived.

"I'd like that," she answered without delay, her eyes locked tightly on his. He read the look on her face as an additional sign of encouragement. "I'd like that a lot."

He watched as she stepped into the elevator and the doors closed behind her. Despite his best efforts to think only wholesome thoughts, he couldn't help noticing the slimness of her hips and thighs, and the gentle rise of her buttocks underneath her suit jacket.

Chapter Thirty

Nova could tell something was up just from the look on Tami's face. She had come to court Friday morning dressed to make a statement. Another two thousand–dollar suit, this time a soft heather gray, diamond stud earrings, enough gold around her neck and wrists to fund a small town's annual public-works budget. And for the first time since the custody hearing had commenced, she truly had the "look."

He'd seen the look often enough before; he even had a name for it. He called it Tami's "X-ray stare." When she was really out for blood, she had the unique ability to meet his eyes and stare straight through them, casting condemnation and judgment all in a momentary glance, penetrating to his vulnerable inner core, remaining cold, aloof, and superior while he was reduced to a creature devoid of moral standing, somewhere between a tree dweller and a simple vertebrate on the evolutionary scale.

From a practical standpoint, the problem with the X-ray stare was that invariably it was a prelude to something else—a high-decibel dressing-down, the delivery of a nonnegotiable domestic demand, an announcement from Mount Olympus about the future of their lives together. She'd had the X-ray stare on

the afternoon she discovered he was having it off with
Jennifer Sawyer and first threatened to take Jamie
away from him. She'd worn it the first time she accused him of trying to stifle her career, and just
months ago, when she told him she was leaving L.A.
and taking Jamie with her. First the stare, then the
sucker punch, ever and always in that order.

As he took the measure of Tami sitting at the opposite counsel table, Nova could only wonder if the pattern would hold true today. He didn't have to wait
long to find out.

"Your Honor," Brockman announced after Goldstein
had taken the bench and called the case to order, "we
have a rebuttal witness we wish to examine before
our closing argument—Yolanda Ortega, Ms. Dawson's
housekeeper." Dressed in basic black and with his
dark eyes even more hooded and shadowed than
usual, Brockman delivered his remarks with the gravity of an undertaker.

Judge Goldstein tapped the long fingers of her right
hand on the bench, frowning in disappointment as she
listened to Brockman. "I have a motion calendar set
for this afternoon, counsel," she said impatiently, referring to the fact that she had set aside part of the
day to deal with preliminary matters in some of the
other cases pending before her. "This case has already
taken up a great deal of my time."

"I'm well aware of that, Your Honor, and I do intend
to be brief. But in view of the testimony that both my
client and Mr. Nova have given thus far concerning Ms.
Ortega's relationship to Jamie, I thought it vital for the
court to hear from Ms. Ortega herself. I might remind
the court that both parties have asked Ms. Ortega to
move in with them and help care for Jamie."

"The court doesn't need any reminding, Mr. Brockman." Goldstein's frown hardened into a scowl. "I've had the best seat in the house for the past week."

Molly rose to object that Yolanda had not been placed on the petitioner's witness list, but the judge brushed aside the protest with a sweep of her robed arm. Since she had come this far, the last thing Goldstein wanted to risk was an abuse of discretion that might invite an appeal of the final order she issued. "I'll hear from Ms. Ortega," she said stiffly. "I assume she's standing by."

"Yes, Your Honor," Brockman answered. "She should be in the hallway with one of my associates even as we speak."

"I smell a rat," Molly whispered to Nova as the bailiff left his post to open the courtroom doors. "I hope you haven't been holding anything back from me." Nova replied merely with a shrug and raised eyebrows.

After a short delay Brockman's associate, a thirty-year-old woman in a lightweight beige business suit, entered. By her side was Yolanda Ortega.

Outfitted in a pair of polyester navy slacks and a red shortsleeve cotton pullover and toting a black vinyl handbag the size of a small suitcase, Yolanda had the manner and appearance of a Hispanic nanny taken straight from central casting. Plump, olive-skinned, full-breasted, and round, with a closely cropped gray perm and deep smile lines at the corners of her eyes, she stood just under five feet tall in her flat slip-on walking shoes. Every eye in the courtroom focused on her as she ambled down the aisle and took her seat on the witness stand.

Like many Central American immigrants, even after more than three decades in this country—spent variously as a wife, mother, grandma, and domestic servant—Yolanda was still only partially acculturated. She visited her native Guatemala every other year and continued to cling to the dream of returning there one day to buy a retirement home where she could spend her remaining days reunited with her large extended family. She had attained proficiency in English largely through her work, but spoke haltingly and with a thick accent. In the form of slang known as Spanglish, her speech was often peppered with terminology drawn from both her native and adopted tongues. Still, she was more than able to make herself understood as long as she wasn't overly rushed or flustered.

Brockman moved quickly to assure the court that no interpreter would be required and launched right into his examination. Yolanda's lack of sophistication and guile was immediately, and refreshingly, apparent. Responding slowly but effectively to Brockman's questions, she explained that she was sixty-two years old and a graduate of the polytechnic institute of Guatemala City, the equivalent roughly of a community-college degree. "My husband was—*como se dice*—a drill-press operator in a big factory," she added with a soft heave of her ample bosom and a little sadness in her eyes. "He pass away three years ago. I have three children, all grown now, one here in Los Angeles, one back home, and one in Feel . . . Feela . . . del . . ."

"Philadelphia?" Brockman offered helpfully.

"Yes." She nodded in appreciation.

"We're dead meat," Molly hissed under her breath. "Why didn't you tell me?" she asked, huddling close to Nova.

"This is news to me," Nova replied. "I knew that one of her kids lived in L.A. and one was back in Guatemala, but the other kid—"

"You never bothered to ask about," Molly completed his sentence for him, shaking her head. "The last time I looked on a map, Philly was only ninety miles from New York."

Back in center court, Yolanda's testimony proceeded. "I have known *Doña* Tami for more than eight years," she said, using the reverential Spanish form of address to refer to her employer. "I came to live with her and her *esposo* . . . her husband"—she nodded toward Nova—"when Jamie was still a baby—still under two years old—and my youngest was grown."

"Was that on a full-time basis?" Brockman asked.

"At first it was just three days a week, but later it was full-time, except for one day each weekend, I went home to stay with my husband. When he die, I still keep a small apartment in the city, but I stay with *Doña* Tami practically all the time, except Sundays, when I visit with my relatives."

"And when Ms. Dawson and Mr. Nova separated, you went to live with Ms. Dawson in Malibu, is that right?" Brockman asked, completing the relevant chronology.

"Yes, I care for Jamie when she is at *Doña* Tami's home and take care of *Doña* Tami's house other times. It is very big, and there is much cooking and cleaning to be done."

"During the time that you have worked for Ms. Dawson, how well have you gotten to know her daughter, Jamie?"

Yolanda's almond eyes widened with incredulity. "How well do I know her? I know her like my own *nina.* I do everything for her. Change diapers and feed her when she was little, rock her to sleep, sing to her. Now I make her food, wash her clothes. We play cards, watch TV together, go to stores. I listen to her play piano." She stopped, as if considering whether to add to the inventory of activities she shared with Jamie. "I give her love. That is very important."

"Yes, I'm sure that's something on which we all agree," Brockman said reassuringly. "Are you aware that Ms. Dawson is moving to New York in the autumn?"

"Of course." She moved her pocketbook off her lap and wedged it between her hip and the side of the witness chair as she folded her short, dimpled arms together. "And I am going with her and Jamie."

"Bingo," Molly sighed quietly, shooting an anxious glance at Nova.

"When did you make that decision?" Brockman asked.

"I feel that way ever since *Doña* Tami first ask me, some time ago now." She straightened her back and turned her face toward Judge Goldstein. "But yesterday Tami say it was very important I give her an answer, and come to court to tell the judge. And so I am here."

"Why have you decided to go with Tami?"

Yolanda raised her eyebrows and shrugged. "There is really noting to decide. My son here is grown and has a good job. It is Jamie now who needs me. And if I am in New York, I will be close to my Rita. She is the one who lives in Feel . . ."

"Philadelphia."

"Yes. She is a nurse. *Doña* Tami has promised to ask her sister's husband—he is a doctor—to get for her a job in a big hospital in New York or with another doctor there. She has also promised to send me here for Christmas to be with my son and his *familia*."

Staying with the subject of New York, Brockman spent a few more minutes bringing out the details of the new domestic arrangement that awaited Yolanda on the East Coast. She would have her own room, in the rear of Tami's new flat, and would be in charge of getting Jamie ready for school and putting her to bed each night, in addition to her general duties cooking and cleaning. "I would do the same things I do now, only in a new home," Yolanda said confidently. "I am sure everyone will be very happy. It will be a new . . . *como* . . . adventure."

"What about Mr. Nova?" Brockman asked, gesturing toward the respondent's counsel table. "Hasn't he asked you to move in with him if he wins custody of Jamie?"

The question instantly struck a nerve. Yolanda took a hard swallow and wrung her hands together, hesitating before answering. "He ask, but I say no."

"When did Mr. Nova ask if you would move in with him?"

"Once, when he brought Jamie home on a Sunday, and again when she leave for summer camp. Each time I say no."

"Are you sure you didn't tell him that you'd think about his offer and get back to him? It's important that you tell the complete truth."

Yolanda seemed to bristle at Brockman's brusque tone, her face reddening. "Yes, I am sure, very sure."

Reacting instinctively, Nova leaned over to Molly. "That's not true," he hissed. "She's lying."

Said with just enough emphasis to become a distraction, Nova's utterance caught the attention of Judge Goldstein. Staring down from on high, she raised her elongated right hand in the fashion of a traffic cop motioning a lane of cars to hit the brakes. The courtroom fell silent as her gaze settled on the respondent's table. "Would you care to share that observation with the rest of us, Mr. Nova?"

"I apologize, Your Honor," Nova answering sheepishly. From out of the corner of his eye he could see a thin smirk creasing Tami's lips. It was the first sign of human emotion she had shown all morning, he thought to himself. It figured that it would come at his expense. "It won't happen again."

"See that it doesn't," Goldstein admonished before directing Brockman to wrap up his examination.

"Can you tell the court, Yolanda, why you told Mr. Nova that you wouldn't move in with him?" Brockman asked.

Yolanda fidgeted with the sleeves of her blouse. She glanced at Nova and then looked at Tami, as if seeking some kind of protection. "I tell him Jamie is becoming a woman. She belongs with her ma-ma."

Ending on a high note, Brockman passed the witness to Molly for what promised to be a most difficult cross. "Just try to contain yourself," Molly whispered to Nova as she rose from her seat. "If she's lying, we'll prove it."

Molly paused for a moment at the lectern, then began. "You like Tami very much, don't you, Yolanda?"

"Oh, yes. *Doña* Tami has been very good to me."

"She's given you a good-paying job and provided you with a beautiful place to live?"

"Yes."

"And now a member of her family—specifically, her sister's husband—has promised to use his connections to help one of your children get a job in New York."

"That is what *Doña* Tami says. I believe her."

"And in return for the way Tami has treated you and your family, you've agreed to move to New York, true?"

"Yes, I think it is best."

"And Tami has asked you to come to court today to tell Judge Goldstein about your decision. Yes?"

"Yes."

"Has she also asked you to come to court and lie?"

Yolanda's face reddened and her hands began to

shake. *"Dio mio,* may God strike me," she said three times, shaking her head through each invocation of the Almighty. "Tami never say any such thing."

"But isn't it true, Yolanda, that until this morning you never told Mr. Nova that you would not move in with him if he won custody of Jamie? You're lying about that, aren't you?" Molly waited for an answer, tapping her fingers lightly on the lectern. When none was offered, she added, "Or perhaps you're simply mistaken or confused."

"No, I no lie and I no confused," Yolanda managed to say after enduring Molly's verbal assault. "I tell the *señor* what I say."

"I think you've made your point, counsel," Judge Goldstein cut in just as it appeared Yolanda was becoming flustered and tongue-tied again. "Time to move on."

Heeding the court's admonition, Molly shifted her focus. "You've observed Mr. Nova with Jamie over the years, haven't you, Yolanda?"

"Yes."

"Then you know how involved Mr. Nova is with Jamie in helping her with sports, and in making sure she keeps up with her homework. He takes her to movies and hosts parties for her. They even go hiking together, don't they?"

"That is so."

"It sounds to me, then, Yolanda, that you have no problems with the way Mr. Nova treats Jamie, do you?"

As she had seemed just a moment ago, Yolanda appeared tongue-tied and unable to reply, prompting Molly to rephrase her question. "He's a good father, isn't he?"

Thinking that a little judicial intervention was again appropriate, Judge Goldstein cut in. "You have to an-

swer counsel's question. Is there anything about Mr.
Nova's ways as a parent that you don't like?"

Yolanda shifted in her seat until she was face to
face with Goldstein. "*Sí*, Your Honor."

"What don't you like?" Goldstein asked.

"I no like how he have so many girlfriends. That is
not good for Jamie to see."

"Anything else?"

Yolanda took a deep breath and almost choked out
the words. "I no like sometimes how he touches Jamie."

"You've seen him touch Jamie in an improper manner?" Goldstein asked. Both the tone of her voice and
the tension in her face indicated that she intended to
continue to question the witness until she got to the
bottom of the potential bombshell.

"Yes, when he come to the house to take Jamie to
the airport for summer camp, I see him touch her here
and here," she said, moving her dimpled right arm to
her buttocks and then to her breast to illustrate the
breach of parental propriety. "They were in the driveway and I was at the front door. I hear him say to
Jamie that she is getting big and soon will have boobies. That's when he touch her here." She laid her
hand again on her breast.

"Mr. Nova used the word 'boobies'?" Goldstein
asked, casting a disapproving gaze at Nova.

"*Sí*, I hear him."

Goldstein nodded toward Molly to resume her
cross, but there was little she could do to recover from
the damage Yolanda had inflicted. She established that
Yolanda could recall no other specific instance of inappropriate touching and then agreed to have the witness excused.

For Nova, the rest of the morning passed in a burn-
ing haze. Struggling to contain his rage at what he

alone knew were Yolanda's lies, he barely listened as Brockman and Molly summarized the evidence in their closing arguments and made their respective pitches for primary physical custody of Jamie. Finally, even though it was already past noon, Judge Goldstein announced her decision.

"After due consideration of the evidence, both oral and documentary, and the arguments of the parties, I have decided to permit the minor to relocate with her mother to New York, commencing with Ms. Dawson's move in the autumn. Under the circumstances presented, where one parent will be moving out of state and the other will remain behind, it is not possible for both parents to be awarded joint physical custody. Given the living arrangements that the court anticipates will be created for the child in New York—in particular, the fact that she will have a large extended family there, as well as the attention of her mother and her longtime nanny—it is my opinion that the child's best interests will be served, and served well, by permitting the move and awarding sole physical custody to Ms. Dawson."

Goldstein paused to assay the parties and their lawyers, her eyes drifting from each face to the next, as if to emphasize the solemnity of the moment and to discourage any undue displays of emotion. "My ruling in no way implies, however, that I consider the child's father, Mr. Nova, unfit, or that I have given the allegations of Ms. Dawson's housekeeper any considerable weight. To the contrary, I consider both Mr. Nova and Ms. Dawson to be adequate, though by no means ideal, parents. The court recognizes that both parties love their daughter and that love is reciprocated by the child. For that reason I have also decided to continue the current status of joint *legal* custody over the child. This means that while Ms. Dawson will have physical custody of Jamie, Mr. Nova's legal parental rights to be consulted and to make decisions affecting the health, education, and welfare of the child shall remain unaltered.

"I am also going to order the parties to submit to me, by the first week of September, a schedule of visitation, which shall provide that Jamie is to visit her father for either the Christmas or Easter vacation periods and for all, or part, of each summer, the exact amount of time to be agreed upon by the parties. Ms. Dawson shall bear the cost of providing the child's airfare for such visits. I think that's only fair. Each party shall pay for the child's support when the child resides separately with them. Given the sound financial positions of the parties, no further support payments need be made.

"Finally," Goldstein added, staring at Brockman and Tami, "I want to remind the petitioner and her counsel that this court shall retain jurisdiction of the issue of custody throughout Jamie's minority. Should the petitioner disregard this, or any subsequent order issued by the court, I will not hesitate to entertain a motion to reopen the entire question of custody."

Goldstein took one last, long look at the parties through the heavy lenses of her glasses, then brought down her gavel and called the proceedings to an adjournment.

Against Molly's strenuous advice that he wait in the courtroom for Tami and Brockman to exit and find their way to the elevator, Nova managed to remain seated only long enough to see the doors behind Tami's heather gray business suit. Then, driven by adrenaline and impulse, he took off after her, leaving Molly and his own briefcase in his wake. By the time Molly caught up with him in the middle of the outer corridor, a small crowd of court personnel and litigants from other courtrooms had gathered around Brockman, Tami, and Nova like a group of school kids intent on viewing a playground fight.

Brockman had inserted himself between the two combatants, his palms pressed flat against Nova's chest in an effort to avoid a physical confrontation. Nova, oblivious to the public spectacle unfolding, looked past Brockman. The ligaments in his neck stretched to the point of snapping, and his eyes flashed with single-minded malice. Pointing an accusatory finger at Tami much as a stickup man angles the barrel of a gun in the face of his victim, he shouted, "You put Yolanda up there to lie. I know it. You know it, and your scumbag attorney knows it, too."

"You're just going to have to learn to live with the judge's order, David," Tami snapped back from behind Brockman. For someone so small and physically vulnerable, she sounded surprisingly poised and unafraid. "You lost. Get used to it, and get over it, or I'll have all of your parental rights completely terminated."

Tami's calm in the face of his fury only caused his anger to swell. "If there's any way to pay you back, I'll find it," he screamed back at her. "I promise."

Finally, with Molly tugging on one arm and Brockman shoving hard now against his upper arms, Nova began to relent. He took a couple of backward steps and allowed Tami and her attorney to board the elevator without further incident.

"We only lost the battle in Judy's courtroom," Molly said with measured irony after the rubberneckers around them had dispersed. "I thought for a moment there we were about to lose the war, too."

Chapter Thirty-one

A phone call after midnight usually meant one of two things—a wrong number . . . or Tami. Even with half a bottle of single malt dancing in his brain, Nova was certain it was the latter. She probably wanted to gloat over her victory, to see if he was really suffering or just pretending, or maybe just to get in one more dig she had forgotten to deliver in the courthouse hallway before Brockman had ushered her out of their private war zone and onto the waiting elevator.

Dressed only in his slacks and undershirt, Nova struggled out of the high-backed easy chair in his Topanga living room and flicked off the *Tonight Show* rerun he'd been half following on the tube. The blue glow of the TV faded with a slight sizzling sound, leaving the sixty-watt lightbulb in the table lamp by the phone stand as the room's sole source of illumination. With Nova's jacket, dress shirt, and tie flung on the room's big sofa and the half-eaten remains of a hastily prepared frozen dinner of chopped steak, green peas, and mashed potatoes congealing on the coffee table next to a nearly extinguished bottle of Glenfiddich, the den had the look of a set from *The Lost Weekend*. And the weekend was only beginning.

Nova poured himself the last of the Scotch and

picked up the phone on the fifth ring. "I thought you'd call," he barked into the receiver, gearing up for another shouting match.

"Really?" the male voice on the other end asked. "That's downright flattering."

"Who the fuck is this?" He was almost disappointed not to hear his ex-wife's voice.

"Sounds like a rough afternoon is becoming a rough night, Davey."

"Who the fuck is this?" Nova asked again, growing impatient and hostile.

"I'm hurt you don't recognize me, Davey. Really."

Nova suddenly felt sick to his stomach. "Sturgis?"

"Long time, Davey. The she-devil gave you a good run for it in court, huh?" The southern twang was in his voice. He sounded happy-go-lucky, supremely confident, and malevolent all at the same time.

"How the hell would you know?"

"How do you think I know? Take a good guess."

Unwilling to take the bait, Nova waited for Sturgis to elaborate. Hearing only the sound of Randy's breathing on the line, however, he quickly gave in. He uttered the first name that came to mind. "Tami?"

"She's fucked over both of us, buddy," Randy said consolingly. "Makes us members of the same exclusive club. We should have some kind of secret handshake. I don't know about you, but for me it's kind of a love-hate thing. Anyways, you have my heartfelt sympathy."

"I don't believe you," Nova countered. "You're a lying sonofabitch."

"Not so, partner. The little gal was one of my biggest fans at Folsom. Used to brighten up ol' Randy's mood on visitin' days real good. Got me straight in a big way, if you understand what I mean."

"That was just business, and I know all about it." Fearing that any display of anger would only add to

Randy's fun, Nova made a conscious effort to calm himself.

"Then I'll tell you something that has nothing to do with business. You and me, partner, are probably the only two who ever brought that little spitfire to a climax just by pinching her nipples. Nice round pink ones. A little on the small side, but real classy." He laughed to himself, then added, "Am I right? Or am I the only one who can lay claim to that honor?"

"That's bullshit, Randy. Tami may be a cunt, but she'd never let a scum like you put his hands on her."

"Is that so? She used to come to Folsom all gussied up, wearing them expensive suits and silk blouses. But you know what? She never wore no bras underneath. I could tell right away she liked the feel of a man's hand, the way she murmured and squirmed, the way her petite nostrils flared and her blue eyes seemed to roll right back into that high forehead of hers. We had a little table in the corner where the guards looked the other way."

Randy paused until he was certain his remarks had registered. "Say, I wonder if little pumpkinface will turn out the same way. I hear she's having a fine time at summer camp back East. That is what you call Jamie, now, ain't it?"

"How the hell do you know that, Sturgis?" The anger was back in his voice, and he was shouting louder than ever. His eyes darted to the wall above the phone stand and the bright color photograph of Jamie standing on the edge of a diving board above a deep blue pool, dressed in a little girl's one-piece swimsuit. The shot was taken in mid-summer two years ago at the daycamp she had attended before heading off this year to the Catskills. More than ever Nova wished he had never let her go.

"Do I detect just a tad of desperation in your tone, Davey?" Sturgis asked. "And here I remember you as a cool and collected one. You've changed, Davey. But then that little cunt, as you so aptly described our mutual playmate, will do that to a man. Tell me you believe me, Davey, if you want an answer."

"Just tell me how you know," Nova insisted, refusing to yield to Randy's demand. "I've got to know."

"You disappoint me, Davey, and this isn't the first time. You were a disappointment at trial and—"

"Sturgis!" Nova screamed into the phone.

"No need to strain the vocal cords, Davey, and anyways, I gotta go." He spoke quietly, as if addressing a tantruming child. "We've been shooting the shit awhile, and you never know who else might be listening. I suggest you run your query by the talk-show hostess. She's the best in the business at tellin' all."

Nova heard the click on the other end before he could say another word. He thought for a moment about phoning Agent Ross, but the impulse to push the speed-dial button for Tami's private number was just too great.

Tami picked up on the third ring, sounding groggy and irritated. "Are you crazy, David?" she asked when she realized it was Nova on the line. "It's after midnight, and we have nothing to say to each other."

"Oh, yes, we do," Nova snapped back. "I know about you and Randy Sturgis."

"*That* again? I thought you'd be moving on to something else by now."

"Cut the crap, Tami. It's just you and me talking now. No more games."

"You know, I think you really *are* crazy, David. And you sound like you've been drinking, too."

"You're the one who's crazy, Tami. You told that scum about Jamie. Don't deny it. I want the truth, and I want it now."

"I thought you said you already knew the truth," she replied in that catty voice that irritated the hell out of him. "Why bother me in the middle of the night if you already know?"

"How could you put Jamie at risk like this?"

"Jamie's on her camping trip, David, and she's perfectly fine. And besides, I don't have to tell you anything. In fact, I don't have to talk to you at all," she said icily before slamming down the receiver.

For the second time in less than five minutes, the line went dead in Nova's hand. He hit the redial button three times but received only a busy signal. The bitch had taken her phone off the hook, he muttered to himself. He wasn't about to let her off that easily, not when she was only a half hour's drive away and he could confront her face to face.

His frustration and anger multiplying with each heartbeat, he slipped on his shoes and reached for his shirt, hastily throwing it over his shoulders without bothering to button it. Then he grabbed his car keys and made his way quickly to the garage.

Driving ten to twenty miles an hour over the speed limit, he made the trip down the canyon in record time. Even with his head still buzzing, he was able to negotiate the sharp switchbacks and keep pace with his own escalating sense of urgency. The motorists he encountered in the canyon and beyond were generally a laid-back and cautious lot, and in no particular hurry to get home in the small hours of the morning. They did their best to accommodate the onrushing Lexus, even to the point of pulling over when Nova came too close for comfort. The local cops also obliged, keeping both out of sight and out of mind. Nova managed to steer his way free of harm, without putting himself or others in danger.

The same could not be said, however, of the two

young men in the Ford pickup traveling south on Pacific Coast Highway en route to the intersection with Topanga Canyon Boulevard. Nova flashed his right-turn signal a good ten yards from the intersection, preparing to enter the highway's northbound lane to Malibu. He made a wide turn, assuming as he swung the steering wheel that the Ford would stop at the red light and allow him to proceed unmolested. With his mind riveted on the anticipated confrontation with Tami, he took his eyes off the Ford. He neither saw the pickup accelerate or noticed that it had crossed the median into his lane of the highway. Nor did he see the open can of Coors the young driver lifted casually to his mouth as the truck slammed hard into the passenger side of the Lexus.

The force of the collision, coupled with the angle of the turn, sent the Lexus spinning back into the intersection, where it was rear-ended by an older Hispanic man driving a beat-up Toyota. The Lexus' air bags deployed on contact, preventing major injury to Nova's chest and face, but doing little to mitigate the damage to his left temple as Nova's head was whipsawed into the driver's-side window like a spring-necked dashboard figure. His ribs bounced violently against the door's armrest. The force of the impact against the side window shattered the glass and opened a deep gash above his left eye. Nova lost consciousness instantly, never knowing what had hit him. Blood seeped past his eye and down his cheek, forming tiny scarlet rivulets as it dried.

Randy checked the ammo clip of his 9mm handgun for the sixth time and glanced again at his watch. It was past one. He had been waiting in the turnoff down the road from Tami's beach house for more than an hour and was becoming bored, angry, and impatient.

There were only so many trips he could make to the 7-Eleven down the street for coffee before the night clerk became suspicious. Had he figured Nova wrong or was Davey just too plastered to make the drive to Malibu? Nova had seemed more than a little fucked up on the phone.

Thinking his plans for the evening had been foiled, he placed the 9mm under the front seat of his Chevy, started up the engine, and pulled onto the southbound lane of PCH. He'd keep his eyes peeled for Nova's Lexus and double back behind him if possible. Or, if prudence dictated otherwise, he'd call it a day and go back to the drawing board. Either way, he was still way ahead of the game.

At the edge of Las Tunas State Beach, just a stone's throw from Topanga Boulevard, traffic started to back up. For a jam to take place at this late hour, Randy knew there either had to be a landslide or an accident. He crept forward slowly, and another minute passed before he caught his first glimpse of the two California highway patrol cars that had responded to the scene. One of the officers, wearing a trademark CHP wide-brimmed khaki green hat, had positioned himself in the middle of the highway to direct traffic. Obeying the CHIPPIE's hand signals, Randy followed the slow line of cars in front of him as they moved past the crash site. To his left, as he approached the intersection of Topanga and PCH, he saw a big blue-and-white tow truck in the last stages of hooking up a late-model steel gray Lexus. The car had a badly dented door and a window shattered like it had been hit by a large heavy object.

Randy recognized the Lexus almost immediately as Nova's. "Davey, Davey, Davey," he said softly to himself, shaking his head. "You should have taken a cab."

Chapter Thirty-two

The expression on Jamie's face was one of intense concentration, the kind of unfettered attention that only a six-year-old who has yet to experience the tedium and distractions of the adult world can achieve. Her pigtails dancing in the blustery March wind, a hard-plastic Dodgers batting helmet on her head, she stood at the plate, her pint-sized aluminum bat raised to the ready, waiting for him to toss another pitch.

"Keep your eyes on the ball and your feet still until you swing," he instructed. He tried to remain equally focused himself, but he couldn't keep himself from smiling at the picture-perfect setting. He was teaching his little girl the great American game, and she was taking to it like a natural. Even Tami, in the days before her leap to TV stardom, was into it, outfitted in sweats and running shoes, no makeup, pounding her mitt in the role of catcher behind Jamie. They were a family, and the future seemed unbroken.

"Throw the ball, Daddy," Jamie shouted. "Come on, I'm ready."

"Okay, here it comes." He raised his right arm and twisted his torso, imitating the motion of a big-league hurler.

And then the pain came again. A shooting, searing

ache in his left side so deep that it seemed rooted in his very breathing, occupying his entire consciousness, jolting him awake.

"You're lucky you weren't killed."

Nova heard the sound of the wry adult female voice and opened his eyes, slowly focusing on Molly. He felt the throbbing at his forehead and traced the Steristrips along his left temple with his fingers before letting his hands fall to the foam-rubber brace on his neck. Then he reached for his ribs and the Acebandage wrap that had been taped around his torso. "Where the hell am I?"

"Kensington Memorial in Santa Monica," Molly answered from the chair beside Nova's hospital bed. "They brought you in early this morning with a pretty bad concussion. You've also got a laceration on your head, a neck sprain, and some bruised ribs, but nothing's broken. I guess God really does protect idiots and fools. What on earth possessed you to take off for Tami's house?"

"How did you know that?" He tried to prop himself up on one arm to face her, but another jolt of pain made him give up on the effort.

"The cops called her after the accident. She called Brockman, who in turn called me—at home, I might add, at four in the morning. I agreed to see to all your paperwork. That seemed to calm them down a little."

"Thanks," Nova muttered, managing a weak smile, grabbing at the foam-rubber cervical collar under his chin. "What time is it?"

"Nearly six o'clock. You've been out like a light until now. The docs have you on a lot of pain medication."

"Christ! We've got to stop her while there's still

time." He tried again to prop himself up, and this time barely succeeded. He gave Molly a imploring look.

"Stop who, David?"

"Tami. The bitch has been helping Sturgis all along. That's why I went to see her. We need to call Tony Ross."

Molly folded her hands in her lap and spoke softly. "Listen to me, David, you've just suffered a bad head injury. This is no time to go off on another tear against Tami, not after that fight at the courthouse and not after she cooperated with the police in contacting Brockman about your accident. You should be grateful for that."

"But—"

"But nothing," she continued. "If you really insist, I'll phone Agent Ross myself. In the meantime, your first and only concern should be getting well."

Realizing that he was in no condition to argue, he began to relent. "Maybe you're right," he said, pawing at his ribs. He took a look around the room and noticed his was the only bed. "How did I manage to score a private room?"

"That's another thing you can be grateful for," she answered. "I represented the hospital awhile back in a little licensing tiff. You might say they owe me one. They've promised to bill your insurance at the double-room rate. They've also agreed to keep you in until Monday or Tuesday instead of giving you the bum's rush like an ordinary patient. They'll write up the medical report to make sure the insurance covers it." She stood and leaned over him, rubbing his forehead gently with her right hand. "So, you've got nothing to do but get better."

"I don't know how I can ever repay you," he said, taking her hand in his. "I certainly don't deserve this."

"No doubt about that, Jack." She withdrew her

hand. "I'm thinking of making you my law clerk when you're released. I need a good indentured servant. I also expect that you'll retain me in your personal-injury claim. The kid who hit you has been booked for DUI. We could be looking at a six-figure settlement."

She started to say good-bye, then added, as if suddenly remembering the most important piece of news, "There's one other thing. I took the liberty when I was here earlier of taking your house keys. There's a fresh change of clothes in the closet—a pair of jogging shoes, jeans, underwear, T-shirt, and a lightweight jacket from your hall closet. I've also checked your wallet. You've got a hundred bucks and some change. And everything's fine up in Topanga. The place is locked up tight."

It seemed as if Molly wanted to say more, but the arrival of Nova's nurse and his dinner brought their conversation to an end. Molly stayed just long enough to hear the nurse, a pleasant Korean woman in her mid-forties, tell Nova how important it was for him to try to eat something.

"Then I want you to take these pills," the nurse said, pointing at the silver medicine cup on the tray. "The blue one is for nausea. The two white ones are for pain. I'll be back later to look at your bandages and to give you a shot to let you sleep."

Nova did his best to find some enjoyment in the overcooked chicken and rice on his plate but was able to consume only a child-size portion. He washed down his meal with a cup of filtered apple juice, which he used to swallow his pills as well. Despite Molly's advice, he thought about phoning Ross on his own and at one point had even lifted up the receiver on the nightstand next to his bed. But the details of his late-night conversation with Sturgis were increasingly hazy in his mind as he tried to recall them. He decided he would make the call later, or perhaps let Molly take care of everything after all. In due course night fell, and the Korean nurse reentered the room, a large syringe in one hand and a small vial of clear liquid in the other, putting an end to his thoughts of contacting anyone.

"Time for your shot," the nurse said cheerfully. She rolled up the right sleeve of his hospital gown and swabbed his left arm with alcohol. "You're doing just fine," she said, inserting the needle and releasing its contents into his bloodstream. "You'll be on your feet and out of here in no time."

The nurse fluffed up his pillows and pulled the blankets over him as he lay on his back. He shut his eyes as she left the room, trying without much success to find a sleeping position free of pain. He passed the remainder of the night fitfully, his sleep interrupted both by the pain and at regular intervals for additional medication, administered each time by a different nurse. At roughly four a.m., after finally settling down, he was startled out of yet another dream by the moans and cries of a patient across the hall.

With the soreness in his ribs dulled by the medication, he managed to struggle out of bed and walked to the door. Despite the lateness of the hour, the bright overhead lights were on in the moaning patient's room. Nova could see two nurses, an Asian woman and a male nurse, either a dark-skinned Hispanic or a light-skinned black, inside the room. Another nurse, a heavyset female Anglo, was hurrying down the hallway, preparing to join her colleagues by the moaning man's side.

Nova took a small step into the hallway. "What's happening?" he asked.

The Anglo nurse looked at him, annoyed and surprised. "What are you doing out of bed?" she scolded.

She shooed him back into his room and bustled after him as he turned around. "Your neighbor's been in a car wreck, like you, only much worse. He has broken bones and some burns." She helped him back under the covers and admonished him to stay put.

Nova muttered something about how nobody ever got well inside a hospital but obeyed the nurse's order without protest.

By early Sunday afternoon, however, he did feel better, well enough, in fact, to sit up in bed, do a little reading, and catch a few innings of the Dodgers' game on TV. The pain in his ribs was still there, but he found he could lie down without the cervical collar, and he managed to get through most of the day without it. Under the watchful eyes of his nurses, he even took a long stroll down the hall. As part of a little mental exercise designed to clear his head as much as to relieve the boredom, he tried to count the number of patient rooms on the floor (he lost interest at twenty) and made a mental note of the location of the nursing stations, the small staff lounge, and the stairway exits, including the one at the corner two doors down from his own room.

The highlight of his day was a call from Sandy just before dinner. She had been at home last night, she told him, thinking about her visit with him when Molly phoned with news of the accident. "I can imagine how agitated you must be after what happened in court," she said, "but the best thing for you now is to put that out of your mind until you're back home and really on your feet again." She promised to call again on her next trip to L.A. and gave him a standing date for "lunch, dinner, or whatever" in the Bay Area. She sounded like she really meant it. And unless he was very much mistaken, moreover, her interest went far beyond the bounds of simple friendship.

His spirits lifted by Sandy's invitation, he was at last able to eat a full meal. Even the mystery meat on his plate—some kind of pressed turkey, he surmised—and sauteed potatoes tasted palatable. With the aid of another dose of painkillers at eight-thirty, he was able to drift off to sleep until another one of the night nurses came to check on him at two in the morning.

A large black man dressed in a neatly pressed short-sleeve uniform, the nurse was well built, with a clean-shaven bald head, a closely trimmed goatee, and the broad, flat nose of a boxer. Along with a medical clipboard, he carried an aluminum medication tray loaded with a pitcher of water and another steel medicine cup. He set the tray down on the nightstand by the bed, and switched on the small table lamp on top of it. "Time for your medication," he said with a smile, gently shaking Nova by the shoulder. "Here, take these."

Nova sat up and took the two pink-colored capsules from the nurse. "These are a different color," he said matter-of-factly. "The others were white."

"They're a little stronger," the nurse replied, pouring a glass of water and handing it to Nova. "You're going to be discharged tomorrow afternoon, and the doctor wants to make sure you sleep through the rest of the night." He watched as Nova swallowed both capsules.

Nova handed the glass back to the nurse. For a split second his eyes met the nurse's. The big man's eyes were light brown, almost hazel, an odd hue for an African American. Even in the soft light, the eyes had a sharp-edged glint that Nova found disconcerting. From the eyes, Nova let his gaze drift down to the name tag pinned above the nurse's heart. The tag read, "Noah Chamberlain." Nova took another, longer look at the nurse's face. His mind and heart began to race.

"I'll be back in a little while to check up on you," Nurse Chamberlain said, turning off the light on his way out of the room. "I'll try not to wake you." He closed the door behind him as he left.

Nova waited until he heard the sound of Chamberlain's footsteps disappear. Then he switched on the nightstand lamp and pushed himself out of bed and over to the closet. Fighting both the pain in his ribs and the first effects of the painkillers, he found his wallet and money and struggled into the clothes Molly had left for him. He remembered from his afternoon walk that the nearest stairway exit was but a few yards away. From there it would be three flights to the ground floor. Olympic Boulevard, if his long-term memory could be relied upon, was only a couple of blocks from the hospital entrance. He knew that it would only be a matter of minutes, a half hour at the outside, until the painkillers really kicked in and he would be unable to walk, much less think clearly. There was no point in reporting what he had seen to the hospital staff, he told himself in a flicker of paranoia. At best they would humor him and take him back up to his room. At worst, they would shoot him up with Thorazine and strap him down good and tight. As his panic mounted, he was driven only by the thought of making his way down the exit stairs and out of the hospital.

Still, there was a part of himself that wanted to stop and turn around before he did something truly foolhardy, like tumbling down a concrete and steel stairwell. There was no rational explanation for what he had just seen. He knew that. He also knew that he might well have misread the name tag on the nurse's uniform. It wouldn't be the first time that an accident victim, particularly one with a concussion and hopped up on painkillers, had thought he'd seen something that wasn't really there. He had been asleep, after all, when the nurse had entered his room.

In the end, it was the nurse's eyes that convinced him of the improbable truth and propelled him forward into the hallway and through the exit door. He'd seen the eyes before, up close and personal, in jail and in court. As impossible as it seemed, he was certain they were the eyes of Randy Sturgis.

Chapter Thirty-three

"You look like shit, mister," the weatherbeaten little man with the raspy voice said.

Nova rubbed his eyes and opened them slowly. His head throbbed and his ribs ached. His mouth tasted like the inside of a dumpster. "Jesus, I must have passed out." He stared at the little man. The deep creases in his forehead, the ragged clothes and worn tennis shoes, and the plastic bag by his side filled with aluminum cans instantly identified him as homeless.

"I saw a couple of skinheads coming after you up the street, and I helped you in here," the man said. He made a sweeping gesture with his right hand to refer to the alley where both he and Nova had passed the night. "If I hadn't seen you, you'd either be dead or back in the hospital."

Nova pulled himself to a standing position and brushed the dirt from his denim jacket and jeans. "How did you know I was in the hospital?" he asked.

"You didn't get them stitches from a quilting party." The man pointed at Nova's temple. "Looks like it smarts a bit." The man looked at Nova again and added, "I thought I saw you get out of a car before you started walking. That true?"

"I don't think so," Nova answered groggily. "My

car was wrecked over the weekend." His mind clearing, Nova reached for his back pocket to make sure he still had his wallet.

"Don't worry, mister, I ain't the kind to rip off someone in his sleep." The little guy looked genuinely offended.

Nova pulled out his wallet just the same and took a quick inventory of his cash. "I'm sorry," he apologized after he was certain he hadn't been robbed, "but this is a new experience for me." He took out a five-dollar bill and offered it to the man. "Here, I owe you a lot more."

The man put up a mild protest but in the end wound up accepting the money. "Well, take care," he said, stuffing the fiver in his right front pants pocket.

"Do you know where I can find a phone?" Nova asked.

"Up at the corner by the bus stop, outside the drugstore. There's also a phone inside the store, but the owner don't like for street folk to use it." The old man grinned broadly, exposing a set of incisors so stained from years of neglect they looked as though some exotic variety of tree moss had taken up residence on them. "Maybe your luck will be different."

Nova thanked the man again and walked off, wincing as he lifted his feet but finding the going a little easier with each step. His appearance inside the drugstore a few minutes later aroused a few worried looks from the counter help, but no threats of expulsion. A quick glance in one of the store's mirrors provided ample explanation of the employees' concern. In addition to the stitches over his left temple, a nasty red welt had begun to rise over his left cheek, the result, no doubt, of a tumble to the pavement before passing out in the alley. He purchased a pair of heavy dark sunglasses at the counter and made his way to a phone booth located near the front of the store.

He punched in his credit card number and phoned Molly, but managed only to draw her answering machine at home and her secretary at the office. "Ms. Carpenter won't be in until late this afternoon or, depending on how things go, possibly not until tomorrow morning," the secretary told him. "She's in a deposition in San Diego." A glance at the clock on the store wall told Nova it was just nine-thirty. He left word only that he was no longer in the hospital and would call back later. Then he punched in his credit card number again and dialed Tony Ross' direct line at the FBI office in Westwood.

"Where are you, David?" Ross asked immediately on picking up the receiver.

It was a simple question but an odd one to kick off a conversation with someone you hadn't talked to in nearly a month. Ross wasn't interested in how he was or even how his custody hearing had gone. He sounded, in fact, almost as if he had been expecting Nova to call.

"I'm in a phone booth, Tony, in Santa Monica," Nova answered warily.

"Good."

"Good? What the hell's good about that?" Nova asked testily. "I've just escaped from the hospital."

"I know," Ross said.

"How could you have known that? It only happened last night." Nova couldn't be sure, but it seemed, from the muted background sounds he thought he heard, as if Ross had placed his hand over the mouthpiece and had begun speaking with someone else.

"Because Tami was murdered last night, David. The housekeeper found her early this morning."

The news hit Nova like an electric shock. His body stiffened, and for a few agonizing seconds he was unable to speak.

"I want you to tell me where you are, David, and I'll send someone to pick you up." Ross' voice was calm and deliberate, the way cops often sound when negotiating the release of a hostage or talking a potential suicide into taking the gun barrel out of his mouth.

"You think that I did it, don't you?" Nova's voice began to quaver. His sense of paranoia also returned, escalating beyond all previous limits as he put together what he regarded as the only possible explanation for Ross' overly solicitous tone. "You want me to come in so you can take me into custody, don't you?"

"We can talk about what happened when you get here," Ross said reassuringly. "Strictly speaking, this isn't a Bureau matter, but we've been contacted by some of the agencies working on the Tanner joint task force and I've promised to help the local authorities. I know you'll want to cooperate, too."

"But there's no reason to cooperate," Nova protested. "At least not in the way you're implying. I couldn't possibly have killed Tami. I didn't leave the hospital until after two in the morning."

"The last recorded bed check the hospital made on you was at eight-thirty, David, and from what I've been told there were several reports of stolen cars in the general vicinity of the hospital last night, including one from the lot right in front of the main entrance. Just tell me where you are, David, and we'll take things one step at a time."

Ross' words were followed by another vexing silence. Thinking again that he heard another voice in the agent's office, Nova's thoughts continued to spin out of control. "You're trying to tap this call, aren't you, Tony?"

"There's no reason to get agitated, I'm on your side. Really." Before Ross could offer any more reassurances, the line went dead in his hands.

Nova rushed out of the drugstore.

On the street, a small column of people had queued up to board an MTA bus. The roll-away sign on the upper front window indicated that it was an express departing for downtown L.A. Nova hesitated, contemplating his next move. As his thoughts raced, he saw a muscular-looking middle-aged black man strolling down the block toward the bus stand. A quick double-take succeeded in allaying his fears that Sturgis had donned yet another disguise and was heading his way. Within another heartbeat, however, a new disaster scenario appeared on the horizon as a black-and-white police car cruised past at what seemed an unusually slow rate of speed. Were the occupants of the car looking for him, or were they just looking in general? There wasn't any time to ponder the question. Even if the FBI hadn't succeeded in tapping the pharmacy's phone, he knew it wouldn't take the feds long to trace the credit card number he had used to call Ross to the drugstore's pay phone.

Nova jumped in the bus line and handed over the fare to cover the ride downtown plus a transfer to the Greyhound station on East Seventh Street. He had about seventy-eight dollars in his pocket and no idea where he might go. He only knew he had to keep moving.

In the light mid-morning traffic, it took just forty-five minutes for him to arrive at the Greyhound station. Like most well-heeled Angelenos, Nova normally had little reason to travel by bus. He had, in fact, visited the central station only once before, to pick up a witness who had come from San Diego to give a deposition in a civil case. The witness, a middle-aged Hispanic woman who had seen a car pileup on the Golden State Freeway, was one of those persons who was afraid to travel by plane and inexplicably preferred the bus over the train.

As it had been on his single prior visit, Nova found the station teeming with people—mostly lower-income individuals, considering their clothing—an equal mix of Anglo, black, Asian, and Hispanic. Some were lugging suitcases to and from taxicabs and cars; others were lining up to purchase tickets. Even more were fidgeting restlessly on the long wooden benches in the oversized main waiting room. Not surprisingly, it was the young single women with kids who seemed to have the hardest times, with their infants tugging at their breasts, their toddlers screaming from boredom and their school-age children galloping through the aisles, oblivious to all exhortations for better behavior.

Nova walked through the big waiting room, stopping a few steps from the central ticket window to study the overhead electronic board on which the day's arrivals and departures were posted in block gold letters. Given his cash situation and the need for a fast decision, the choices came down to a noon departure for Las Vegas or an express trip to San Francisco, leaving in twenty minutes. He chose the latter, for a fare of thirty-two dollars, leaving him with just enough time to buy a sandwich, a Coke, and a big bottle of Advil.

He found a corner seat on the last row of the Greyhound and laid his head against the rear wall as the bus pulled out of the station and followed a path on the surface streets to the northbound Golden State Freeway. It took another half hour for him to begin to relax, but as the bus approached the outer limits of the county and the surrounding traffic thinned out, he was finally able to eat his sandwich and make an assessment of his situation.

His most immediate concern, of course, was for his safety on the bus, and his prospects for making it to San Francisco without being apprehended. A quick look around told him he had little to worry about along either line. He remembered how one of his former clients—a con man he had defended almost fifteen years ago on a series of grand-theft charges—once had told him how easy it was to evade detection as long as you kept your cool and took care to blend in with others around you. In any other setting Nova knew he might have stood out like a sore thumb with his dark glasses and facial bruises. Here on the bus he seemed to be just another member of the downtrodden multitude. There was a forlorn young woman with even more prominent facial bruises than his, sitting with a two-year-old in one of the front rows, and a middle-aged man whose left leg was in a cast not more than three rows from him. The other passengers, and the driver as well, took no special note either of them or of Nova.

Trying to make sense out of what had happened to him in the hospital, or with Ross on the phone, was another matter. Nova was a man accustomed to being in control of his life. His actions were measured, his thoughts always carefully organized and logical. His thoughts now were jumbled, his actions impulsive and perhaps even self-destructive. Try as he might, he could not account for the time between his escape from the hospital and his early morning encounter with the homeless man back in the alleyway. He knew in his heart that he could not have murdered Tami in Malibu and have traveled back to Santa Monica in time to wake up on the hard ground. Still, he had no alibi, and the homeless guy had said something about seeing him get out of a car. He also knew that in Ross' eyes, the absence of an alibi, coupled with his troubled marital history, made him a prime suspect.

He flashed again on Tami. Had she told him the truth about her involvement with Sturgis, or was there more to it? Surely, it was Sturgis who had murdered her, but why? Had the killing occurred during a lovers' quarrel, or if Randy had lied about their relationship, was the killing his way of paying Tami back for rejecting his advances at Folsom? Then again, perhaps Randy had planned the whole thing to make it seem that Nova had murdered her in a jealous rage. Was that also part of Randy's "game," along with the Tanner kidnapping?

The questions kept flying at him, but he knew there were no answers to be found on the bus. He knew, too, that he would eventually have to give himself up. The only unresolved part was where and when. As easy as it had been for him to board a Greyhound out of town, he could not remain on the lam for long.

What he needed now was a place of refuge, if only temporarily, a place to clear his mind, adjust the bandage around his ribs, and plot his next move. Besides Jamie, who was in the midst of her camping trip to the Adirondacks and in all likelihood unaware of her mother's death, there were only two people in the world he trusted—Sandy and Molly. Molly was in San Diego, and Sandy was in the city to which he was heading at that very minute. From Nova's perspective, that made Sandy his only option.

Chapter Thirty-four

The Greyhound depot in San Francisco was located on Mission Street just a few blocks from the Promenade and the Embarcadero in an immense concrete terminal that housed the city's central Amtrak station as well. Like its L.A. counterpart, the Bay Area station was rundown, chaotic, and crowded, filled with people far too busy and preoccupied with their own daily hassles to take any notice of Nova as he stepped off his bus at ten minutes after six. Confident that his anonymity had not been compromised, Nova quietly found an empty phone booth and rang Sandy's office, betting correctly that she would still be at her desk. Her office, as luck had it, was only a short distance away by cab.

He knew he had made the right decision in phoning almost immediately from the concern in her voice. There was a certain measure of anxiety in her tone, to be sure, but not a trace of anger or alarm over the potential problems his call might cause for her. "I've heard about Tami, David," she said, letting him know straight away that she knew what had happened.

"How?"

"It's been on the radio, and the sheriffs from L.A. called a few hours ago to ask if I'd seen you. I told them I hadn't, of course." She paused a moment. "Where are you?"

"At the Greyhound depot."

"You're running from them, aren't you?"

Nova tried to tell her about his brush with Sturgis and how he was nearly drugged to death in the hospital, but quickly realized how incoherent he sounded. "I had nothing to do with Tami's murder; somebody's setting me up, Sturgis and maybe somebody else," he added, half in desperation and half in an effort to hold on to his sanity.

"I don't know about the setup, David, but I can't see you killing anyone."

"I just need a place to calm down and clean up before I turn myself in. Molly's in San Diego, and I couldn't think of anyone else—"

"But me," she cut in.

"I'm sorry, Sandy. I don't want to lay my troubles on you, but they're not going to bust you for talking to an innocent man, if that's what you're thinking. And I promise to be out of your hair by tomorrow morning. I look like shit, and my head and ribs feel like I've been slow-dancing with Mike Tyson."

"It's okay," she answered after a long pause. "I'll pick you up outside the station in fifteen minutes. Just don't do anything stupid until I get there. I'll be driving a red Camry."

It took a little effort for Sandy to pick Nova out of the crowd in the bus station parking lot, but by six-thirty they were safely on their way, driving up the Embarcadero past the World Trade Center before cutting across Broadway to Columbus Avenue and eventually making their way along the Presidio and onto the Golden Gate Bridge en route to Sandy's home in Mill Valley. Sandy made a few sympathetic remarks about how dreadful he looked, but otherwise remained silent, keeping her eyes trained on the road until they had safely crossed the bay. Then she turned on the radio and punched in one of the area's all-news stations.

The traffic and weather reports were followed by commercials for Pepsi, Chevron, a local dairy specializing in hormone-free milk products, and finally an update on Tami. "Details are still sketchy in the murder of television talk-show hostess Tami Dawson. As reported earlier, Ms. Dawson was found early this morning in her Malibu home by her housekeeper. A Los Angeles Sheriff's Department spokesperson has confirmed that authorities are seeking Dawson's former husband, Los Angeles attorney David Nova, who appears at this hour to be missing after escaping last night from an area hospital."

Sandy switched the radio off as soon as the report was completed. "We'll go back to my place and have some dinner," she said, apparently unshaken by what she had just heard. "I can put your clothes through the wash." She gave him an appraising look. "You probably could use a shower, too."

"I don't know how to thank you," Nova replied, easing his head against the Camry's neck rest.

"There will be time for that later," she said perfunctorily. "I also want you to call Molly. Okay?"

"As soon as we eat," he promised. He closed his eyes and drifted off to sleep for the last part of the ride.

Like many other successful Bay Area businesspeople, Sandy had left the city for the rustic affluence of Marin County. Mill Valley, where she had relocated two years earlier, was just one of the county's many bedroom communities, but when it came to being quaint and precious, it stood at or near the top of the list. A one-time lumber camp situated on the eastern slope of Mount Tamalpais, the town had managed to redefine itself over the decades, retaining the folksy ambience of its past, with plenty of tree-lined lanes, redwood groves, and riding stables, while attracting a bustling array of trendy restaurants, coffee houses, art galleries, and specialty shops, not to mention a liberal selection of custom-built million-dollar homes. It was a place not unlike Topanga, as Nova recalled from the few times he had driven north of San Francisco, where investment bankers, lawyers, and stockbrokers could be found taking long weekend hikes in flannel shirts and jeans like college kids before tooling back to their offices on Monday mornings in new Jags, Land Rovers, and Porsches.

Sandy's home was an attractive split-level redwood affair at the end of a cul-de-sac in a small nest of secluded houses on a hillside above the town. A narrow black-topped driveway flanked on either side by mature oleander and barberry bushes climbed steeply from the street before leveling off in front of a two-car garage and a neatly kept flagstone patio. An ornate sundial on a green marble pedestal, its face cast in bright bronze leaf and its gnomon, or shadow-producing device, of black obsidian, stood at the center of the patio. The sundial was surrounded by a pair of rough-hewn stone benches, a small koi pond, and three crescent-shaped flower beds stocked with a dazzling array of multicolored roses, daylilies, gladioluses, and tulips. The dwelling itself had a decidedly open-air flavor, accented by a gently sloping chalet-style roof above the lower level, a roomy wooden deck over the garage, and a cozy breakfast-nook balcony outside the master bedroom on the second story.

Sandy brought the Camry slowly up the drive and parked it carefully just inches away from the far corner of the garage door. "Until I find the right contractor to add on another room in the back, the garage is serving as a second studio," she said by way of explanation for leaving the car outside.

She opened the car doors and led Nova onto the patio. It was twilight, and the birds had begun to kick up their evening chorus in the lofty fir, oak, and redwood trees that bordered the property on every side and gave it a feel of genuine privacy. "This is one of my favorite times of day around here," she said, stopping to listen. She was prepared to give him the standard walking tour she provided all first-time guests, beginning with the history of the sundial—the former owners were the publishers of a well-known Bay Area gardening magazine, with a strong side interest in astrology—but saw that he was in no shape to enjoy the experience. "Actually, I've kind of grown to like the old sundial, even though it isn't much use with all the fog we get," she added with a little laugh as she unlocked the front door. "Maybe I was a druid in another life."

The home's interior was bright and clean, with high-gloss herringbone hardwood floors, expensive oriental area rugs, two bubble-domed acrylic skylights fitted into the living room's slanted beamed ceiling, and woodsy views available from every window. Richly rendered reproductions of Cockrill's *Heart,* Almaraz's *Greed,* and O'Keeffe's *City Night* shared space on the living room walls, flanking a big red-brick fireplace with a hand-carved teak mantel and an antique gold-rimmed mirror above it.

"Why don't you relax while I fix some dinner?" Sandy said, depositing her handbag and keys by the door on top of a narrow single-drawer entry stand made of distressed pine. She guided Nova across the living room and helped him ease into the overstuffed white sectional in front of the fireplace before adjourning to the kitchen. "There's a *Newsweek* and a *Time* on the coffee table. The latest *Vanity Fair* and

New Yorker should be there, too, if they're more your thing," she said on her way out. "I'll get a couple of chicken breasts started."

Nova sank into the cushions and took a good look around. His eyes passed from the Maloof rocker by the far end of the fireplace to the Cockrill and O'Keeffe paintings and finally to the *Greed*. Set in a surreal desert landscape of nightmarish red sand and mountains, the painting depicted two wild black dogs, their teeth bared and fur raised, preparing to draw blood over a small and very ordinary-looking bone lying on the sand between them. All the while, two other bones, every bit as nourishing and attractive, lay unclaimed just steps away. Nova had seen the painting once before, in an art magazine, and was quite taken with it. Back then he had seen it as an allegory of modern man's darkest impulses—the relentless drive for power over others, the addiction to savage competition without regard to costs, the inability to share nature's bounty. If only for an instant, he saw himself and Tami as the two warring dogs, with Jamie caught in the middle. Now that Tami was dead, did that make him the victor? Suddenly, he felt ashamed for thinking she had been in league with Sturgis.

Disgusted by the image he had cultivated of himself, he made a halfhearted effort to read the current issue of *Newsweek,* but his attention was drawn away by a thick scrapbook of photos that was also lying on the coffee table underneath the *New Yorker.* He picked up the scrapbook, plunked it down on his lap, and began to leaf through it.

The first few pages contained photos of a recent party at Sandy's office in San Francisco, a semi-formal affair with plenty of well-dressed clients with champagne flutes in one hand and color promotional brochures in the other. One shot of Sandy showed her mugging for the camera, cheek to cheek with a dark-haired fortysomething guy dressed in an expensive suit. Nova wondered if the guy was the boyfriend Sandy had told him about at the Regency Hotel. He didn't seem like the type who would desert a woman after she had suffered through a pregnancy that ended in disaster, but you could never tell. The office-party pictures were followed by recent shots of Sandy's parents and siblings back in Minnesota, and a few interior and exterior photos of what Nova assumed was Sandy's vacation mountain cabin.

The last few pages of the scrapbook contained mostly older photographs. In addition to some vintage Kodaks of Sandy as a kid, dressed in a cowboy outfit and a Halloween skeleton suit, there was one very old black-and-white portrait of a young couple standing in front of a large wooden farmhouse surrounded by rolling fields and tree-lined hills in the distance. The man had a broad, strong face and a dark handlebar mustache. He also appeared slightly uncomfortable, dressed in an undersized formal dark suit with high lapels, a bowtie, and stiff shirt collar. The woman, by contrast, had a sweet smile on her face—not unlike Sandy's, in fact—as she gripped the man's left arm tightly with her right hand. Like Sandy, too, she had long hair, which she braided and wore tied back in a bun. She was outfitted in a light-colored long-sleeve dress, with a lace collar buttoned up to her throat and no jewelry, except for a single strand of pearls around her neck. Judging from the couple's apparel, and the photo's frayed brown edges, Nova guessed the portrait dated from the last decade of the nineteenth century. Although he remembered the pictures of Sandy from the early days of their marriage, he couldn't recall if he had ever seen the old portrait. His lack of recollection was troubling, and he made a mental note to ask Sandy about the photo.

As he studied the curious couple in the early evening quiet, he could hear Sandy talking on the phone in the kitchen. From the pitch of her voice, she seemed to be in the midst of a heated argument. "I think what you did was impulsive and inexcusable," she said, almost shouting. "No . . . just wait until tomorrow. There's no need to hurry. It can all be taken care of then. Okay?" She paused, as if to listen to the party on the other end. "All right, I'll see you tomorrow, early."

A few minutes later, Sandy was back in the living room, carrying a tray loaded with crackers, Gouda slices, Brie, and Camembert spreads, and two glasses of cold Sonoma chardonnay. "The chicken's in the broiler," she said, placing the snack on the coffee table. She slid onto the sofa next to him and spread a few crackers. "I hope I wasn't too loud just then on the phone. One of my associates and I have run into a little disagreement over a project."

Nova assured her that he had taken no notice and helped himself to a cracker. He took a sip of wine and for a long moment just looked at her. Here she was, his first wife, and just possibly his newest best friend. She had a career and a home many women would kill for, yet she was as unpretentious and warm as when they first met. And just as beautiful, if not more so, sitting there in her jeans and boots, her thick black hair hanging loosely about her shoulders, her blue eyes soft and soothing, alluring and sexy all at the same time. He had been a fool ever to have let her go, he thought to himself.

The snack was followed by a quick dinner and a shower, after which Sandy helped to rewrap the Ace bandage around his ribs and, as promised, washed his clothes while he lounged in an old bathrobe. By ten-thirty, he was dressed again, sitting once more on the

living room sectional, feeling almost like a free man.
Even the pain in his head and ribs had subsided.
Sandy made them each a cup of herbal tea and lit a
small fire. "Well," she said, turning toward him
expectantly.

"I was browsing through your scrapbook," he replied, trying to forestall the inevitable discussion about
when and how he would surrender himself to the authorities. "I hope you don't mind."

"No, not at all." She picked up her tea mug and
cradled it in her hands. "See anything interesting?"

"Lots, actually," he answered, opening the book
and turning to the office-party shot of Sandy and the
guy in the three-piece. "Anybody special?"

She laughed and shook her head. "He's a very successful plastic surgeon, and quite rich, too. He's also
very married—to one of my best and most satisfied
clients."

"Then he isn't the shithead you told me about?"

"No, and I've told you enough about the shithead
before. I prefer not talking about him, if you don't
mind."

There was no particular reason to press for an answer, so he flipped ahead to the photos of the mountain cabin. "I take it that's the vacation home you're
selling?" She nodded, prompting him to add, "Seems
pretty sweet."

"It's too much like this place, but in the other end
of the state. Actually, it's in the mountains outside
L.A. I bought it because I spend so much time down
south, but with the mortgage here, it doesn't make
sense to keep it." She cocked her head to one side as
though an idea had just popped into her head. "If
you're interested, I could put you in touch with my
realtor."

"I don't think it's the right time for me, but thanks

anyway." He touched the stitches over his temple. "I have a few minor problems to work out before I can think of any new investments."

"Maybe we should put some Neosporin on that," she offered sympathetically, making a closer inspection of the wound. "I think there's some in the bathroom down the hall." She stood to accompany him but resumed her seat when she saw he wasn't ready to get up.

"There's one other picture I'd like to ask you about first," he said. He turned to the old portrait. "I take it you're related. The woman has your smile and your hair."

"That's my great-grandmother Marjorie and her husband. The portrait was taken outside of their farmhouse in Minnesota just after they were married around the turn of the century. You've seen the picture before, David."

"I don't think so."

"Of course you have." She put her cup down and gave him a little reproving frown. "I brought the photo into your office before we were divorced. My younger brother sent it to me. He had just completed a family tree for one of his college classes. He found the photo in the attic at my uncle's home and wanted me to have it. I had never seen a picture of my great-grandparents before, and I was very excited. Don't you remember?"

"I must have been preoccupied," he apologized.

She touched the image of the young couple affectionately with her fingertips. "That's my great-grandfather Oswald Nash. Marjorie's family was originally named Olafsen, but they changed the name to Olsen at Ellis Island when they immigrated to America."

"So your great-grandmother was Marjorie Olsen?"

"That was her maiden name."

All the color drained from Nova's face as he took in her reply. A barely containable wave of nausea convulsed his midsection. He might have forgotten seeing the picture all those years ago in his office, but he knew the name from a far more recent context—the computer printout Tony Ross had shown him of the women who had visited Randy Sturgis in prison. Marjorie Olsen had been Randy's number one fan at Folsom Prison.

"You really don't look well, David," Sandy said with some concern. "I was going to suggest we turn on the TV, but maybe we should give the news a rest until morning."

"I'm just tired, that's all," he answered. His fatigue, though undeniable, was the least of his worries. He tried to appear natural but was unable to look directly at her.

"Me, too. I've been up since six." She stood, stretched her back, and began to yawn. "Time for bed, then. Why don't you take the guest room down the hall? It's already made up and, there's a phone you can use to call Molly. She should be in by now, and given the circumstances, I don't think she'd mind hearing from you, even at this hour. She'll probably know more about what's going on than you'd find out from the news, too."

She took his hand in hers, patted it gently, and gave him an encouraging smile. "I'm sure everything will work out."

He thanked her and watched as she walked into the kitchen and then upstairs.

Back in the guest room, he tried to contain his thoughts but entirely without success. The thin hold he had regained on his sense of security earlier in the evening had yielded to a new and uncontrollable sense of apprehension and suspicion, all focused on Sandy.

There were just too many coincidences to dismiss: the name Marjorie Olsen. The boyfriend Sandy refused to discuss who had gotten her pregnant and then supposedly had dumped her. The fact that Folsom Prison was a mere two-hour drive away. The mountain cabin she owned. Hadn't Ross told him the feds thought the Tanner video had been made in just such a setting? And then there was the angry phone conversation she'd had earlier that evening with her associate. Whoever she had spoken to was going to see her tomorrow morning. Could that person have been Randy Sturgis? Even the slightest chance that it was placed Nova in mortal danger. Was the plan to have Randy show up here while he was still asleep and finish the game? What if, on the other hand, Sandy decided to turn him into the police? That could happen literally at any moment, and there was no telling what she might say to them.

He picked up the guest-room phone and began to punch in Molly's home number but abruptly placed the receiver back before completing the call. There was no point in telling Molly he was with Sandy, because he had no intention of staying with Sandy any longer than his wits and resources would allow.

He waited another hour, pacing and plotting, before returning to the living room. Certain that Sandy was asleep, he found her handbag on the entry-room stand and removed the keys to her Camry, along with three twenty-dollar bills from her wallet. In another half minute he was behind the wheel of the Camry, letting it glide down the drive in neutral before starting the engine at the bottom. The dial on the fuel gauge told him he had a good three-quarters of a tank as he pulled away from Sandy's home, never casting a backward glance.

Chapter Thirty-five

"I'm at a truck stop in Salinas," he said into the phone. "I know I have to turn myself in, but I can't do it alone. I need your help."

Molly tried to wipe the sleep from her eyes as she switched on the night light by her bed. She propped herself up on a pillow and took a bleary look at her alarm clock. "Jesus, David, it's four-thirty in the morning. Why didn't you call earlier?"

"Listen, I don't think anyone's spotted me. I took Sandy's car. She's the one, not Tami." He uttered the words breathlessly, like a person in an old spy movie on the run from the KGB, invoking a secret code.

"Wait a second, you're way ahead of me. You're referring to Sandy Nash?"

"She's the one who's been helping Randy Sturgis. I know it sounds crazy, but it's true. Sturgis has found some way of dyeing his skin black. He nearly killed me in the hospital. That's why I had to leave." He paused to deposit another four quarters in the pay phone. "And I didn't kill Tami. I swear."

"David, you're not making a lot of sense. You've been to see Sandy in Mill Valley, and you've stolen her car. Is that what you're telling me?"

Nova stroked his chin. He hadn't shaved at Sandy's

and had a three-day growth of black and gray stubble. "I've taken her Camry and sixty dollars in cash. I know it looks bad and I'm prepared to surrender, but I'm in no shape to do it alone. If we go in together, you might be able to straighten things out before they get any worse."

"You want me to surrender you?"

"If you're willing to help." His voice cracked with desperation as he made his plea.

She answered without the slightest hesitation. "Of course I am. Just give me a minute to think."

"Maybe we can meet somewhere," he suggested when she failed to come up with a quick answer. "Some place between here and L.A."

"It would have to be somewhere quiet where we can talk and won't be noticed." She grew silent again, then suddenly added, as though she had thought of the perfect spot, "How about that place where you and Jamie went hiking last summer near Santa Barbara?"

"Mineral Springs Canyon. You know the area?"

"I know the coastal mountains pretty well. They were one of my dad's favorite getaways. Mine, too, for a while."

"There's a dirt clearing that people use as a parking lot where the trail head into the canyon begins," Nova said, eagerly embracing the idea. "It's just a few miles above the highway. I could meet you there."

"Good. I'll find it. If you leave now, you could get there by nine or nine-thirty at the latest. The place should be deserted at that time of day."

"What can I say, Molly? 'Thank you' seems so inadequate."

"Just tell me you'll be there, and that you'll let me deal with the authorities. Don't say a word to anyone."

"I've got gas money, a map, and enough Advil to numb a horse," he replied, trying to chase away the hollow sensation rising in his stomach with a feeble attempt at humor.

"Okay, and if you take a minute to use the rest room, you shouldn't have to get out of the car until you get there."

He started to say good-bye, but the thought of being pulled over by the highway patrol prompted him to ask about Sandy. "What if she's already reported the Camry?"

"Don't worry about Sandy. She's probably still asleep. If she *is* involved with Sturgis, she won't want to bring in the cops. And if she isn't, we'll just have to hope that she's so fond of you she'll wait awhile before making any calls. Just make sure you take good care of her car. You hear that? I want you and the Camry both in one piece."

He promised to drive safely before hanging up and making a beeline for the men's room.

With the traffic light and the skies dry and clear, Nova made good time driving south on Highway 101, the main artery through the lettuce, artichoke, and almond fields of the Salinas Valley. Apart from an occasional pocket of fog and the odd eighteen-wheeler passing him like a runaway elephant, his primary concern was staying awake. He had slept on the Greyhound before hooking up with Sandy, but he had not enjoyed a really good night's rest since the beginning of the custody case. That seemed a small eternity ago.

To keep himself from drifting off, he cranked the Camry's air conditioning up full blast and at the same time rolled down the driver's-side window. The wind swept against his face, sending his hair dancing across his forehead and filling his nostrils with the sour scent of fertilizer from the adjacent fields. When even the fertilizer began to lose its punch, he turned on the radio and tried to tune in a news station. Finding mostly static out in farm country, he settled for a Spanish-language station playing festive *banda* music. He turned up the volume and self-consciously shifted his eyes from one side of the roadway to the other to fight against "highway hypnosis," just as the driver-safety manuals he had read as a teenager recommended. Still, he felt an overwhelming urge to doze.

Finally, as he reached Paso Robles, he pulled into a mini-mart off the freeway for a new tank of gas, a large cup of coffee, and a cherry Danish. It was a little after six, and the sun was beginning to peek over the oak-studded hills to the east, bathing the fields and the highway in muted shades of green, yellow, and brown. Nova had never been much of a morning person, and he was somewhat surprised to see how crowded the mini-mart was with a diverse assortment of businessmen in jackets and ties, truckers in oil-stained jeans, and tourists in jogging shoes and short pants, getting an early start on treks to the beaches of the central coast.

He knew that by entering the store he was violating Molly's first admonition, but he felt little risk as he mingled freely with the other customers. A young couple with a pair of toddler-age kids walked to the check stand just ahead of him, holding a red plastic shopping basket filled with soft drinks, chips, cheese snacks, and the morning edition of the *San Francisco Chronicle* fresh off the delivery van. Nova waited for the couple to complete their transaction before adding a copy of the paper to his own purchases.

Back in the parking lot, after topping off the Camry with unleaded premium, he found the story on Tami's murder on the lower left columns of the first page.

"Police Looking for Talk Show Star's Ex-Husband,"
the headline announced.

The article that followed jolted him awake far more
than any cup of coffee ever could.

> *Los Angeles County Sheriff's deputies have issued*
> *an all-points bulletin for attorney David Nova,*
> *the former husband of television talk-show host-*
> *ess Tami Dawson. Nova is wanted in connec-*
> *tion with the slaying of his wife.*
>
> *Dawson's body was discovered at her Malibu*
> *beach home early Monday morning by her*
> *housekeeper, who was returning to the residence.*
> *A sheriff's spokesperson stated that Ms. Daw-*
> *son died either late Sunday night or early Monday*
> *from multiple blows to the head with a blunt*
> *instrument.*
>
> *Although details of the crime are being with-*
> *held pending further investigation, a confiden-*
> *tial source within the Sheriff's Department*
> *confirmed that Ms. Dawson was struck at least*
> *six times with an aluminum baseball bat. The*
> *source also confirmed that robbery has been*
> *ruled out as a motive, as no valuables were taken*
> *from the home.*

The article jumped to the back page, where it continued alongside a recent photo of Tami—taken at one
of her live broadcasts—showing her wading into the
studio audience, microphone in hand, full of life and
energy. The story went on to note Tami's meteoric
rise to the top of the talk-show circuit, and her show's
impending move to New York. There were the usual
quotes from celebrities and associates, mourning the
loss of such a young and vibrant talent, and expressing
the hope that her killer would be apprehended soon.

Nova was just coming to the part about the "acrimonious custody hearing" that had concluded in a "hallway screaming match only days before the slaying" when his attention was drawn to another murder story at the bottom of the page. "In a grisly crime that the FBI believes may be connected to the recent kidnapping and murder of Ninth Circuit Court of Appeals judge Lawrence Tanner, the partially decomposed body of an Altadena woman was found Monday afternoon in her home by a neighbor. The woman, identified as Vera Fletcher, was the judge's longtime clerk at the court. The sheriff's department is treating the death as a homicide."

Nova closed his eyes and took a long, deep breath. He opened them just in time to see a CHP patrol car pull into the parking lot.

In the presence of the black-and-white, his mind began to race again. He remembered how Sandy had dissuaded him from phoning Vera when they were together back in L.A. at the Regency Hotel. Had she known that Vera was already dead? Did she share some kind of complicity in that crime as well as Tanner's abduction? And what about Tami's murder? Sandy always had hated her. Perhaps she secretly hated Nova as well. The possibilities spiraled through his mind, endless and maddening. He was tempted to stay with them, to examine each at length on its own terms, to arrive somehow at the whole truth, but there was no time. There was no time even to mourn.

He dropped the paper on the Camry's front seat without finishing either article and followed the patrol car through the rearview mirror as it came to a stop in a parking space near the minimart's main entrance. Two uniformed Chippies exited the vehicle and began to talk. Unable to discern what they were saying, Nova's heart pounded and his breathing quickened.

He told himself aloud to "stay calm" and started his engine. He was just another working stiff, for all anyone else knew, out for his first coffee of the day. There was nothing even remotely conspicuous in that.

The Chippies were still talking when he drove the Camry slowly out of the parking lot and flashed his turn signal to renter the freeway. Whatever the officers were discussing, they clearly weren't looking for a middle-aged guy with a heavy beard in a red Camry. He was fully awake again, and his rendezvous with Molly remained on schedule.

Glued to the wheel for the duration of the drive, he passed San Luis Obispo by seven and in another ninety minutes had reached downtown Santa Barbara. At nine o'clock sharp he was in the foothills of the Santa Ynez Mountains, heading for the trail head to Mineral Springs Canyon.

Apart from a solitary jogger near the freeway exit, Nova had the road into the mountains all to himself. On any other mild summer morning he surely would have stopped to savor the expansive views of the Pacific, which became ever more inspiring with the climb in elevation. He remembered stopping at several points along the way with Jamie last year. Three, maybe four times they pulled over the side of the road, scrambled up a steep hillside, and trained their binoculars on the white sails of the tiny boats lazing on the ocean, and the dark green outlines of the Channel Islands beyond. He remembered, too, the long hike they took through the sheer rock walls of the canyon, traversing the creek that ran along the canyon floor as it twisted through thriving groves of pine, bamboo, eucalyptus, agave, and palms. Along the way they explored the ruins of an old resort hotel that had been destroyed by fire in the 1920s. They pretended they were archaeologists discovering a lost world.

He had meant to return with Jamie to the Santa Ynez this summer, to check out the Chumash Indian cave paintings to the north, but the allure of a summer in the Catskills proved to be a far stronger attraction for his daughter. It was the height of irony that he was returning to the canyon today alone. Perhaps if he had refused to let Jamie go to New York, the nightmare from which there now seemed no escape would never have come to pass. Tami would still be alive, and he would not be on the run in a stolen car, wanted for her murder, burdened by the oldest of motives, without an alibi to confirm his whereabouts at the probable time of her death. It was funny how you crossed a line, almost without realizing it, and then suddenly there was no turning back.

Recalling what might have been, Nova reached the canyon trail head at nine-thirty, just as Molly had forecast. As she had also predicted, the area was deserted. He sat in the Camry for at least a minute, just staring at the jagged sedimentary outcroppings that formed the canyon's sheer flanks. The rocks were a warm golden brown color in the morning light. Later in the day, as the sun passed over the ocean and the canyon grew shrouded in shadow, they would become haunted shades of purple and gray before finally fading to black.

Driven more by nervous energy than any consideration of where it might be best to wait, he exited the Camry and walked across the dirt parking strip to the cement drainage apron, about thirty yards away, at the tip of the trail head. To the left of the trail, under a tall, leafy alder, there was an old cement picnic table. He took a seat on the top of the table, his legs resting on one of the benches. Soothed by the sun, he slipped off his denim jacket and rolled it into a makeshift pillow. Then he gently reclined against the table until his back was completely flat and his head was on the jacket. He lifted his gaze to the sky, azure and still, and he waited.

Of all the concerns that had been darting through his mind, the most important was the one he had most avoided. What would he ever say to Jamie? How would he tell her that her mother had been murdered and that the police thought he had killed her? Even if he were quickly exonerated, she might be scarred for life. And if he wasn't quickly exonerated, the possibilities were nearly unimaginable. In that event he would surely lose legal custody of her, perhaps forever.

The prospect of losing Jamie was too grim to contemplate, and he tried to push it aside. There was, in any case, nothing he could do to right the situation until Molly arrived. There was nothing to be gained by beating up on himself any more than he already had. Seeking a brief respite from the self-inflicted torment, he closed his eyes and gave in to his fatigue. *Sleep purifies the soul,* his nana used to say. In almost as much time as it took for him to recall the stern expression on the old woman's wrinkled face as she delivered her homespun homilies, he drifted off into a fitful slumber.

"Wakee, wakee."

Nova heard the sounds and stirred to life. He opened his eyes and squinted into the sun. Slowly, the image of Randy Sturgis came into focus. He was smiling, like an old friend, standing no more than a few feet away.

"Death fires, Davey, time to die," Randy said tonelessly.

Nova felt a visceral current of fear shoot through his chest and stomach. Acting on pure survival instincts, he reached behind his head for his rumpled jacket and threw it into Randy's advancing face. Then he rolled to his left and scrambled off the table. The maneuver bought him only the smallest of reprieves. He made a dash for the trail head, but without any real hope of escape.

Sturgis tackled him from the rear just before he reached the drainage apron, driving him hard into moist earth near the creek bed, sending a shiver of pain radiating from his still tender ribs down his torso and into the middle of his thighs. In his weakened condition Nova was no match for Randy's rage. He managed to struggle onto his back and even to aim a punch at his attacker, but his strength was lacking, and in a moment of surrender, his will to resist seemed also to fail.

Sturgis blocked the intended blow as though it had been thrown by a child and pinned Nova savagely to the ground. In one brutal motion he grabbed Nova by the ears, lifted his head, and drove his own forehead into the bridge of Nova's nose. The force of the head butt split Nova's septum and unleashed a river of blood spilling over his lips and chin. Nova lay back, barely conscious and half choking as the bleeding spread to the back of his throat.

Pleased with his handiwork, Sturgis straddled his prey. He reached into the rear pocket of his pants for the straight-edge razor he had taken from Vera's home. "I want to feel this one almost as much as you will, Davey," he said, beginning to breathe hard as his excitement mounted.

Nova could see the feral glint in the eyes of his former client. He could see the muscles in his face and jaw tighten, and his chest heave with abandon. Randy Sturgis was an animal preparing for the kill, reveling in the ultimate act. The ritual was clear and simple, like the laws of nature taking their course.

The pain in his face and torso became so unbearable that Nova could only hope that death came quickly. Awaiting that outcome, his mind was reduced to a state of unalloyed anticipation. Not even a thought of Jamie intruded.

The shot that rang out sounded initially like the backfire of a car engine. Still kneeling, Sturgis turned his head in the direction of the report. His facial expression, at first simply one of curiosity, hardened into a contorted mask of confusion and surprise. He seemed to want to cry out, but his lips parted and froze, as if he was at a loss for words. Only a mournful groan came from somewhere deep in his throat. Then his body began to buck and the razor dropped from his hand. He slumped on top of Nova, two hundred pounds of sinew and bone, blood oozing from a walnut-size hole in his back.

It took most of Nova's remaining strength to push Sturgis aside. When finally he succeeded, he had an unobstructed view of Molly walking toward him. Looking shaken and grim, she was carrying a large black pistol in her right hand.

Chapter Thirty-six

"Thanks for coming, David," Ross said, extending a beefy hand across his desk and motioning Nova with the other to take a seat. "You're looking better. I see the bandages have come off."

Nova touched the bridge of his nose lightly. The bandages had been removed, but the swelling had yet to subside completely, and it still hurt sometimes to breathe normally. He returned the pleasantry. "You're looking well, too. And the papers are making you out to be a hero. That must make you feel pretty good."

"The papers can say what they want, but they don't change the truth." A blush rose in Ross' face. He seemed genuinely embarrassed by all the publicity he had garnered since the death of Randy Sturgis. "Actually, I wish that we could take more credit for the way things turned out, but I'm afraid it was the Riverside sheriffs that really broke the case. Can you believe that? Fucking Riverside. They were investigating a death by overdose of Demerol at the Alpine Convalescent Home up in Idyllwild."

With Nova hanging on his words, Ross curled the ring and middle fingers of his hands into simulated quotation marks. "When Noah Chamberlain suddenly resigned from the convalescent home, they had a search warrant issued for the little apartment he rented in Banning. They found three sunlamps and enough Oxsoralen to let him live the rest of his life looking like an African American. When you combine that with the plastic surgery he must have had to flatten out his nose and throw in a few cheap hairpieces for special occasions, it was the perfect cover. We might never have found him."

Nova gazed out of Ross' office window. It was still eighty degrees outside at three-thirty, but it was mid-September and the days were growing noticeably shorter. Even the way the sunlight and shadows fell upon the streets and the green lawn outside the federal building seemed to signify that summer had all but run its course. Sinking back into his chair, he sighed heavily through his mouth. "*Black Like Me*," he said, almost as an afterthought.

"How's that?" Ross asked.

"*Black Like Me*. It's the title of a book written in the early sixties by a white civil-rights activist named John Howard Griffin. He turned his skin black using Oxsoralen and ultraviolet light treatments. Then he toured the South in order to see what it was really like to live as a black person. They made a movie out of it."

"I guess I must have missed it." Never one to enjoy being made to look uninformed, Ross frowned.

"I read the book in college," Nova added. "The drug is used to treat vitiligo. It darkens the skin's pigment and heightens its sensitivity to the sun. Sturgis must have read the book, too. He was always the literary type."

Ross raised his right forefinger to his lips. "The autopsy report mentioned that his forearms were badly burned. Maybe he spent too much time in the sun.

Serves the asshole right. He was laughing at us right until the end."

"And Molly?" Nova asked, wondering when the special agent was going to get around to the reason for their meeting. "I assume you called me in here to talk about her. You told my secretary it was important."

"That was yesterday," Ross replied, sounding slightly apologetic, "before she worked out her plea agreement with the U.S. attorney. We thought you were going to be our star witness."

"She pleaded out?" Nova asked.

Ross paused to savor the astonishment on Nova's face. "A little over an hour ago, to aiding and abetting the kidnapping of Larry Tanner. The government dropped the murder charge in exchange for an early resolution of the case and for her cooperation in providing statements on the other charges that would have been filed against Sturgis had he lived. I got a phone call from the trial deputy in Judge Anderson's courtroom. Surprised the hell out of me. The news hasn't even hit the radio yet."

Nova shook his head in disbelief. He thought about leaving but decided to stay put awhile longer. There were still too many mangled pieces of his life, and Ross owed him some candid answers. "You know I never did understand how you came to suspect Molly."

Ross flipped through the large case file on his desk. "The Riverside sheriffs who raided Randy's apartment also found a stack of old letters that Molly had sent to him on her legal letter head while he was still at Folsom."

"What kinds of letters?"

"On the surface, just regular lawyer letters. It seems that Sturgis remembered that she had been one of

your young associates at the time of his trial. About
five years ago he wrote her asking for help with his
Ninth Circuit writ petition. She started to write back,
giving him various pointers on what issues might be
raised and the procedural pitfalls he'd encounter in
federal court. Their correspondence became rather
chummy."

"That might have been stupid, and even unethical,
given her prior association with me," Nova commented, "but she wasn't breaking any criminal laws."

"No, she wasn't. But one of the Riverside guys—an
up-and-comer who told me he'd like to join the Bureau someday—remembered reading a joint-task force
memo where we suggested Randy was being helped
by a woman. The guy took a closer look at Molly's
letters and saw that in one of them she wrote that she
liked his idea of paying him a visit under an assumed
name. That way she could get to know him better
without revealing her true identity. She told him to
get ready to meet a new friend named Marjorie—"

"Olsen," Nova completed the special agent's sentence
for him. "Marjorie Olsen was the great-grandmother of
Sandy Nash, my first wife. Molly was still one of my
associates when Sandy brought a photograph of her
great-grandmother into my office. She showed it
around the staff. Molly went on to represent me in
our divorce, and I guess she and Sandy got to know
each other fairly well."

"Maybe a little too well," Ross observed.

"Molly must have remembered the name all these
years."

"Clever girl. Anyway, we got our tip about 'Marjorie' the day you had your run-in with Randy up in
Santa Barbara. Then we had Molly's handwriting
checked against the signature cards at San Quentin

for Marjorie Olsen." He tapped the file with his right hand. "It was an easy match."

For the most part, the remainder of the investigation was public knowledge. Two days after Nova and Molly had returned from Santa Barbara, while Nova was still in the hospital and technically in custody for Tami's murder, the feds arrested Molly at her law office for aiding and abetting the kidnapping and murder of Larry Tanner. A few days after that the local authorities followed suit, charging her as an accessory after the fact in the murders of Rosalee Aquino, Vera and Tami. A subsequent search of Molly's cabin in Idylwild turned up a treasure trove of incriminating evidence, including a bogus driver's license with Molly pictured in a blond wig and heavy makeup, under the name of Marjorie Olsen, listing a nonexistent mail drop for an address. The frozen tip of Tanner's right ring finger was discovered wrapped in a piece of paper towel in the freezer. The judge's headless body was found a week later, buried in a shallow grave in a mountain ravine about a mile from the cabin.

"You know," Ross said with a thin smile, "I really thought at first that you were the one who killed Tami. Apart from your little girl and Tami's housekeeper, yours were the only prints we found on the bat that Randy used to crush her skull."

"When I was in the hospital, Molly took my house keys to get me a fresh change of clothes. Sturgis must have gone with her, put on a pair of nylon gloves, and taken the bat."

"Crazy bitch," Ross said. "I can understand why a bastard like Sturgis would want Molly for a girlfriend. She got him a phony nursing certificate under the name of Noah Chamberlain, supplied him with job references, gave him a place to hide out, and it had to have been her who arranged for the nose job."

"She was very well connected," Nova observed.

"But what was the attraction for her?" Ross asked, palms upturned.

"I don't know," Nova answered thoughtfully. "Maybe she just wanted to be needed and loved."

"Yeah, needed and loved . . . by a psychopath. That's great."

"I'm not about to make any excuses for her," Nova said, "but I don't think she planned any of this business with Tanner, Vera, or Tami. She probably found out about the kidnapping after the fact and just got swept along until things got out of hand."

"That's what I'm told her fucking lawyer said when she worked the goddamned plea," Ross snapped back. Even without saying it, it was obvious he was pissed that the prosecution had arranged a deal without consulting him. "You attorneys are something else. Her sentencing hearing should occur early next month. She'll probably get upward of ten years is my guess. With time off for good behavior, she'll be able to walk out of prison before she's old and gray. From my point of view, she's getting off easy."

Nova raised his eyebrows and tilted his head. "That doesn't make what her lawyer said any less true. I understand from personal experience how you can lose control over your life."

"You mean to tell me you forgive her? She didn't drive Randy up to Santa Barbara to picnic with you, David."

"She thought that I was the only one who knew that Noah Chamberlain and Randy Sturgis were the same person. In her mind, if Randy was to stay free, I had to be eliminated."

"So, love makes us do crazy things. Is that what you're saying?"

"All I know," Nova answered, "is that in the end she couldn't go through with it. She saved my life."

"You know, she still might face trial on the state charges."

"If she does, I won't testify against her, at least not voluntarily. Her federal time for the kidnapping's going to be more than sufficient."

"Suit yourself. That one's out of my hands."

Their business apparently concluded, they fell silent. When Ross next spoke, the hardness was gone from his face and voice. "There's just one other thing." He reached into the middle drawer of his desk and pulled out a black plastic audio cassette. "I found this myself at Molly's home."

Nova took the cassette from Ross. He stared at it and his pulse quickened. The label bearing the date of his old jailhouse interview with Randy Sturgis was still pasted on the outside, but the magnetic tape had been removed and the cassette itself was completely hollow. Nova could only surmise that Molly had come across the tape in his home study and taken it. He slipped the cassette into his jacket pocket and turned his eyes back to Ross.

"It was like that when I found it," Ross explained. "I thought you might want it back. It's no use to us."

Nova began to thank Ross, but the special agent raised his hand to stop him. Any other G-man would have accused him on the spot of obstruction of justice for removing the tape from Sturgis' trial file, but not Ross. Maybe he wanted to prove he was a cop with a soul, or that he thought Nova had been through enough without having to face a bullshit rap for something that no longer mattered. Or maybe he just wanted to show that despite their differences on the law and life in general, he regarded Nova as a friend.

"The less said the better, for both of us," Ross said

matter-of-factly. "Just tell me one more time. The bit about the death fires that Randy liked to recite for his victims. That was from Coleridge?"

"*The Rime of the Ancient Mariner*," Nova answered.

"I think I'll pick up a copy at the library." Ross wished Nova the best of luck and told him "to stay in touch, on personal things, from time to time." The special agent watched Nova leave the office without getting up from his desk.

Had Molly destroyed the tape or had Ross? Nova would never know the answer, and for the time being at least, the answer didn't matter. There was someone far more important than Molly or Ross who warranted his immediate attention: Jamie.

Nova found Jamie and Sandy standing on the front lawn of the federal building, feeding bread crumbs to the pigeons and sparrows. He hurried to them and threw his arms around his daughter, hugging her tightly to his chest.

Jamie hugged him back with every fiber in her little body. To Nova's great surprise and everlasting relief, she had proven to be far more resilient than he ever could have hoped. She had taken her mother's death hard, as any child would, but with some intensive early counseling from Dr. Engstrom, she had begun to turn the corner and was now back at her old school. The counseling not only helped Jamie recover, but it also laid to rest the sexually volatile lies Yolanda Ortega had told at the custody hearing. After only a single session Engstrom had concluded that Jamie's relationship with her father showed absolutely no evidence of sexual impropriety. It would always hurt to know that Tami had pressured Yolanda to lie, but with all that had happened, Nova eventually found his way to forgiving his former housekeeper. He discarded the notion of pressing perjury charges, and after an emotional confrontation at Yolanda's apartment, he even raised the possibility of one day inviting her to return to work.

Sandy, too, had proven to be a source of enormous support and forgiveness. Visiting nearly every week, she and Jamie had gotten to be good friends. Although she would never take Tami's place in Jamie's heart, it was already plain that she and Jamie had formed a lasting female bond that Nova could appreciate only from a distance. It didn't exactly hurt either that Sandy had never reported her Camry as stolen.

"We've counted over a hundred different birds," Jamie said as Nova released her from his grasp. "Want a try?"

Nova took the bag of crumbs and tossed a handful onto the lawn, inviting a frenzied landing of yet another flock.

"Sandy says there are lots of birds and other animals up around her cabin in the mountains," Jamie said. "She's invited us there this weekend. Can we go?"

Nova turned to Sandy. "But I thought you were close to a sale."

"The escrow fell through, and I decided to take the place off the market," she answered. "I'd love to have you."

Sandy looked at him and began to laugh. "Just remember, the cabin's in Big Bear. That's in a whole different county from Idylwild." She leaned against Nova, and he put his arm around her.

"I want you to trust me, David," she whispered. "If we're to have any kind of future together, that's a must."

"I know," he said, moving his face close to hers.

There were so many things he might have added, but
his nana had a saying for such moments. *Love is about
doing, not talking.* Following the old woman's advice,
he pressed his lips against Sandy's, kissing her with
passion for the first time since they had separated all
those long years ago. With the sounds of rush-hour
traffic rising in the background and Jamie by his side,
he felt certain it would not be the last.